Lyn Andrews is one of the UK's top one hundred bestselling authors, reaching No. 1 on the *Sunday Times* paperback bestseller list. Born and brought up in Liverpool, she is the daughter of a policeman and also married a policeman. After becoming the mother of triplets, she took some time off from her writing whilst she raised her children. Shortlisted for the RNA Romantic Novel of the Year Award in 1993, she has now written twenty-eight hugely successful novels. Lyn Andrews divides her time between Merseyside and Ireland.

By Lyn Andrews

The White Empress
The Sisters O'Donnell
The Leaving of Liverpool
Liverpool Lou
Ellan Vannin
Maggie May
Mist Over the Mersey
Mersey Blues
Liverpool Songbird
Liverpool Lamplight
Where the Mersey Flows
From This Day Forth
When Tomorrow Dawns
Angels of Mercy
The Ties That Bind
Take These Broken Wings
My Sister's Child
The House on Lonely Street
Love and a Promise
A Wing and a Prayer
When Daylight Comes
Across a Summer Sea
A Mother's Love
Friends Forever
Every Mother's Son
Far From Home
Days of Hope
A Daughter's Journey

lyn andrews

Maggie May

headline

First published in 1993 by Corgi Books
an imprint of Transworld Publishers

First published in paperback edition in 2009
by HEADLINE PUBLISHING GROUP

1

ISBN 978 0 7553 4181 8 (B-format)
ISBN 978 0 7553 5673 7 (A-format)

Typeset in Janson by Avon DataSet Ltd,
Bidford-on-Avon, Warwickshire

Printed in the UK by CPI Mackays, Chatham, ME5 8TD

Headline's policy is to use papers that are natural, renewable and recyclable products and made from wood grown in sustainable forests. The logging and manufacturing processes are expected to conform to the environmental regulations of the country of origin.

HEADLINE PUBLISHING GROUP
An Hachette UK Company
338 Euston Road
London NW1 3BH

www.headline.co.uk
www.hachette.co.uk

For my dear friends
Pauline Gallagher and Jean James,
who have shared the ups and downs with me,
as only true friends can.

And for a very special school friend,
Margaret Upritchard (née Connell).
We shared those happy, carefree, fun days,
Marg, and you'll always be with me,
if only in spirit.

Author's Note

The song 'Maggie May' is a traditional Liverpool sea-shanty and tells of the days of the sailing ships, of crimps and press gangs and 'ladies of the night'. The original 'Maggie' was transported for her crimes for the song tells us,

> The Judge he guilty found her,
> Of robbing a homeward-bounder,
> And paid her passage out to Botany Bay.

Which is probably why her true identity has been lost in the mists of antiquity, or the early and often unrecorded annals of Australian history.

This book is not my version of the life of 'Maggie May' but the story of a girl given the same notorious name.

My thanks go again to Mr Derek Whale of the *Liverpool Daily Post and Echo* for his help and advice, to Caroline Sheldon, my agent, for her unstinting support, and to my husband, Robert, for the hundreds of cups of coffee and the always available shoulder to lean on.

Prologue

Bowers Court 1889

A GIRL! A USELESS, WHINGING girl! Nago May looked down with contempt and increasing anger at the figure lying on the straw pallet on the floor in the corner of the room. He was oblivious to the thin, sweat-drenched body of his exhausted wife, heedless of the unhealthy pallor of her cheeks and the dark circles of sheer exhaustion beneath the pain-dulled blue eyes.

His malevolent gaze was fixed on the tiny scrap of humanity, bundled in the grubby remains of a towel, that lay in the crook of Dora's arm. Already it was waving a tiny fist in the air and yelling its protest at being thrust so harshly into an unfamiliar and increasingly hostile world.

'Nothin' wrong with 'er lungs an' she's got your 'air!' Ma Jessup, self-appointed local midwife from the room above, had announced with forced cheerfulness.

It didn't need much nouse to see that its father was far from pleased with the new baby.

'She has, it's goin' to be red, like yours.' Dora tried to hold the child out but her strength failed and she bit her lip. One glance at her husband's face had sent her heart plummeting. She knew what was wrong. He'd wanted a son, not a daughter. After so many miscarriages and dead babies who'd never even taken a first gasp of air, he'd set his heart on a son.

Tears welled up in her eyes. Suddenly, Dora felt a great wave of despair wash over her. It wasn't going to be easy to cope, but life had never been easy, particularly over the last few years. Her gaze wandered slowly around the miserable basement room. The only light came from the small window, set high in the wall, two of whose panes were broken and stuffed with rags. The walls were stained with dark patches, for the spluttering fire in the grate could do little to remove the chill of the place, let alone keep away the dampness.

She shivered as the cold, fetid air seemed to press down on her and mocked the spitting, crackling green twigs and bits of rubbish that passed for a fire.

Bowers Court was one of the maze of courts and alleys that criss-crossed Hurst Street and Salthouse Lane which ran down to the docks and the River Mersey. In winter, the raw dampness and heavy fogs seeped into the houses. They crept through badly fitting doors and windows, down chimneys where often no fire burned to dispel it, and up under flagged floors. In summer, it was a stinking, airless hell-hole. Vermin were always present, but in summer clouds of flies increased the misery and the threat of pestilence.

They had little in the way of possessions, for Nago spent more time out of work than he did in it. What little he did earn was mainly spent on beer and tobacco. His only bit of pleasure, he always yelled whenever she remonstrated with him. Some weeks there was nothing left to pay the rent and buy scraps of food and they were always in debt. There was nothing much in the way of furniture. The few ornaments which had given the room a bit of a homely look had all been pawned long ago. The straw pallet, with its two threadbare blankets, an old, battered table and an equally decrepit food press, a couple of rickety stools, a kettle, a black stewpot, three tin plates and mugs were all she could call her own.

She'd found work when she could and sometimes she'd gone begging in the more prosperous streets but that hadn't been often because of the constant miscarriages and stillbirths before the birth of this new baby. The first she'd ever managed to carry. Sometimes, when she'd been desperate, she'd borrowed or begged from the neighbours. It was a course of action that couldn't be repeated often for the residents of Bowers Court were in the same position as themselves. She knew there were thousands of other families in the festering slums of Liverpool who were living on the edge of starvation and despair, but they didn't concern her. Her own battle for survival needed all her depleted energies.

'Well, aren't yer goin' ter pick 'er up then?' Ma Jessup questioned belligerently. Her opinion of Nago May wasn't very high at the best of times, but after poor Dora had gone through searing agony for the last six hours, during which time there had been no sign of him, she thought the least he could do now was to show some interest in the child. Instead he was standing there as though an even worse stink than that which came from the open midden at the end of the Court, had been wafted under his nose. At least this one looked healthy, there wasn't much doubt about that, kicking and crying she was, full of life, she thought. Her coarse features constricted into a frown. Dora wasn't strong, all those miscarriages and still births had taken their toll and Nago May was a thoughtless, selfish sod.

Nago ignored her and continued to glare at his wife. His brown eyes, under straggly, auburn lashes, were hard and cold. He wanted nothing to do with the brat. He'd wanted a son. A man could be proud of a son. The birth of a lad was something to have a laugh and a drink with your mates about. He wanted nothing to do with a bloody girl!

He shifted his gaze, stared down at the cracked flags beneath his feet, and pulled his greasy cap further down over his shock of wiry, unkempt hair. He must have been mad to have saddled himself with a wife and kid. If he hadn't then he wouldn't be stuck in this hovel with never enough money in his pocket, never enough food in his belly or decent clothes on his back. Never a good fire in the hearth and Dora forever tired, nagging, complaining. He shouldn't have stayed in Liverpool at all. When he'd finally been released from the Dublin orphanage, he should have headed for America.

His frown deepened, as did his resentment. He'd been a bloody fool. But he'd been young and alone, the repressive and often brutal regime of the Christian Brothers had been in the past. He uttered a snort at the memory. Christian Brothers – that was a laugh! There had been little Christianity or charity about them. They'd inflicted the name Ignatius on him. Then they'd beaten him – for his own good, so he'd been told. They'd worked him to death – also for his own good and had tried, and failed, to instil in him a respect for the Church and a fear of God and His Commandments. Little wonder he'd found freedom from their domain so heady and intoxicating. Then, when he had been so vulnerable, Dora had come along. Pretty, buxom and always laughing and that had been that. He balled his fists in his pockets.

The laughter hadn't lasted long nor had her looks. Now she looked a hag – an ugly, nagging old hag.

He'd worked hard in the early days and they hadn't been doing too badly. Then they'd been beset with troubles. Work, on a regular basis, had been hard to find. She'd had so many miscarriages and still births that he'd begun to think she was incapable of bearing him a healthy child. He kicked at the edge of the broken flag and the dirt in the crack loosened. It wasn't his fault, he'd always told himself. It couldn't be, the pity of his mates reinforced that belief. It was Dora's fault. There must be a weakness in her. When she'd said she was pregnant again, his hopes had been raised – and now dashed.

He realized that both his wife and Ma Jessup were staring at him and he felt the hair on the back of his neck rise. What the hell did they expect him to do or say? Fall on her neck and tell her how bloody marvellous things were? Not a ha'penny to his name and another mouth to feed. Well, he was finished with them all. To hell with trying to be honest and respectable, two of Dora's favourite words. There were other, easier ways of making a living. Aye, and a better living than this. To hell with honesty and decency, hard work and whinging, bloody women!

Ma Jessup, seeing she was not going to get a response from Nago, turned back to Dora with contrived cheerfulness. 'Let's get you comfortable, luv. Bit of a wash down, like, an' you'll feel better. Then I'd feed 'er. What are yer goin' ter call 'er?'

Dora looked down at the baby and felt a great surge of tenderness, the agony of the last hours forgotten. Nago would get over his disappointment in time, when he saw how strong the baby was. 'I was up in Church Street a few weeks back an' I heard a woman call her daughter Laura. I liked it. It's different . . . it's sort of "pretty".'

Before Ma Jessup could reply, Nago emitted a roar of laughter. They both stared at him.

'Laura! Laura May! What kind of a name is that? Sounds like somethin' painted on the side of an owld fishin' boat!'

A flush crept over Dora's pallid cheeks and her thin shoulders straightened a little. 'I think it's a lovely name!'

A malicious smile crept over Nago's face as a thought occurred to him. 'I'm the one who 'as to register 'er, an' she's 'avin' no fancy names. She can 'ave somethin' plain.' He jerked his head in the baby's direction, although he didn't look at the child. He took his hand from his pockets and folded his arms across his chest. 'Maggie, that's what it'll be. Just plain Maggie.'

Ma Jessup looked quickly towards Dora but she was staring up at her husband, an expression of horror on her face. 'No! NO! You can't do that to her! You can't, Nago, please! Not Maggie! Mary, Sarah, Jane, anything but Maggie! Not with your . . . our family name!'

Nago felt strangely elated and he stared at the two women with contempt. 'I'll call 'er what I bloody well like an' there's nothin' you can do about it!' he yelled, then, turning on his heel and laughing, he sauntered from the room and slammed the rickety door after him.

The feeble crackling of the fire was the only sound in the room for the baby's cries had ceased, as though she were afraid of drawing down more wrath upon herself.

'Jesus! 'E won't do it, girl!' Ma Jessup cried, her features registering shock and concern as she saw Dora clutch the baby to her.

'He will!' Dora choked. 'I know him. It's . . . it's his way of gettin' back at me, 'cos she's not a boy.'

'God blast the evil bugger to hell an' back! I 'ope 'e gets run over on the way! Knocked down and trampled on, but if 'e don't, then God 'ave mercy on the poor little mite.' Ma Jessup passed a grimy hand over her forehead.

Dora closed her eyes and a large tear oozed from beneath her sparse lashes and slipped down her cheek. He'd changed so much lately, he'd become hard and uncaring, but this . . . this was an act of pure spite. She'd sooner have taken a beating from him. She'd sooner he desert them, bad though that would be, than to do this. Life was hard enough for babies in this city but to be called Maggie May! Dear God, it didn't bear thinking about. The tears flowed faster. To start life with the same name as a whore, and Liverpool's most famous whore at that! What kind of a start was that? What kind of a life would she have? 'Please God, don't let him do it! Let him change his mind! Let him see sense. Let him have some pity!' she prayed, but in her heart she knew her hopes would be dashed, her prayers unanswered. This tiny, helpless little girl would have to shoulder a crushing burden before she even had the strength to hold up her head which was covered with the soft, downy, auburn hair she'd inherited from her cruel and vindictive father.

Chapter One

1905

A COLD, DAMP MIST WAS stealing up from the river. Slowly it shrouded the buildings on the waterfront and was dimming the glare of the street lights. Maggie, standing at the top of the floating roadway, shivered and drew her shawl closer to her. Another ten minutes and then she'd head for Canning Place to meet Tommy. She'd had enough and she was bone weary. After the arrival of the next ferry she was going home.

She poked around in the pocket of her skirt and drew out a few coins. Threepence ha'penny. Not much for two hours spent standing in the bitter cold of a February evening but it was better than nothing. At least it would help Mam out a bit. She began to walk up and down, stopping occasionally to stamp her feet, before resuming her little promenade. At sixteen she was tall and slim, although she thought of herself as skinny. She was all arms and legs her Mam said. Her thick auburn hair was scraped back and tied with a piece of twine. Her face was oval, her nose a little tilted; her skin very pale and in some lights it looked almost translucent. But her eyes were her most alluring and unusual feature. They were large and the colour of amber flecked with gold and were fringed with thick auburn lashes. A fine-looking girl, was how Dora described her.

She stopped her preamble and peered into the increasing gloom, trying to ascertain whether or not it was the squat shape of the ferry boat she could see or was it just the roof of the Riverside Station. She shifted the tray of matches to her hip. Her hands were so cold they were numb. She didn't really have to stand around selling matches, she told herself, for she had a 'proper' job. She worked at Bibby's where animal feed was made and the place stank to high heaven, so it did her good to get some fresh air. She had been lucky to get the job and she didn't mind continually brushing the floor in the bagging room all day. It was better than breaking your back filling bags and sacks. It was only to earn a few extra coppers a day for Mam that she touted her wares on the streets. And to help out Tommy, of course.

Her eyes softened. She loved Tommy, he was more than just a brother. They were friends. From the day he'd been born she'd been close to him. They'd been drawn together by a mutual bond. They were both great disappointments to Da. She because she was a girl and Tommy because he'd been sickly and weak. Not the strong lusty lad her da had wanted. Mam had watched him like a hawk in the early days, praying he wouldn't catch any of the diseases that so frequently decimated the squalid courts.

Da was no help, even when he was there. Which wasn't often. She knew he had no time for any of them. But she was very often the butt of his anger and he called her terrible names. It was probably because she was his firstborn, his first disappointment, that he took out his spite on her. When he was drunk he yelled at her, saying she was a whore, that she was useless, that she should go into the workhouse out of his sight. It was at times like that that Maggie had to bite her tongue to stop herself from yelling that the best place for him would be the workhouse. There they'd get some work out of him. After all, Mam, Tommy and herself seemed to do nothing but work while he did nothing. Well, nothing honest. She took grim satisfaction from the fact that he had to work hard when he was in prison, and he'd been in and out of Walton Jail since she'd been born.

She stamped her feet and blew on her numbed fingers, then began to walk again. Mam had had to work, beg and borrow to keep a roof over their heads when he'd been inside, but she'd noticed that the atmosphere at home became lighter, less fraught when he was in jail and though Mam was permanently worn out, she'd seemed happier. Sometimes, she even sang. There had been times when Da hadn't been caught and then there had been more money for food and coal and clothes, but Mam never sang then.

She peered again into the gloom. The ferry was late, probably because of the fog that was becoming denser by the minute. The sound of foghorns blaring punctuated the eerie stillness and she shivered. It was strange how all the sounds of the street and the river had become muted and muffled. As though the fog really was a blanket that distorted all the noises and shut out the light, so that she could have been standing alone in the middle of a field. It would take her ages to get to Canning Place now. She just hoped Tommy would wait. She pursed her lips and began to whistle, more to cheer herself up than because she was happy. Then she remembered what Mam always said about whistling. 'A whistling woman and a crowing hen, bring the devil from his den.' There was one song she never sang or whistled, she thought savagely. The song about the woman she'd been named after. Maggie May. The famous whore who had walked these streets in the days when there had been hundreds of sailing ships on the river and no sign of the new, steam vessels. She hated that song and she hated her name. She hated her Da, too, for being so spiteful. She'd been six years old when she'd found out why the kids in the neighbourhood laughed and jeered at her. Katie Murphy from the top landing had told her and she'd run, crying, to her mam. Dora had tried to calm her, tried to explain gently but it had been Ma Jessup who had said, 'Don't beat about the bush, Dora, girl, give it to her straight, she's going to 'ave ter know about that doxy an' why that sod gave her the same name.'

So Dora had told her but she'd been too young to know what a 'whore' was. A bad woman who took money from men, was what Mam had said, but as she'd grown older the true meaning of the word was made patently and painfully clear to her. She'd learned how to fight then. Mam did all she could to protect her from the worst of the sneering and taunting, but Mam couldn't be with her all the time and so she'd learned how to deal with most of her tormentors. It was just the older lads and girls and some grown-ups she couldn't cope with. Her name was part of the reason why she and Tommy were so close, for no one wanted to be friends with someone called after a whore. Sometimes she was lonely, but usually Tommy was there to cheer her up.

When she'd started at Bibby's she'd come up against the familiar jibes and she couldn't fight there, for she'd lose her job. So, instead, she'd tried to make a joke of it. It was hard for her to do but it seemed to be the right approach. The other girls had stopped tormenting her, a couple of them had sympathized with her and defended her when some of the lads had begun to annoy her.

'Just because she's got that bloody awful name, doesn't mean she's a whore so bugger off!' Jinny Tate had yelled at one of the carter's lads one morning. Maggie had thanked her, but her cheeks flamed with rage, just the same.

The dull clanking of chains followed by a heavy thud brought her out of her reverie. The ferry had docked at last and the first passengers were making their way up the steeply sloping, cobbled roadway. Maggie settled her tray firmly and arranged her features in what she hoped was a cheerful expression. 'Matches! Matches! Buy your matches, here! Two boxes for a farthing! Best on the market! Made in Liverpool! Matches!' she yelled.

People pushed past her, all eager to get home to warm kitchens and hot dinners. The crowd thinned and Maggie pursed her lips in disappointment at the wasted effort. There would be no more sales tonight. She started to fold up the tray, engrossed in her task until someone spoke to her. Looking up, she saw a middle-aged man staring down at her.

'Do I get my matches or not, girl?' he asked impatiently.

Her cold fingers fumbled with the boxes. 'Sorry, sir, I didn't hear you.' He wasn't short of a bob or two she thought, taking in the heavy wool overcoat, its collar trimmed with fur, and the shiny, black beaver on his head. She was struck by his craggy, handsome face and dark, kindly eyes.

'Is this all the work you can find? A girl of your age should be in more gainful employment.'

Maggie didn't miss the note of disapproval in his warm but cultured voice. What would the likes of him know about employment, gainful or otherwise, she thought indignantly, although she didn't know what 'gainful' meant. 'I work at Bibby's as well as this! I do this to help our Tommy out . . . and me Mam!'

'Tommy is your brother I take it?'

Maggie nodded, still holding out the box of matches.

'And what does he do? Does he work?'

''Course he does,' she shot back. 'He sells papers, bundles of kindling, runs errands, anything he can get. He's no shirker, isn't our Tommy. An' he finished school!'

'How old is he?' The voice was less censoring and she thought he looked kind.

'Just fourteen.'

'And what does your father do, girl?'

Maggie hesitated and shifted her weight on to her right foot. 'He . . . he . . . left us,' she replied. Well, it was partly true, she thought. He did leave them a lot. There was no need for her to say: he's nearly always in jail.

'He deserted you?' The tone was now concerned.

Maggie nodded slowly. He hadn't deserted them, he just put himself first. He was selfish and that was as bad as being deserted in her eyes.

'How does your mother manage then?'

Maggie began to feel uncomfortable, wondering why he was taking such an interest in her. 'She goes out cleaning, she scrubs floors.'

'So, you all work then?'

Again she nodded. 'We have to, to pay the rent and buy . . . things.' To keep a roof over their heads and some food in their bellies, but mainly to keep Nago May in beer money, she thought savagely. The fog had become so thick she could barely see his face and she was very uneasy.

'What's your name, girl?'

Maggie drew away from him. She wasn't going to tell him. She wasn't that stupid. There were all kinds of odd people around these days. 'Laura,' she said flatly. It was what her mam had wanted to call her and she hated her name so much that often she thought of herself as actually being 'Laura'.

'Well, Laura, I admire people who try to make the best of their lives, improve their circumstances, despite all the difficulties. Take this and go home now. It's a bad night to be out alone.'

Maggie breathed a sigh of relief and took the coin he held out, then she bobbed a curtsey. Strange feller, that, she thought as she watched him disappear quickly into the gloom. She had begun to feel afraid of him. She peered hard at the coin but the street-lamp was so obscured by the fog that it was difficult to see it. Then she gasped aloud. It was a sixpence! A whole sixpence for a box of matches! He must have more money than sense! Quickly she pocketed it. She'd best get going in case he'd made a mistake and came back to rectify it.

She'd hurried as quickly as she could along the dock road and past the Goree Piazzas until the outline of the warehouses on the Albert Dock loomed faintly on the other side of the road. Then she turned into Canning Place, making her way past the squat buildings until she came to 'Mrs Mac's', the alehouse on the corner. It wasn't its real name, but it had been called after the landlady for so long that everyone had forgotten its proper one. 'Tommy! Tommy! Are you there, Tommy?' she called, for the cold, murky fingers swirled around her and she could see nothing.

'I'm here, Maggie. Where've you been? I'm froze to the marrer!'

Maggie grinned at the pale, thin lad, dressed in shabby trousers and jacket, a piece of red flannel wrapped around his throat, serving as a muffler. At least he had good strong boots on his feet tonight, she thought, for there had been many nights when his feet and her own had been bare. Before she had time to reply he was shaken by a racking cough and concern replaced the look of excitement on her face. 'I'm sorry, Tommy. You shouldn't have waited. You should have gone home, standing in this dampness is bad for your chest.'

'I'm all right! You and Mam are always fussing over me!'

'Well, you've always been sickly, like.'

'I haven't! I'm all right!' Tommy May said belligerently. He wished they would stop treating him like a baby, mollycoddling him all the time. He just got a bit of a cold now and then. He was small for his age, he knew that, but it didn't matter for he had brains. Miss Cumberland had said so, and she knew everything. He'd worked hard at school and had hoped to get an apprenticeship. Then he'd earn good money and have a trade too. It was his burning ambition, but he'd found no one to take him on and his days were now spent working on the streets. Miss Cumberland had helped him a lot. She'd given him extra lessons. She'd provided books and paper and pencils, things they could never afford. If he could just go on hoping he knew one day he'd get a fine job. He'd told his mam how good his teacher was, of course, but not his da. He knew what his reaction would be. He was ashamed of his da and he knew that both Maggie and Mam were too, although Mam would never admit it.

'Look what I've got.'

He realized his sister was smiling at him. 'What is it?'

'Some toff gave it to me, he must be mad. A sixpence! A whole sixpence!'

Tommy was incredulous. 'How many boxes did he buy then?'

Maggie laughed, her eyes sparkling. 'Just one. He started to ask me a lot of questions, about you and

Mam and Da. I told him Da had left us, made it look as if things were really bad so he'd cough up the money, but I was gettin' a bit scared of him, like.'

'Why? Did he look . . . well, you know . . .'

'No, he didn't look strange. It was just the way he kept talking to me. Anyway, I can look after myself.'

Tommy accepted her statement. She'd fought many of his battles as well as her own in the past. He slung the small bundles of kindling wood over his shoulder and linked his arm through hers. 'What are yer going to do with the money then?'

'First off, we're going to call in the chippy, to get three big helpings of fish, chips an' peas. I'm going to give Mam the change. She saw some good thick blankets down at Paddy's Market she said. Not worn too thin either, a real bargain. Won't that be great, Tommy? Nice warm blankets to keep us all snug at night. I'll keep the coppers I got tonight, for my bit of carry-out. Save Mam having to get me some. How did you do then?'

Tommy looked crestfallen. 'Only sold two. You'd think with this weather folk would be only too glad to get dry chips to start their fires up.'

Maggie sighed, 'Never mind. You know they can get the same in the shops. The fellers don't buy them 'cos the women get them with the shopping. It's mainly fellers that buy the matches and the papers so we should be thankful for that. I tell you what, you do the papers and the matches and I'll do the wood. I'll go down to St John's Market, round the back where they sell the monkeys and parrots, I might do better there.'

'We can try it out but better not tell Mam, she goes on and on about me standing at the Pierhead. Bad for me chest by the river, she says.'

Maggie looked down at him. She knew he was right but she hated to think of him walking the streets and selling nothing. That was desperate.

'Come on then, let's get a move on, I can smell them chips already and it's making me mouth water!'

Chapter Two

THE CHIPS AND FISH were wrapped in layers of newspaper and Maggie hugged them to her, savouring the warmth of the package against her chest, eager to get home, for the aroma was a torment to an empty stomach. It took much longer to reach Bowers Court because visibility was so bad and, as they hurried through the narrow alley that led to the courtyard, they could hear the drunken shouts and curses, then the yelping of a dog.

'Oh, hell! It's Da an' he's drunk!' she hissed with annoyance.

'Maybe we can creep along the wall an' he won't see us.' Tommy tugged at her arm, pulling her towards the wall of the house that formed the left side of the square.

'He's gorra nose like a bloody ferret, he'll smell the chips. Come on, let's make a dash for it!' Maggie advised.

As quietly and as quickly as they could, despite the

piles of debris, they reached the doorway to the house and rushed inside.

'Here, you take them and this and get upstairs! Sit on the landing outside Murphy's till he's gone to sleep!' Maggie pushed the warm, greasy parcel and four pennies into Tommy's hands.

'But they'll be cold by the time he goes to sleep!'

'Then eat yours. Mam can warm ours up. I'm not going to watch him scoff the lot an' he will. Now go on!' She pushed Tommy towards the flight of rickety stairs as she heard Nago's stumbling footsteps below.

They had moved out of the basement room last year, after Ma Jessup had died of the influenza. It was a far better room. It was bigger, with a proper window and a range and it was not so damp. It was still crowded of course, but that was normal, they expected nothing more. Everyone lived in one or two rooms. As Maggie pushed open the door Dora turned to greet her. Her face was set as though she were continually facing the icy winds from the river. Once she had laughed a lot and her expression had been cheerful, her cheeks plump. It was a long time since she'd laughed and her face was drawn, the frown lines deep and permanent.

'Thank God, I was getting really worried about you, where's Tommy?' Dora's voice rose as she realized Maggie was alone. She looked far older than thirty-seven. She was painfully thin, her shoulders rounded and her hair was peppered thickly with grey. Her pale-blue eyes were darkly circled with fatigue. She had borne life with resignation, if not tolerance, but tonight she felt even worse than usual. Her head was aching, her eyes burned and yet she felt hot and cold at the same time.

'He's on the landing upstairs. Da's on his way up, he's drunk – again. I had a bit of luck, Mam, and got us all fish an' chips and he's not havin' any, I told our Tommy not to come down until me da's asleep.'

'I ain't goin' to sleep until me belly is full!'

Maggie and Dora both turned to see Nago leaning heavily against the doorframe. He, too, looked far older than his years and his face was bloated with drink.

'Where's me dinner then, woman?'

Maggie turned away from him, thinking that his belly was full enough already but not with food. Dora bent over the range and ladled out a helping of thin, meatless stew into a dish and placed it on the table. At least now she had some decent bits and pieces, she thought. All bought with her wages and those of Maggie and Tommy, or 'obtained' by Nago, although what he brought to the house often disappeared along with him when the police arrived.

Nago stared down at the dish, his lip curling with distaste. 'Can't you cook anythin' other than bloody scouse?' he yelled. 'And blind scouse at that!' With one swipe he sent the bowl hurtling across the room. The dish smashed against the wall and its contents ran down on to the floor.

Dora didn't speak. Instead she continued to ladle

out the meal for Maggie.

Biting back her temper, Maggie took a cloth from beside the range and began to wipe up the mess. There were times when she positively hated her da. He was cruel and wicked.

'And you're just a useless girl,' he raged on at Maggie.

'Nago, you know she can't help being a girl. It's not . . . fair to blame her for that,' Dora said quietly. It was always the same. It had a pattern, did this abuse. She knew what was coming next.

'I do bloody well blame her and he's no bloody use either, is he? Sickly, weak, no use to a man is a son like that! Get rid of the pair of them! Then I'd get some peace!'

Be better if you never came home at all! Better if they kept you in Walton for ever, Maggie thought savagely, but she dare not say the words aloud.

'I'll wet the tea. A good, strong cup of tea will make you feel better, Nago,' Dora said, placatingly.

'Aye, sit down on the bed, Da, and I'll take your boots off.' Maggie added, praying he would submit to their combined coaxing.

'Tea! Bloody tea!' he spat, glaring at them both.

Maggie thought of Tommy, crouching on the cold, dark landing above and of the cooling chips and fish. 'Will I go and get you a jug of stout then, Da?' she asked brightly. She had no wish to go out again, but for the sake of peace, she would.

'An' have yer got the money for it, too?' he sneered.

'You know I haven't, Da.' She lied steadily. With him it came easily, she'd had plenty of practice.

His bleary, bloodshot eyes narrowed. 'Then where did yer get those boots then? Been whoring, have yer?'

'Nago, that's enough! You know she bought them from Paddy's Market last week! Used her own few coppers, too, she did. She's a good girl!' Dora cried, her patience exhausted after working a fourteen-hour day.

He laughed before lashing out and catching his wife across the side of her head with his open hand.

Maggie's eyes narrowed and a protest sprang to her lips but one look from her mother silenced it.

Nago staggered across the room and sank down on the bed, pulling the dirty muffler from around his throat. Then he began to sing raucously.

'Maggie, Maggie May,
They've taken you away
An' you'll never walk down Canning Place no more.
For she robbed so many sailors
An' captains of the whalers
That dirty, robbin', no good, Maggie May!'

Maggie dug her nails so hard into the palm of her hands that it hurt, but the pain was nothing to the shame and fury she felt. Wave after wave of it washed over her and, at that moment, she knew she could kill him. Dora caught her by the shoulders and propelled her towards the door.

'Get out, luv, for a few minutes!' she hissed. 'He'll go to sleep. Take no notice of him, he's not worth it!'

'I'll swing for him one day, Mam, so help me. God, I will!'

'Hush, luv! Go on, get out and sit with Tommy.'

With fury driving her, Maggie took the stairs two at a time.

'Maggie, what's goin' on? I can hear Da's yelling and swearing up here!'

She crouched down beside him. 'I hate him! I hate him! He belted Mam, yelled at me, then he called me a whore and starting singing that . . . that . . . song!' She couldn't bring herself to name it.

'Maybe he'll go thieving again and get nicked!' Tommy said hopefully, trying to console Maggie.

'We should be so lucky! He's getting too crafty for them. We haven't had any peace for ages.'

Tommy nodded glumly. 'Here, you might as well eat yours before they're stone cold.' He thrust the parcel of chips into her hands and she unwrapped it. The food was cold already but she was too hungry to care. She began to break the battered fish into pieces and cram them into her mouth.

Tommy went to the head of the stairs and leaned forward. 'Seems to have gone quiet.'

'Well, I'm not going down there until I've finished these!' she replied thickly, her mouth full.

The sound of footsteps was heard below and Tommy rushed back to his sister's side.

'Someone's coming up! It must be him!'

Maggie got to her feet. 'If he thinks he's going to start again, he's got another think coming! I'll push him down the flaming stairs first!'

They huddled together in the darkness as the footsteps came nearer, but Maggie sighed with relief as she realized that they were those of a woman.

'Jesus, Mary an' Joseph! You frightened the livin' daylights out of me!'

'Keep your big mouth shut, Katie Murphy! Do you want the whole house to hear you, screeching like that!' Maggie hissed loudly.

'Don't you tell me to shut me gob outside me own door, Maggie May! What are yer doing up 'ere anyway an' what's that you've got there? Been pinchin', 'ave yer?'

Katie pushed her way forward. She was a big, raw-boned girl, older than Maggie by three years.

'Nothing to do with you and we never go thieving!'

Katie laughed raucously. 'So, yer da's a bloody saint now, is he?'

'You know full well, Katie Murphy, that we don't follow me da!'

'What are yer doing up here?' Katie pressed.

'Minding me own business!'

'Snooping more like.' Katie made a grab at the newspaper parcel. 'What's in 'ere? I bet you've been in our room, haven't yer?'

'I haven't!' Maggie shot back, ducking the blow the

older girl aimed at her and then passing the chips deftly to Tommy. She caught Katie by the front of her blouse and pushed her hard against the wall.

Katie, taken by surprise, let out a yell and a curse then ran at Maggie, her fingers curved like talons. Tommy flattened himself against the door of the Murphys' room as Katie and Maggie scratched and tore at each other, both yelling at the top of their voices.

It was only a few seconds but it seemed like half an hour to Tommy, before running feet were heard on the stairs and the light from an oil lamp illuminated the scene.

Dora, with her free hand, caught Katie by the hair and yanked her backwards, and Maggie, seeing her mother, let her arm fall. 'Stop it, the pair of you! Stop it! Carrying on like a pair of Mary Ellens! Look at the state of you both. Hair like birds' nests and scratched faces!'

'She started it, Mam! She called us thieves! We were only waiting here, doing nothing wrong!'

'Never mind who started it. Do you want to wake your da up after the trouble I had getting him asleep?' Dora put out a hand to steady herself, feeling light-headed. The antics of these two she could well do without.

'She was skulkin' outside the door, Mrs May, what was I supposed to think?' Katie whined.

'Get in with you, Katie Murphy! Hasn't your poor mam got enough on her plate without you and our

Maggie rousing the whole damned house! Go on, get inside and get to bed and you two, get down those dancers before you feel the back of me hand!'

Katie put out her tongue at Dora's retreating back and went inside, slamming the door after her.

Maggie was incensed at the injustice of her mother's words. 'Mam, she went for me! I didn't start it, I didn't, isn't that right, Tommy?'

'It's the truth, Mam.' Tommy stoutly defended Maggie.

Dora paused outside her own door and brushed back Maggie's thick straggling locks. She felt awful. 'I'm sorry, Maggie, but I'm worn out and I hate to see you fighting like some common tart. God knows I've tried to bring you up decent.'

'Then you shouldn't have let him call me Maggie, should you!' Maggie cried. Her head hurt where Katie had pulled out a handful of hair and the numerous scratches were beginning to smart and she was tired and cold and hungry. She let out a startled cry as Dora's hand made contact with her cheek.

'Mam! What was that for?' she cried, the tears springing to her eyes.

'For being hardfaced!' Dora said, but already she felt sorry for her action. 'Oh, you know full well I couldn't do anything to stop him, luv. Come on, let's get those chips warmed up and I'll make a fresh pot of tea. It's been a long, weary day and I feel quite poorly.'

Instantly Maggie forgot her grievances. She peered

closely at her mother. 'You look flushed, Mam. I'm sorry. You sit down and I'll get the tea,' she said contritely.

Dora smiled but her head was bursting and her throat felt like sandpaper. She shook herself mentally. It was just a bit of a chill, she could shake it off. She would have to. She couldn't afford to lose her job, there were too many waiting to take her place. For the hundredth time that day she wished that Nago would make an effort to find honest work. It was such a burden trying to be breadwinner, mother and housekeeper, and his frequent spells of imprisonment made it hard for her to hold up her head amongst the decent families in the neighbourhood.

As she eased her aching body down into the chair by the range, Tommy held out his hand. 'What's this, lad?' she asked, puzzled.

'It's what's left over from the sixpence, Mam. You can get those blankets now. The ones you saw in the market,' Maggie said.

'What sixpence?' Dora asked.

As she made the tea and shoved the parcel of food into the side oven, Maggie recounted her piece of good fortune. When she'd finished she smiled down at her mother but then her expression changed, for Dora looked terrible. 'Mam! Mam! What's wrong?' she cried but barely were her words out than Dora had slipped from the chair to the floor.

Chapter Three

MAGGIE SAT UP WITH Dora all night. Frequently, during those long hours her eyelids drooped, while Tommy slept and Nago snored loudly beside his wife, who tossed and turned restlessly.

Dora had never felt so ill in all her life. Her whole body ached as though she had been kicked all over and her head felt as though a tight band of iron was crushing her skull. Her chest felt tight and her breathing was laboured. She had bouts of intense shivering and then her body burned as though it were on fire.

By morning, Maggie was worried sick. Her father she totally ignored. He could take care of himself, she thought. It was her mam who concerned her. 'You get off to your work, Tommy, I'm going up for Mrs Murphy. I don't like the look of Mam at all.'

Tommy's concern showed in his eyes. 'Will I wait until you get back?'

'No, I'll only be a minute or so.'

Tommy wound the red flannel muffler around his throat and pulled on his cap and then hovered by the door.

'Go on with you!'

'I'll get home as soon as I can, Maggie.'

When she was sure he'd gone, Maggie left the door ajar and ran quickly up the stairs and hammered on the door of the Murphys' rooms.

It was a bleary-eyed Katie who opened it and she glared at Maggie. 'What do yer want?'

'Your mam. Will your mam come down with me, our mam's sick and I'm worried. I've been up all night with her.' She ignored the girl's malevolent stare.

Mrs Murphy came to the door, her hair hanging loose, a man's old coat around her shoulders covering a grubby nightgown. 'Maggie, what's up, girl?'

'It's her mam. Took bad she is,' Katie informed her mother in a tone that made it clear she didn't care much for either Maggie or Dora.

'I don't know what's the matter with her but she's bad. Will you come down, please?' Maggie begged.

Mrs Murphy gave her daughter a shove. 'Get in with yez an' see to yer da now.'

Maggie breathed a sigh of relief as she followed the woman downstairs.

After leaning over Dora and placing a hand on her forehead, Mrs Murphy stood up, shaking her head.

'She needs a doctor, Maggie. I'd say it was the influenza. Sounds like it's got to her chest, too.'

Maggie looked at her with concern. 'We haven't got the money for a doctor. Isn't there anything I can get for her . . . do for her?' She knew there was the fourpence left from the sixpence but that wouldn't be enough. A doctor charged at least two shillings.

'I'd get that idle sod out of the bed for a start. Then try and prop 'er up, so she can breathe easier. Get the kettle boiling and keep it boiling, the steam is good. 'Ave yer got any flannel an' goose grease?'

Maggie shook her head. 'But I can go and get some and some medicine, I've got a few coppers. Would you stay with her? I won't be long. I'll run all the way.'

The woman nodded. No one in Bowers Court refused such requests, in times of trouble they all helped out. Then she shivered as she remembered that it was in this very room, only a year since, that Ma Jessup had died of the same disease that now held Dora in its grip. She was a superstitious woman and she hastily crossed herself. 'Ask the feller in the chemist shop for some Balsam an' something to rub her chest with an' don't let him rob yer blind!' she called as Maggie, wrapping her shawl around her and taking the money from the old tin box that had once held boot blacking, ran from the room.

When she returned after running all the way up Salthouse Lane and back, she was gasping for breath, but she was clutching a small bottle and a roll of flannel. There was no sign of Nago.

'I sent himself off with a flea in his ear all right!

Told him to get out, unless he wanted to go down with it, too.'

Maggie bent worriedly over her mother. 'I hope she'll be all right.'

'I've used a few old clothes and things, rolled them up to get her head up, see. She's still burning with a fever. Did yer get the things?'

Maggie placed them on the bed beside her mother, then bit her lip. 'She looks proper bad, Mrs M.'

'She's worn herself out tryin' to keep you lot an' with no help from that idle, useless get either! Shouldn't you be at your work, girl?'

For the first time Maggie remembered her job. 'I can't go and leave her like this!'

'You'll get the push and then where will yer all be? She can't work any more and himself won't, so what will yer do for money, Maggie?'

'Our Tommy has his papers and wood.'

Mrs Murphy shook her head. 'That won't keep body an' soul together. Get off with yer. I'll see to 'er. If yer run you might not be too late.'

Maggie hesitated. Mrs Murphy was right, she knew that. She might already have lost her job and they did need the money and would continue to need it until Mam was better and could work again. 'Will you send for me if . . . if she gets any worse?'

'That I will, now get off with yer. Herself will be in good hands, don't you fret now.'

* * *

Maggie had pleaded eloquently to the foreman. When she'd arrived she'd been so out of breath she could only gasp out a few words, but as her breathing had calmed, she had gasped out the whole story and she thanked God that he was in a good mood, for after wagging his finger at her and saying, 'All right, I believe you, girl, though thousands wouldn't, get to your work and don't be late again or I won't be so generous,' he'd walked off and she grabbed her brush and had begun to sweep the floor with great vigour.

As the day wore on her anxiety increased and at the dinner break Tommy came looking for her. She was sitting on the wall in the yard with three of the other girls.

'What's the matter? Did Mrs M. send you?' she cried as she saw Tommy.

'No. I came home and she chased me out, so I came here.'

'How was Mam?'

'She looked the same, Maggie, but she was moaning, sounded as though she were sort of . . . choking.'

'Oh, Tommy! Did Mrs M. say anything?'

'Only told me to clear off from under her feet.'

Maggie jumped down from the wall. 'I'm coming home.'

'Don't be a fool, Maggie. Owld Johnson will give yer the push for sure,' Lily Mabbs said.

'She's right, Maggie. Mrs M. will see to Mam,' Tommy added, wishing now he hadn't come, but he'd felt miserable and he'd wanted Maggie to cheer him up. To reassure him and tell him Mam was going to be fine.

'No. I'm going home.'

'Jesus! You're a fool, Maggie May! Well, don't come crying to me when you've no job and no brass! Your mam'll get over it, hundreds do!'

'Well, Ma Jessup didn't, Lily, and she was a fine strong woman. Me mam isn't strong.'

Lily gave up and stared resignedly out over the pewter-coloured waters of the Mersey. Maggie was making a mountain out of a molehill and she'd live to regret it, but she'd get no thanks for saying so.

They both ran home as quickly as they could but Tommy often had to stop for a pain in his side made him double over. Halfway up the stairs Maggie met Nago coming down. She caught his arm. 'Da! Is Mam all right? Is she?'

'How the hell would I know, that old bitch won't let me in me own home! I'm goin' down to the Baltic Fleet, get a bit of peace and a bit of cheerful company down there!'

Any other time Maggie would have tried to stop him but now she just shrugged and let him pass. He wasn't the one who was ill. As soon as she entered the room she could see that Dora was worse and panic gripped her heart. 'She can't get her breath! Why is she making that noise?' she cried.

Mrs Murphy got to her feet. 'The fluid's got to her

lungs, Maggie, ain't nothing to be done, except for her to go into the Infirmary.'

Maggie's eyes widened with horror. 'No! No! She's not going in that place, no one comes out of there alive! It's terrible, they just leave you.'

'You've been listening to gossip, girl. Course folk come out, they have proper doctors there.'

'No! Mam always said if she were going . . . going to . . .' She couldn't say the word. 'Then she wanted to be at home, that place is no better than the workhouse!'

'Suit yourself, but she needs help, proper help.'

Tommy tugged at Maggie's arm. 'Will I go for the doctor?'

Maggie nodded. She didn't care whether they had money or not, she *had* to do something for Mam.

'He won't come unless he sees the colour of your brass first, don't I know that for a fact!' Mrs Murphy said, grimly.

Maggie delved into her pocket and drew out the few coins she had left. 'That's all I've got, Tommy, give it to him and tell him I'll give him the rest as soon as I can. Go on, hurry!' She pushed her brother towards the door, ignoring his pale, worried face and turning back to her mother.

'Mam! Oh, Mam! Can you speak to me?' she whispered hoarsely.

Dora opened her eyes. She was too tired to fight any more and it was hard to breathe, harder still to speak. 'Maggie!' It was little more than a whisper.

Maggie bent closer. 'What is it, Mam?'

'Promise . . . promise me . . . you . . .' She fought for her breath while Maggie clung to her hand. 'You . . . you won't ever be like . . .'

'Like who, Mam?'

'Like *her*. The Maggie in the song.'

The tears spilled down Maggie's cheeks, unchecked and unheeded. 'Oh, Mam, how can you think like that? How can you think I'd do . . . anything like . . .' She choked.

'Promise?' Dora pleaded.

'I promise, Mam! I promise! You mustn't talk. You must save your breath!'

Dora closed her eyes, she felt more at peace now.

Maggie was so distraught that when Tommy returned with a young doctor, she was almost in tears. 'Oh, please, do something to help her! She can't breathe!'

She stood, clutching Tommy's hand, while the young man bent over her mother, listening to her chest with a stethoscope. Then he stood up and turned towards her, the look on his face striking pure terror into her heart.

'I'm sorry, there's not much I can do, it's pneumonia and she's so weak and undernourished.'

Maggie clutched at a straw, her fear wiping out her prejudice. 'The Infirmary! Will she be better there?'

Again he shook his head. 'I'm sorry, it's too late for that.'

She stared at him, her eyes wide, her hair tumbling

loosely around her stricken face. It couldn't be true! It couldn't. Mam wasn't too bad last night and now . . . now he was telling her . . .

The doctor was struck by her obvious grief and took pity on her. He was tired, for the influenza was raging and he'd been up nearly all night and in rooms like this one, and many that were far worse and when he had time to think, he raged at the futility of it all. Animals lived in better conditions than some of his patients, yet nothing was being done about it. These filthy, festering courts needed pulling down, their occupants needed proper housing with decent sanitation. He felt that all his training had been a waste for he was powerless to make any impression on the diseases that made vast inroads in such appalling conditions. 'Will it help if I stayed with you?'

Relief surged through Maggie. Perhaps he was wrong, perhaps that was what he meant. He was going to stay to see if he had been wrong. 'Yes. Oh, yes, please.' The tears sparkled on her lashes and the young man was suddenly struck by how lovely she was. In decent clothes, with a bit more flesh on her, she would be quite stunning, especially with those large, amber eyes, now luminous with tears. He smiled tiredly. 'Get some fresh water to sponge her down and make her as comfortable as possible. I'll hold her up.'

Maggie went to the task with rapidity, so eager that she splashed the water from the kettle down her skirt. Tommy stood next to her while Mrs Murphy told them she was going to find that 'Gobeen of a father of theirs, the devil take him! Down the alehouse at a time like this!' And sure wouldn't they all be better off without bloody men, 'except the likes of yourself, Doctor, an' the clergy, of course,' she added hastily.

Nago was too late. When Mrs Murphy had finally harangued and harassed him to leave the Baltic Fleet and he'd got home, he found a young man gently drawing the blanket over his wife's face and Maggie and Tommy clinging together, sobbing as though their hearts would break.

'For Christ's sake, can't you do something to shut those two up? Wailing like bloody banshees!'

'Don't you want to know about your wife?' The young man's tone was cold and accusing.

Nago looked abashed. 'What was it then . . . that . . . took her?'

'Pneumonia is what I will put on the death certificate. But I would say it was malnutrition, worry and this . . .' He threw out his hand to encompass the room.

Nago shuffled his feet. 'I did me best,' he whined.

Maggie lifted her head and glared at him. 'No you didn't. You never cared about Mam! You took all the money she earned and drank it! We were better off when you were in jail!'

Nago made to lash out at her but the doctor stepped quickly between them. 'That won't help anyone, especially your wife! I'll give you the certificate and then I suggest you go and register the death and make the necessary arrangements. I'll send my bill on.'

The insolent young devil, Nago thought. He felt no sorrow at Dora's death, all such feelings had gone long ago. 'We ain't got no money for bills or funerals.'

'Then I suggest you go down to the Parish Relief Office. You can't just leave her . . . leave things like this,' he quickly amended, before turning away in disgust from Nago. He touched Maggie on the shoulder.

Again she looked up, her eyes red and streaming. Mixed with her grief and shock was hatred for her da.

'I'm sorry about your mother. Will you be able to manage? Will you be all right?'

She choked back the sobs. 'I . . . we . . . we'll manage. Mrs Murphy will help us.'

He nodded slowly as he gathered up his bag. What chance had she? What a terrible waste of such beauty, spirit and, he guessed, intelligence.

When he'd gone, Nago stood staring at his children with distaste. They were still crying and it grated on his nerves. He lashed out at Maggie, catching her a hard blow across her head. 'Shut your bleedin' mouth before I shut it for you!' he yelled.

Something inside Maggie snapped and she launched herself bodily at her father, her fingers clawing at his face. 'Don't you hit me! Don't you touch me again or I'll kill you! I'll kill you! It's all your fault! You killed Mam! You did!'

Nago fell backwards, taken off guard, then he grabbed her hands and shoved her as hard as he could. She was thrown across the room and fell against the wall.

Tommy faced his father, his pale cheeks flushed, his eyes full of tears. 'Don't you belt Maggie! Don't you dare or I'll go for the scuffers! I will!'

The appearance in the doorway of Mrs Murphy, accompanied by three of the other neighbours, saved Tommy from a beating.

'Jesus, Mary an' Joseph! Isn't this a fine way to be carrying on, Nago May, an' herself hardly cold! Get out of here, while we lay her out, God rest her. Have you no respect for the dead? Clear off!'

'Aye, bugger off, Nago May!' another cried.

Before this concerted attack and the fact that the other women were all scowling at him and he knew they were all capable of violence, Nago fled.

Maggie picked herself up. Her head was aching where it had hit the wall but it was nothing to the ache in her heart. She just wanted to run away. Take Tommy and run. Anywhere. Anywhere that would offer her a little peace to grieve for her mam.

One of the neighbours made a pot of strong tea and gave them each a cup. Maggie and Tommy huddled together while the women worked.

When the work was done, Mrs Murphy looked down at them. 'Come and look at her.'

Tommy drew back and Maggie put her arm around him.

'She loved you both, God bless her soul. No need to worry about her now.'

'What will we do now, Mrs M?' Maggie asked.

The woman shook her head sadly. 'It will have to be a pauper's grave, Maggie girl, and then . . . then you'll have to look after Tommy. You'll have to take her place now.' She took Maggie's hand and drew her to her feet. 'Come an' see her, say a little prayer for she won't never be cold or sick again.'

Maggie clutched Mrs Murphy's hand tightly as she stood gazing down at the face she loved so much and she smiled through her tears. Mam looked so . . . different. Younger and . . . happier. She had loved them so much. 'Oh, Mam, why did you have to leave us?' she said quietly and then she felt a great weight settle on her shoulders. Mrs M. was right. She'd have to look after them now. She would have to be a mother to Tommy and she'd have to contend with her da and that prospect filled her with dread. She reached out and gently touched Dora's cheek. 'Help me, Mam. Help me to be like you and I won't forget my promise.'

Chapter Four

MAGGIE PAUSED ON THE landing to get her breath. Her back and shoulders felt as though they were on fire they ached so much, and she was freezing cold. She'd had to wait in line at the standpipe in the centre of the Court for the water was late being turned on. The delay had infuriated her for it was time she could ill afford to waste. She pressed her hands into the small of her back and grimaced, tucking the ends of her shawl into the waist of her skirt. Usually it was Tommy who dragged the heavy buckets up from the yard below but he was still out.

She resumed her task, thinking that it didn't seem like any time at all since Mam had died and yet, in another way, it seemed like years. It would be Christmas at the end of the month and she wasn't looking forward to it. It would be even more cheerless, with less to celebrate than there had been in the past. Two of those long-ago Christmases had been good though, she reflected. Da had been in jail and they'd had a big parcel from the Goodfellows' Fund and another one from the fund the scuffers paid in to. They'd had a whole goose, vegetables, biscuits, apples, oranges, and a stone bottle of ginger beer. Mam had got them some nearly new things to wear and a penny toy each. The ghost of a smile hovered around her lips for a second before it disappeared as she reached her front door.

Now her days had settled into a routine of pure drudgery, for there was so much to do. Shopping, cooking, cleaning, washing and always trying to make the pennies stretch further and further for Da demanded all their wages and only after many hard battles had been fought had she got any money to keep house with. She was always tired when she got home when another day's work faced her.

She'd lost her job at Bibby's, but at the time she hadn't cared. Da had made a bit of an effort to get honest work, labouring on the site that was going to be the big, new Liver Building, down at the Pierhead. But that hadn't lasted long. So, she'd had to go looking again and it had taken her nearly a month before she was taken on at the match works. Selling matches had been bad enough, but making them was far worse. Her head ached and her stomach heaved with the fumes of the phosphate, but that was nothing compared to the terror of contracting 'phossy jaw', the disease that the chemical caused, which ate into the jaw bone and for which there was no cure.

The room was dim and drab she thought as she looked around. It was a far from welcoming sight. She did her best but there wasn't much she could do, with her limited resources, to dispel the dampness or disguise the large cracks in the walls and ceiling. She tried to keep it clean and tidy, but with three people living, eating and sleeping in it, she felt it was a total waste of energy. But she went on trying, for Mam's sake. Dora had managed and so would she, she often told herself resolutely.

She filled the kettle and pushed it on the hob. Then she poured a little water into a chipped enamel bowl and began to scrub the potatoes. She'd bake them tonight, they were just the thing on a cold early December evening and they were filling. With a bit of bread and dripping and a mug of tea it wasn't a bad meal.

It was Tommy she felt sorry for. He worked like a Trojan all day and late into the evenings.

'What use will all that book learning be to him, anyway? It's time that lazy young bugger got some proper work and brought some decent money into the house,' Nago had commented, acidly, when Tommy had got the job with the coal merchant. She'd said nothing about the money Tommy had been bringing in for years. The yard was down near Wapping. He helped fill the sacks from the great mounds stored up on the dockside. At first she'd been terrified that the work would kill him but he seemed to have gained strength. He'd grown, too. He was still thin, but he was what Mrs M. called 'the greyhound breed'. He was wiry and had stamina. More stamina than anyone imagined for he'd even tried to keep up his lessons after work with Miss Cumberland, his old schoolteacher, but he was so dog-tired in the evenings that he could hardly put one foot in front of the other, let alone try to take in all the facts and figures.

Maggie had gone to see Miss Cumberland, to explain the situation, for she knew Tommy wouldn't give up and throw the woman's generosity in her face. She liked the teacher enormously.

'Tommy uses the brains God gave him and he works hard and under very difficult circumstances, I know that.'

'The circumstances are nigh on impossible, miss. He's dead on his feet when he gets home from work. But he's stubborn as a mule, too, and he wants to have a trade so badly.'

Miss Cumberland had looked thoughtful and Maggie had felt a little uncomfortable, wondering what she should do or say next. But then Miss Cumberland had smiled and said, 'I think I have the answer. What about Sunday? He doesn't work on Sundays and he can't possibly be absorbing much the state he comes in on Tuesday and Thursday nights.'

'He helps me in the morning, miss.'

'Well, what about the afternoon?'

Maggie had nodded. 'A few hours when he ain't so

tired would be just fine. I don't want to see all his hard work going to waste, miss, and I just know he'll get an apprenticeship one day. But . . . but . . . we can't afford . . .' she'd muttered, embarrassed, her gaze flitting around the small parlour, noting the good quality carpet and hide-covered sofa, the heavy curtains at the window and the many ornaments and pictures.

'Maggie, I don't want paying! I've never asked for money before, have I? If only you knew how wonderful it is to teach someone who really wants to learn! Most of the time at school it's as much as I can do to keep them under control and teach them to write their name and read a little.'

So Tommy had gone every Sunday afternoon to the neat little house in Cleveland Square until last week when there had been another row because Da had followed him there and had made a show of Tommy in front of Miss Cumberland and most of Cleveland Square as well.

As she placed the potatoes in the oven beside the range, the door opened and she turned. 'Stand there, till I get some newspapers. I've just finished scrubbing the floor.'

Tommy stood where he was. He was covered from head to toe in coal dust and the whites of his eyes stood out in his blackened face like a minstrel from a music hall revue. When Maggie had put down the papers he began to strip off his clothes. She only washed them once a week and then down in the yard because of the mess.

'Leave them there, I'll go and beat them on the wall downstairs afterwards. The water's ready. Don't look at me like that, Tommy May, it's hard enough dragging those buckets up here, without wasting water.'

'What's to eat, Maggie?' Tommy asked, soaping his hands with the block of carbolic and attacking his face vigorously, feeling ashamed of himself. Maggie had enough to do seeing to the place and Da without him complaining about having to get a good wash down every day.

'Baked tatties and bread an' dripping.'

'When I've finished washing, shall I take those down for you?' Tommy jerked his head towards two big buckets standing in the corner.

'You're a good lad, Tommy.'

'No sign of Da?' Tommy asked, scrubbing hard at his arms with a bit of cloth. The water had turned a dirty grey with a thick rim of coal dust adhering to the sides of the bowl.

Maggie looked at him scornfully. 'Don't be daft, it's too early for him. I'll leave him some bread and dripping because he'll have had a meal. Oh, he thinks I don't know that he gets a hot pie either in the morning or afternoon, but I've seen him coming out of Sullivan's.'

'You going out then?' Tommy questioned.

'Only along the road. Garrity's stays open late and

I might get some fades cheap and maybe a bit of scrag end,' Maggie replied. Garrity's was the grocer's on the corner of Carpenter's Row and Mr Garrity was always good to her. When all her chores were done, she knew she wouldn't feel like traipsing out, she'd be ready for her bed, but there was nothing for a meal tomorrow so she had no choice.

'I'll walk with you as far as Grayson Street. I'll take the sack.' One of the perks of Tommy's job was that, once a week, he was allowed to take a sack down to the coalyard, after working hours, and fill it with the lower grade of coal and slack. It was something Maggie was very grateful for for it meant they had a good fire all winter. Sometimes, one of the older men helped Tommy to carry it back and up the stairs.

It was nearly ten o'clock when Maggie at last walked back along Hurst Street towards home. She was exhausted but satisfied. In the hemp bag over her arm was a bit of scrag end, some bones, which would make some broth, a few potatoes and some carrots. Mr Garrity had slipped a small bag of lentils, a twist of tea and one of sugar into the bag too, and when she'd begun to thank him he'd brushed aside her words. 'You're a good girl, Maggie, and I always admired your mam. A fine, good woman, she was, and she had a hard time of it. Knew her when she was a young lass, I did. She wasted herself on him! Everyone thought so,' he'd finished bitterly. She'd nodded her agreement before leaving the shop. She'd make a big pan of scouse which would do them for a couple of days, until she got her wages and then the housekeeping, if Da didn't owe it all.

There was no sign of Tommy and she sighed. He must be lugging the coal home by himself tonight. As she reached the door she stopped, hearing the sound of voices coming from within. She placed her ear against the widest crack. There was little that could be kept secret in the ramshackle old house. It was her da but she didn't recognize the other voice. Da had had a couple of jars, she could tell by the way he was slurring his words slightly. She caught the words 'scuffers out of sight' and 'always money' and then 'only an owld cocky watchman'. She held her breath, then her da said, 'Mr effin' bloody Robinson's as tight as a duck's arse', and she knew what was going on. A robbery was being planned. Robinson's, the big ships chandler's and supplies yard at the corner of Pownell Street and Park Lane was obviously the target. She stood very still wondering what to do. If Da went to jail they would have a bit of peace for he'd go away for a long time, if he was caught. If she were to go to the scuffers . . . She caught her breath and bit her lip. No, no she couldn't do that. No one in their neighbourhood ever went to the scuffers for help and no one ever grassed on their neighbours, let alone their family or relations. If anyone found out she would be hounded out of the area and her da would kill her.

Thankfully, she heard the sound of Tommy dragging the sack up the stairs and she breathed a little easier. She must have been mad to even think of it. It was just wishful thinking. Like the way she often dreamed of running far away before common sense took over, and she asked herself who would take care of Tommy.

The sound of the voices within fell silent as she opened the door and helped Tommy drag in the coal. Maggie looked innocently at her da and the dark-haired, thickset man who sat opposite Nago. An empty jug and two dirty beakers were before them on the table.

Nago got to his feet. 'Oh, so you've finally decided to come home, the pair of yez! Where's me dinner?'

'I left it on top of the press. I've been down to Garrity's and Tommy's been for the coal,' she stated flatly.

'Bread an' drippin'! Call that a meal!' Nago demanded.

'It's all we had, Da,' she answered, taking the vegetables from the bag and shoving them quickly into the press, shooting a surreptitious look at her father from beneath her lashes, trying to judge his mood.

'What's that?' Nago asked.

'Only a few fades, bits for tomorrow. There'll be scouse for you tomorrow night and it'll be pay day soon.'

Tommy engrossed himself in building up the fire, placing the larger lumps of coal carefully, his back to

Nago for he didn't like his da's friend. He knew him; Mick Devanney was known to be a hardened criminal, and one who often used violence to gain his ends. In fact he was someone to avoid like the plague.

Nago looked at his mate. 'No use stoppin' here, Mick, too many flappin' ears and waggin' tongues and nowt to eat either!'

The other man nodded his agreement. 'I'm off to the Queen's Dock. I'll see yer termorrer, Nago.'

Neither Maggie nor Tommy spoke as he left but, when he'd gone, Tommy whispered to Maggie, 'He's a real bad 'un, that Mick Devanney.'

Maggie grimaced. 'I know. I heard them talking, I think they're going to have a go at Robinson's.'

Tommy sucked in his breath. 'When?' he hissed.

Maggie shrugged.

'What will we do?'

Maggie looked at Tommy with surprise. 'What can we do?'

'What's goin' on between you two? What's all the whisperin' about? Don't think I'm bloody daft an' can't hear you!' Nago demanded.

Maggie wiped her hands on her sacking apron.

'Da, you . . . you won't go doing anything . . . well . . . wrong?'

Nago glared at her suspiciously. 'Who have you been talking to, girl?'

'No one, Da! Honestly! it's . . . it's just that we . . . we don't want you to . . . get into any more . . .

trouble.' She didn't mean it and her lack of sincerity was evident in her tone but Nago didn't notice.

He seized her by her shoulder and dragged her roughly towards him. 'What have you heard? Come on, don't beat about the bush! Tell me who's been blabbin' to you or by God I'll beat it out of yer!'

'No one, Da! That's the truth, it is!'

'It is, Da. We just thought, seeing him here, that . . .' Tommy interrupted and then fell silent.

'An' why shouldn't he be here. It's my place an' I'll have who I like in!' He released Maggie suddenly and sat down, the colour draining from his face.

'Da, what's the matter? You've gone a funny colour.' Tommy asked as both he and Maggie stared at Nago, Maggie ruefully rubbing her shoulder, her amber eyes dark and resentful.

'Dunno. Feel . . . feel sort of queer. Dizzy, me legs 'ave gone numb, too, an' me fingers.'

Too much ale, serves you right! Maggie thought grimly. 'You're just tired, Da. Come on now, get to bed. A good night's sleep and you'll be fine,' she coaxed, praying there was nothing more seriously wrong with him than a few jars too many. It would only mean more work for her.

Nago let Maggie and Tommy help him to the bed and take off his boots and jacket. He did feel ill but it was nothing like any illness he'd ever experienced before. The ale must have been off, he thought before he sank into a deep sleep.

'It might be a blessing in disguise, Maggie. If he's bad then he can't go knocking off Robinson's with Devanney, can he?' Tommy whispered, hopefully.

Maggie sighed. There was that way of looking at it, she supposed. She frowned as the sound of voices drifted up from the stairs, increasing in volume. She cursed, thinking that Devanney had come back and would wake Nago, but then she realized it was Katie and her mother and that they were laughing uproariously. She grinned at Tommy. 'At least someone's got something to laugh about,' she said, jerking her head towards the door, but her grin disappeared to be replaced by a look of annoyance as someone hammered loudly on the door,

'Open it quickly, Tommy, or they'll have him awake!' she hissed.

Tommy did as she bade him and opened the door to reveal Katie and her mam, their faces flushed and eyes dancing with merriment.

''Ere Maggie, girl, we've got to tell you this! Dead funny it is!' Mrs M. pealed with laughter, her eyes almost disappearing into the folds of loose flesh.

Katie screamed with mirth. 'Oh, Mam, you're a case! Dead funny!' she shrieked.

Maggie could see they had both been drinking and her irritation increased. 'Me da's not well an' I don't want him waking up.'

Katie peered at her and grinned. ''E been out boozing tonight, Maggie?'

'Don't ask daft questions, Katie Murphy!'

'This will teach all the no-good, drunken gets in this city!' Mrs M. roared, leaning against the door frame, her ample bosom shaking.

'What will? What are you both talking about?' Maggie demanded, wishing they would shut up and go away.

'Someone has put arsenic in the beer! Thousands of barrels have been emptied into the bloody river!'

Maggie's mouth dropped open.

'It's true,' Katie laughed. 'Half the drunken sots in the city have been poisoned! Serves them right! Good job me da only drinks the hard stuff!'

'But . . . but . . . you . . .' Maggie stammered, not knowing what to think.

'There's no harm to us, Maggie. Can't stand ale. Our Katie and me only have a nip of gin. Got expensive tastes in our 'ouse.'

'Da. Da's been drinking ale,' Tommy cried.

This statement had the effect of sending both Katie and her mother into fresh spasms of laughter. 'Serves him right! Got his comeuppance at last! God bless the feller what did it, I say, an' I bet there's plenty other women that would second that. Quite a few should be shut of idle drunken husbands! There'll be a few fine wakes around here before the week is out, Maggie girl!'

'As long as they don't get ale in, Ma!' Katie again screamed with laughter.

Mrs Murphy tried to arrange her features into a more decorous expression and failed. 'Come on now, Katie, an' let poor Nago May get his sleep! It might be his last, if these two get lucky!' she laughed, taking Katie's arm and dragging her away towards the stairs.

Maggie closed the door slowly and looked at Tommy. 'Do you think she's right? Or was she just having a bit of a laugh? They're both a bit tipsy.'

'Why would she joke about something like that? It must be true. Do you think he's . . .' Tommy jerked his head in the direction of the bed.

Maggie bit her lip. 'I don't know.' She picked up the empty jug from the table and sniffed it. 'It smells all right.'

'He might not have had much of it. Maybe Devanney had most of it. I hope he did. At least this will put paid to their plans for Robinson's, Maggie.'

She nodded slowly. Mam used to have a saying. 'The Lord works in mysterious ways.' Well, maybe this was His way of keeping Nago out of trouble or of keeping Mr Robinson from being burgled more like, she thought, for she was certain that the Lord had given up on Nago May long ago.

Chapter Five

WHEN NAGO AWOKE THE following morning his head felt heavy and his legs a bit weak but that was all. Just a few aches and pains, he told himself. No wonder, living in this damp hovel, he thought, completely dismissing Tommy's welcome addition of free coal and the fact that the room was far warmer and brighter than many in the house. He'd have a bit of a wash, go out and get a bite to eat in Sullivan's eating-house opposite the Albert Dock gates and then get round to see Devanney about the plans for tonight.

He looked around the room, which was tidy enough he supposed but he scowled at the rack of washing, suspended from the ceiling, that was slowly drying in the rising heat from the fire which Maggie had banked down with slack, so it wouldn't burn away too quickly. A fine mist of steam was rising from it and he wrinkled his nose with distaste at the smell of damp wool and cotton. There was nothing to be gained by staying here and he slammed the door hard behind him, knowing it would be heard upstairs by Mrs Murphy. Nosy old biddy, that. She probably knew everything about them by now. She probably knew how many cracks were in the ceiling. Nosy old cow. Still, if the job went well tonight, he'd have enough money to get away from here, away from Liverpool altogether. He might even go back to Dublin, he speculated. Get himself some fancy duds, a nice place up in Stephen's Green and then go back and cock a snoot at the Christian Brothers. He'd show them how well he'd got on despite them, and that honesty didn't pay.

He felt his spirits rise as he contemplated that rosy future, heightened further by the excitement generated by the forthcoming job, and it wouldn't go wrong this time. Devanney would make sure of that, he was too smart and he himself was no novice now either. There were ten or fifteen minutes when there would be no scuffers about, when they went for their tea break and Devanney would make sure that that doddering old fool of a watchman wouldn't stop them. Devanney also knew where the money was kept. He'd made it his business to find out. It was in a tin box in a cupboard that was kept locked, but that presented no problem – it was nothing that a quick wrench with a crowbar wouldn't sort out and then . . . His eyes lit up at the thought. On Fridays the box would be full to bursting with crisp white five-pound notes and golden guineas. Old Robinson was not only a miser but he was a fool, too. He told everyone how he distrusted banks and what he actually did with the money had been open to speculation for some time.

His step was lighter, his head clearing and he pushed his cap to the back of his head and began to whistle. Tomorrow, Nago May – no, Mr Ignatius May – would be kitted out and on the midnight mailboat to Dublin. He'd just have a quick glass or two on his way to Devanney's. Set him up for the day, that would.

As he entered the saloon bar of the Brunswick, known locally as the Seven Steps he looked around. The place was unusually empty. 'What's up, Jacko? All your customers deserted you an' gone to the Queens?' he said good-naturedly to the barman.

'No. Business is bad for everyone.'

'Since when?' Nago demanded, sarcastically.

'Since some bleedin' fool put arsenic in the beer!'

Nago's mouth went dry. 'Christ, yer jokin'!'

'Wish I bloody well was. It's no joke!'

'Who the hell would do that?' Nago began to feel alarmed, remembering how peculiar he'd felt last night.

'My bet is it's some bloody temperance society. The Brewery's not too happy either. They've lost a lot of money, but they can afford it. You never see a poor brewer! Just a poor landlord.'

'An' not many of them either,' Nago replied cuttingly.

'I'll be on the Parish at this rate. My ale's not

poisoned. I've just tapped a new barrel, but try telling that to me customers! Are yer drinking or have yer just come in to gloat?'

Nago ran his tongue over his lips. He had a powerful thirst, but could he take a chance?

The landlord noticed his hesitation. 'I'm telling you, Nago, on me mother's grave, there's nowt wrong with my ale! I've sampled it meself and I'm still standin'!'

'Oh, all right, give me a glass then.' His mood of optimism returned. 'Take more than a bit of a bloody scare to put me off me drink!'

'That's the way, lad, and be sure when you leave to tell everyone you see that the ale in the Brunswick is good and pure.'

Nago's fears diminished as the day wore on and he felt no ill effects. He began to boast to all his mates that he wasn't a man to sign the pledge. It would take more than a bunch of bloody miserable temperance fellers to frighten him off his ale. Just to prove his point he had three more glasses in three different pubs and basked in the open admiration he attracted, although there were mutterings behind his back about what a bloody eejit he was.

He spent the afternoon and early evening with Mick Devanney in the room Devanney rented in a house off Jamaica Street, a house in a worse state of decay than that in Bowers Court. They went over and over the plan until they both felt it was foolproof, then to set themselves up and kill the last few hours, they had a few more glasses in the Flying Dutchman on the corner of Canning Place and Litherland Alley and Nago slipped a bottle in his pocket, just in case his throat got dry, he told Devanney.

At the appointed time, after waiting to hear the chimes of St Nicholas's at the Pierhead, they crept down Pownell Street flattening themselves against the wall. It was a clear, frosty night. The sounds of the ships on the river and in the nearby Salthouse Dock carried clearly. The stars glittered brightly and the moon was full, circled with a milky white aura that foretold more frost, but Nago was sweating and his heart was hammering against his ribs. Just a few nerves, he told himself. He always felt like this just before a job.

They both shrank further back into the shadows of a doorway as the policeman on his returning beat stopped to chat for a few minutes with the watchman, stretching out his hands to the warmth of the brazier that crackled in the sharp air. Then he continued on his way to the station. Nago heard Devanney let out his breath slowly with relief, then, when the street was deserted, he whispered 'Now!'

Nago ran quickly and quietly down the street, then turned off and scaled the wall that ran around the back of the building, a wall that threw deep shadows that afforded him plenty of cover. He didn't want to know what Devanney was up to, but he hoped he didn't kill the old man, just knock him senseless. He slid down into the yard and, by the light of the moon, quickly found the door, just where Devanney said it would be. So far so good, he thought with relief, his nervousness diminishing. One wrench of the crowbar broke the lock on the door and he was inside. It was pitch dark but he remembered Devanney's instructions and directions and felt his way cautiously around until he found what he was looking for.

He crouched down behind the counter, searching clumsily for the padlock, wishing he'd had the foresight to bring some matches. He gashed his hand against a sharp corner and cursed but there was not time to waste worrying about it. Again he tried to ease the crowbar behind the lock and again it slipped. His breathing became ragged. He was all fingers and thumbs. Yer bloody great fool! he cursed himself. Precious seconds were ticking by but at last he felt the lock give. One more wrench would do it. The lock gave suddenly and he fell backwards with the sudden movement but, scrabbling on his hands and knees, he reached inside the cupboard. His fingers closed around a metal box and he grinned to himself. That was it! That was it! He'd made his fortune now, so to hell with everyone!

He staggered to his feet and suddenly the room tilted sickeningly. He let out a yell and tried to clutch at the top of the counter but the solid surface eluded him and he was slipping down. Then it seemed as though all hell had been let loose. He heard yells and shouts from outside, accompanied by the sound of pounding feet and the shrill blasts of a whistle! There was more yelling and cursing and he recognized Devanney's voice. The scuffers! The scuffers were back and there must be dozens of them, judging by the noise! Panic engulfed him and a cold sweat broke out from every pore in his body. He had to get out – and fast – and not the way he'd got in, for they'd be waiting for him! He tried to open the box, but his fingers felt stiff and numb. At last he managed it and frantically he tried to stuff the notes into his pocket, but his fingers were inflexible and the notes slipped. There was no time to pick up those he'd dropped.

All Devanney's instructions were forgotten as he staggered and blundered into coiled piles of hawsers, bales of sailcloth, buckets and lamps, metal parts for pumps and winches. The commotion outside was growing louder and he was becoming frantic when at last he found a door. The small side door that led into the jigger that ran into Shaw's Alley.

Once outside he gulped in the cold, stinging air. The sweat was pouring down his face. He managed to get the bottle of ale from his pocket and took a deep swig. He must think and think quickly. If he ran they were sure to hear his boots on the cobbles. He must take it slowly, keep close to the wall, no matter how much his senses urged him to run. But could he run? His legs felt shaky and he couldn't feel his feet. In fact, everything seemed to be freezing up, including his insides. Devanney must have killed the old man and someone had seen or heard him, or maybe the scuffers had got wind of it somehow. All that careful planning down the drain. Still, at least he had some of the money. To hell with Devanney, it was his own fault for being so bloody heavy-handed and vicious. He had his own skin to think of now, for if he was caught it would be ten years' hard labour this time or he may even be charged with being a party to the attack on the old watchman.

He had nearly reached the end of the entry. Soon he would be out in Shaw's Alley. Then he could run to Salthouse Lane, then to the safety of Bowers Court. When he got home he could think more clearly, calm down and make plans. Just a few more yards and he would be safe. He took another swig from the bottle and stumbled on.

No one had chased him as he'd staggered up Shaw's Alley or Salthouse Lane, but he felt it had taken him hours. He was ill, but he had to get home. As he reached the entrance to the court he leaned against the wall. His throat felt as though someone was squeezing it hard. He dragged himself slowly up the stairs and collapsed against the door which opened so suddenly that he went reeling into the room.

Maggie screamed, startled by his sudden appearance and his contorted face. 'Da! Da! What's wrong?' She caught him by the shoulders and steered him towards the bed.

'Maggie! Take . . .' Nago couldn't speak. He shoved the screwed-up notes towards her.

She stared at them as though they were pieces of rock from the moon.

'Hide . . . scuffers . . .' His whole body was rigid and Maggie pushed him on the bed.

'Oh, God, Da! What have you done?' Maggie stood staring at him, her eyes wide with fright. They'd all go to jail if the money was found here. Frantically she looked around the room. There was nowhere to hide it. Nowhere where they wouldn't look anyway. They tore the place apart; she knew that from bitter experience and most of the time they had no search warrant. Hastily she folded it neatly and pushed it inside her blouse. They'd have to search her, but she didn't think they would. Maggie turned her attention to Nago. 'Da, what's the matter with you? Are you hurt? Did you fall?'

He didn't reply and she stood there, twisting her hands helplessly. He'd got home and climbed the stairs, so he couldn't have broken any bones. She'd have to go up for Mrs M., she'd know what to do.

Tommy had come in when she got back and he turned frightened eyes towards her. 'What's the matter with him, Maggie? What's he done? The Lane is full of scuffers, hundreds of them. I heard that the old watchman's dead. Battered over the head with an iron bar.'

Maggie gasped and clapped her hand to her mouth. Behind her, Mrs Murphy eyed Nago grimly.

'Jesus, God and the holy saints! He'll swing at the

end of the rope this time!' Mrs M. yelled, crossing herself. 'The poor old man, he never did no harm to anyone!' She pushed past Maggie and walked over to the bed, glaring down at Nago. 'Do yer hear me, Nago May! You'll swing this time!' She turned quickly as she heard Maggie scream, and saw the doorway blocked by the towering figure of a policeman.

'Got the bastard!' he shouted over his shoulder and they heard the pounding of heavy boots on the stairs.

Maggie and Tommy clung together, shaking, but Mrs M. was made of sterner stuff. Much as she hated Nago May and condemned what she was sure he'd had a hand in, she wasn't going to give him away to the scuffers. 'Get out, the lot of yez! Can't yer see the man's sick? In agony he is, poisoned beer, it is!'

'Don't give me that, Ma! He was seen running here. Poor old Fred Blake is lying with his skull smashed in and there's money gone, too! It was him all right and Devanney. But we'll get that bastard too. Move yourself!'

Mrs M. held her ground. 'Look at him, yer daft sod! How could it be him? He can't even stand up! He's been here this past hour, ain't that right, Maggie?'

Maggie nodded, not trusting herself to speak, terrified that they would all be carted off to the police station. The sergeant pushed his way into the room.

'Ma here swears it wasn't him. That he's been here for over an hour and that he's ill. Some of that beer laced with arsenic,' the constable informed his superior.

'Don't give me that, Ma. I wasn't born yesterday. He was seen by one of my lads!'

'Then whoever saw him needs bloody eyeglasses! He's been here with me and his kids. We was just going to go for the doctor when you lot barged in here without a by-your-leave, never mind a bloody warrant!'

'We don't need a warrant for a murderer and I've got a reliable witness,' the sergeant replied grimly, bending over Nago who looked ghastly.

'It's his word against ours!' Mrs Murphy cried.

The sergeant turned to Maggie. 'You, girl, will you swear in court that he's been here for over an hour?'

Maggie's heart dropped like a stone but she nodded, praying she would never have to do it, praying that Mam would forgive her for she knew that her da was guilty.

'Now will you let the girl go an' get the doctor before he dies an' it'll be your fault! Go on, get out an' leave honest folk in peace!' Mrs M. yelled.

Their faces grim and set the police left and as soon as the footsteps had died away, Mrs M. turned to Maggie. 'I wasn't joking, girl, he's bad. Go and get that young doctor who came out to your mam. Go on, move yourself. They'll have left someone behind to see if you do go out.'

Snatching her shawl from the back of the chair, Maggie ran.

Chapter Six

IT HAD ALL HAPPENED SO suddenly that Maggie was dazed. Da was dead. The kind young doctor had shaken his head yet again and repeated his regret. He'd asked questions, which hostelry had Nago spent the evening in? He seemed more concerned that there could be more deaths than at the loss of this patient. Maggie couldn't answer him. Da could have had the fatal pint in any one of dozens of pubs in the area.

She went through the motions, not really feeling anything other than a sense of unreality, as though all this was happening to someone else. She'd made a little bag into which she put the stolen money and she pinned it to the inside of her blouse. She'd stared at the two large, white pieces of paper for a long time. Ten pounds! Ten whole pounds! More money than she'd ever imagined anyone could have.

There hadn't been time to discuss what they would do with it, for the day after her da had been buried, the plainclothes police had arrived with a warrant and had searched every inch of the room. She had stood and watched them, her face set. They hadn't found what they were looking for.

Mick Devanney escaped, but they'd soon find him, they'd told her. Devanney was a murderer and there was a manhunt under way. Maggie prayed that they would, but there were so many places a man could hide in this neighbourhood, and he had friends. He may even have managed to get aboard one of the ships in dock and stowed away. Either way she didn't care. It was after their visit that she discussed with Tommy the matter of the money.

'What will we do with it?' Tommy asked, earnestly.

'There's nothing we can do with it yet. There's too many scuffers watching us, watching everyone.'

'We could get away from here, Maggie.'

She sighed. It was exactly what she wanted to do, but they would have to wait a while. The risk was too great.

'Couldn't we get a few things?' he persisted.

'I wish Da had managed to get a few coins. No one round here has five-pound notes. The first shop I went into they would know where I got it.'

'Not if you went into town and got stuff from Church Street or Lord Street.'

'And how would I explain away coming back from town, laden down with parcels? Don't be daft, Tommy. We'll just have to wait. Oh, I know it's hard. I keep dreaming of wearing nice clothes, living in a quiet, clean little house and getting us all the things we've ever wanted for Christmas. We could have a really grand Christmas, Tommy.'

They both looked wistfully into the dying embers of the fire.

'I've got an idea, Maggie. Why don't you go and have a look in Anfield or Everton for a little house. You could pay the rent in advance, then we could do a moonlight flit. We don't have much to take with us anyway, we could leave all this junk.'

Maggie's face had lit up but then the light in her eyes faded. 'When would we be able to leave? It could be months before they finally give us some peace and what about Devanney?'

'What about him?'

'He'll know Da got some of the money, he'll want it, need it. Then we'll never get away from here.'

Tommy felt that there was blood on that money, maybe this was God's way of not letting them gain from it.

Maggie brightened. 'I *will* go into town. I'll just get a few bits and pieces, just to change one of the notes. It will be easier to spend then.'

'Be careful, in those shops they might think you've stolen it.'

Maggie felt irritated. 'It was you who said go to town!'

'Don't snap my head off. I was just telling you to be

careful. What will you get?' he finished, to change the subject.

Maggie looked thoughtful. 'A nice piece of meat.'

'Is that all?'

'Yes. If I come home with more than one parcel, tongues will start wagging. Now who's being daft?'

The next morning she walked into the centre of Liverpool. She was aware she was being followed but she walked briskly just the same, her head held high. She stopped and gazed into the window of Frisby Dyke's, mentally picking out what she would buy for herself when she could spend the money. That green, fine wool dress would suit her and that lovely shawl with thickly fringed edges, that's what she'd buy. She resumed her journey, crossing into Church Street and she stood for three minutes gazing into the window of Bunnies, then she threaded her way between the trams and carts and bicycles to the opposite side of the road and went quickly into Cooper's.

She sniffed appreciatively, for the aroma of coffee was like perfume. She'd never tasted coffee but now wasn't the time to experiment. As she passed the artistically arranged mounds of fruit, a lot of which she had never seen before, her mouth watered. There was so much food that you could dine like a queen in here. She was filled with impatience and longing, but common sense prevailed.

There was quite a crowd around the meat counter

and she edged her way into it. If whoever it was who was following her was still there, it wouldn't be so easy to pick her out in a crowd, she reasoned. When it was her turn she pointed to a piece of brisket and nodded. She watched as it was weighed and wrapped, then she slid the folded note across the counter.

'Come into an inheritance, girl?' The butcher grinned at her.

'No. The lady I work for gave it to me, to buy the meat. She didn't have change and she said I was to be extra careful of it. As if I need telling, it's more than a year's wages!'

'Too right. She's not short of a bob or two then, is she?'

'No. Some people have all the luck,' Maggie agreed, wishing he would get a move on and stop asking questions. Carefully, he counted the change into her hand and, hastily pocketing it, she picked up her meat and slipped it into the hemp bag. She held the money tightly in her fist within her skirt pocket. This city was full of pickpockets and she hadn't taken such a big risk only to have it pinched.

Pausing before a counter displaying a vast variety of cheeses in all shapes and sizes, she deliberated whether to buy some. It was very tempting. Then, reluctantly, she thought better of it.

She wandered along Church Street, gazing into the windows of every shop she passed. She hesitated on the corner, opposite Central Station, wondering if she should include Bold Street in her ambling. She decided against it for she was cold, so she made her way along Hanover Street, heading for home.

She'd cooked the meat slowly, and the tantalizing aroma filled the dingy room and permeated out on to the landing. It would do them two meals, she thought, and she could use small amounts of change to buy groceries, but not from Mr Garrity for he'd be suspicious as to where she'd got the money.

She'd washed the few dishes and put the remains of the brisket into the food press, covered with a piece of cloth, and was about to bank up the fire when she heard a scratching at the door. What was the matter with Tommy, couldn't he knock properly? she thought irritably. Her nerves were on edge, but there was no need to take it out on Tommy, she scolded herself.

It wasn't Tommy. In that first instant when she opened the door she didn't know who it was, for a figure just shoved past her and entered the room. But, as she closed the door, recognition dawned and she shrank back, her hand going to her mouth.

Mick Devanney glared at her. 'Where's the money, girl?'

He was a terrifying sight. His clothes were torn and covered in mud, he hadn't shaved and a thick black stubble made him appear even more evil and menacing.

'What . . . what money?' Maggie said, her heart thumping against her ribs.

'Don't give me that. Yer da got some of the money, I found that much out.'

Maggie's thoughts were racing. He was a murderer and he was on the run, but there was no way she was going to give him a single penny. If he touched her she'd scream blue murder. She shook her head. 'He didn't!'

He grabbed her arm and pulled her towards him. 'I need that cash, the scuffers are after me. I've got to get away!'

She tried to keep her voice steady. 'I know. They came here and turned the place inside out but they found nothing.' She was trembling but she forced herself to go on. 'Because there never was anything. Da must have dropped it.' She took a deep breath. 'You must be mad coming here! They've been watching the place and they've followed me and our Tommy! They'll be waiting for you!' She saw the flash of naked fear in his eyes and breathed a little easier. Even if the police found him here, they couldn't pin anything on her because no one had found the money, the only evidence that linked her to Devanney.

'You're lying, you bitch! Nago wasn't that much of a bloody fool. He must have got something!'

The pressure on her arm increased. He was hurting her and she screamed, trying to twist away from him. 'Get out and leave me alone or I'll scream the place down. I will, then they'll come running and they'll get you, Devanney, and you'll hang for killing that poor old man!'

Devanney knew he was defeated. He couldn't let her start yelling, it *would* bring the scuffers down on him. He could almost feel the noose tightening around his throat. He raised his arm, but then let it drop. 'They won't get me! But I won't forget this! You bitch! I'll get you for this! I've still got mates around here, good mates, too, and they'll be watching you so don't think you can get away with holdin' out on me or grassing me to the scuffers. If I don't get you, they will!'

He'd gone as quickly as he'd arrived and Maggie sat down, for her legs had gone weak. She knew Mick Devanney's mates and they were some of the worst criminals in the city. She went to the window and stared out but the street was deserted. She'd have felt better if there had suddenly been a hue and cry. She went back to her seat by the fire.

She was still sitting, trembling and shocked, when Tommy arrived home.

One look at his sister's face spoke volumes. 'Maggie, what's the matter?'

'He's been here. That Mick Devanney.'

'Oh, God, no!'

'He knew Da had got some of the money and he wanted it.'

'Did you give it to him?'

'No! I told him the scuffers had been and searched for it. Oh, Tommy, I hope they get him! I hope they hang him!'

'They will, Maggie, he's so thick he'll give himself away. They might even have him now, the streets are still swarming with them.'

Maggie raised her terrified gaze to Tommy's face. 'He said he'd get me, or his mates would and you know what they're like, every bit as bad as him! We've got to get away now, Tommy. Now, tonight!'

'Where to? You said we couldn't go yet.'

She stood up and pressed her fingers to her throbbing temples. 'Let me think, Tommy. We've got to make some plans. Maybe we can get a ride from a cart on the Dock Road but we'll have to wait until later.'

'Do you think we'll get that far?'

'Oh, don't go saying things like that, Tommy. I'm scared to death as it is!' Maggie began to pace up and down the room and Tommy watched her helplessly, gnawing his fingernails.

'Just get a few things together, only the things you will really need and I'll do the same. We'll take the blankets but nothing else. No furniture or pots,' she instructed. Then, upon glancing around the room, she realized there was precious little to take.

'We'll have to wait until it's very late, until everyone's in bed.'

'If we leave it too late there won't be any carts by the dock,' Tommy argued.

'There are always one or two, and anyway we can hide down there. Don't worry, we'll get away from here.'

Maggie busied herself bundling together some clothes and food, darting to the window every now and then. Just after midnight, when the streets were silent and all noise in the house had subsided, Maggie wrapped her thick shawl around her and covered it with one of the blankets. Tommy wrapped the other one around himself. They looked like two shapeless bundles, Maggie thought, hoping the blankets would disguise them to some extent.

'We're going to have to be careful we don't trip up on these things.'

'Oh, stop being so flaming awkward! We'll meet the worries when we get to them!' Maggie replied, exasperated, her taut nerves making her snap at Tommy.

They crept slowly down the stairs, trying to avoid the boards that creaked and the piles of rubbish that had accumulated on every turn of the stair but, thankfully, no one heard them. Tommy peered out into the courtyard. There was no one in sight, for it was a bitterly cold night and, to his relief, ragged clouds covered the moon.

They made their way through the dark and silent streets as quickly as they could, avoiding the pools of yellow light thrown out by the spluttering gas lamps. At each sound they jumped nervously and every second Maggie was expecting to feel a hand on her shoulder.

The moon appeared for a few minutes from behind

the clouds as they skirted the wall of the Salthouse Dock, keeping well away from the gate and the policeman stationed there.

'There's only one cart, Maggie,' Tommy hissed.

She nodded, biting her lip but quickening her steps towards it.

'Where are you going?' she asked the driver who was sitting up in front, so heavily swathed against the biting cold that only his eyes were visible.

'Not going anywhere for another hour or two. Why?'

'We're looking for a ride. I can pay you.'

'A ride where to?'

Maggie felt like screaming. 'Anywhere, away . . . away from here.'

'I'm going out as far as Kirkby. The boss is expecting some new machinery. Some newfangled foreign rubbish, it's supposed to be on that old barque. Can't go back without it, he said. I've got to see to it personally. He should have come himself but then why should he when he can get me to come all this way and sit in the freezing cold, like a bloody idiot,' he grumbled.

'Where's Kirkby?' Tommy asked.

'A long way from here, lad. Out in the country, it's only a village. The boss rents his land from the Earl of Derby, like everyone else.'

Maggie only heard the words 'a long way from here' and she leaned forward eagerly. 'Can we go with you, when you're loaded up? I told you I can pay.'

The man looked down at the odd pair. The thin lad, his face pale and pinched beneath his old cap, the young girl, her shawl beneath the blanket wrapped tightly around her, her eyes pleading.

'Both of you?'

Maggie nodded eagerly. He deliberated. 'Three pence – each.'

'Three pence!' Tommy exclaimed but Maggie shot him a warning look. They had little choice.

'All right, I'll give you sixpence when we get there,' she agreed.

'No. Do I look daft? You'll get the ride and then run off without paying.'

'How can we run off? We've nowhere else to go.'

'Sixpence now or no ride.'

'Oh, all right.' Maggie fumbled down the front of her bodice, then counted out the pennies. All she wanted to do was to get herself and Tommy into the cart quickly. They were too obvious, too vulnerable, standing here.

'Get up in the back but you'll have to leave room for the stuff.'

They huddled together in a corner, trying to keep warm and wishing that whatever it was that was being unloaded would soon be clear of the dock.

Tommy had fallen asleep but she had fought to keep her eyes open, watching for any advancing policemen. There had been none and at last the crate from the ship was loaded and the horse moved off. The sudden movement jolted Tommy awake.

'Are we off at last then, Maggie?'

'Aye, I don't know how long it will take us but at this pace it will be hours and hours and I'm half frozen now.'

Tommy shifted his cramped limbs. 'At least we'll be safe when we do get there.'

Maggie didn't reply, she was wondering what lay ahead of them. All they had were a few clothes, a bit of food and the money. She smiled bravely to herself. It had to be better than staying in Liverpool. Things would turn out fine, she just knew they would. She had enough money to pay rent and buy furniture and pots and new clothes, and they'd be together, well away from Bowers Court and the dirty city streets. Away from the choking fogs and damp mists of the river. Life could only get better now.

Chapter Seven

IT WAS ALMOST DAWN WHEN the cart finally drew to a halt. They had both slept fitfully, being bumped and jolted over the cobbles and then the rutted frozen roads that in places were little more than cart tracks. They seemed to have left the streets of the city behind hours ago, Maggie thought as she sat up, groaning as she eased her cramped and cold limbs.

She gazed around her apprehensively. The first thing that struck her quite forcefully was the silence. There were birds singing but there were none of the familiar sounds of an awakening city. Fields stretched away to her right for as far as the eye could see. Their flat patchwork of greens, ochres and browns relieved by clumps of trees, whose bare branches reached like skeletal arms towards the pink-streaked sky. On her left a few low, stone cottages were huddled together by the side of a stream over which there was a little, humped-back bridge beneath which the water flowed swiftly over its stony bed. Away in the distance she could see the solid, turret-like tower of a church and a large house which stood by the side of it. More cottages were grouped together beyond the church and then the bare fields rolled onwards towards the horizon.

'Down you get, this is as far as you go,' the carter announced.

Maggie and Tommy climbed down stiffly. Maggie turned to him hopefully. 'Is there a cottage anywhere we can rent, or a room maybe? Not too far away,' she added. They couldn't go wandering around out here all day just looking and hoping. They were cold and hungry.

'Well, there's the Farmer's Arms. They might have a room. Best ask the vicar at St Chad's about renting though.' He pointed towards the church.

'Where's the Farmer's Arms?' Tommy asked. 'Is it far?' He hoped it wasn't, the sight of so much emptiness was bewildering to his city-bred eyes.

'About a mile and a half along there.' The carter pointed in the opposite direction of the church.

'But all I can see are fields!' Tommy stated.

'You can't see it from here. There's a footpath over there, beyond those bushes.'

Maggie stared at him dejectedly, not looking forward to the prospect of walking so far and it must be a fair way because he'd said you couldn't see it.

'Can you take us there, please?'

'What do you think I am, a bloody public transport

service!' He, too, was cold and hungry and he knew that a good fire and a big breakfast would be waiting at home and he didn't trust these city urchins.

'I'd pay you.' She really didn't want to have to part with any more money, but at her offer Tommy lost his weary, apprehensive look.

'How come you've got so much money?' the man demanded, suspiciously.

'We worked for it. We worked damned hard, too. We've saved up. We always wanted to live somewhere . . . nice.'

'I can't blame you for that. Dirty, stinking place is Liverpool.'

'It's not! There are lots of really big grand buildings!' Tommy cried, stung by the slur and suddenly defensive of his birthplace.

'Oh, aye, there are, I'll give you that, but not for the likes of you and me. I bet you didn't live in Rodney Street or on Princes Avenue!'

Maggie stared up at him, pleadingly. 'Oh, please? We'll get lost and could be wandering around in circles all day!'

The carter sighed heavily. 'Get back up then, I can't sit here wasting time talking about Liverpool or you wandering around lost.'

Maggie thanked him profusely.

It was a small inn that they finally drew up outside and it was very isolated. Maggie thought it looked as though some giant hand had picked it up and placed it down in the middle of the fields. It was a single-storeyed, low building with a grey slate roof and small, leaded windows. A low, whitewashed wall ran around its perimeter and a painted sign, depicting a farmer dressed in a smock and moleskin trousers, creaked mournfully in the wind. There was a yard at the back and, as they drove into it, the carter called out, 'Is there anyone at home?'

A small, thin woman emerged from the back door. Her greying hair was confined in a bun at the back of her head, and her features were sharp, her dark eyes bright and bird-like. She wore a plain dark blue dress, over which was tied a crisply starched white apron.

'Oh, it's you, Dick Fletcher! What's all this then?' She eyed Maggie and Tommy with open curiosity.

'I brought them from Liverpool. She's looking for somewhere to rent but first off she needs a room and board.' He got down and leaned closer to the woman. 'She seems to have the brass. God knows where she got it though, but you know me, Mrs Garvey, ask no questions and you'll get no lies.'

Mrs Garvey pursed her lips disdainfully. 'That's news to me, Dick Fletcher. You're worse than Ma Stokes, and there's not many know more than she does about other folk's business.'

Abashed, the carter turned away. 'Well, I've done my bit, so I'm off! My Nora will think I've deserted her.'

'From what she tells me there's times when she hopes you would!'

He ignored her and clucked to the horse.

They all watched him go, then Mrs Garvey turned to Maggie, her expression softening. 'Is that the truth of it, lass? You want a place to rent and bed and board?'

Maggie warmed to her. 'Yes, please. We've been travelling for hours. He said we should ask at the church about renting a cottage.'

Lizzie Garvey scrutinized Maggie closely. She didn't look as though she had two ha'pennies to rub together judging by the thin, faded skirt and the old black woollen shawl around her thin shoulders. And, she wore no hat. 'You're not in any kind of trouble are you? Not running away from the law?'

'Oh, no! We've been working and saving for ages to come to live somewhere like this. Please, missus, can you help us? I'd be ever so grateful.'

There was something in the girl's face that touched the older woman. It couldn't have been easy saving up, yet she believed Maggie's story. The girl had a determination and she seemed to have an air of authority about her. 'No mam and dad then?'

'No. They're both dead. I've been looking after Tommy. How much do you charge, please?'

'It'll be half a crown a week for the room.'

'Each?' Maggie interrupted, looking horrified.

'No, for both of you and that includes linen and a fire. It'll be two shillings for your meals – a week,' she added hastily, seeing Maggie's eyebrows shoot up again.

Maggie was relieved. Four shillings and sixpence

wasn't too bad, but she'd have to get a place to rent soon. She couldn't go on paying that for weeks on end or there wouldn't be much left at the end of a month.

Mrs Garvey looked around her. 'No bags? No luggage?'

Maggie's heart missed a beat. 'No, there was nothing to bring except that.' She pointed to the bundle in Tommy's arms. 'We sold what we had.'

This explanation seemed to suffice. 'Right. Around the back it is then.'

Maggie felt much better after she'd seen the room. It was clean and welcoming and it surpassed anything she'd expected. The walls were whitewashed. Print curtains hung at the window and polished lino covered the floor, with bright rag rugs placed by the narrow beds. Heavy white quilts covered the beds, and the chest of drawers and big wardrobe glowed as a result of much polishing with beeswax, the aroma of which still lingered. On the washstand was a bowl and jug decorated with a blue willow pattern.

They'd had a wash with the water Mrs Garvey brought in a big earthenware jug. The fire crackled merrily, the flames reflected in the shiny brass fender, and they had begun to thaw out. Two bowls of steaming hot, thick porridge, made with fresh milk had been brought next, along with a big brown pot of tea and two mugs. As her hunger abated, Maggie relaxed. Yes, things were looking up now, she thought happily.

She waited until they'd finished their tea and then she gathered up the dishes and went to find the kitchen. Halfway along the passage she found it. A young girl of about thirteen was scrubbing at a large, black pot in the sink by the window.

'Where's the Missus?' Maggie asked.

The girl turned and eyed her curiously. 'Who wants to know?'

'We've just arrived. We've got bed and board here. I wanted to speak to her.'

The girl rubbed her nose with a soapy hand, then yelled, 'Ma! Ma!' so loudly that Maggie stepped backwards.

Mrs Garvey bustled into the room.

As far as Maggie could see she ran the place with the girl who was obviously her daughter.

'What have I told you, Florrie, about bawling like a fishwife? What's the matter now?'

'I . . . I wanted to have a word with you, please,' Maggie interrupted, ignoring the hostile gaze of young Florrie.

'Oh, that's different. Put those pots down and come with me.'

Maggie followed her out into the passageway and through into the bar, which was empty.

'Right, now sit yourself down. But if you've decided to tell me that you've no money then out that door you go, the pair of you!'

'No. It's not that! Here's the money for the week.'

Maggie held out the silver half crown and florin. 'But I think we should try and find somewhere to rent – we can't afford to stay here long.'

Mrs Garvey pocketed the money. 'If I were you I'd go over and see his reverence at St Chad's about renting a place. The church and the earl have all the land and property around here and as far as I know Derby's got no houses standing empty right now.'

'We wouldn't want much. A bit of a cottage. Just two rooms and a scullery would do.'

Mrs Garvey looked thoughtful, her head nodding slightly. 'There's an old cottage over towards Simonswood. It needs a bit doing to it though. It's half falling down for it's been empty for a while. So isolated you see, no one wants to live out there. It's too far from the village and certainly from here.' She jerked her head towards the long counter. 'His reverence might be glad to have someone to rent it.' She got to her feet. 'I'll come with you. That way he won't get out of doing it up a bit,' she said firmly.

Mrs Garvey had done most of the talking, for Maggie was overawed by the size and furnishings of the vicarage. The vicar had agreed to a rent of a shilling a week but the price had gone up when Mrs Garvey demanded that the repairs be done and done quickly for he couldn't expect a soul to live with half the roof missing in this weather.

'Jesus Christ was born in a poor stable, don't forget,' he'd impressed on them.

'Aye, but He didn't stay there and His mother didn't have another child to see to as well,' had been the tart reply, for Lizzie Garvey thought the rent was too high and in her private opinion she thought the man a pompous prig.

'Maggie here has enough to do, looking after herself and her brother,' she said, making it clear by her tone that if the Lord had seen fit to place this burden on Maggie's shoulders, then he, the Lord's servant, could see to it that they were not condemned to live in a barn at one and sixpence a week.

Maggie had told Mrs Garvey about her name on the way to the vicarage. The woman had shaken her head and raised her eyes to the lowering skies at the wickedness of some men. Her man had been a good one, she told Maggie. He'd died five years ago when he'd been dragged along the lane, his foot caught in the shaft of a haywain and the stupid horse had panicked even more and had bolted. Maggie had shuddered. Runaways were frequent and she'd witnessed many a fatal accident in the crowded streets of the city. Obviously such accidents happened out here as well.

At first sight the tiny cottage didn't look too bad, but it did look very isolated. There wasn't another building in sight. It seemed to huddle close to the gnarled old blackthorn for protection against the wind and its door creaked and banged on broken hinges. As they drew closer, she saw that it was badly in need of repair, but then so had been many of the houses in Bowers Court. At least this wasn't surrounded by other buildings that blocked out the light, nor was it covered in soot and grime.

There were three rooms. A big kitchen with low beams and a flagged floor that was covered in debris. On one wall was a big, old-fashioned range, dull and rusted in places and covered in sooty dust. Above it was a wide overmantel of dark oak. Beneath the small latticed window was a brown stone sink with a wooden draining board and to the side were shelves. There was no running water, a pump outside was the source of supply. A small dark musty pantry with a cold slab and a few narrow shelves led off the kitchen.

The other two rooms had either been bedrooms or one a bedroom, the other a parlour. One had a flagged floor but the other was hard-packed earth. Both had fireplaces, that in the room with the earth floor was just a hole in the wall, but the other one was cast iron, dirty and dull. It was above this room that the roof was missing, and the window didn't close properly and dead leaves and twigs swirled in small eddies on the floor, blown by the wind that rushed through the gap in the roof and the chink in the ill-fitting window.

Maggie followed Mrs Garvey outside and inspected the low outhouse at the back that was a sort of storeroom. At the bottom of the overgrown garden was an earth privy.

Mrs Garvey shook her head and tutted loudly. 'It's not fit for anything except to house animals! He's got a nerve wanting that much rent, he should be paying you! You can't live there, at least not until that roof is mended – you'll both freeze!'

Maggie didn't share her views, she was looking at the cottage with enthusiasm. 'It only needs the roof fixing and that window and a good lock on the front door. The rest just needs a good scrub out and a bit of whitewash.' She was imagining how it *could* look. The kitchen range gleaming with black-lead, the flags scrubbed and covered with bright rag rugs, a big table and some good chairs, a food press or maybe even a dresser with some nice dishes, and she'd have a rocking chair by the range. She'd put a curtain up to divide the room with the earth floor and they could both sleep in there and she'd have the other room as a parlour. Her cheeks flushed with excitement and longing. A parlour. What wouldn't Mam have given for a parlour. It set you above your neighbours, gave you standing, did a parlour, and she could work miracles with the room.

'There's not a stick of furniture though.' Mrs Garvey's statement brought her out of her daydream.

'That doesn't matter. There must be somewhere that I can get the things we'll need.' She rubbed her hand over the range. 'A good scouring with wire wool and then some Zebo blacking and it will come up a treat.'

'Well, I admire your enthusiasm but won't you be very lonely out here?'

Maggie sighed. 'No. It will be wonderful. No one yelling and fighting half the night. No babies screaming or dogs howling and fighting. No foghorns or ships' whistles waking you up all night long. No-one banging about upstaiars. No kids pounding up and down the stairs by the minute. No queuing up at the standpipe. No muck and filth in the yard. No having to dry the washing indoors all the time, making the place damp and smelly. It's . . . it's wonderful!'

Mrs Garvey shrugged. No wonder she thought it heaven if that's what she'd left behind, but she wouldn't fancy taking this place on or being stuck out here with the nearest neighbour nearly three miles away.

Maggie's optimism was not to be quelled. 'Wait until our Tommy sees it! He's good with his hands, is our Tommy. He'll help me fix it up.'

'And what will you both do with yourselves all day?'

Maggie frowned. 'We'll have to get work. Maybe I could try to grow things.' After all that's what farmers did, she reasoned.

'Grow your own vegetables, you mean?'

It was an idea that had occurred to Maggie on the spur of the moment but the more she thought about it the more sense it made. 'Yes. I could, couldn't I? Then we'd have good, fresh, homegrown stuff. It would help out with the groceries. Do you think I could manage a few chickens, too? Are they a lot of work?'

Mrs Garvey smiled, not wishing to put a damper on the girl's spirits, but wondering what on earth a girl born and bred in a city would know about growing things and keeping fowl. 'No, you just let them scratch around. But give them a bit of meal or bread now and then and see they don't wander too far. I might be able to help out as far as Tommy's concerned. I have a lot of farmers who come in. It might only be a bit of casual work to start with, until spring when things get busier, and then when it's harvest time it's all go and everyone helps out.'

Maggie had a vision of herself and Tommy, glowing with good health and rosy with the sun, helping out in the fields for the harvest. Oh, this was the life. This would be such a pretty cottage when it was fixed up and they'd live happily ever after. What more could anyone wish for?

'Well, we'd best be getting back now. I'll get someone to take you into Ormskirk for marketday. You should be able to pick up some pieces of furniture there, pots and pans and the like. There's plenty of shops there, too, and they don't all charge the earth.'

Maggie smiled at her, thinking that Devanney had done her a big favour in starting the chain of events that had led her to this wonderful place.

Chapter Eight

MAGGIE STOOD IN THE open doorway and gazed wonderingly at the great draperies of scarlet and gold that hung across the October sky. Like a huge ball of molten fire the sun was sinking slowly behind the horizon. The fields, now shorn of their crops, turned stubbled faces towards the fading rays. The summer was over, she thought sadly. The hours of daylight were getting shorter. There was a nip in the air and, in the mornings, the mist hung over the fields and hedgerows. The pungent, earthy smell of falling and decaying leaves heralded the changing of the seasons.

It had been a good year, she mused. A year full of new experiences. A time for adapting to a way of life very different to that she had known. In many ways it had been hard, yet in others it had been easier. There was no constant, futile battle against dirt and overcrowding and she had become used to the peaceful silence of the long evenings.

They'd worked hard, very hard. Especially these last few weeks, for everyone was needed to get the harvest safely in and when she'd worked in the fields with her neighbours, she'd felt that now, at last, they were being accepted. Her brow furrowed as her gaze rested on the patch of ground beyond the window that bordered the path. Her vegetables hadn't been very successful, except for the potatoes. She thought of all the weary hours she'd spent digging, hoeing and weeding, often on her hands and knees. The results had been scanty and disappointing, for there seemed to be so much she didn't know. She'd asked Mrs Garvey's advice and had followed it to the letter, but all she had were potatoes and carrots. She sighed. She'd just have to buy her vegetables.

She'd had more success with her chickens. Mrs Garvey had been right, they were easy to keep and had supplied them well with eggs. Tommy was now making a proper, wooden coop for them for the winter. She'd been warned about marauding foxes. True to her word, Mrs Garvey had found Tommy work with a farmer who lived four miles away and Tommy trudged to work on foot each morning at six. He'd grown, she thought with satisfaction. He had filled out and his pallor had gone, replaced by a healthy, golden colour and each time she looked at him she felt happiness stir in her. It was the best thing she'd ever done getting him away from the unhealthy squalor of Bowers Court. A frown creased her forehead. Tommy didn't agree with her on that. Lately he had been grumbling more and more about their life. There was nothing to do after work, he complained, although in the early days he'd been so exhausted he'd only wanted to sleep. You could end up going mad in a place like this, he'd said heatedly. 'All this silence would drive a person to distraction,' had been his exact words. 'It's so boring!'

'I don't have time to be bored!' she'd retorted.

'It's different for you, Maggie, you go to market.'

'Once a week!' she'd interrupted.

'Well, you see other people. Mrs Garvey, Mrs Fletcher, Florrie and that Billy Roberts has come sniffing around a few times!'

'Oh, so that's it, is it? You're jealous!' she'd cried. Billy Roberts was the son of the farmer who was their nearest neighbour. He was a tall, dark-haired, taciturn lad, of an age with herself. No one had been more surprised than she when he'd appeared one afternoon on the pretext of 'checking the boundary walls'.

She'd offered him some tea and there had been a stilted conversation, but she'd seen the way his eyes followed her as she'd moved around the kitchen. She liked him and no boy had ever been interested in her before and the knowledge had lifted her spirits.

He'd called twice since. Uninvited on both occasions and with barely credible excuses, but she'd made him welcome. The last time he'd called she had just washed her hair and had been sitting in the sun, brushing it dry. It had been spread around her shoulders like a veil of silk burnished by the sun. Haltingly and with his colour rising, he'd told her of the fact and she'd ducked her head, suddenly shy and tongue-tied.

'I'm not jealous! I was just saying that you *see* people!'

Winter was drawing on and there would be even less to do and people would forgo visiting, Maggie thought. She wouldn't admit, even to herself, that she wasn't looking forward to the dark months ahead. There would be little to do except sit by the fire and listen to the wind and the rain. Yet she should be grateful for her lovely, warm home. The stone walls were thick, which made it warm in winter and cool in summer. She couldn't read well enough to tackle a book and her sewing was limited to mending and the straight seams required for curtains and the like. With Tommy at work all day she would see no one, except perhaps Billy Roberts, especially if it snowed. Last winter there had been no snow, only heavy frosts and driving rain, but Mrs Garvey had warned her that sometimes when the drifts were deep she would be cut off completely and she'd advised her to make provision for that.

It had been some months since they'd heard, via Dick Fletcher, that Mick Devanney had been hanged in Walton Jail. She had shuddered, but a feeling of relief had also filled her.

She stirred herself, it was no use being so miserable

and down. Tommy would be in soon, starving hungry. She busied herself setting the table and cooking the meal. As Tommy's frame filled the doorway Maggie looked up and smiled. 'Have you had a good day then?' she asked. She could see that he was excited about something from the colour in his cheeks and the sparkle in his eyes.

'Better than usual, but it's not work I'm so happy about.'

'What then? Get those boots off, they're covered in mud and I scrubbed this floor this morning!'

Tommy grinned as he removed his working boots and placed them just outside the open door. 'There's a fair coming soon.'

'A fair. Here?'

'Well, at St Chad's, it comes every year.'

'Who told you?'

'A lad I met today. Dinny his name is. He's with the fair people. He said there are great larks to be had here and he was surprised I didn't know it. He goes hunting for rabbits and pigeons and all sorts of things.'

'I bet he's not very popular with farmers if he goes tramping over their fields!'

Tommy ignored her remark. 'He says people come from miles around. Won't it be great, Maggie, to have a bit of fun at last?'

She placed a plate of smoked ham and potatoes on the table and sat down opposite him. 'Aren't you happy here, Tommy?'

He shrugged. 'It's not bad but . . .'

'But what?'

He laid down his knife and fork. 'It's so . . . it's so quiet, Maggie. Nobody ever *does* anything except work. I never go anywhere or do anything interesting!'

'We went to the harvest supper and the dance in the big barn,' she reminded him. 'And I saw you clodhopping around with Mary-Ann Kelsey.'

'I mean . . . well, we were used to seeing a lot of people, all day and all night. I used to have good times with my mates, we always had a bit of a lark around and there were things to do. We could walk into town, or watch the ships on the river and in the docks. Have a ride on the ferry if we had a penny, and when we didn't. It was great hiding when we got to Seacombe so we could sail back free!'

'You've got a short memory, Tommy May! Oh, we were *seeing* people all right, hundreds of them packed into half a dozen houses around the Court and the noise of them driving you mad day and night. And as for things to do, there was all that coal you had to hump around. All that tramping the streets trying to sell matches, papers and kindling. All those chores you had to do, all that dodging out of Da's way and giving him every ha'penny you earned for his ale! That was really great, wasn't it? Well I like it here,' she finished resolutely.

'I didn't mean all that! I know it's better . . . healthier here, Maggie, but you'd go mad with boredom and the silence in winter, Dinny said so.'

'Oh, so he's the expert now, is he? I thought you said he travelled from place to place?'

Tommy felt guilty and, because he did so, he was irritated. 'I didn't mean anything . . . I was just repeating what he said.'

Maggie got up from the table. 'Well then, let's hear no more about going mad with boredom.'

She learned next day that Tommy had been speaking the truth when she walked to the Farmer's Arms, to hitch a lift to market. Mrs Garvey was full of it.

'It's the event of the year, Maggie girl. A sort of celebration after the harvest. His reverence has a special church service, mind, but then there's the fair. There's sideshows and a carousel with painted horses, fortune-telling – not that you can take any notice of that – they're not real Romanys, more Irish Tinkers and you've to keep a watch on your purse and other belongings when they're about. Light-fingered lot they are. But for the fact that the fair's been coming since the year dot, I know there's many folk who would like to see the back of them.'

'Our Tommy's met one of them. A lad called Dinny.'

'Aye, there's quite a few of them Tommy's age. I'd keep my eye on Tommy, Maggie, they'll be having him up to all sorts of devilment.'

Maggie sighed. It looked as though the excitement

of the fair would be tempered with anxiety, for if what Mrs Garvey said was true, then anything they suggested Tommy was bound to agree to go along with.

She met Dinny the following day when Tommy brought him home with him. She took in the sharp features, the quick, bird-like eyes, the thatch of untidy hair and the old, tattered clothes. She took an instant dislike to him. She didn't like the way his gaze darted quickly around the room as though searching for something but noting every item just the same. He looked younger than Tommy and yet she sensed he was far more crafty and knowing. He reminded her of the street urchins in Liverpool.

'So you come here every year?' she said.

He nodded, watching her as she ladled out a large helping of rabbit stew for Tommy.

'Put your eyes back in your head, there's some for you. Sit down.'

'Thanks, missus, I'm starving.'

'I'm not missus, my name is Maggie.'

'Thanks, Maggie.'

'Where else do you go, with the fair?'

'All over the county.'

'Don't you go to school?'

He laughed, wiping his mouth with the sleeve of his torn jacket. 'I ain't never been to school, it's a waste of time for the likes of me.'

Reluctantly she saw his point. 'Our Tommy was good at school, he's clever is our Tommy.'

Tommy looked embarrassed, but she continued to smile at him fondly.

Tommy sensed her animosity towards his new friend. 'Dinny has a great life. He helps a bit with the fair but then he's free to do whatever he likes.'

'Is he now?' Maggie ignored the note of envy in Tommy's voice. 'What does your ma do?'

'Same as all the other women, cook and wash, things like that and she sells things when we stop over in a place.'

'What sort of things?'

He shrugged again. 'Clothes pegs, bits of lace and ribbons. Lucky charms. She tells the cards and the tea-leaves too.'

It sounded like an easy way of living to Maggie.

'We're off up to the village later,' Tommy ventured.

Maggie shot a quick look at him. 'And what will you do there?'

Tommy looked towards his new friend with a little trepidation. He hoped Dinny would have the right answer for he could see Maggie didn't like him, although she was being polite.

'Oh, just hang around and see what's going on. Might walk along to the station and watch the trains,' Dinny answered, mopping up the remaining gravy with a piece of crusty bread.

'There won't be many of them at this time of night and it'll be dark soon.' Maggie's gaze rested on Tommy. 'And I don't want you hanging around the door of the Railway.'

Tommy got to his feet impatiently. 'We'd best be off then, before the light goes.'

Dinny seemed reluctant to leave but Tommy urged him towards the door. 'I won't be late, Maggie, I promise,' Tommy called over his shoulder.

Maggie watched them walking down the path, pushing and shoving each other and laughing. The chill evening air made her shiver. There was something about that lad she didn't like. She'd have to watch him. She bit her lip worriedly. Tommy was all the family she had and he was only sixteen, a lad looking for a bit of company and a bit of excitement to lighten his evenings. But he wasn't a fool, he wouldn't do anything stupid. At least she prayed he wouldn't.

She'd banked up the fire and washed up and her thoughts turned to her mam. She sighed. Mam would have loved this place. It was easy to keep clean. The air was fresh and there was peace and quiet, room to breathe. No matter what Tommy thought, they were both healthier and life was good. She felt weary and suddenly down and a wave of grief washed over her. 'Oh, Mam, look out for our Tommy. Don't let him get into any kind of trouble, please,' she prayed.

She was sitting dozing by the fire when Tommy came in and she jumped up, startled for a second. 'Oh, you gave me a fright, Tommy.'

'Who did you think it was? Billy Roberts come calling?'

She ignored his jibe. 'No one, I was half asleep. Where's your mate?'

Tommy shrugged. 'Gone back to the fair. I'll see him around tomorrow.'

She could see that Tommy was restless. He wandered up and down the small room, his hands in his pockets.

'All right, what is it? Out with it!'

'What?'

'Don't give me that, Tommy May. I know when you've something on your mind.'

'Maggie, Dinny was saying . . . well, when they leave here, he was saying why don't I go with them. There's always work to be done.'

She was so stunned she just stared up at him. He'd only met this Dinny, who appeared to have no second name, such a short time ago. 'You want to go . . . off . . . with them?' she stammered, unable to take it in.

Tommy nodded solemnly.

Maggie's heart began to race. 'Tommy, you're all I've got. What will I do? How will I manage without you? Have you thought about that?' Shock was being replaced by anger.

Tommy was not to be deterred. 'I hate it here, Maggie! It's boring and too bloody quiet! I hate it! There's no one my age and old man Johnson hardly says two words to me all day.'

She was visibly shaken. She'd known he wasn't completely happy but she'd never realized he disliked it here so much. 'It's better than Liverpool! We agreed it was.'

'Only in the beginning, when I didn't know any better! But there's nothing here, Maggie. Nothing at all. Not for me!'

'Well, you're not going traipsing off with those . . . those tinkers! I promised Mam I'd look after you, and you're not going off with them!'

'What do you expect me to do all my life, Maggie? If I stay here I'll go mad.'

'You're not going and there's an end to it.'

'You can't make me stay here,' Tommy cried, his chin jutting forward stubbornly.

'I can. You're only sixteen. I'll go to the constable in Ormskirk and tell him you want to run off with the tinkers. Then they'll have the whole county watching for you and I don't think that's something they'd be very happy about.' She had no idea if the police would even take notice of her but it was the first thing that came to mind and she could see by his face that he, at least, believed it. She tried another tack. 'And what about the great plans you had? Getting a trade, getting a good, steady job?'

'Don't talk daft, Maggie! What chance have I here? There's no trades here, unless I want to learn how to thatch or do hedging and ditching or hang around the forge.'

She knew he spoke the truth but she persevered. 'You could go and see about learning to work the forge, that's a good trade and they're always busy.'

'Aye, and Mr Ramsden has three sons of his own to follow him. He won't want the likes of me.'

'Something will turn up, Tommy, I know it will. Don't give up on your dream, think of all that time Miss Cumberland spent with you. You're smart, Tommy, you've got brains. Don't give up.'

He looked sulkily around the room. 'Can we move from here then? Live somewhere nearer a town. Somewhere where I'll have friends and a good chance of work. Work I want to do.'

'I'm not going back to Liverpool, Tommy.'

'I didn't say Liverpool, did I? Just . . . just somewhere else!' He ran his hands through his hair, making it stick out in tufts.

Maggie smiled. 'You look like a walking hayrick.'

He grinned reluctantly and she knew that she'd won this round of the battle. But if he was so unhappy she'd have to try and think of something for him, yet she was loath to move. The cottage was the first decent home she'd had and she was so proud of it. The rent was cheap and with his wages and the bit of money still left, they were doing just fine. 'I'll have a good think on it, but cheer up, it's fair day the day after tomorrow. We can have a bit of fun then.'

He nodded and grinned and she breathed a sigh of relief but the sooner the fair people left here the better, she thought.

She was bringing in the last of the washing late the

following afternoon when Mr Roberts, accompanied by Billy, pulled up in the pony and trap. She smiled at Billy. 'It's been another grand day!'

'Where's that brother of yours?' the older man demanded.

Maggie was surprised at the hostility in his voice. 'On his way home from work I should think.'

'He hasn't been at work since noon! Mat Johnson's not best pleased about that I can tell you!'

Maggie's heart began to race.

'He's off with that young savage from the fair. Bloody great boot prints all over the wife's kitchen garden and across my field of winter wheat! None of the hens are missing – yet!'

'Tommy wouldn't steal! Even when we were on our uppers, he never took anything that wasn't his!' Maggie cried defensively.

'I'm not saying he would, girl, but they've been over in the copse too, where the pheasants are. I keep my eye on all the game birds in this neck of the woods and his lordship don't take kindly to poachers!'

'But what makes you think Tommy is up to no good?' Maggie looked pleadingly at Billy, hoping for support, but he was examining his hands.

'This. I found it caught on a bush by the house. It's his.' He handed Maggie a blue and white checked handkerchief.

It *was* Tommy's. She'd used the scraps from the curtains to make handkerchiefs. She didn't know what to say or think, but she was feeling slightly sick.

'You'd best watch him. I'll forget it this time but only if nothing goes missing. They're a bad lot. God knows why his reverence allows them here, the trouble they cause! It's the same every flaming year, so you keep an eye on that lad, you hear me?'

Maggie nodded. There was nothing else she could say. She looked again at Billy but he just shrugged.

She'd folded the washing into a pile and had the flat irons heating up when Tommy arrived home. She'd been so terrified that he'd run off with Dinny that every second had seemed like an hour.

'Where've you been? And don't lie to me!' she yelled at him. 'Mr Roberts has been here creating about trampled vegetables and the Earl of Derby's pheasants!'

Tommy looked shamefaced. 'We didn't do anything, Maggie, honestly! Dinny only wanted a couple of rabbits for his mam!'

'You left work! Mr Johnson's good and mad about that, and why go stamping around Mr Roberts's place if that Dinny was only looking for rabbits? I could kill you, Tommy May, I really could! You know it's only lately that people have started to accept us and now . . . now you go and get mixed up with that lot and ruin everything! I'll have to go and see Mr Johnson and beg him to keep you on. Why did you have to spoil everything?' She slammed the flat iron down hard on the sleeve of Tommy's Sunday shirt.

'It was only a bit of fun! It seemed like a good idea. I'm sorry, Maggie, but I swear to God we didn't pinch anything! I didn't even know there were pheasants in that place!'

'But he did! Oh, he knew all right!'

'I've said I'm sorry, Maggie, what else can I do?'

'You can get yourself over to Johnson's and apologize and tell him it will never happen again. And you can stay away from that Dinny!'

Tommy hung his head. He really hadn't meant to cause so much trouble. 'Can I go after supper, Maggie?'

He looked so contrite that some of Maggie's anger evaporated. 'All right, at least it will keep you out of mischief for tonight.'

'It's fair day tomorrow, Maggie, and I was so looking forward to it. Don't spoil it by going on at me, please?'

Maggie let out her breath in a sigh of impatience. 'There's ham and cheese and pickles in the press and I'll put the kettle on. Honestly, Tommy, you've got me heart-scalded! I was looking forward to a day's enjoyment, too.'

'It'll still be a great day!' he enthused, fearful in case she changed her mind.

She smiled. She *was* looking forward to it. Everyone was going. Mrs Garvey had arranged a ride for them and they both deserved a treat, she thought.

Chapter Nine

FAIR DAY DAWNED CLEAR and bright. The sun was rising slowly in the sky, its golden rays dappling the hedgerows that were aglow with hips and berries. On the trees, whose foliage was turning slowly from green to vibrant orange and russet, the early morning dew sparkled. It clung to the cobwebs in the grass and on the bushes, making them look like necklaces of silver and pearls.

Maggie was up and dressed just after dawn. She wore an apron over her good dark blue skirt and the sleeves of her white blouse were rolled up to the elbow. Her hair was caught at the nape of her neck with a dark blue ribbon and she'd admitted to herself that she looked well.

She'd just finished getting ready when Tommy came into the kitchen, struggling with the stud of his stiffly starched collar.

'Come here and let me do it,' Maggie said.

He grinned at her. He was looking forward to the day's entertainment. 'At least it's fine and dry.'

'Aye, thank God. It's a grand day and don't we look well? You in your Sunday best and me done up to the nines. Do I look . . . nice?'

'Of course you do,' Tommy replied enthusiastically.

'Now, have we got everything?'

'Well I have.'

'Mr Rosbotham will be here any minute,' she said, giving him a gentle shove. Sometimes she didn't understand Tommy at all. He seemed quite happy most of the time and then he would surprise her with his sudden fits of dejection. She supposed he was growing up, but she had no time to reflect on this for the sound of cart wheels and hooves told her that their ride had arrived.

A carnival atmosphere seemed to prevail, excitement was in the air, Maggie thought as they drew nearer the village green. Perched on the back of the farm cart, she looked around her with a feeling of mounting anticipation. People were calling out, greeting each other and she could hear the sound of piped music. She looked at Tommy and saw the vitality, the eager expectation in his eyes. Yes, it was time they all had a bit of enjoyment. A day off from the routine of work in all its guises.

The cart came to a halt beside the church wall.

'Right, everyone out,' Mr Rosbotham said jovially, as he and Tommy helped Maggie down. 'Be back here by four, Maggie. I can't wait. I've got cows to milk and they won't wait until dark, fair day or no fair day.'

Promising to be back on time, they made their way slowly across towards the enclosed piece of field where the fair had been sited. Maggie turned to Tommy. 'Go on off with you. I know you want to be with all the lads of your own age. There's no need to worry about me, I'll have a great time.'

He breathed a sigh of relief and grinned at her. 'Thanks, Maggie.'

She grinned back and delved into her pocket. 'Here, take these few coppers and enjoy yourself, but no getting into scrapes now.' She watched him disappear and looked around her, wondering what to see first.

'Isn't it a fine day, Maggie?'

She turned to see young Florrie Garvey in her best Sunday suit, a wide straw hat trimmed with a pink ribbon, set jauntily over her curls.

'I didn't recognize you, Florrie, you look so smart. Where's your mam?'

Florrie coloured prettily and pointed to one of the stalls. 'She's in charge of the cakes. I'm off for a ride on the painted horses.'

Maggie laughed as she watched Florrie push her way through the crowd, then she turned and made her way to Mrs Garvey's stall.

'Maggie, don't you look nice. You'll be turning a few heads today if I'm not mistaken. Now would you like to buy a cake? All home made with best ingredients.' She bustled efficiently, rearranging the confectioneries.

'I will later on. I want to see everything first.'

'Well, there'll not be much choice later on, maybe none left at all.'

'Oh, I didn't really want to have to carry it around with me, it will get all squashed.' She looked closely at a rich, spicy fruitcake.

'That's no problem, girl. I'll keep it for you, under here.' Mrs Garvey indicated a large basket under the white cloth that covered the stall.

Maggie nodded. 'How much is it?'

'Threepence, it's a good buy. It will keep, no need to eat it all at once, not like a Victoria sponge.'

Maggie handed over the coins and the cake was duly wrapped in greaseproof paper and deposited in the basket.

She wandered around the sideshows slowly and returned the greetings of neighbours with a smile and a few cheerful words.

'Maggie, will you try your hand at the Aunt Sally?' Billy Roberts asked, looking down at her and smiling.

She looked up at him feeling a little embarrassed, remembering his father's visit. 'What do I have to do?'

'You hit that dummy, the Aunt Sally, with one of those balls and you win a prize.'

'Is that all?'

'You have to hit it hard to knock it over, it's not as easy as it looks.'

He was smiling at her and she felt the colour rise in her cheeks. 'I'll have a go.'

She paid her money and pitched the coloured balls as hard as she could, laughing at her bad aim.

'Never mind, have another go,' he urged.

She shook her head.

'I will then and if I win a prize I'll give it to you.'

To both their disappointments he failed to win anything and they moved on.

'I'm sorry our Tommy caused so much trouble the other day,' she said.

Billy shrugged.

'He apologized to Mr Johnson.'

'I heard.'

'You might have said something to your da, told him that our Tommy isn't bad,' she said reproachfully, for his attitude had hurt her.

'It wouldn't have done any good. They're a bad lot.' He jerked his head in the direction of the carousel.

'But you know our Tommy!' she persisted.

'I don't – not very well.'

Maggie said nothing. Perhaps she had been reading too much into his visits. Perhaps he'd just been curious about her – about them both – and his last words seemed to reinforce that deduction. Her chin jerked up. She didn't care.

'Where will you be eating then?' Billy asked.

'I don't know. I brought some things in a basket. I'll find somewhere a bit quieter than this, I suppose. Well, I'd best move on, there's so much to see and do.'

He looked put out but shrugged and she walked away feeling annoyed. Damn him. He wasn't going to spoil her day.

She watched children roll ha'pennies down a chute on to coloured squares. At another stall young men and older ones were shooting at rows of coloured ducks and cursed when they missed, saying there was nothing wrong with their aim, it was the guns. They were 'fixed'. Quite an argument was developing between the stall owner and Mr Roberts who was demanding to use his own shotgun. She watched Mary-Ann Kelsey, blindfolded and shrieking with laughter, trying to attach the tail to a cardboard cut-out of a donkey.

She had her fortune told by a very dark-haired, dark-skinned woman, dressed in a vivid purple, blue and gold outfit. She hadn't believed a word of what the woman said. Where was she going to find a rich husband and a big house? And she wasn't very happy about what the woman had said about her future being filled with darkness and people who would work against her. She shivered as she walked away.

When the sun was high in the sky she walked towards the side of the field and sat down beneath a huge oak. She'd wait for Tommy, he must be starving by now, unless he'd stuffed himself full of sweets. It wasn't long before she saw him coming towards her. His collar was undone, his cap pushed to the back of his head and he was perspiring.

'You look as though you're having a high old time,' Maggie laughed.

He flung himself down on the grass beside her.

'I am. This is the life, Maggie. You should try those swinging boats. Your stomach turns right over! The harder you pull on the ropes the higher they go! It's like . . . like . . . flying.'

He crammed the cheese and crusty bread into his mouth hungrily yet not wishing to waste a precious minute.

'You'll choke yourself! Eat it slowly.'

'Got to hurry up, Dinny's waiting for me.'

Her face clouded. 'I thought you said he was helping his da?'

'He was, now he's helping on the boats. If it gets a bit slacker, he says I can have a couple of free turns.'

'Have you spent all that money I gave you?'

'Aw, Maggie, it was only a few coppers. Can you spare a few more?'

She nodded in mock despair. 'You'll have us out on the road at this rate. You'd spend the rent money if I let you!'

'I wouldn't do that, but before we know it it will be time to go.' He paused, turning the coins she'd given him over in his hand. 'Maggie . . . can I . . . well, can I stay on a bit longer?'

'You'll have to walk all the way home if you do!'

'I don't mind that, it's only as far as I walk to work. Please, Maggie, go on! Just until supper time.'

She was weakening. After all it was only one day. 'All right, but I don't want you coming home at all hours. It's work in the morning, remember.'

'I know.' He was torn between the relief that she'd agreed to let him stay and the depressing thought of the grinding, boring hours at work. 'They'll be gone in the morning,' he added glumly.

'I know. Well, get off with you then.'

She watched him as he elbowed his way through the crowd around the swinging boats. She didn't like the look of them, they looked sort of dangerous, but she would love a go on the carousel. She wandered back towards Mrs Garvey's stall and saw that the supply of cakes had been considerably depleted.

'I told you they'd all go, didn't I? Having a good time?'

'Yes, and so is our Tommy, he's been after me to let him stay on.'

'Did you agree?'

'Yes. It's only a day, let him enjoy himself.'

'And what about you?

'Oh, I'll have had enough by four o'clock. I was up at the crack of dawn.'

'Oh, get off with you. You're a young lass, go and have yourself a bit of fun on the rides.' Mrs Garvey laughed, turning away as more customers approached, smiling and rubbing her hands together.

Maggie had two rides on the carousel and it was exhilarating, although she refrained from screaming like Florrie and her friends. But she did wave and call out to Nora Fletcher when she spotted her. She felt carefree, happy and daring as she made her way towards the painted boats, trying to pluck up enough courage to have a ride. There was no sign of Tommy or Dinny. The man who was in charge had dark hair and eyes and a red handkerchief around his neck. He saw her hesitancy. 'No need to be afeared, Miss, jump in here with this young 'un.' She looked up to see young Florrie sitting inside, holding tightly on to the sides.

'Come on, Maggie, it's marvellous, you'll love it.'

She smiled at the girl and was helped up by the man.

'You have to pull hard on these ropes,' Florrie instructed earnestly.

She nodded and followed the girl's lead and soon she felt as though she really were flying. She closed her eyes tightly and, forgetting all decorum, screamed with delight as the boat swung higher and higher. When the time was up she was flushed and laughing.

'Have another go?' Florrie pleaded.

'No, thanks, I don't think my stomach could stand it and I've spent enough. I'll go back and have a bit of a gossip with Mrs Garvey.'

Her legs still felt a little wobbly as she began to walk back towards the carousel and the stalls. She'd get a drink of cordial with the few coppers she had left. She hadn't brought a lot of money in case she'd be tempted to spend too much.

As she drew nearer she wondered what was going on for a crowd seemed to have gathered and people were shouting. She pushed her way forward and then stopped. A crowd of young lads and older youths were grouped around little Daisy Pope, who was stunted and slow; half-witted was what Lizzie Garvey called her, though not unkindly. The lads were laughing, skitting and jostling the poor creature and in the background she saw Billy Roberts and Tommy, just standing and watching. Anger gave her strength as she pushed her way roughly to the front.

'What do you think you're doing? Stop it! Stop it! She can't stand up for herself you . . . you rotten cowards! Leave her alone!' she yelled.

A youth she had never seen before stepped forward. 'What's it to do with you?'

The sound of her hand as it met his cheek was like the shot from a rifle and he fell back surprised. 'She suffers enough without you adding to it. You should be thankful you weren't born like her. You should have some pity for her! Come on, Daisy luv, I won't let them hurt you.'

He recovered and stepped forward but she held her ground, her eyes flashing with pin-pricks of amber fire, her arm around Daisy's shoulder. And then there was a ripple of noise on the fringes of the crowd and

Mr Rosbotham with Mrs Garvey and the constable appeared.

'Now, what's going on here then?' the constable demanded.

Maggie turned towards him. 'It's him and . . . and that lot! They're making a mock and a jeer out of poor Daisy Pope!'

The constable advanced purposefully and the group fell back.

'I blame myself, I could have stopped the cruel little fiends. Mrs Halliwell forgot her change, I ran after her and she kept me talking!'

'It's not your fault, I can't bear to see anyone jeered at or tormented. I know what it's like.'

The group had all slunk away, except for the youth who was being interrogated by the constable, and Dinny and Tommy. At the sight of her brother, anger consumed Maggie and she dashed forward and caught him by the ear. 'You! You should have known better! I'm ashamed of you, Tommy May! Mam must be turning in her grave to see you joining in with them! How could you stand there and let them torment that poor girl? How could you? You're coming home with me, now! There's no more treats for you and if there's any more of this then the constable can take you away with him!'

Tommy's cheeks burned and he winced with the pain in his ear. 'I . . . I tried to . . .' he stammered.

'You didn't try hard enough, did you! Oh, fine friends you have, picking on a poor, harmless, witless girl! Get home and I don't care if we have to walk the whole way, it will serve you right!'

'No need for you to walk, girl, I've had enough of all this myself.' Mr Rosbotham was standing beside her, his face grim.

She nodded, 'Thanks.' She turned her back on Tommy who hung his head in shame at the mutterings of sympathy that came from the thinning crowd. He'd certainly never intended to get involved, and now the day was ruined.

Maggie fumed all the way home, irrationally angry at Tommy but upset at the callousness of Billy Roberts who'd just stood by and watched. And to think she'd liked him! She didn't speak to Tommy and began to prepare the evening meal, banging pots and dishes loudly, venting her hurt and anger.

'Make yourself useful and go and fetch me some water from the pump!' was the only instruction she gave Tommy.

She was still seething when the meal was over but before she could clear away the dishes there was a tapping on the door.

Her mouth tightened into a thin line when she opened it and saw Dinny and the fortune-teller standing there.

'What do you want?'

The woman gave Dinny a little shove. 'Go on, tell her you're sorry for the way you behaved today. Say it properly.'

Dinny shuffled his feet. 'I . . . I really am sorry. Can I come in and see Tommy?'

Maggie hesitated, then she shrugged. They'd be leaving tonight anyway and it was good riddance. She opened the door wide and they trooped in. Tommy stood up, his hands thrust deep into the pockets of his trousers, while Maggie sank down in the chair beside the table. She felt so tired.

Dinny mumbled something and Tommy nodded, then the woman turned to them both.

'Ah, get out of me sight the pair of yez. I want to talk to this girl here.'

Maggie looked up at Tommy who stood eyeing her with trepidation, but she nodded. Thankfully they both left the room.

'Say your piece, then will you go and leave me alone,' she said to the woman who was obviously Dinny's mother for she had the same dark eyes and sallow skin.

'I came to warn you, girl.'

'What against? I don't believe you have any powers of any kind.'

The woman looked down at her steadily. 'I'm not a full Romany, but me mother was and her mother before her and you can believe what you like, but be careful, girl. Be careful of a man who is connected with distant lands for he'll bring you grief.'

Maggie was openly derisive. 'A man who is connected with distant lands! How will I ever meet someone like that stuck in the middle of the country, miles from anywhere? Take your warnings and get out.'

The woman continued to stare at her and then she shrugged and turned away. 'It's up to you if you believe or not, I've done me duty.'

Maggie watched her leave and then drew the curtains tightly across the windows. It had been a far from perfect day but she would never have believed that Tommy could have been so cruel. He'd always stood up for her when she'd been the butt of jeers and taunts.

She was still sitting at the table when he came in.

'Has that Dinny gone then?'

'Aye.'

'And good riddance to the whole flaming lot of them! I've a good mind to go and see the vicar about all this!' Inwardly she was relieved, for at the back of her mind was the nagging fear that Tommy would go with them, but he was easing off his best boots.

'Best get yourself to bed, you've work in the morning and I won't be unhappy to see the end of this day I can tell you!'

He looked very shamefaced as he left the room and well he might, she thought. He should never have got mixed up with that lot, their kind always seemed to spell trouble.

It was after lunch the following day when she discovered that the money had gone. She'd looked with pure disbelief at the empty cocoa tin in the bedroom where the remains of Nago May's larceny had been kept. Dinny! That dirty, thieving Dinny! It must have been him for his mother had stayed in the room with her all the time. He and Tommy had gone out – into the bedroom! How could Tommy have been so stupid? He must have left that tinker's lad alone in there!

She sat down on the bed with her head in her hands. All they would have now was what Tommy could earn and that wouldn't keep them. She'd have to try to find some kind of work, anything, to earn the extra money they would need.

She was still trying to get over the shock when she heard the gate creak as it opened. She jumped up, hope springing into her heart. If it was that Dinny or his mother or any of his friends or relations, she'd make them give it back to her. It was Tommy.

She searched his face anxiously. 'What's the matter?'

'I got the push, Maggie. Six of Mr Johnson's hens and two guineas have been stolen. He . . . he said it was the tinkers. He said that Dinny was my friend and that I knew my way around the place. He thinks I helped them.'

It was all too much for Maggie. 'You fool! You bloody fool, Tommy May! That Dinny has robbed us too. All the money has gone and so are they . . . long gone! No one will believe you now, Tommy, not after the carry-on of you and that Dinny the other day!' She sat down, for her legs felt weak.

'He said he won't go to the police about me, 'cos he knows you're a good girl, but . . . but that's my job gone.'

She leaned back and pressed her fingers against her temples. Oh, it would soon be bandied around by Mr Johnson and Mr Roberts that he had been in cahoots with the tinkers. The rumour would be believed and he'd never get another job for there were still a lot of people who considered them 'outsiders' and viewed them with suspicion that would now turn to hostility.

'What . . . what will we do, Maggie?' Tommy asked, wishing now he'd never set eyes on Dinny or the fair.

She looked up. 'I don't know, Tommy. I honestly don't know.'

Chapter Ten

WINTER WAS DRAWING ON and the fields lay fallow beneath leaden skies. Tommy had tried to get work. He'd gone cap in hand to every farmer for miles around, but, as Maggie had predicted, no one trusted him. Maggie had also tried to get work but there was nothing, for all the women did their own washing and cleaning and mending. Mrs Garvey had been the only one to offer help and that was just a few hours behind the bar on Saturday nights.

Piece by piece she'd had to sell the furniture and it had broken her heart to see her little parlour now bare and forlorn. Mrs Garvey had been kindness itself, making sure she got the highest prices, sending over the occasional pie or pudding, but as Christmas approached Maggie knew they couldn't hang on for much longer.

'There's hardly anything left to sell, there's no choice. We've got to go back to Liverpool,' she said with a catch in her voice. She dreaded going back. Oh,

Mick Devanney was dead, but his mates were alive. That knowledge terrified her. They would be forever looking over their shoulders, living in fear of strangers, of footsteps in the dark streets, yet what alternative was there?

They would have to live in a different area and hope and pray they wouldn't be seen, but in her heart she knew that even in so large a city anonymity wasn't guaranteed, yet they had little choice, they couldn't stay here.

Lizzie Garvey sighed deeply. 'I wish there was more I could do, lass, just to see you over the winter, but there's barely a living here for Florrie and me.'

'You've done more than your share. You've been so good to us, from the first day we arrived here.' Maggie took her hand. 'I hate the thought of going back, I really do, but it's no use moaning and complaining about it.' She tried to keep her voice steady and she blinked rapidly to keep the tears at bay. 'Hate' wasn't a strong enough word for how she felt. She'd cried all night long after she'd finally realized that she had to accept reality. She knew only too well what she was going back to.

She withdrew her hand from that of the older woman and stood up, preparing to leave. 'So, there it is. I'll sell everything that's left.'

Lizzie Garvey stood up. 'I'll ask around and see if anyone's going to Liverpool. I'll get you transport. That will save you a few coppers.' She didn't say that there would be many people who would say good riddance. It took a lifetime to be accepted in these parts.

Maggie thanked her again and had trudged the miles back to the cottage that would soon be just a memory, and, as she turned her face into the wind, she swore to herself that it was the biting blasts that were making her eyes water, for she had no tears left.

She watched the familiar landscape of narrow streets and factory buildings pass by from the window of the tram. They'd only managed to get a lift as far as Walton-on-the-Hill. The sight depressed her terribly. This was her home. The city where she'd been born, yet there was no feeling of belonging. She had no fond memories and she didn't relish what lay ahead of her: searching for lodgings and jobs, the daily battle against poverty, dirt and noise. Her secure and tranquil world had gone.

The conductor had helped them off with their few bundles. A fine drizzle was falling as they stood on the pavement in Hanover Street. It soaked into their clothes and turned the cobbles a dull pewter colour and made them slippery. People pushed past them, caps and hats pulled low, staring impatiently from beneath umbrellas at the brother and sister who were impeding their progress.

'Where do we go now, Maggie?'

Maggie looked at Tommy with annoyance. 'We'll

have to find somewhere to live and that's not going to be easy, is it?'

He hung his head and kicked at a stone. He didn't dare tell her that in a way he was glad to be back. That the activity around him uplifted his spirits, despite their dire circumstances. He couldn't have stuck it back there in that cottage, year after year. Nothing ever happened, except the fair once a year and look where that had got him? No, he was glad to be back. 'I'll soon get a job, Maggie. We'll manage, just like we did before.'

She'd begun to push her way through the press of people. 'Oh, aye, we'll "manage". We'll somehow keep body and soul together,' she said sarcastically, for she was too heart-sore to care about Tommy's feelings. She was already cold and wet and the day stretched before her endlessly.

She decided that it was hopeless trying to drag their few belongings with them so she left them, giving a penny to the attendant in the ladies' waiting room at Lime Street Station, promising to be back as soon as possible.

It was mid-afternoon, a grey, damp, miserable afternoon, when they finally found a room in a house in Brick Street off Chaloner Street, near the docks. It was as bad as Bowers Court, Maggie thought, as she rubbed her hand over the dirty, flyblown panes of glass in the long, narrow window.

'It's not much,' she commented.

'You don't 'ave to take it, there's others waitin',' Ma Nevitt said shortly.

Maggie knew there were, so reluctantly she nodded. 'We'll take it.'

Ma Nevitt rubbed her fat, grimy hands together. 'Right, that's half a crown a week.'

'Two and sixpence for . . . for this.' Maggie remembered the room at the Farmer's Arms and Lizzie Garvey's kindness. Ma Nevitt was repulsive. She was a fat, dirty, greedy woman and the few tenants she'd seen seemed to be far less friendly than her old neighbours.

'Take it or leave it, that's what I charge for everyone and this is a respectable 'ouse. There's no whores living here.'

Maggie paid her and then she returned to Lime Street for their bits and pieces and then, squaring her shoulders, she turned to Tommy who was looking very dejected. 'Go and get some soda and soap and a couple of scrubbing brushes and then you can help me pitch all this stuff out.' She counted out a few coins into Tommy's hand. 'I'd sooner sleep on a scrubbed floor than on that filthy, stinking thing!' She pointed to an old, sagging mattress covered in dirty ticking that lay beneath the window.

When Tommy had gone she squatted down beside the small fireplace in which she would have to cook and boil water for washing. She'd become accustomed to taking a bucket and going to the pump and she'd had her lovely big range. We won't be here long, she told herself. Tommy will soon get work and then we'll find somewhere nicer. But we'll never get anywhere as nice as our cottage though, she thought, fighting back the tears.

She got up and walked again to the window. She could see out over the roof tops, their slates shining dully in the rain, and beyond towards the docks where a forest of masts and rigging stood out bleakly against a sky the colour of gunmetal. It was a far cry from the soft, rolling meadows that had been her vista for the past year. Impatiently, she dashed away the tears with the back of her hand. No matter how miserable and defeated she felt she mustn't look back. It hurt too much. Now she must be practical and look to the future.

When Tommy returned they set to, but it was eight o'clock before they were finished. Maggie leaned back on her heels and pressed her hands into the small of her back. It didn't look much better but at least it was clean.

'Maggie, I'm starving,' Tommy complained. 'And you must be hungry too.'

'We'll have to get something from the chip shop,' Maggie said wearily. 'There's nothing to cook with. Tomorrow I'm going to have to walk to Great Homer Street to see what I can get.'

It was the worst night Maggie had ever spent. She had sat with her back to the wall, trying to get comfortable. Tommy leaned heavily against her shoulder and she prayed desperately for dawn to creep into the room. The candle was burning lower, and somehow things never looked as bad in the morning.

When at last the first fingers of the December dawn lightened the dismal room she shook Tommy. 'Come on, Tommy. There's things to do, lad. I want you to go and get some coal and cadge a few old boxes. I'm going to get a few bits and pieces and some food.'

He looked pale and drawn, she thought as she handed him some money, but then they both did. 'Best try and ask after work, too. At the rate we're going we won't have this for much longer.' She shook the purse and pulled a despairing face.

She felt so awful that she didn't have the strength to walk to Great Homer Street and she couldn't afford the tram fare. So, at the local pawnshop, she'd bought six coarse, grey woollen blankets, a kettle, some pots and some crockery and two straw-filled mattresses. She had also persuaded the shopkeeper to lend her a handcart to bring it all back on. She'd paid the most money for the pots, so they'd been left behind to ensure that she returned the handcart. It entailed another journey but she didn't mind too much.

She'd arranged their pitiful belongings with care, pushing from her mind the memory of her treasured parlour. When Tommy returned she made up the fire and set the kettle on it. 'We'll have a nice hot cup of tea when this has boiled. I'm about to drop. What did you find out?'

Tommy sat on one of the empty orange boxes. 'There's not much work, Maggie, things are bad.'

'Things are always bad for the likes of us.'

Tommy held out his hands to the flames. 'I was thinking last night, Maggie.'

'What about?'

'About work and well . . . I'm going to try for a good job, like Miss Cumberland always said I could get.'

'You mean a trade?'

He nodded. 'It will be better than selling things, or labouring.'

'You've got plenty of sense in that head of yours, when you want to use it that is. Where will you try?'

'The shipyards. That's my best bet.'

'Cammell Laird's? Won't it be easier to get something around here? There's plenty of factories and workshops. It would be better than having to get the ferry backwards and forwards every day.'

'I don't mind that, Maggie. If I get taken on at Laird'd we could maybe go and live in Birkenhead.'

She didn't really relish the thought of living 'over the water' as people called the opposite bank of the Mersey, but then anything would be better than living here. 'Maybe we could.'

'I met a feller on the way back. Well, I didn't meet him, I almost knocked him over.' He looked edgy and plucked at the frayed cuff of his jacket.

'What kind of a feller?' She had noticed the quick flash of fear in his eyes.

'He said he was a friend of . . . Devanney's.'

Maggie felt her heart turn over sickeningly. 'Oh, God!'

'I told him I'd never heard of anyone called Devanney. I said we'd been living miles out in the country for years.'

'Did he believe you?'

'I don't know. I think so. He looked at me closely, like, and then shook his head, saying something like he must be mistaken, thought I looked like Nago May's lad. I told him I'd never heard of him either, that my name was Davie Rosbotham. It was the first name that came into my head.' He placed his hand on Maggie's arm. 'I'm sure he believed me and no one knows we're back.'

'Not yet but it won't be long before someone recognizes us.' She felt cold as she remembered Devanney's words about his mates and how they'd wreak vengeance on her. Devanney had been hanged in Walton Jail, but she was certain his malevolence would reach out beyond the grave. 'We've got to get out of here, Tommy. Maybe it would be better if we went to live over the water.'

Tommy stood up.'Then I'd best be off and get the ferry. Can I have the tuppence, Maggie?'

She smiled at him shakily. 'Aye, I'll get you something to eat and then you'd better get going.'

Chapter Eleven

TOMMY HAD RETURNED, DISPIRITED. He'd managed to have a few words with a foreman who'd told him that he had little chance of getting taken on.

'There are a hundred lads for every single vacancy. Two hundred for each apprenticeship. You've no qualifications and you're a bit too old, though that sometimes doesn't matter.'

'But I finished school and got a certificate to say so! Doesn't that count?' Tommy had pressed.

The man had shaken his head. 'Your best plan is to get yourself into a mechanics institute.'

'I can't do that. I need work now. I'm desperate.'

'I can't help you, lad. Try somewhere else. There's plenty of factories and workshops back there.' He'd inclined his head in the direction of the river. 'Or you could go north. Up to the Tyne or even the Clyde, there's plenty of big yards up there.' He didn't add,

'And plenty of lads waiting on jobs, too.' He felt sorry for the earnest lad.

Tommy had thanked him and walked away. Shoulders drooping, hands in pockets.

All the way back on the ferry he thought about the advice. It was becoming an obsession with him. He didn't want to go back to humping coal or worse, wandering the streets trying to earn a few pennies a day. He wanted more from life and a trade would give him opportunities he'd never even dreamed about.

He'd stared out across the glaucous water, rippled with the dirty, cream-coloured wash of the Seacombe ferry boat and that of the tugs pushing the *Ivernia* towards the landing stage. He'd barely noticed the activity on the river, his thoughts had been totally absorbing. All his life he'd wanted one thing – to be a skilled craftsman. Oh, he'd known all the odds were against him, but he'd worked so hard at his books. Fate hadn't dealt him a good hand in any aspect of his life, so far, but surely his luck must change for the better soon?

He'd pulled his cap more firmly down over his forehead as the wind had tugged at it. He'd try the local places first. It would be better for Maggie if he could get something in Liverpool, but he'd made up his mind. If he had no luck he'd go north. He'd be seventeen soon, no longer a kid. He could look after himself. The more he'd thought about it, the more determined he'd become and more certain that his future – a better future – lay in the north of England or Scotland.

Day after day he'd set out, tramping around the city, but he had no luck. The fact only strengthened his resolve that it was time to leave Liverpool. He said nothing when Maggie sympathized and tried to bolster his spirits. He knew it was a decision she wouldn't agree with.

Every time Maggie went out she found she was looking over her shoulder, to see if she was being followed, or being stared at. She was too well known in this part of the city to be anonymous for very long.

She'd tried everywhere in her search for a job. There were no vacancies at all in the factories she tried. It was the same story in the shops. She had tried to get an evening cleaning job. She visited all the offices in Castle Street, Dale Street, Tithebarn Street and the whole of the business sector of the city. At most of them she'd received a curt, 'Sorry, nothing!' but at a few they'd told her to keep on calling, sometimes jobs became vacant.

To make what little they had go further, she'd taken to walking into town late in the afternoon. She visited the small street markets and St John's Market where she could get fades, scraps of meat and stale bread at the end of the day. The other reason for her daily trips was that she was less likely to meet anyone she knew at that time.

She'd settled her hemp bag over her arm with a sigh

of relief, thankful for the vegetables, the loaf and the few bits of meat she'd been able to scrounge. She gazed up at the sky and was glad that it was clear. Thankful too that spring was on its way. The days would be warmer and the evenings lighter which would make life slightly easier.

She'd reached the corner of Church Street and Whitechapel and was preparing to pick her way between the congested traffic when someone tapped her on the shoulder. She spun around.

'I thought it was you, Maggie May! Turned up again like a bad penny! That was nice, doin' a moonlight on us like that. Me Mam was dead put out. Where've you been then?'

Maggie stared at Katie Murphy open-mouthed, her heart racing.

'Well, cat got your tongue then?' Katie jeered.

'No. Well . . . we had to get away, that Mick Devanney came round!'

Katie's eyes widened. 'What did he want?'

'He said Da had managed to get some of the money from Robinson's, but he didn't. He didn't have a penny!'

'Oh, aye?' Katie was openly suspicious.

'He didn't! Didn't the scuffers come and tear the place apart?'

Katie nodded grudgingly. 'They hanged him, you know, that Devanney feller. Served him right. Me mam and me went and stood outside Walton Jail an' we cheered with everyone else. Pity they won't let you in to see it properly, they used to in the old days.'

Maggie shuddered at Katie's ghoulishness. 'I heard he'd been hanged.'

Katie had fallen into step with her as they walked up Lord Street and Maggie glanced at her surreptitiously from beneath her eyelashes. She'd have to get rid of Katie somehow or the girl would follow her all the way home and then everyone would know where they were living. Katie had a mouth like a parish oven and a voice like the steam whistle of the *Mauretania*.

'So, where did you go then?' Katie pressed.

'We got a ride on a cart to Kirkby, a long way it was too.' Maggie's eyes misted. 'It was lovely there. Quiet and peaceful. Green fields and fresh air. We had a beautiful little cottage, you should have seen it, Katie.'

'Catch me being buried out in the sticks. If you liked it so much what did yer come back for?'

Maggie gathered her wits quickly. She couldn't say they'd had the money stolen. 'Our Tommy hated it,' she replied tersely.

Katie nodded. That she could understand. 'What did he do?'

'He worked on a farm. Just labouring.'

'Sounds dead boring. What did you do all day?'

'The usual things. Cleaning, cooking, washing, but I had chickens and I grew vegetables. I didn't mind the cleaning, it was a pure joy to see everything gleaming and know it wouldn't get all mucky again in half an hour. I even had a parlour. Me, with a parlour!'

Katie cast her eyes towards heaven. 'Sounds like a laugh a minute!' she said, sarcastically. 'All that housework wouldn't be a "joy" to me!' Mentally she'd noted everything Maggie had said to repeat to her mam. Especially the bit about the parlour. Her mam would sell her soul for one. 'So, where are yer livin' now then?'

'Oh, up by Catherine Street,' Maggie answered vaguely, knowing it was far enough away from Bowers Court for Katie not to go snooping around.

They had reached the corner of North John Street and Maggie stopped. 'I've got to go now.'

Katie looked at her quizzically. 'What for, that's not the way to Catherine Street?'

'I've got a job, cleaning in an office, up there.' She pointed up the street.

'So has me mam, she'll be here any minute now. I think I'll wait for her.' She thinks I'm bloody thick, Katie thought grimly. Well, two can play at that game, girl, she added to herself. Katie was curious as to why Maggie didn't want her to know exactly where she lived. She didn't believe the bit about Catherine Street. It was posh up there. Oh, there were some streets of small, terraced houses but not many and the rent was certainly more than Maggie could afford, judging by the state of her clothes.

'You wait then, I've just got time to dash home with these few bits. I'll get a tram up there. I don't start until half past six. Tarrah then, Katie.' She concealed a grin of satisfaction as she saw the swift look of chagrin that crossed the other girl's face. There was nothing else that Katie could do now, except give substance to her lie by waiting.

Maggie crossed North John Street and began to run. She wanted to put as much distance between herself and Katie Murphy for, Katie being a blabbermouth of the first order, by seven o'clock the whole of Bowers Court would know they were back and the rest of the neighbourhood by midnight.

Katie's eyes were fixed on Maggie as she darted between the traffic. She'd always been a devious one, had that Maggie and now she felt sure there was far more to their coming back to Liverpool than met the eye. She remembered her mam saying that there was something very queer about the way they had up and done a moonlight flit. The whole court had been in uproar what with the scuffers breathing down everyone's neck and then, when things were easing off, those two had up and run. There had to be more to it, her mam had always said. Now they were back and Maggie seemed determined to be secretive about just where they were living. Maybe they did have the money after all. Maybe it had been so well hidden that the scuffers just hadn't found it.

Katie quickly crossed the road, finding a gap in the traffic, her eyes fixed on the tall figure ahead of her. She wasn't going home until she had found something out, even if it was only where Maggie lived, for that might turn out to be something of an eye-opener. Perhaps they did have a house up near Catherine Street and wouldn't that be a turn-up for the book?

Maggie was panting when she got home, her breath coming in ragged gasps.

'What's the matter?' Tommy cried as she leaned against the door, her chest heaving.

'I met Katie Murphy and she tried to follow me.'

'Oh, Maggie, you know the mouth she's got! We might as well put an advert in the *Echo*.'

'Don't worry, I told her it was up around Catherine Street. Said I was getting a tram. I gave her the slip.'

'But . . . but she'll tell everyone she's seen you.'

Maggie had begun to unpack the bag. 'I can't help that, Tommy, and besides, someone was bound to see us sooner or later. But if she tells everyone the wrong area they won't be looking for us around here, will they?'

Tommy sat down on one of the boxes. He was very uneasy. 'Devanney had mates, Maggie.'

'I know, but what else can we do? Where can we go, we've no money!'

Tommy began to press his hands together, the knuckle bones cracking, it was an old habit but it grated on Maggie's nerves. 'Stop doing that, you know how it sets my teeth on edge. Come on, give me a hand, get the kettle on.'

Tommy stood up but before he put the blackened

kettle on the hob he turned to his sister, biting his lip. Now was as good a time as any to tell her his plans, he deduced. 'Maggie, I've . . . I've been thinking.'

She looked up. 'Come on then, out with it. I can see something is eating you.'

'I'm not going to get any work, let alone a trade, around here.'

'You've just got to keep trying, Tommy,' she urged. 'I know it's hard, it's always been hard.'

He shook his head. 'I've made up my mind, Maggie. I'm going up north to try, there's plenty of shipyards up there, on the Tyne or the Tees or even the Clyde. The feller I spoke to at Cammell Laird's said I'd stand a better chance at one of those yards.'

Maggie sat down suddenly, the hemp bag still clutched in her hands. 'But you can't do that, Tommy! You can't go all the way up there, not on your own!'

'I'll be all right, Maggie! I'm not a kid! I'll be seventeen next month. I'll get a job, an apprenticeship, and then you can come up. We'll get a few nice rooms. You'll see. It will be better than staying here and no one will know anything about us. They probably won't even have heard of that other Maggie May.'

'But you might not get a job. There must be hundreds of lads who live up there, who need jobs too and they'll get first chance.'

'I know that, but I just *know* I'll get something, Maggie! I've never had any luck here.'

'Neither have I, but it's no reason to up stakes and go chasing after dreams.'

He'd spent the last two days working it all out in his mind and he wasn't going to be swayed by any arguments she used. 'I won't change my mind, Maggie.'

'But where exactly will you go? How will you manage? Where will you live?'

'I'll go up to the Clyde first. If I can't get anything there then I'll move down to Newcastle. I'll find somewhere. Someone will have a bit of a room I can have, it won't cost much. Then I'll start and look for somewhere decent for us, Maggie. We can't go on living like this.'

'What do you mean? I'll get a job soon, a few places told me to keep on calling. Something will turn up, then we can move,' she cried.

'I don't mean that, though it's bad enough living here. I mean having to look over our shoulders all the time. Frightened to go out. Terrified of Mick Devanney's mates. I wasn't going to tell you, but . . . well, that feller I saw a week ago spoke to me again. He said he was sure I was Nago's lad. I swore blind I wasn't. I don't even look like Da. I tried to sound Welsh so he couldn't connect me. But you, with your hair the same colour as Da's . . . Maggie, we've got to get away from here.'

A cold fear gnawed at her guts and she gazed up at Tommy with terror in her eyes, knowing that there was sound sense in his words. She'd enjoyed living in Kirkby so living on the Clyde might not be so bad. She began to nod slowly, biting her lip, reluctantly resigned to the fact.

'When . . . when will you go?'

'Tomorrow morning. I won't need much.' He laughed, a harsh bitter sound. 'I haven't got much. Do you think you could spare me something towards the fare? I can try and cadge rides, but that may not work and it will take me ages to get there.'

'How much will you need for the train?'

'If I can get a ride as far as Preston, I won't need too much, Maggie.'

She got up wearily and drew the battered purse from the pocket of her skirt. There wasn't much in it but she took out most of the coins and handed them to Tommy.

'Don't leave yourself with nothing, you've got to eat.'

'Don't worry about me. The rent is paid for another week and I do quite well, cadging stuff at the market. I'll manage.' If everything else failed she could beg in the streets, she thought. There had been times when Mam had been forced to do it. Pride didn't fill empty bellies, Mam always said.

She'd bustled about, making a meal from the things she'd brought home, and rolling up Tommy's few belongings in a bundle. But when he was asleep she lay staring at the cracks in the dirty ceiling and was near to tears. He was all she had. Her only family, her only friend and he was just a lad, no matter what he said. He was too young to go on the road alone, and to go so far away. Yet, she could see no other course open. There were many shipyards up north, here there was only the one and the chance of a skilled job was at a premium. And they needed to get away for there was nothing but danger lurking in the streets of this city.

It would be lonely without him to talk to, for she spoke to no one else in the house and dare not speak to anyone on the street. She'd have to get some kind of a job for, despite all her brave words to Tommy, the rent wasn't paid and she had left herself short. She could have laughed at that if she hadn't been feeling so miserable. Short, it was an understatement. All the money she now had in her purse wouldn't keep her for more than a few days. It was just enough for coal, her main priority. Without coal she couldn't cook or do anything to try to keep herself clean.

She'd risen weary and heavy-eyed, heedless of the shafts of sunlight that slanted in through the narrow window, thinking only that it was a blessing that it wasn't raining. The sight of Tommy standing in the dismal and austere room, clutching his bundle, brought a lump to her throat. He was so full of hope, she could see it in his eyes, in his face. Hope and ambition filled him. There was no fear of the dangers that might lie ahead of him or the total uncertainty of his future. He believed in himself, in his hopes and ambitions and she must let him go on believing.

'As soon as I get fixed up, Maggie, I'll let you know. I'll write.'

'No, come back. Come back for me, Tommy, please?'

'All right, I'll come back, if I can. When I get a job I can't go asking for time off straight away, now can I?'

'No, but try, Tommy? Promise?'

'I promise.'

She hugged him quickly, her eyes over-bright with tears, her smile forced. Then she watched him clatter down the stairs and bang the front door after him. Such an empty, final sound, she thought. Only then did she let her tears flow freely.

Chapter Twelve

THE SPRING SUNLIGHT SLANTED down between the tall buildings of the waterfront and caught the ripples of the grey, turgid river, turning them to wavelets of molten gold. The canvas and rigging of the old sailing ships in the docks flapped and creaked lethargically, as though in protest at being prodded from their rest by the playful breeze. From the steam packets and tugs, spirals of smoke curled towards the sky which was a bowl of blue, washed with the fluffy white fingers of cumulus cloud.

The Pierhead was crowded, bustling with activity, for the first real day of warm spring weather seemed to have put everyone in a good humour. Everyone except Maggie. She was too worried and preoccupied to notice anything. She walked with her head bent, lost in anxiety. She had threepence in her purse and Tommy had been gone for nearly four days. She had begun to worry, imagining him lying weak or hurt by the roadside, or even worse . . . But no, she refused to think of worse fates.

She'd had no luck in finding work. She'd tried everywhere. Factories, shops, laundries, private houses and offices, there was nothing and she had no money for the rent. Bad as Brick Street was, it was better than the streets, which is where she'd be if things didn't look up soon. She *had* to find work today. Things just couldn't get any worse, she thought desperately as she pushed her way down James Street and towards the city centre.

St John's Market was busy and she wandered through slowly, gazing longingly at the huge slabs of cheese, the rows of freshly baked bread, the smell of which brought tears to her eyes, and the stalls fairly groaning with meat and poultry, for those who had the money to buy, she thought bitterly.

At last she stopped before Starkey's. Mr Starkey was a good-natured man who often gave her scraps. She stood to one side while, with bellicose charm and wit, he served the two women in front of her.

'There yer are, girl, put hairs on yer owld feller's chest that will!'

'Aye, well, he's gor enough of them already. 'E looks like a flamin' bearskin rug me mam says.'

'The poor feller! Who's he married to then, yer mam or you?'

'Shurrup, Albert Starkey, an' give us a nice ox tail!'

Maggie ignored the banter, thinking only of the

oxtail. The strong meaty smell of the thick soup it would make and the tasty nourishing meat. She was half tempted to snatch the meat Albert Starkey held out for his customer's approval and run. Mentally, she shook herself and traced a pattern in the sawdust on the floor with the toe of her boot. The women moved away.

'You're here early, girl. What can I do yer for?'

Maggie realized that Mr Starkey was speaking to her. 'Something cheap, really cheap.'

'It's too early in the day for bits, girl, sorry. Come back later on.'

Maggie shook her head. 'I can't. I'm starving. I've had nothing but cups of tea.'

'That's a crying shame, luv, but the best I can do is a bit of liver or an ox heart.' He grinned cheerfully. 'That's not too bad. Nice heart, stuffed with parsley and thyme and roasted, a good nourishing filling meal is that.'

Again Maggie shook her head. She didn't have enough coal to keep the fire going long enough to roast or even boil anything. 'Just a half pound of dripping then.'

He sighed heavily and weighed out the beige-coloured solidified fat. He felt sorry for her, but then if he went giving away his meat to half the poor of the city he'd soon find himself joining them. 'Come back tonight if yer can, or tomorrer,' he said kindly as he waved away the coins she held out. At least he could spare half a pound of dripping.

She moved on to the next stall. She'd get a large loaf and some tea and on the way home she'd buy some milk and a bit of coal. She'd also try and cadge some firewood to try to keep the fire in for the night, try to make the coal last out to boil enough water to do a bit of washing.

At the back of the market were the open stalls and here she purchased the milk, slipping the last few coins back into her purse. Only the coal now and then she'd get home. There was a crowd around the open-fronted shop that sold parrots and monkeys and many other exotic birds and animals that the sailors brought in on the ships. She stopped, distracted by the efforts of the owner, hindered by the antics of two young lads, who were trying to catch a small, black-faced monkey that had obviously escaped and was perched on the awning, chattering abuse at everyone. She would have liked to have stayed to have seen the outcome but she had to get back.

She retraced her steps and walked along The Strand towards the Albert Dock. She'd call at the place where Tommy had once worked to buy the coal. Mr Soames might be persuaded to part with a bit more if she piled on the misery. The thought depressed her further, she certainly had enough miseries, there wasn't any need to add to the list.

The huge piles of coal glittered in the sunlight, like mountains of jet. A thick cloud of dust rose from where three young lads were working, industriously shovelling the coal into sacks. Two wagons were drawn up and the huge horses waited patiently, their heads lowered, tails swishing to and fro. As she walked towards the boys she could taste the coal dust and her skirts trailed on the blackened cobbles.

One of the lads detached himself and she pointed to a depleted pile. He filled a small sack from its edge. She could only afford slack which was good enough for banking down but not for warming the room or cooking.

'Take it over to the boss, he'll weigh it and take yer money,' the lad said laconically, before resuming his place in the group.

Maggie clutched the bag to her and walked to the wooden shack that served as an office.

The bag was weighed. 'Tuppence ha'penny, girl,' Mr Soames stated.

Maggie rummaged in the hemp bag and found her purse. She counted the coins out to him. They were the last coppers she had. Her purse was empty.

She made her way home by instinct, for tears blurred her eyes. There was no money now. All she had was a loaf, the dripping, a twist of tea and the milk. She wished Tommy would come soon, or even write. Anything to alleviate the terrible fear of the predicament that faced her. The streets or the workhouse. Oh, how she missed him. He was someone to share her troubles with, someone who just might have an idea how to get them out of the mess they were in.

Well, she'd just have to try to hang on, she'd have to make the bit of food last.

Although the following day was fine, the night had been cold and, after eating some bread spread with dripping, she'd wrapped herself in all the blankets.

She'd hardly had a wink of sleep, she'd been too cold, too hungry and too worried. There was nothing left now but to go to the offices of the Parish Relief and plead her case. Oh, if only a letter would come from Tommy to give her some hope. If only he would walk through the door and say he'd got a job and money and a place for them. But she couldn't live on 'if onlys'.

The office was situated in an austere building set back from Byrom Street. The wooden floor was scuffed and dirty, a long wooden counter divided it in half and four middle-aged men in shiny suits and high, starched collars were attending to the long queue of people who were waiting. People all dressed like herself, all with worry and despair etched on their faces. It was cold and grim and impersonal but there was nothing she could do but wait her turn.

She felt as though she had been there hours and in that time the queue had grown longer. Her stomach rumbled emptily and she felt light-headed, but at last it was her turn.

'Name?'

The question was barked at her.

'May . . . Maggie,' she stammered.

The clerk looked up and peered at her suspiciously

over his spectacles. 'Don't waste my time, girl, with your stupid jokes. What's your name?'

'That is my name, though I wish to God it wasn't!'

'Don't blaspheme! Address?'

'Twenty-three Brick Street.'

'Circumstances?'

'What . . . what does that mean?'

He gave her another icy glare. 'Are you married, do you have children, do you live with your parents, why do you want money?' he snapped impatiently. He was tired. Sick and tired of the never-ending line of ignorant, illiterate, dirty and often itinerant humanity with their hard luck stories. He tapped the nib of the pen impatiently against the inkwell.

'Mam and Dad are dead. There's only me and our Tommy.'

'Can't your brother work?'

'He's gone up north to look for a job. He went last week.'

'So, there's just you?' He scribbled something down on the sheet of paper in front of him. 'There doesn't look as though there's anything stopping you from getting a job.' He didn't look up at her.

'I've tried, I've tried everywhere. Truly I have.'

He stared at her hard and she felt the colour rising in her cheeks. She wouldn't be here if she could have found work, she was desperate, couldn't he see that? What must she do, go down on her knees and beg?

'Seems to me you've got an answer ready for every

question. I've met your sort before, we get hundreds in here, scrounging, looking for handouts, too lazy to work. There's not many genuine cases.'

'No. I want to work, honestly I do! Oh, mister, please! I'm at my wits' end. I haven't got a penny, I've no food, no coal, no money for the rent!'

He was unmoved by her pleas. 'Then the best thing you can do, young woman, is to go and try harder to find a job.'

The weight of officialdom that this cold, unfeeling martinet of a man represented terrified her. Turning, she pushed her way through the waiting queue and ran out into the street.

She ran all the way down to the corner of Trueman Street and Dale Street before her strength gave out and she leaned against the wall of an office block, gasping, tears streaming down her cheeks. What was she going to do now? She felt so beaten . . . so lost. Oh, why didn't Tommy come back!

'What's up with you? Whinging like a baby who's had her sweets pinched?'

Through her tears Maggie recognized Katie and hope surged through her and she grabbed the girl's arm. 'Oh, Katie! Katie! Thank God, it's you!'

'What's up?'

'I've no money, not a farthing! I can't get a job, our Tommy's gone and the Parish turned me away.' It all came out in a rush, the words tumbling over each other.

'You've been the Parish?'

Maggie nodded. 'Oh, Katie, you've got to help me. Lend me a few coppers, just till I get a job. I'll pay you back, I swear I will! But I'm starving and I'll be chucked out on the street soon!'

For once Katie looked perturbed. Maggie's situation was one they all lived on the edge of, yet she had no liking for Maggie. 'I haven't got any money. Been laid off I have.'

Maggie's grip tightened, her fingers biting into Katie's flesh. 'Katie, please? Do you want me to go down on my knees?'

'Gerroff me arm, you're hurtin' me! It's the truth, Maggie, I ain't got no money, but I know where there's a job going.'

Maggie released her. 'Where?' she asked eagerly.

'The Yankee Clipper on the corner of Sparling Street and Wapping. They want a barmaid. Me mam won't let me go for it, she says they're all whores in there, but you ain't got much choice. I've got me mam and da to see to me,' she muttered, thankful that she wasn't in Maggie's situation.

Maggie nodded. She knew the place. It had been one of Nago's haunts and it had a terrible reputation but, as Katie had said, she had no choice.

'Best get off home and tidy yerself up a bit, they won't take yer looking like that,' Katie advised, rubbing her arm ruefully.

Maggie ran a hand over her untidy hair. 'Thanks, Katie. I'll do that.'

Katie turned away. 'Good luck then,'

'Thanks,' Maggie called after her.

'Aye, you'll need it, girl,' Katie muttered as she quickened her steps.

Chapter Thirteen

BY THE TIME SHE HAD done what she could to tidy herself up, the sun was beginning to slip in the sky, bathing the new buildings on the waterfront in a roseate glow. She prayed that no one had got there ahead of her as she moved quickly down Wapping. Gone was the fear of being seen and recognized by any of Mick Devanney's mates, she had too many worries to dwell on that particular anxiety or its repercussions.

Even though it was still daylight, lamps burned inside the Yankee Clipper and the door stood wide open. Beyond the doorway, Maggie could see a room crowded with people, mostly sailors, but there were women too, although she didn't look too closely at them. The air was so thick with tobacco smoke that her eyes smarted and she began to cough, but she elbowed her way towards the bar determinedly, ignoring the coarse remarks and the grasping hands.

Charlie Gannon, the landlord, was a huge, thickset

man, with short, dark, close-cropped hair. His arms and what she could see of his chest beneath the open, collarless shirt, were heavily tattooed.

'What do yer want, girl?' he shouted to make himself heard over the din.

'A job. I was told you wanted a barmaid.'

'You don't look strong enough to lift a pint of ale, let alone cart trays of them around all night, or were yer thinkin' of er . . . lighter duties?' He bellowed with laughter at his own joke.

Maggie's cheeks flamed and she bit back the retort. She needed this job desperately. 'I'm strong enough and serving ale is the only job I want to do! I'm not like that lot!' She jerked her head in the direction of two girls at the end of the bar. Their faces were painted, their clothes cheap and gaudy and they were hanging around the necks of two sailors.

'Too bad, the job's taken and I'm happy with Matty. Aren't I, girl?' Charlie Gannon called out.

Maggie followed his gaze and saw a buxom, dark-haired girl wearing a bright red dress, grinning boldly at the landlord. Her heart sank as she turned away and as she elbowed her way through the crowd she was very near to tears. It was a terrible place but it had been her last hope. Now, she was at her wits' end.

She leaned against the wall and stared unseeingly at the ships in the dock across the road. It was nearly dark so there was no use going to Church Street or Bold Street. The shops would be closing and the shoppers going home. She'd have no luck there. She had no choice now, she must beg for money on the streets.

She debated going to the Pierhead. There would be people coming off the ferries and the trams, but there would also be hoards of street urchins who would gain more sympathy than she would. She was tired, lack of food, disappointment and sheer wretchedness had sapped her remaining energy. She'd stay here, there were bound to be sailors coming to the alehouse all night.

After an hour she was cold. Her pleas had fallen on deaf ears. Twice she'd been offered money but only for 'services'. Her cheeks had flamed at the coarse expressions and she'd sent them off with fleas in their ears. She'd been approached by a girl with a painted face and flashy clothes and told to 'gerrof me pitch'. She'd moved further down to the edge of the dock road, but it had been the same story there. No one wanted to part with money unless she became what she'd promised her mam she'd never be – a whore.

She'd decided to go home. She was freezing cold, and so hungry that she felt sick and faint. The tears now slid unheeded down her cheeks. Through their haze she saw a man approaching, well dressed by comparison to the sailors and labourers she'd accosted.

'Sir! Sir, could you spare a copper, please? I've had nothing to eat all day. Please, sir, spare a few coppers? I'm starving!' The tears flowed freely now.

Callan O'Shea looked down at the girl blocking his

path. There was something strangely familiar about her. He shook himself. He was imagining it. 'Can't you find work, girl?' he asked, not unkindly.

Maggie looked up into the face of a man who was in his forties. His dark eyes were full of concern. His bowler hat was pushed back, revealing thick dark wavy hair. 'I've tried and tried, sir. I even tried in there but the job was taken.' She pointed in the direction of the Yankee Clipper. 'I'm a decent girl, I won't . . . won't be like them.' She motioned with her head to where two girls were lingering under the streetlamp. She found it hard to speak for her teeth were chattering and a fog kept clouding her brain.

Callan O'Shea was filled with compassion for the girl. She looked to be the same age as his sons and was obviously desperately upset. He was also familiar with the effects of malnutrition. 'How long is it since you've eaten?'

'I don't know. I . . . can't remember.'

'Come on then, let's get some food inside you. You'll feel better then.' It was only common decency, he thought. A few coppers for something to eat, any man with an ounce of Christianity in him couldn't just leave her here.

'I won't hurt you. A girl like you shouldn't be here, whatever the reason.'

She felt a strong arm encircle her waist and she leaned heavily against him. She caught the faint smell of good soap. She knew what it must look like. People would think she was a drunken tart who'd been picked up, but she was past caring.

Katie Murphy had been on an errand for her mam but had decided to go home via Wapping, to see how Maggie was faring in the Yankee Clipper. She'd have to come down off her high horse in there, she thought spitefully. She'd never liked Maggie, she'd always thought she was better than anyone else in Bowers Court.

As she turned the corner Katie stopped dead, her eyes narrowing. The two-faced little bitch! she thought. Pretending she was decent, going to the Parish, begging from herself when all the time she intended to pick up a feller. She watched as Callan O'Shea supported Maggie and they walked slowly up the road and turned the corner. She'd tell her mam all about this, Katie thought malevolently. Miss Goody-Goody May was really a whore, just like her namesake.

The smell of hot foods brought tears to Maggie's eyes, as they entered Sullivan's Eating House. Callan sat her down on a wooden chair at a scrubbed table and she heard him order two meat and potato pasties and a large portion of chips. She supported her head with her hand and closed her eyes. She didn't care what happened to her now, just as long as she could eat. Then she would feel stronger, she would be able to cope should he want a 'favour' in return for the food. She opened her eyes as a steaming plate of food was thrust before her.

'Now eat,' Callan instructed, and watched her devour the food, cramming it into her mouth like a starved animal. He still had a feeling he'd met her before. 'Where do you live?'

'Brick Street,' she replied, thickly, her mouth full of pastie. She was feeling better already. Warmer and less faint.

'What's your name?' he asked.

'Maggie. What's yours? Who are you?'

'Callan O'Shea. I'm a cattle agent. I'm supervising the loading of young breeding stock, over the road in the Queen's Dock. I just left for a few minutes to get a drink.'

'Oh,' Maggie replied before attacking the chips.

He smiled at her. She was such a timid little thing but possessed of a strange, haunting beauty. Her eyes fascinated him for he'd never seen eyes that colour before. Or had he? They were like clear forest pools reflecting the russet leaves of autumn. 'I know what you're thinking, Maggie, but I don't want anything in return. Sure, I'm old enough to be your father. How old are you anyway?'

'Nineteen.' He looked kind and if he really meant what he said . . . She began to relax a little.

'What's your pa doing letting you beg in the streets around here for God's sake? And outside the Yankee Clipper, too. It's one of the worst rough-houses I've seen, and believe me I've seen quite a few.'

'I haven't got a da, he's dead. So is my mam.'

'Do you live on your own?'

She shook her head. 'Our Tommy, me brother, he went looking for work, up north. I gave him most of my money. I thought I'd get a job but I couldn't. Even the Parish turned me down.'

He tutted softly, it was a pitiful little tale, but not an unusual one in Liverpool – or Dublin, come to that. He thought of his own home. The airy house with its fine views of Killiney Bay. He thought of Breda, his wife, a homeloving but frail and nervous woman, the daughter of a cattle breeder. It was due to his late father-in-law's position and connections that he'd risen in his job so quickly. He was grateful to Breda for her support and understanding and for his sons, Richard and Sean, who were of an age with this little waif.

He shook his head, trying to clear it of the image of Breda's rather plain face. They seemed to have drifted apart these last few years. But she'd known that separation was inevitable. She'd seen little of her own father in her childhood and early years. She had created her own life, her own friends and pursuits, now the boys were more independent. It was a life that held no interest for him, nor did she seem to expect it to but she'd looked tired and much thinner on his last visit and she'd been impatient with him.

It might have been different had they lived here on Merseyside where most of his business was done. Either at the company offices, the docks or over at

Woodside where the huge lairages and abattoirs were situated and where the cattle he purchased in Europe, America, Argentina and even Australia were landed. Oh, it was only a ten-hour crossing to Dublin, but often it was time he didn't have. Time he couldn't or wouldn't spare, if he was truthful.

He glanced through the window at the squalid buildings. The narrow alleys and courts of dilapidated houses. The bulk of the many-storeyed warehouses that almost blotted out the night sky. The dark, snaking track and girders of the overhead railway. No, he could never have brought Breda to a city like this, it would have killed her.

Maggie leaned back replete. She felt sleepy now but she couldn't afford that luxury for she was still wary of him. She glanced at him surreptitiously from beneath her lashes. He was old enough to be her father. He was a handsome man with only a few silver hairs at his temples. He was well dressed and his dark eyes regarded her seriously.

'What does a cattle agent do?' she asked. She'd never heard of such an occupation before.

'Oh, I go and look at stock – cattle – in Argentina, America, Ireland, all over the world really. I buy animals on behalf of the company who employ me. Then I arrange for them to be transported here, to Woodside, to be exact. I have to ensure they are well looked after on the journey so that they arrive in a fairly good condition, although on long trips they do suffer. The company doesn't pay me for those that die or are maimed. Sometimes I buy breeding stock here and transport it abroad to improve foreign herds. It's not the easiest job in the world.' He smiled at her. 'Now, I think I'd better get you home.'

Maggie clutched the edge of the table. 'No. No, I'll be all right now.'

'You don't believe me, do you? I won't hurt you, I've told you that. It's not safe for you to be walking the streets.'

'I've lived around here all my life. I'm used to it. I can take care of myself,' she replied firmly.

'I see, but it's only manners to see a lady home,' he said with a smile.

She was still wary. She wished Tommy were back at Brick Street.

Her face was vaguely familiar and it was still puzzling him.

'What's the matter?' Maggie asked, noting his expression.

'I'm sure I've seen you before.'

'You haven't. I'd remember.'

'I never forget a face. Sometimes a name, but never a face.'

Maggie got to her feet. 'Thanks . . . thanks for everything. I'd best get home. Sometimes at night it gets misty, foggy like, around here. It's 'cos it's near the river.'

The word 'foggy' triggered a memory for Callan.

The memory he'd been searching for. 'Now I remember. You were selling matches at the Pierhead on a foggy night . . . Oh, two, three years ago. You told me your name was . . . Laura?'

Maggie's mouth dropped open and her eyes widened. 'You . . . you gave me sixpence.'

'I was on my way to an important meeting but you looked so . . . so vulnerable and it was a miserable night.'

Maggie smiled as she remembered how that money had been spent. 'I bought fish and chips for me, Tommy and Mam, and the rest I spent on medicine. Mam died the next day.'

'I'm sorry, but at least I provided you with some help.'

Maggie nodded.

'Our paths seem destined to cross.'

Again she nodded.

'Why did you say your name was Laura?'

'I didn't quite trust you. It was the name Mam wanted to call me but Da registered me as Maggie.' She pushed back a wisp of hair and drew her shawl around her shoulders.

'Come on, I'll see you home,' Callan stated firmly.

She trusted him now for he hadn't wanted anything in return last time, except the matches.

'This is it,' Maggie announced when they reached Brick Street. She suddenly felt shy and wondered why she felt like this. One part of her wanted him to turn around and go, the other part wanted him to stay. She wanted someone to talk to, confide in, to sympathize.

'I'll see you safely in,' Callan said, leading her into the narrow entrance hall. 'Show me the way.'

They passed one of her neighbours on the stairs and the woman smirked. Maggie ignored her but Callan tipped his hat and said, 'Good evening.' The place was abysmal but it was probably all she could afford. She seemed to have had a raw deal from life.

He'd experienced spars and often grim conditions in some of the places he'd travelled to and he'd seen, only too often, the festering slums of Dublin, but when she opened the door and lit the tiny stub of a candle, he drew in his breath, appalled. Quickly he noted the bare floor, the lack of furniture, the empty hearth. The dark stains of damp on the wall were not masked or hidden by the shadows, nor was the creamy-brown fungus on one corner of the ceiling. 'Begod, it's as cold as the grave in here!'

'There's no coal,' she replied flatly.

With a quick glance he accurately summed up the situation. She hadn't been lying. She was totally destitute. There wasn't a bite of food in the place, no coal and not even the barest necessities. He couldn't leave her like this. A man would have to have a heart of stone not to be stricken by her plight. If he left her in these dire conditions he'd have not an ounce of luck, of that he was certain. 'I don't want you going out again, Maggie, do you hear me?'

'I won't,' she said quietly.

'I have to go. We're away with the early tide.' He delved into his pocket and brought out some coins. 'Take this. Get food and coal and buy yourself some things. It will tide you over until your brother gets back.' He looked down at the waif-like face with its creamy, petal-soft skin and beautiful amber eyes. She was a lovely girl, despite the dirt and the rags. It would have been easy for her to make her living the way many girls in such circumstances did but she hadn't – not yet. If he could save her from that then it would be one blessing he could count on when he finally met his Maker. Although Catholic, he wasn't a deeply religious man. There had been too many temptations in too many places that he'd succumbed to over the years, especially when he'd been younger. But not since he'd risen in the company. The delights of the flesh-pots of the world had lost their appeal. He was required to be a serious, sober, blameworthy man with a position of high responsibility that commanded respect. 'I'll maybe call and see how you're getting on, when I get back.'

Maggie nodded, tightly grasping the coins. He didn't appear to want anything in return. He was leaving. She watched him close the door behind him and then she looked down at the coins. Two sovereigns! Two whole sovereigns! She bit the edge of each coin in turn to make sure they were real. Her luck had changed. This was more than enough to tide her over until Tommy got back.

Her mind leaped ahead, planning how she would spend the money, what she would buy. First she'd pay the rent, then she'd buy food and coal. Enough coal to last two weeks, Tommy was bound to be back by then. Blankets, some towels and soap, washing soda and Jeyes Fluid, they were necessities in a place like this. Then she'd go to the pawnbrokers and get some clothes. Luck had certainly smiled on her. God only knew how long she would have had to work to earn this much money, even if she'd managed to get a job.

Her eyelids began to droop with exhaustion. What was his name? O'Shea. Callan O'Shea, that was it. He was the kindest, most generous man she'd ever met. What had he said before he'd gone? Something about coming to see her when he got back? Her eyelids flew open. Would he expect his . . . reward then? She hadn't thought of that! She shifted her cold, cramped limbs, the joyful speculations gone from her mind. Then she sighed with relief. Tommy would be back by then, she knew he would and maybe they'd have left Brick Street. With that solution easing her anxiety she fell into a deep sleep.

Chapter Fourteen

MA NEVITT HAD LOOKED AT her speculatively but she'd ignored it. Someone had probably told the woman she'd come home with a man. She'd slapped the coins down on the table and had walked out without a word.

When the coal was delivered and the food she'd bought was carried up by the delivery boy she knew that everyone in the house thought she'd gone on the streets, but she didn't care. She'd soon be gone from Brick Street. From the pawnshop on the dock road she bought for herself a dark green worsted skirt, a print blouse, a dress of fine grey flannel with a small white collar, stocking, buttoned boots and a shawl.

She'd taken twopence and had gone to the public baths. She'd been given a large, coarse towel, a piece of lye soap and a heavy, stiff-bristled brush and had been shown into the white-tiled cubicle by the big, raw-boned woman attendant. She'd looked in awe at the bath tub. It was huge and almost filled the cubicle. The enamel was chipped and stained in places but she hadn't cared. Never in her life had she had a proper bath. She'd never totally immersed her body and she'd watched in wonder as the hot water instantly gushed and splashed from the tap the attendant had turned on with a special key.

When she'd eased herself into the tub, she lay back and relaxed; the water had seemed to draw all the tenseness, all the bone-weariness and the aches away. After a few minutes of sheer bliss, she'd sat up and had scrubbed herself from head to toe. Then she'd washed her hair and rinsed it. She'd rubbed herself dry with the coarse towel until her skin had glowed and tingled. As she'd dressed she felt she was totally clean, almost a new person. It had been a heady feeling. She'd felt fresh as a daisy as she'd stepped out into the street.

On the stairs she'd met one of the women who lived up in the attic.

'God, 'ave yer come into a fortune, Maggie? Yer dead lovely, do yer know that, all dressed up in good clothes.'

Maggie had smiled, surprised and pleased at the compliment.

Her pleasure had given way to the gnawing anxiety when she'd reached their room. There was still no word from Tommy. She'd become really afraid, feeling certain that something terrible had happened to him. Oh, why, why, didn't he come or even write? He could have got a bit of paper or card, and stamps didn't cost the earth. If he had been illiterate it would have been different, but Tommy could write very well. Miss Cumberland had seen to that.

A couple of times she'd gone to Lime Street Station, hoping against hope that maybe Tommy would arrive by train, that his silence was due to the fact that he'd made good and had the money for the train fare home. She'd scanned the faces of the crowds that alighted from each train, but all in vain. Each time she'd returned home dejected, disappointed and increasingly worried. It was ten days since he'd gone.

She'd turned away from the station concourse and headed towards Ranleigh Street, ignoring the crowds of shoppers pushing their way in and out of Lewis's. With her head down she walked on towards St Luke's Church at the top of Bold Street. There were gardens there, maybe she'd sit for a while and try and work out what she could do. There *must* be a way of finding missing people, and she didn't feel like going back to Brick Street.

'Begod! Wasn't I on my way to see you!'

Maggie looked up startled and her eyes widened. 'It's . . . it's you!' She backed away instinctively. He'd come back and Tommy wasn't home to protect her.

'Aye, it's me. What's the matter? You look like a frightened rabbit. I'm not going to hurt you,' Callan said quietly. He hadn't been on his way to see her. In fact they'd had a bad trip, the weather in the Bay of Biscay had been foul, but he couldn't just ignore her, not when he'd nearly collided with her. 'What's the matter, Maggie?' he repeated.

She looked up into his face. His eyes were kind, his expression concerned. 'It's our Tommy . . . he . . . Oh, I'm that worried about him!'

Callan took her arm and guided her across the road towards St Luke's Gardens. There was something obviously very wrong. She didn't look half-starved, dirty, cold or ragged now. In fact she looked very different. The weak sunlight played on her auburn hair, giving it the appearance of a burnished halo. Her pale skin had a clear, translucent quality and her large eyes looked up at him, bright with incipient tears. The plain grey dress emphasized her slimness. She was a very lovely girl. He eased her down gently on a bench and sat beside her, still holding her arm.

'What's wrong, Maggie? Is it money? You haven't gone back to begging?'

'No! I'd sooner die first! And . . . and it's not money . . .' She looked down. 'You were . . . you were dead . . . kind to give us so much.'

'Then what is it?' he urged.

She began to twist the edge of her shawl. 'Our Tommy. Me . . . brother. He's been gone over two weeks now and I'm so worried about him! I keep thinking he must be hurt or . . . had a terrible accident . . .'

'Maybe he's working hard and saving up to send for you?' he suggested.

'But he could write and let me know that, couldn't he?'

'Not if he can't write.'

'He can write! He's clever, is our Tommy! Oh, I'm at me wits' end!' A tear rolled slowly down her cheek and she dashed it away with the back of her hand.

Callan looked perturbed. They appeared to be close, being orphans it was natural. It was also natural that she should deny any question of his capabilities. He knew many men who were unable to write and sometimes he'd been asked to write a few lines for them, but if the lad could write and was, as she said, clever, then he felt her fears had some foundation. 'Ah, don't be making yourself ill now, girl. Give him a bit more time. It's a long way.'

She looked up at him hopefully. He was an educated, well-travelled man, surely he must be right.

Reluctantly she drew her shawl around her and prepared to get up. 'I'd better be off.'

He stood up. 'It's a fine day, would you like to go for a walk in Princes Park?'

She hesitated. It was a tempting offer. She didn't want to go back just yet and he was someone to talk to. She missed that so much. She nodded.

'Come on then, we'll get a tram. It's not a bad day, some fresh air will do us both good.'

* * *

She'd enjoyed herself. They'd walked in the well-laid-out park with its trees and shrubs, neat pathways and large lake. She'd looked with new eyes at the imposing houses of the very rich that bordered it. Wouldn't it be wonderful to live in a house like that and never have a moment's worry about money or work, she'd said to him. Gradually, she began to tell him of her parents, her childhood, the time they'd spent in Kirkby and how much she'd loved it there. And how heartbroken she'd been to have to come back to the city.

He'd found himself describing his home and Dublin, with its fine buildings and its slums. He told her about the places he'd been, the exotic sights and sounds, the conditions at sea, the storms, and finally about Breda and his sons. He also felt strangely drawn to her. She was so young, so lovely, so vulnerable. It was only how he would feel if she'd been his daughter, he told himself. No man would want someone as gentle and beautiful as she was to be alone in such a city as Liverpool.

'When will you be going away again?' Maggie asked, knowing that soon she really must get back.

'Tomorrow. But it's only a short trip. To Friesland.'

'Where's that?'

'Holland – it's a great cattle-breeding area. I'll be back in a week.'

'Our Tommy should be back by then, or he should have written.' The nagging worries were back. The sun had gone in, the wind was cold and the burden of anxiety had settled on her shoulders again. She'd forgotten her plight for the past half hour. She shivered.

Callan stopped and pulled her shawl up closer around her throat, a gesture of affection and concern. 'If he's not back by the time I come home, I promise I'll try and help.'

She felt a surge of gratitude towards him. 'Will you? Will you really?'

'I will, it's a promise, but he'll be home. I'm sure of it, and we'll all have a drink to celebrate!' The words were spoken with a cheerfulness he didn't feel. He was certain something had happened to the lad. It didn't take two weeks to get to Glasgow. And even if he was wrong, he had a very alien feeling of resentment. As though he didn't want her to be no longer dependent on himself.

When they alighted from the tram on the Strand, he pressed another sovereign into her hand.

'No! I've still got some left!' She pushed the coin back towards him.

'No. You keep that just for . . . emergencies. I'll feel happier knowing you're not short of money.'

She put it into her pocket reluctantly. 'Why are you so . . . good to me?'

'Because I think you've had a rotten deal from life. I want to help . . . to give you a bit of a chance.'

She smiled and it transformed her face. 'I've never met anyone as kind as you.'

'Maybe you've been mixing with the wrong people,

Maggie. The world isn't full of thieves and drunks and villains, there are plenty of good people too.'

She smiled shyly. 'Thanks, but I won't spend it unless I'm desperate. I'd best get back now. Will . . . will I see you . . . again?' She felt awkward asking such a question. Yet she liked him, she trusted him. He was the first man who had shown her kindness, consideration and compassion. And he treated her with . . . respect. Yes, she did like him. He was easy to talk to, he seemed to understand her. He was old enough to be her da but that didn't matter. She wished her da had been more like Callan O'Shea. She didn't feel quite so alone now.

'Yes. Didn't I say so, Maggie. I'll be back in a week. No time at all.'

He watched her cross the road and he smiled. Her shoulders were back, her head held high. She carried herself well, he thought. He'd not break his promise. He'd see her again. He refused to listen to the small voice in his head that told him he was a fool and an old fool at that. He was captivated by this slip of a girl with her mass of auburn hair and doe-soft eyes. A girl he didn't really know very well. A girl whose surname had not been revealed to him, he thought with a sudden jolt.

For the next seven days Maggie wished that Callan O'Shea had not gone. There was still no word from Tommy and she was frantic. She had no one to turn to, no one to even confide in and her nerves were shredded. She began to listen and pray for footsteps on the stairs. Tommy's or Callan's.

When at last she heard them, she flung open the door, tears streaming down her cheeks.

'Oh, thank God! Thank God you've come! I've been going mad!'

Callan led her gently inside and closed the door. He'd walked from the dock with some dread, wondering what he would find. The trip had been uneventful and he'd alternated between cold reason, that told him not to seek her out, to leave her alone for that way only led to unhappiness and rejection, and increasingly confused feelings of longing and tenderness. 'He's not back then? No word either?'

'Nothing! Nothing! He's dead, I know he is!' Maggie sobbed.

Callan pulled her to him and held her as she sobbed against his shoulder. 'Hush, now! He's not dead, you mustn't think that, Maggie!'

She raised a tear-streaked face. 'What else can I think?'

He pulled out his handkerchief and wiped her face, trying to keep his voice steady. Her slim, trembling body in his arms had brought a wave of longing, tinged with fear and self-loathing. How could he take advantage of her when she was in such a state and trusted him so much? 'Dry your eyes, Maggie, and get your shawl.'

Maggie's sobs had diminished a little. Now that he

was here she felt calmer, more relieved, she splashed her face with cold water then picked up her shawl.

His arm firmly around her waist, they descended the rickety stairs.

'Where . . . where are we going? What will we do?' she asked when they were in the street.

'There's only one place we can go. The police station.'

She pulled away from him. 'No! No! We can't go to the scuffers!' She remembered vividly the visits the police had made to Bowers Court.

'Maggie, don't be an eejit! They are the only ones who can help! You've nothing to be afraid of!'

'I can't! I can't go there!'

He caught her firmly by her shoulders. She was trembling. 'Why? What have you done?'

'Nothing! I swear it! But . . . but my da . . . I told you about him! I can't go to the scuffers!'

'Maggie, you're with me! Besides, if you've done nothing you've nothing to fear.'

Oh, he just didn't understand! He didn't understand the fear and suspicion, she thought.

'Don't you want to try to find Tommy?' he persisted. He was very aware of how the slum dwellers viewed the police.

She managed to nod.

'Come on then. Hold on to me, I won't let anything harm you. You should know that by now, Maggie.'

She was so terrified that she could hardly speak.

Callan informed the desk sergeant of her fears for her brother.

The policeman looked hard at her. 'I know you, girl.'

'She's done nothing wrong, I assure you,' Callan interrupted firmly.

'I didn't say she had. When did he go, your brother?'

'Over three weeks,' Callan answered for her.

'And it was Glasgow he was heading for, you say?'

Maggie managed to nod.

'I don't really know that we can do anything.'

Callan felt his temper rising at the man's indifference. 'Can't you get in touch with the Glasgow police and ask if there have been any . . . accidents or the like.' He didn't want to have to say 'suspicious deaths' or, worse, 'murders' in front of her.

'That will take time, time we haven't got. You should know how busy we are around here. The place is a thieves' kitchen!'

'You'd soon find the time if she lived on Princes Avenue!' Callan snapped.

The man tapped the end of his pen on the desk top. 'I don't like what you're implying, sir. Can I ask what er . . . relation she is to you? You seem to be taking a very keen interest in a lad you've never even met.'

'You can ask and think what you like, Sergeant. I'm concerned for her and for the lad, that's all you need to know. I'm a concerned citizen. Will you try and find out something? Anything?'

Recognition dawned on the sergeant's face and he ignored Callan. 'I know who you are now, girl! That copper nob gives you away!'

Callan lost his temper. 'I asked you a question and a man in my position expects answers! What the hell does it matter who she is! It's no wonder these poor souls are afraid to come to you when they need help!'

The sergeant looked at him coldly. 'You can be His Holiness the Pope for all the ice it cuts here! We'll do what we can. Now I'd advise you to take yourself and your . . . friend . . . out of here, sir!'

Maggie broke free from a furious Callan and ran.

He caught up with her halfway down the steps, after venting his anger on the sergeant with a few well-chosen epithets.

'I knew they wouldn't help! I knew it! They don't care! No one cares about Tommy!' she sobbed.

'Maggie! I'm sorry, I really am! The man should be sacked!'

She was sobbing brokenly now and he took her in his arms, ignoring the amused and censuring glances they attracted. He couldn't take her home in this state. Someone was bound to accuse him of molesting her. Glancing around he caught sight of a hackney cab and hailed it. He helped her inside.

'Where to, sir?' the cabbie asked.

Callan thought quickly. 'The Avon Hotel, Mount Pleasant.' It was a quiet place where he sometimes stayed if business demanded a protracted sojourn in

Liverpool, and he didn't have the time or the inclination (if he was truthful) to go home. It was the sort of shabby, genteel place frequented by commercial travellers and the like.

The porter was a discreet man. He nodded to Callan in recognition as he handed him the room key. He neither looked nor spoke to Maggie who was still crying quietly.

Callan asked for a half bottle of brandy and this was produced and paid for.

Maggie sat on the over-stuffed chair, the only one in the room. She hadn't asked why he'd brought her here. She didn't care. All she could think of was Tommy.

'Here, drink this up. Slowly, sip it now.'

She looked at the glass at though it contained poison.

'It will calm you down, Maggie, please,' he urged.

Slowly she sipped it. The fiery warmth burned her throat and she gasped.

'Go on, another sip.' he coaxed.

She obeyed him. He was the only person in the whole world she could trust. She'd known the scuffers wouldn't help her. 'What . . . what can I do . . . now?'

'I'll go to the Main Bridewell and see if I can get some sense out of someone there.' Seeing her eyes widen he went on, 'I said I'll go, Maggie. Not you.'

'They won't help.' She felt calmer.

'Then I'll ask around. I have colleagues who visit

many places.' He knew it was futile. What would anyone hear or know about a young lad from Liverpool looking for work?

She heard the note of insincerity in his voice and the tears started in her eyes.

He gathered her into his arms. 'Don't cry, Maggie. Please, don't cry.'

'I'll never see him again! He's gone and I've got no one! No one!'

He gently lifted her chin. 'You have me, Maggie. I'll look after you. I swear I will!'

She felt so drained, so utterly desperate that she clung to him. 'Don't leave me! Don't go away and leave me!'

'I won't. I'll never do that, Maggie!' His heart was pounding. All reason, all common sense fled, and he kissed her gently on the lips. He felt desire flood through his veins like wine, but desire tinged with a tenderness he'd never felt before.

Maggie was trembling, from sorrow but not fear, at least not fear of him, she thought. She was afraid of herself, of her own feelings. Strange feelings that were coursing through her, making her sweat and tremble and yet burn with fire. As his lips sought hers more urgently, more passionately, it was as though the whole world was spinning and she was carried along with it, in its rushing whirling dance. A myriad of colours shattered inside her brain and she clung to him, all the sorrow, all the worry banished.

'Maggie! Maggie! My sweet, innocent little Maggie.' Gently he lifted her as though she were a child and then laid her on the bed.

She reached out and touched his cheek, her fingers trembling. 'I'm . . . I'm afraid,' she whispered.

He caught her hand and pressed it to his lips, then swept her into his arms. 'There's no need to be afraid, Maggie. I'll look after you, I promise.'

She lay curled in the circle of his arms, her head resting on his chest, utterly exhausted by the events of the day. She could think of nothing but this present moment, she didn't want to think of anything, anything except him and the fact that he said he loved her. That he would never leave her. That she'd never know poverty, pain or grief ever again.

He lay, watching her, still struggling to understand his own feelings and make sense of them. She was young enough to be his daughter and yet she'd become a passionate woman in his arms, a woman he could not now abandon, nor did he want to. It filled him with such a feeling of wonder and reverence to know that he was the first man to have loved her. There was no doubt about that and it made him want to cherish her and protect her. 'Maggie, I never meant this to happen, I couldn't help myself, but I'm not sorry. Are you?'

She turned her head and looked up at him. 'No. I never thought of you . . . like . . . like this, but it was so . . . easy . . . it seemed . . . right. I needed you so much, in every way, not just . . . Oh, I can't find the right words,' she finished, the colour tingeing her cheeks. It was the truth. She'd only ever thought of him as someone who was kind, and who did care for her, but when he'd held her and kissed her she'd felt so . . . so different. She loved him. She must have been falling in love with him without knowing it, just the way he said he'd fallen in love with her.

Those words seemed to break the spell that held her entranced. Abruptly she sat up and for the first time the reality of what she had just done dawned upon her. Her words 'I needed you so much' now sounded shameful. The words of a cheap tart. The image of Dora's face flashed into her mind. The hot blood rushed to her cheeks, she turned away from him and pulled the blanket higher to cover her nakedness.

'Oh, Mam! Mam! What have I done? Oh, God! Oh, Mam, I'm sorry!' Her cry was like that of a lost soul and Callan winced as though he'd been physically struck.

'Maggie! Maggie, don't think like that!' He tried to gather her to him, but she jerked away, her eyes wide and swimming with tears of self-loathing.

'I promised! I promised her on her deathbed . . . that . . .' The words choked her and the tears spilled down her cheeks. She'd failed Mam! Tommy was lost . . . probably dead. She'd let him take her virginity without a thought, without a struggle, and she'd . . .

she'd gloried in it! She'd said she 'needed' him! God would strike her down for her wickedness and Mam, oh, Mam would rise up and haunt her! Her terrified gaze darted around the room, as if expecting to see Dora's shadowy form appear. She was trembling again and she let him draw her into his arms. Great racking sobs shook her as he held her, rocking her, making soothing noises, as though she were a baby.

'I'm . . . I'm no better than . . . *her*. And I promised Mam I wouldn't . . . Oh, God! I promised!' she sobbed.

'Hush now, mavoureen! I'll not desert you. I'll look after you, Maggie. My sweet little Maggie!' he soothed.

She looked up at him. 'But you don't understand! I promised! I promised!'

'You promised your mother you'd be a good girl and you have been, Maggie. Don't think that I've just used you, taken advantage of you and that I'll fling you aside. I won't! I couldn't leave you now, Maggie.'

She was feeling a little calmer for his tone was so sincere. 'It's not . . . that.'

He stroked the auburn hair away from her hot flushed cheeks. 'Then what is it?'

'It's my name.' Her words were almost a whisper.

He was mystified. 'Your name?'

'Da wanted a boy not a girl, so he called me Maggie.'

'But hundreds of girls are called Maggie, it's short for Margaret, isn't it? Will I call you Margaret?'

'No, and it's not short for Margaret, not for me, it's just plain Maggie. Maggie May.'

Slowly understanding dawned. So that's why she'd never volunteered to tell him her surname. 'The bastard!' he said grimly.

'Oh, I know it's wrong to speak ill of the dead, but I hate him! I hate him! That's why I promised Mam I'd never do anything . . . anything like this! I promised I'd never be like *her*.'

He drew her to him. He could only imagine the taunts she must have had to endure all her life and his eyes darkened as he thought of the type of man who could put such a burden on a helpless child and for no other reason than pure spite. 'Your mam would understand. You're not like her. You're not like that . . .'

'Whore,' she finished, quietly.

'Oh, Maggie! That's something you could never be! You're too sweet, too trusting, too gentle.'

'But I did! I was so miserable and desperate and you were here and I forgot . . . everything.'

He held her away from him, his expression severe. 'Never let me hear you talk like that again! Something, destiny, fate, call it what you will, drew us together. I didn't even think that anything like this would happen when I first met you. You were just a poor, starving girl and I couldn't have left you like that. I only wanted to help you, the way I did that foggy night all those years ago. I never intended . . . I never realized that I'd come to love you, Maggie. And I do love you. I won't desert you! Everything I said I meant, I swear it before God and all His saints!'

Her lip began to tremble and he wiped away her tears. 'I'd better get you home. I'm sailing tomorrow to New York to look at farm cattle in Buffalo. I'll be away for two weeks, unless the weather's bad and slows us down. When I get back we'll make some permanent plans. Something definite. I won't have you living in that hovel, and I'll make proper inquiries about Tommy. I'll hire someone to find him, if needs be.'

'Do you really mean that?' Her eyes pleaded with him. She wanted to believe him so much.

'Of course I do. I'll look after you and Tommy, too, if he'll let me.' He meant it. If the lad was alive, he'd find him a place in the cattle business. That way he'd have a trade, a future, a wage of his own and he wouldn't need to feel awkward about his sister.

She leaned her head against his shoulder, the terrible guilt fading a little. Surely Mam would understand that he really did care about her?

Callan was certain he loved her, if anyone was certain of what love was anyway. He'd thought he'd loved Breda, but there were many kinds of love and they all demanded care, commitment and loyalty. Things he'd given Breda little of over the years, but he couldn't deny his wife's existence. Basically, he was an honest man and lies and subterfuge he detested. He'd been accused of being stern, inflexible and unforgiving by many of his colleagues, but it was his nature and he hoped he was a fair man. Cheating and deception were alien and abhorrent to him, yet now it seemed he would have to ignore some of his principles. But she was worth it.

Maggie remained silent. She had never trusted a man, especially not with her heart, her emotions. Had she left herself open to misery, heartbreak and humiliation? Despite all her guilt and shame she knew she loved him. She *had* to love him for she'd given herself to him. To admit to any other reason was to torture herself. To drive herself to despair and the edge of madness.

She'd slept fitfully that night although she was exhausted. When he'd gone, she kept telling herself that they loved each other. That it was right. That Mam would understand. That he would find them a nice home, and that they'd find Tommy.

He had insisted on leaving her money to make the room in Brick Street more comfortable until he returned.

Next morning, with the money tucked inside her bodice, she walked down Spalding Street, towards Park Lane, heading for town. There was plenty of food for the next few days, so she would spend some of the money on furniture and maybe something new for herself. The sun was warm on her shoulders and it made her feel better. Even the usually turgid water of the river looked cleaner. The sun's bright rays caught the hundreds of small windows in the dockside warehouses and made them sparkle like diamonds.

She bought two armchairs, stuffed with horsehair and covered in a dark green Linen Union that wasn't too stained. A couple of bright rag rugs, a set of pans and some nice pieces of china. They didn't all match but that didn't matter. She bought a jug and basin decorated with red and pink roses. She bought a bed, a proper bed with a headboard and footboard and an iron mattress frame. She bought two feather mattresses. She had been persuaded to purchase a pair of white cotton sheets and a bolster case. The shop keeper told her he'd have his lad bring them all around on the cart later that day.

She stood looking into the window of Frisby Dyke in Lord Street, bemused by the choice of garments. Astonished that she, who had never had anything but cast-offs in her life, now had the money to buy something brand spanking new. Something that no one had ever worn. She settled for a dark green skirt with black braid around the hem and two large black buttons on the high waistband, and a white cotton blouse, buttoned up to the neck with tiny pearl buttons, the front pleated and pin-tucked, the sleeves wide and full and gathered into the tight cuffs. She chose a green and gold paisley shawl with long, fringed ends. The whole outfit was complemented by a large hat adorned with a curled green feather around the brim. She wore everything and her old clothes were neatly parcelled up.

She also bought some underwear and felt that she must be in heaven to have such soft cotton against her skin, instead of bleached calico. When she stepped outside she was laden down with parcels, but her step was light.

A barefooted street urchin pushed towards her.

'Carry yer parcels, missus? I'm honest me, I won't do a runner with 'em, cross me heart an' hope to die.' He spat on his hand and then crossed himself.

Smiling, Maggie handed him a couple of the larger ones. 'You scarper with them an' I'll set our kid on you! Big as a carter's horse he is, so you watch it, lad.'

He looked at her fearfully. By her tone and manner of speech she was one of his own kind, not the posh lady he'd taken her for, so it would be no good running off with her stuff.

Chapter Fifteen

IT HAD TAKEN TOMMY TWELVE days to get to Glasgow. He'd hitched rides when he could, but he'd had to walk for most of the way. Sleeping rough, doing odd jobs in exchange for food and if he was lucky a roof over his head, when he could get the work. It had all delayed him but he'd got two days' work with a farmer near Selkirk and with what he was paid, and the few pennies he'd grimly saved, he'd paid for a third class train ticket for the rest of the journey.

When he'd asked a lad loitering at the entrance to the station where the shipyard was, his question had been greeted with scorn and he'd been informed that he must travel on to Greenock. When he'd replied that he had no money, the lad had asked him why he'd come to Glasgow. Tommy had explained. The explanation had been met with a shrug and the advice to 'try Dixon's Blazes, it's nearer.' Hope had surged and had given him renewed strength.

That night he'd wandered the city, mesmerized by the unfamiliar dialect which at times he could hardly understand. Glasgow was not unlike Liverpool, he thought. Big and sprawling, with its fine shops and grand buildings and its slums. He begged a few coppers for food and then settled down in a doorway at the back of Argyle Street.

It wasn't quite dawn when he'd arrived at the gates of the big iron foundry, but the sky was illuminated by the great showers of sparks that shot up from the tall chimneys. At least he'd be first in the queue for the day shift, he thought, standing with his nose pressed against the huge iron gates.

He was shivering with cold after an hour but then he heard a strange sound. A muffled rumbling that soon became a clattering that grew louder by the minute. Men from all parts of the city were converging on the foundry, their boots striking the dusty cobbles. Soon he'd been surrounded by a throng, and he'd been jostled and pushed and pressed hard against the gates. Stubbornly he'd pushed back. He'd been here first, he thought doggedly, even though he realized that there was a big difference between himself and them. They had jobs to go to.

The crowd was growing restless but then it had parted to let someone through. A man in a motor car, and from the style of his clothes Tommy realized that he must be someone very important.

He'd made a desperate bid to free himself from the

crush but as he did so, the massive gates swung open and he stumbled. Men pushed past him, roughly elbowing him aside and with the sheer weight of numbers rushing past he was forced to the edge of the crowd and pinned against the side of the car. His chance was slipping away from him but worst of all he was being crushed. The pressure on his chest was so great that his breathing was ragged and painful. Then he'd been seized by the collar of his jacket and yanked forcefully inside the car.

'Don't you know better than to stand there, laddie, holding everyone up? It's a good job I was here or you'd have been trampled underfoot.'

Tommy looked up into the stern, clean-shaven face. Now was his chance!

'I was first! I've been here hours, since before it was light! I came for a job and I wasn't going to let them get in front of me,' he cried, although his voice was shaky.

The man didn't reply and Tommy felt defeated. He fixed his gaze on the back of the uniformed man who was driving. Once inside the gates the car stopped.

'You're not from these parts, are you?'

'No, I've come all the way from Liverpool, sir. I got a few rides but I walked most of the way. I got work when I could, it's taken me nearly two weeks.'

'You must want a job badly, laddie!'

'Not just a job, sir, I want a trade. I can read and write and I'm good with figures,' Tommy said earnestly, knowing instinctively that he would never get another opportunity like this.

'And are there no jobs in Liverpool, then?'

Tommy shook his head. 'No. Things are bad and there's only one shipyard, Cammell Laird's. I know I look a mess, sir, but I've been sleeping rough most of the time. I was going to try at John Brown's but . . . but my money ran out.'

Alasdair Dixon looked at Tommy closely. It took guts to come all the way from Liverpool to look for work and, judging by the state of the lad, he'd not slept in a bed since he'd left home. 'Where did you sleep last night?'

'I don't rightly know, sir,' Tommy answered truthfully.

Probably under the Victoria Bridge, Alasdair Dixon thought. 'What's your name?'

'Tommy, Tommy May and I'm seventeen and I'm good with my hands and willing, like. I slept in a doorway last night, I don't know where, I don't know the city yet. But please, sir, give me a chance, will yer? Me schoolteacher said I'd got brains, that I could get meself a good trade. I finished school an' got me certificate.'

There was something about the boy that had struck him and Alasdair Dixon prided himself on being a good Christian and a fair-minded man. 'All right, we'll start you off in the smelting shop, see how you shape in there. It's not easy work but when you've some food inside you, you'll feel better.'

Tommy couldn't believe his ears. He was being given a chance. The chance of learning a skill, something that would set him up for life. 'Do you mean that, sir?' His pale thin face was alight with eagerness.

Alasdair Dixon laughed. 'Indeed I do. Some of the men walk miles to get here, but none of them from as far as Liverpool. If you want something that badly, laddie, then at least you deserve a chance, but if you're no good, then out those gates you go.'

'Oh, don't worry about me, sir, work until I drop, I will!'

Tommy was given over to the charge of Andy McKinnon, the foreman. He was taken to a low wooden building that was a kind of an office.

'Right, laddie, some details first. Name?'

Tommy gave it.

'Address?'

'I haven't got one, sir, not here anyway.'

The foreman leaned on the table. Mr Dixon had given him a few brief details and instructions. 'Well, in that case you'd better come home with me the night. Until we sort something out.'

Tommy could only stare, so great was his relief.

'Mr Dixon is a great benefactor. A very Christian gentleman who cares about his workers, and he'd not like it if you were left to roam the streets. Have you eaten?'

'No, sir.'

A mug of tea and four thick sandwiches were placed

in front of him and he tucked in heartily, not knowing it was Andy McKinnon's own lunch he was devouring.

'Do you know anything about working iron?'

'No, but I'll soon learn, sir. I want a trade.'

'It's no' really a trade in the strict sense, but it's a skilled job. Oh, aye, it's skilled.'

'Then I'll be grateful, sir.'

There was something about the boy, Andy McKinnon had mused. He thought he could see what Alasdair Dixon had seen. An eagerness, an honesty and great determination. 'Right, we'd better get started then. We've a long, hard day ahead of us and you've a lot to learn.'

Tommy felt almost delirious with happiness. Was everyone in this part of the world so kind and generous or had he just had an enormous stroke of luck? 'Thanks . . . thanks, sir,' he stammered, getting to his feet. He'd been right. He'd just 'known' his luck would change. 'I will get myself fixed up with a place, too. I left my sister back in Liverpool. I said when I got on my feet, like, that she must come up here too.'

'Well, you can tell me your life story tonight, laddie, but now you'd best make a start or Mr Dixon will have us both outside the gates for idling.'

He had been with the McKinnons for two weeks and he'd never been happier in his life. Florrie McKinnon was a homely woman whose only son, on whom she'd doted, had been killed at Mafeking, and she'd taken to

Tommy instantly. She declared that he must stay with them, there was no question of paying good money for a room in a dirty tenement house. An easy prey for all the 'hairies', as she termed the prostitutes. When she'd heard his story her affection for him had grown. And Andy had only praise for him, telling everyone he was a sharp lad and a hard and willing worker. A fine example of Mr Dixon's unerring judgement and faith in his fellow man.

The only thing that clouded Tommy's perfect horizon was the fact that he hadn't written to Maggie. He put it off every day, with some light excuse. He knew it was wrong of him and that both Maggie and Mrs McKinnon would think badly of him. But the truth was that he would be content to stay with the McKinnons. They were offering a life and opportunities he had only ever dreamed of.

Their home wasn't a palace. It was a tall, redbrick terraced house in East Pollackshields. It was plainly furnished but it was spotlessly clean, inside and out. Florrie battled daily against the smuts that marred her whitened front step and windowsills. She was a wonderful cook and he was already putting on weight. His clothes were washed and ironed, his boots cleaned and buffed to a shine, despite the scuffing.

Andy was inclined to be taciturn but his wife made up for his long silences and when, after supper, Andy sat engrossed in his newspaper, Florrie kept up a constant chatter, though her hands were never idle.

She was always sewing or knitting. After the long, hard day of unaccustomed heavy work and a good supper, Tommy found it hard to stay awake. It was then that he thought of Maggie.

They'd have to find rooms and they wouldn't be in a decent area. He had seen his dreams fulfilled a thousandfold and was reluctant to have to revert to his old life style.

'Have you not written to your sister, yet, Tommy?' Andy asked as they sat after supper at the beginning of the next week.

Shamefacedly Tommy shook his head.

'Well, it's about time you did. The poor lassie will be out of her mind with worry.'

'I . . . I don't know what to say . . . what to write. It would be better if I could see her, speak to her, explain everything. She might think I was making all this up, just to stop her worrying.' Tommy gestured with his hand, encompassing the room and Andy and Florrie.

Florrie nodded. 'He's right, Andy.'

'Could you go there and back in a weekend?'

Tommy brightened. 'Aye, I think so. I'll have the money for the fare by Friday.' If he could just talk to Maggie, tell her about how fortunate he'd been and how he would hate to leave the McKinnons. He could send her money every week or if she really preferred it she could come to Glasgow and find work. She would make some friends, girls of her own age.

His gaze went quickly around the room. The

brasses shone brightly, the range was blackleaded and polished. The chenille cloth on the overmantel was bright, with little silken tassels hanging from it. The few ornaments were lovingly dusted and a large geranium in a pot stood on the windowsill, flanked by the neat curtains. The table was scrubbed white and all the dishes on the dresser matched. To Tommy it was as good as living in a palace.

'Then that's settled. Get the train to Liverpool on Saturday and the one back on Sunday. Andy will meet you. Then everyone will be happy.' Florrie beamed at them both, unaware that behind Tommy's smile lay deep apprehension and the beginnings of resentment.

As he walked up Salthouse Lane late on Saturday night Tommy felt depressed. The journey had been long and tiring. There was poverty in Glasgow, he thought, but somehow it seemed different. It didn't touch him. For, except for that first night, he'd lived very comfortably. Here it seemed to reach out and cling to him. Everything looked old and dirty and decaying. Even the smell from the river, a smell bound up in his earliest memories, now seemed alien to him. Liverpool was his past. A miserable past. Glasgow was his future and that looked bright and promising. But what would he say to Maggie? How would he put it to her that he didn't want to leave the McKinnons and if they fell out over it, what would Andy and Florrie think of him? The last thing he wanted was to see disapproval and censure in their faces. They were an honest, hard-working, God-fearing couple and he admired them immensely. Andy was everything his da hadn't been and subconsciously he was modelling himself on Andy McKinnon. He was the kind of man Tommy wanted to be. Upright and respected.

As he climbed the narrow, rickety stairs he wrinkled his nose at the stink of the place and then felt guilty. Maggie had to live here. He knocked on the door, arranging his face in a smile.

'Tommy! Tommy!' she shrieked, throwing her arms around him and hugging him. 'Oh, I thought you were dead! I really thought I'd never see you again! You've been so long! Oh, I've missed you, Tommy!'

Over her shoulder Tommy could see into the room and couldn't believe his eyes. 'What's all this, Maggie?'

She dragged him inside and closed the door and then he noticed her clothes.

'Bye, you've been busy, Maggie. You must have a good job!'

Maggie was smiling at him, her eyes shining with pure joy. 'Oh, Tommy, I've missed you so much and I've got so much to tell you, but first you must be starving. Sit there and tell me all your news while I get you something to eat.'

She did want to tell him about Callan but her joyful euphoria was passing. She felt anxious and nervous, she glanced quickly at him from beneath her lashes. He looked so happy and yet . . . if she told him the truth, would he believe her? She decided not to tell him, not just yet. It would be better if he had a day or two to settle down. Tommy grinned at her with relief. Maybe she wouldn't want to leave Liverpool now. She obviously had had a stroke of luck. She'd got the place looking really nice. The walls had been freshly lime-washed. There were bright curtains at the window and rugs on the floor. The low beds were neatly made up with clean, warm-looking blankets and even sheets. The two armchairs had cushions on them and a small table boasted a white tablecloth. Nor did there seem to be any shortage of food either for she'd set the frying pan on the fire and was deftly turning rashers of bacon.

He sat down in a chair and watched her. 'I was so lucky, Maggie. It took me weeks to get there, to Glasgow. I'd no money so I couldn't get to the shipyards but I've got a skilled job, well it will be when I eventually master it, at the big iron foundry. Dixon's Blazes it's called and a right bonny place it is, too!'

Maggie laughed as she spooned the tea into the pot from a painted tin. 'You've certainly picked up the lingo quick enough, our Tommy!'

'That first morning, I was near crushed to death but it turned out lucky for me. Mr Dixon himself hauled me out of the crowd before I was hurt. Right into his motor car! Then, he gave me a job.' His eyes glowed with pride.

'Well, where are you living?'

'That was another thing. I'd been sleeping rough most of the time but when they took me on at Dixon's,

Andy McKinnon, the foreman, took a shine to me and I've been living with him and his wife. Oh, Maggie you should see it, it's like a little palace. They only had one son and he was killed at Mafeking and they've really taken to me!'

She was so relieved, so happy and so pleased for him and yet she was afraid to tell him that she couldn't leave Liverpool now.

Tommy tucked into the rashers and eggs and fried bread with relish. 'So where are you working or have you got a fairy godmother?' he asked thickly, his mouth full.

Maggie sat down opposite him. 'Things were so desperate, Tommy, after you left. I gave you nearly all the money I had, and I did leave myself short. I managed to get scraps from the market but I was at my wits' end. I went to the Parish but they turned me away. The man said I should get a job, even though I'd told him I'd tried everywhere. I met Katie Murphy and she told me there was a job going at the Yankee Clipper.'

Tommy put down his fork and stared at her. 'You didn't go there!'

'I did but the job had been taken. But then I had a real stroke of luck. I got a job in a laundry, packing. It's not hard and the pay's really good. It's piecework, the more you do the more money you earn.'

Tommy had finished eating. 'I think we should celebrate then. We've both done well. I'll go down to the Baltic Fleet and get us a drink.' He was on his feet and making for the door before Maggie could stop him. She might be more agreeable to him going back alone after a drink or two. Neither of them had tasted spirits or wine. He'd get a small bottle of rum and they could have a drop in their tea. That way it wouldn't taste too strong. He didn't feel guilty at all now. Maggie had a good job and she had the place nicely done out.

On his way out of the pub he collided with Katie Murphy.

'Mind where you're going, yer nearly knocked me flyin'!' Katie yelled.

'Sorry, Katie, I didn't mean to.'

She peered at him. 'Oh, it's you, Tommy May! Where 'ave you been then? I saw your Maggie a while ago, she was desperate for a job she even went down to the Yankee Clipper.'

'I know. The job was taken, but it was good of you to tell her about it, Katie. Even though it's not the place for any girl to work and our Maggie's a cut above all those . . . well, that sort of girl.'

'Oh, is that so? Well, let me tell you something, Tommy May, your Maggie was on the street outside the Yankee Clipper looking for men and she found one, too. She picked up a toff, at least he looked like a toff by the style of his clothes, and he was old enough to be yer da. So don't go tellin' me your Maggie's a cut above anyone!'

'You're a liar, Katie Murphy! Our Maggie's got a good job in a laundry.'

'What bloody laundry? Is that what she told you? Jaysus, you're thick as a plank if you believe that! I saw her, with me own eyes! He had his arm around her and her makin' up to him! Laundry, me arse!' Katie shrieked with laughter.

An icy blast of wind from the river cut through Tommy's coat, but he wasn't shivering because he was cold. Maggie had lied to him. She had no job and there was no laundry. As Katie had said, he must have been thick to have believed her. Katie hadn't seen the way Maggie had transformed the room in Brick Street, or the new clothes she was wearing. Maggie couldn't have earned enough to pay for everything.

After all she'd said and the way she'd promised Mam on her deathbed, she'd gone on the streets, like her namesake. The tide of anger and hurt swelled in him and, with his face set, his lips in a tight line and his eyes full of rage, Tommy strode along Wapping towards Brick Street.

The smile was wiped from Maggie's face as he opened the door and then sent it crashing back on its hinges.

'You lied to me, Maggie! You've not got a job! You didn't buy all this stuff!'

'Who told you that?' It was almost a whisper.

'Katie Murphy, she saw you touting for business outside the Yankee Clipper, so don't try to deny it!'

'I was desperate, Tommy. Yes, I did go to the

Yankee Clipper, but you don't understand. I was begging, Tommy. I had to beg like Mam did, I was reduced to begging but I'd never, never do . . . that! I did meet someone. Mr O'Shea. He buys cattle for the big meat companies and arranges to bring them here, to the lairages over in Woodside. Oh, Tommy, he was so good. He bought food and coal and he insisted on leaving me money. Two whole sovereigns! When he came back I met him again, then the third time he gave me the money to buy all this.'

The ugly red flush began at the base of Tommy's neck and spread upwards. He jumped to his feet, sending the chair crashing over. 'He left you money! He left you money! What did you give him in return, Maggie?'

Maggie was on her feet, her cheeks as red as Tommy's. 'It wasn't like that, Tommy! I was starving! Ma Nevitt was going to throw me out! He's a good, kind man.'

'They all are, once they've got what they paid for!' Tommy yelled at her.

'Tommy, stop it! Let me explain it all!'

'There's nothing to explain, Maggie! Taking up with a common bloody sailor!'

'He's not a sailor, he's a cattle agent!'

'I don't care if he's a bloody duke, you're a whore, Maggie! You sold yourself and you promised Mam, on her deathbed, that you'd never do that! You're a lying, cheating whore!'

'I didn't! I wasn't on the streets, I was begging! You believe Katie Murphy, but not me.'

'Why should she lie? What could she gain?'

'She's never liked me and now she's lying.'

'Is she, Maggie? Well, I don't bloody well believe your story!'

Maggie's hands flew to her cheeks. Tommy's words were like stinging slaps. 'I'm not a whore! I'm not! It wasn't like that, honestly! When he comes back, he's going to look after me, after both of us! He's going to get us a decent home!'

Tommy's bitter laughter echoed around the room. 'You're bloody soft, if you believed that, Maggie! He won't come back, you won't see hide nor hair of him again!'

'I will, I know I will! He came back the other times! I trust him! I love him, Tommy, and he loves me! I didn't sell myself, he loves me!'

Tommy was shaking. On his mind was imprinted the image of Dora's face as she lay dying and he could hear her rasping breath, her painfully laboured voice extracting that sacred promise from Maggie. Fury exploded in his brain as he thought of the McKinnons. How could he tell them this? 'You're a whore!' he yelled. 'You turned out just like her, Da named you well, Maggie!'

Cruelly he began to sing,

'Maggie, Maggie May,
They've taken you away . . .'

With a strangled cry Maggie flew at him, lashing out blindly. 'Stop it! Stop it! I hate you! I hate you, Tommy May!'

He pushed her away roughly. 'After you promised Mam . . . you dirty bitch!'

'I did my best! Didn't I look after you the best I could? It was your fault we had to leave Kirkby and come back! You left me! You could have stayed but you wanted your precious bloody trade! I did my best! I was starving, Tommy. Bloody starving! You could have written! I thought you were dead! I even went to the scuffers. Callan took me! He tried to help find you, Tommy!'

'I hate you, Maggie! I'm going back to Glasgow, there's nothing here for me now. Go out and pick up as many "cattle agents" as you want! I don't care what happens to you! You betrayed me and Mam! Go to hell, Maggie!' he yelled, shaking with anger, shock and disgust. He'd sooner spend the night on Lime Street Station than spend another minute in this room surrounded by the things some man had bought at the price of his sister's honour and his own. He'd go back to Glasgow and tell Andy McKinnon what she'd done and he'd never, ever speak to her again. He had no sister now, for as far as he was concerned Maggie no longer existed. She might as well be dead – like Mam!

As he stalked out of the house and into Brick Street he collided with a lad a few years older than himself.

''Ere, watch where yer going!'

'Sod off!' Tommy yelled.

'Eh, it's Tommy May! Bloody 'ell, we wondered where you'd got to.'

Tommy didn't recognize him. 'Bugger off and leave me alone!'

The lad pushed his cap to the back of his head and grinned slowly. He knew a few people who would be interested to know where Tommy May and his sister were living and they'd pay well for the information, too.

Chapter Sixteen

TOMMY'S WORDS ABOUT Callan O'Shea haunted Maggie. She'd cried herself to sleep the night Tommy had left. If only she could have made him understand that it was not the base, sordid thing he had portrayed, but the beautiful, tender love that it really was. She'd had no time to tell Tommy anything about Callan O'Shea, but what was there to tell – that he had a wife and two sons in Ireland? With a terrible clarity she knew that she'd never see Tommy again. She'd hurt him and hurt him deeply and if his new life was as promising as he'd described it, there was no place in it for her.

Tommy had been her mainstay, her companion, her comfort and support for years and she felt as though a limb had been severed. And what if it had all been in vain? What if Tommy had been right about Callan? No! No! She would never believe that, she had sobbed.

May came in with clear blue skies and warm breezes. The trees and bushes in the parks and squares in the prosperous areas of the city burst into leaf. In St John's Gardens behind St George's Hall, spring and early summer flowers splashed a bright swathe of colour against the grimy buildings. Maggie saw none of the beauty of the season. The days and nights passed increasingly slowly. She argued with herself that Tommy was wrong. Callan had come back to her before, so why not this time. Because he'd got what he wanted from her, made promises for a future, that's why, her conscience would jibe.

In the days immediately after Tommy had left, she'd gone down to the Woodside lairages, her gaze scrutinizing every man. Her inquiries met with disinterested or scornful replies. So she gave up that avenue of hope.

She became pale and thin, having no appetite. Worry and fear gnawed at her constantly as she counted the days. It was Saturday and she knew she should be going to the market to do the week's shopping, for supplies were low, but she had no heart for it. She stood staring out of the window, unseeing. If her reckoning was right he should be back today and one way or another things would be settled. She had two possibilities in life. Things could get better or worse. Often she'd toyed with the idea of going to try to find Tommy and try once more to explain, if the worst came to the worst, but it was something she always ended up dismissing, for it meant that she admitted to herself that Callan would not return.

As the hours wore on and there was no sign of him, the feeling of dread claimed her. She was stiff from standing rigid, staring at the door. Her mind was tired from willing him to come through it. Each noise on the stairs made her jump, her heart leaping to her throat, then plummeting sickeningly when there was no loud knock on the door.

Daylight was fading and soon it would be time to light the lamps. She knew it must be getting late for the evenings were longer now. Slowly, she rubbed her arms, then folded them around herself, as though for protection. The light slanting into the room was a soft misty indigo that heralded the hours of darkness. 'Oh, I'm so miserable,' she thought. 'I . . . I just want to curl up and die. He . . . he's not coming back. What will I do now, I can't . . .' She stopped, her head jerking up, her ears straining. She wasn't imagining it! She wasn't! The heavy tread on the stairs was growing louder and then with a shriek of pure joy she ran to the door and flung it wide and then she was in his arms, laughing and crying and repeating his name all at the same time.

'I thought . . . I thought you weren't coming!'

He swung her off her feet. 'Oh, Maggie! You little fool! Didn't I promise I'd look after you?'

She clung to him, relief racing through her veins like wine, making her dizzy. 'I asked, but no one knew exactly when you'd be back! I waited and waited and our Tommy said . . .'

He held her away from him and traced the outline of her lips with his finger. She was so pale and thin. 'Ah, so the prodigal returned then? Didn't I tell you nothing had happened to him?' he said quietly, though he could see no evidence of male occupancy in the room.

She nodded and pain filled her eyes.

He sat down in an armchair and drew her down on to his lap. 'What happened, Maggie?'

'Oh, he was full of what he'd done. Got a good job and a nice place to live with good people.'

'And he wanted to know where you got all this from?'

'He . . . he called me a . . . whore. He wouldn't let me explain. He believed Katie Murphy's lies. He yelled and shouted at me and then . . . then he left. Oh, Callan, I know I'll never see him again. He hates me now!'

'Hush, hush! He should never have left you alone in the first place. He could have got work here or near here. He was only thinking of himself, wanting to learn a trade, fulfilling his own ambitions, with not a thought for you. He didn't even write and let you know. Has he forgotten everything you did for him?'

'No, it wasn't like that.' Even now she wouldn't let him say anything against Tommy.

'Maggie, he'll come back. He's only a lad, give him

time. No one just cuts and runs like that, burning their boats for ever. He'll be back.'

She was much calmer now. 'I wish I could believe you but he's so stubborn.'

He drew her head down towards him. 'Let's forget about him, for now. I've missed you, Maggie, far more than I ever thought I'd miss anyone. The nights have never been so long or so lonely.' It was the truth. He'd thought about her often during the days but at night, when sleep wouldn't come, he'd stared at the dark sky for hours and pictured her: her fascinatingly beautiful eyes, her laugh, her long white slender limbs that made him ache with desire and longing. He felt young, younger than he'd felt in years. She'd rolled the years away. She'd given him a new, clearer outlook on life and now, as he looked at her, he knew he loved her. The only thing that saddened him was the fact that he wasn't free. During those long nights he'd had many a fight with his conscience, too, but he couldn't, wouldn't, deny his love for her.

Happiness was coursing through her and Tommy and everything else was forgotten.

For the next three days she was happier than she'd ever been in her entire life. She laughed, something she hadn't done for months, and she sang, something she hadn't done for years. He took her for dinner, to the music hall, shopping, walking in the park or along on the waterfront and she saw her city through new eyes, his eyes. He pointed out the fine architecture of the library and museum, St George's Hall where the law courts were. The town hall, which she had passed thousands of times without really looking at it, became a different, beautiful building. He'd laughed at her when he'd told her that the statue perched on the domed roof was that of Minerva and not 'Britannia' or 'that woman on the back of a penny' as she'd described the figure.

They'd sat in Princes Park and Newsham Park and admired the grand houses with motor cars and carriages outside their doors. She'd fed bread to the ducks on the lakes although she'd told him it was a sinful waste when so many people didn't have a crust.

She'd asked him about Dublin and he'd tried to paint a picture with words, of the quays and the bridges across the Liffy, the beautiful Georgian houses in Fitzwilliam Square and St Stephen's Green, the fine shops, the castle, the Four Courts, the Customs House and Phoenix Park. She tried to picture it all for she knew she would never see it. He would never take her there nor would she ask him to.

He'd promised that when he next came home he would help her look for somewhere else to live. He hated her living in Brick Street. 'A nice little house, maybe,' he suggested.

'A house! A whole house just for me!'

He laughed. 'I don't mean a great barn of a place! Just a nice, little red-brick terraced. Now where is a good area far away from here?'

She shrugged. 'Walton, Everton, I don't know.'

'Well then, I'll have to ask Mr Compton for his advice on the matter.'

'Who's he?' she'd demanded.

'My lawyer.'

She'd never known anyone who could afford the fees those 'legal blokes' charged.

'He looks after all my affairs, this side of the water that is. Mr Foley does the same in Dublin.'

She glanced up at him. 'You have two lawyers?'

'Oh, it's a desperate business being a cattle agent, Maggie!' He didn't say that Mr Foley was the family solicitor or that Mr Compton, who did indeed deal with his personal matters, was one of the solicitors in the firm the company he worked for employed. His eyes had twinkled and she'd laughed, but she knew their time together was growing short. His trip would be a longer one this time, he'd be away a month and already she was beginning to dread the long days and nights without him. 'The worst part of being here is that I have no one to talk to. Sometimes I see Rosa from next door, but we've . . . we've not much in common and ever since you and I . . . Well, I know what they say about me!' She jerked her head in the direction of the ceiling.

'Ah, don't fret about it, soon you'll have nice neighbours, plenty of women and girls to be gossiping with. I tell you what, I'll go and see Mr Compton this afternoon, tell him my plans, see what he says and then while I'm away you can go and look at places.'

'I'd like that, I really would!'

'It won't be anything too grand, Maggie. I'm not that wealthy. I wish I were.' He had some savings but not a great deal. The finance was in the house and a bit of land in Ireland.

'I don't mind that. Just to have a place of my own . . .'

She became silent and thoughtful.

'What's the matter?'

'I . . . I don't want to be . . . well, kept. I'm so grateful for everything, I really am, and it was all right when we were so desperate, but . . . but I wouldn't feel right.'

He understood or thought he did. She had her pride. 'What will you live on, then?'

'If I had some spare rooms I could take in a couple of lodgers, ladies,' she added, seeing his expression change. 'It would be a bit of a wage, like.'

He remained silent. He wanted her to himself when he came home. He didn't want a house full of people and yet it did make sense. In a quiet, respectable neighbourhood it would be considered very 'proper' for her to have a couple of lady boarders while he (to all intents and purposes her husband) was away on business. He had already decided that she would suffer no more humiliating speculation. He would buy her a wedding ring and she would be known as Mrs O'Shea.

'Then it's settled, I'll leave everything to Compton.

You just pick something you like and get out of this hell-hole as quickly as you can!'

'Can I come to see you off?' she asked later.

'Do you want to?'

She nodded slowly. 'Yes, at least I can watch you all the way down the river.'

'That won't take very long, the *Apappa*'s steam driven, she can get up a rare speed of knots, if she's pushed.'

'Well, I don't mind, it's better than staying here.'

Next morning she was regretting her words, for the skies were overcast, trapping the sultry heat and the smoke rising from the factories and the three chimneys of the Clarence Dock Power Station, leaving it hanging in a pall over the city. The blue-grey waters of the Mersey looked oily and sluggish with only the white wake of the ferries and dredgers breaking the glassy surface.

There was the usual crowd at the Pierhead, swelled by those waiting at the tram terminus. A train rattled along on the overhead railway, while on the track beneath it a small sturdy steam engine chugged along lugubriously, drawing behind it waggons loaded with coal and pig-iron. Drays and motor lorries were at a halt, blocking the road, waiting for the train to pass.

They'd said their farewells last night and now the *Apappa* stood out in the river, awaiting the tugs to get her under way. A thick black curl of smoke from her single funnel spiralled upwards to mingle with that of the Cunard liner *Ivernia* that was tied up at the landing stage, disgorging her passengers into the Riverside Station.

Maggie stood with a light blue shawl draped around her shoulders over the pale lilac chambrey dress with its frilled collar and wide sleeves. A light straw hat was perched over her upswept hair. Her eyes were fixed on the *Apappa* and she felt miserable, knowing that even though she could make as many forays to the quiet streets on the edge of the Everton district of the city as she wished, it was no substitute for him.

She wondered, idly, if her mam had ever loved her da the way she loved Callan O'Shea. She doubted it. Her love for him was such a precious and wonderful thing that no one in the whole wide world could ever have experienced anything remotely like it. She let out her breath in a sigh as she saw the tugs take up the heavy hawsers and the *Apappa* began to move with the ebb of the tide, picking up speed. Before she was past Perch Rock she would be free of the tugs and then she would pass into the Crosby Channel heading for the Mersey Bar and be out of sight. She knew he'd be thinking of her, wondering how long she would stand – just watching.

The crowds had thinned a little when at last she turned away, her eyes burning from straining to see the vessel that had become a mere speck. The day was still sultry and threatened a storm and it seemed to have sapped her strength.

She walked slowly up Shaw's Alley, so deep in thought that she didn't see the three men blocking her way. When she did, her heart plummeted and she let out a startled cry.

'You're coming with us, girl. Mick Devanney was a good mate,' the tallest of them said menacingly, as the others caught her arms and twisted them behind her back.

Maggie began to scream and kick but they were too strong for her and a dirty piece of rag was shoved into her mouth. Pure terror gripped her. Were they going to beat her up or was there a worse fate ahead?

She'd lost her hat and her hair had come loose from its pins and straggled around her shoulders. Her dress was torn and after what seemed like an eternity, she recognized the surrounding buildings. They were in Park Lane. If she could just attract someone's attention, she thought, frantically renewing her struggles, but she was tired and weak. Ahead of her she could see a small crowd of people and her heart began to race. Someone would surely see what was happening. Help was at hand.

Suddenly she was surrounded by people who were all yelling and screaming but the gag had been removed and her arms were free.

'Help me! Help me! These men are going to beat me!' she screamed, but no one in the crowd seemed to hear her. She heard the sound of breaking glass and she was jostled to the forefront of the disturbance. She looked with horror at the window of Greenburg's, the naval outfitters shop; most of the glass had gone, just a few jagged shards were left. The rest of it crunched beneath her feet. She gazed around frantically not knowing what was happening. The crowd seemed smaller and she caught sight of the ruffian who had said he was Devanney's mate. He grinned at her slyly before melting into the press of people.

She was so disorientated and frightened that she just stood, looking at the broken window and at the people who were dragging jackets, top coats, shirts and anything they could get their hands on, from the shop. She didn't hear the shrill blasts of a whistle nor did she see the two burly policemen who had appeared on the scene.

'Right, girl, what's going on?'

Maggie looked up. 'I . . . I don't know.'

'Then what's that in your hand?' the older of the two asked.

She looked down and screamed. Someone had pressed a large stone into her hand and she'd been so dazed, so terrified that she hadn't even noticed.

'Someone must have put it there, honestly! I don't know any of these people.'

'What people?'

She looked around with pure disbelief. Everyone had gone. 'They were all here! I swear they were.'

'Aye, and I'm the lord mayor of Liverpool. Incitement to Riot is a very serious offence.'

Maggie's expression registered the gamut of emotions she was experiencing. 'I didn't do anything! I was dragged here by three mates of Mick Devanney. They arranged all this, all those . . . people. They must have paid them. I haven't done anything, I swear. They set me up! They did!'

'It's a long time since I heard such a good fairy tale. You've got a vivid imagination, girl,' the older man said acidly.

'But it's the truth! Mick Devanney swore he'd get even with me. He was on the run, he wanted money. Money he said my da had stolen from Robinson's.'

'Who was your da?' the younger man asked.

'Nago May.'

'And you mean to tell me that you were standing here innocently minding your own business, an' you're Nago May's daughter. Come on, we've wasted enough time listening to a pack of lies.'

As the cold metal handcuffs were clasped around her wrists, she began to cry. 'It's the truth. It's the truth. I've been to see Mr O'Shea off, he can vouch for me, he'll tell you I'm not lying.'

'You've just said you've been to see him off.'

Maggie was confused. 'Yes, but . . .'

'What does he do, this mysterious Mr O'Shea?'

'He's a cattle agent, he goes all over the world. Oh, can't you contact the *Apappa* in some way? I've done nothing!'

'We can't go chasing after ships that are already at

sea on the say so of a street baggage like you!'

Her struggles ceased. It was no use. Callan had gone, there was no one to tell them that she was telling the truth. No one to verify her story.

'Let's get her down to the Bridewell at Cheapside and see if she changes her tune in a cell.'

'No! I'm innocent!' Maggie cried, frantically trying to twist away, but they were too strong.

'You should have thought about that, shouldn't you? Don't make it any harder, girl, and don't start kicking up or we'll have to "restrain" you!'

Maggie slumped and, but for the strong arms holding her, she would have slid to the floor. Mick Devanney's vengeance had reached out from the grave. His mates had seen to that. Now she was accused of a crime she hadn't committed.

Chapter Seventeen

BY THE TIME SHE REACHED the police station she'd stopped crying. She'd been bundled into the Black Maria. That in itself had increased her terror, for it was very dark inside and divided up into little compartments like cells. She'd sat cramped and shaking as other prisoners were picked up, mainly drunks and prostitutes.

She tried to think clearly. It was all a terrible mistake, but who did she know who could vindicate her?

The Bridewell was large and cavernous and she was taken straight towards the large countertop upon which were piled heavy books, wads of papers and rubber stamps. A large-faced clock on the wall ticked loudly and hung beneath it was a thick list whose title proclaimed it the 'List of Habitual Drunkards'. That made her think of her da. It seemed as though he too had reached out from the grave to condemn her, to place his crimes on her shoulders.

'So, what have we here, then?' The desk sergeant looked down at her.

'Incitement to Riot, a proper little firebrand. Screaming, shouting and smashing windows. She's Nago May's girl. Remember him, George?'

'Oh, do I. Good riddance to bad rubbish, no regrets over his loss from this quarter.'

Maggie gripped the edge of the counter tightly and fought to control herself. 'I didn't do anything! I swear on my mam's grave and I loved my mam, almost as much as I hated my da! I'm decent and honest. Mam brought me up like that! Please, please, sir, you've got to believe me!'

'It's not a case of me believing you, girl. I'm just doing my job. It's the magistrate you'll have to persuade and he'll take a very dim view of your behaviour and I don't think he'll be too readily disposed to listen to any hard luck stories!'

'I don't know those men. I've never seen them before. They dragged me off and it was them that broke the shop window, not me! Please, it's the truth. I can't help my name and God knows I hate it! That was all my da's doing! I had no choice, did I?' she yelled with a flash of spirit.

'Don't be so hard-faced! Now let's get some particulars down!' The desk sergeant looked annoyed. 'Name we already know, ditto address, age, how old are you?'

'Nineteen.'

'Parents . . . deceased. Any other relatives?'

'Our Tommy, but he's up in Glasgow.'

'God help the Glasgow city police' the desk seargeant muttered.

'Charge?'

'Incitement to Riot. I've read her her rights, George.'

Maggie felt as though everything was unreal, that this wasn't happening to her. 'Look, please, I told you Mr O'Shea will vouch for me. I've been set up! Mick Devanney swore he'd get his mates to get even with me, he did, before he was hanged!'

'Look, Sarge, she's just wasting time. This Mr O'Shea was on the *Apappa* that sailed this morning and as far as the rest of the tale goes, it's all lies. Oh, Nago May and Devanney were very thick, until Robinson's was turned over and the old watchman murdered. May conveniently dies of arsenic poisoning, remember the beer? Devanney was hanged. End of friendship. I think we've had enough fairy stories for today, we had a tip-off from a very reliable source.'

Suddenly Maggie remembered Callan's solicitor. 'Mr Compton!' she blurted out. 'He's Mr O'Shea's solicitor! You go and ask him about me. I'm supposed to be going to look for a nice little house in Everton, he knows all about it! It's true! You'll see that it's true when you ask him!' She clung to the thin strand of hope.

They all looked at each other. 'Is this another

bloody fairy story? If you go sending one of my men off on a wild goose chase, annoying a solicitor . . .' The desk sergeant glared at her.

'No, it won't be a wild goose chase! It won't!'

'Well, we can't go barging into people's houses on a Sunday on the word of a suspected criminal, it will have to wait until tomorrow!' The desk sergeant was loath to think that she might be innocent. This job was far from finished and he had another six on the spike, awaiting attention. He made a decision. 'Right, put her in the cells for the night. She's helping us with our inquiries.'

Maggie made no further protest, she seemed drained of all energy. At least it would only be for tonight, they couldn't keep her any longer, not once they'd spoken to Mr Compton.

She was taken down a wide, dark corridor where four young lads sat on a bench, looking dejected. They were only kids, she thought, ten or eleven years old. She wondered what they'd done. The passageway narrowed and suddenly she stood facing a heavy iron door. Panic overtook her as it was unlocked and opened and she turned and clutched the constable's arm. 'Please! Please, can't you go and see Mr Compton now? He won't mind, I know he won't!'

'Sorry, luv, it's not up to me. In you go, be a good girl now,' he added kindly.

She looked around her fearfully. It was very bare. A wide, wooden shelf ran the length of the wall, ending in a kind of toilet. There was a blanket folded on the shelf and against the far wall stood a small three-legged stool. There was no window and the only light came from the passageway outside, through a small pane of thick glass on the other side of which burned a naked gas jet. It was bitterly cold and she had no shawl. She wrapped the blanket around her and sat on the wooden shelf, trying to bolster her spirits by telling herself that tomorrow she would be out of here and back in her own room.

The hours had dragged and she'd spent a miserable night but by the following lunchtime she was frantic. She'd seen no one since a uniformed constable had brought her a bowl of thin porridge and a slice of bread spread with margarine and a cup of tea. She'd begged him to tell her what was happening but he didn't seem to know.

She began to hammer on the door with her fists and scream until at last she heard approaching footsteps and the door was unlocked.

'What the hell is all the noise about?' the sergeant demanded. She'd not seen him before. He wasn't the one she'd seen last night.

'Oh, please, you must have been to see Mr Compton by now, you've got to let me go.'

'I haven't *got* to do anything! Now shut up. We'll let you know when or if anything happens to alter your case.'

The door was slammed shut and she sank down on to the stool.

When they at last returned she could see by their faces that she wasn't going to be released.

'Mr Compton can't corroborate your story! Oh, he's heard of you all right and this Mr O'Shea did leave instructions with him, but he never saw you with his client. He doesn't even know where you live and he said it was no business of his where Mr O'Shea spent his days or nights! Come on.'

Maggie backed away. 'Where are you taking me?'

'Upstairs to be formally charged. You'll go before the magistrate in the morning.'

As though in a trance she let them lead her back up to the main hall. She heard the charge read out and answered 'Not guilty'. Everything was written down and she had to sign a large book, then she was taken back to the cells. Then the door closed once more and she looked around with horror, the sound had broken the spell of unreality. A cold sweat stood out on her forehead and she began to shake. She'd believed . . . she hoped . . . she'd been so sure that Mr Compton could have helped her and now . . . all this was real, it wasn't a dream!

She began to hammer on the door and to scream but it brought no response and at last, utterly exhausted, she slid to the floor and buried her throbbing head in her hands.

She'd not slept, nor had she eaten anything that had been brought to her. The following morning another, unfamiliar young constable brought her her breakfast and a bowl of warm water, soap and a towel.

'Get yourself tidied up.'

She stared at him blankly. Her face was streaked with dirt and tears, her hair was tangled and her clothes creased and stained.

'You're going before the magistrate this morning, luv, try and make a bit of an effort – it might help,' he advised before he left.

She washed her face and hands and tried to tidy her hair, grasping at the ray of hope. Maybe if she did look tidy and if she tried to speak well, they might believe her.

She'd bitten her nails down almost to the quick when they finally came for her. The cells were beneath the court and she was taken by surprise when her journey ended in the dock. She stood blinking in the brightness, but as she looked around the courtroom and saw the stern, hard features of the magistrate, she went cold and all courage deserted her.

She had no money for any legal help and the atmosphere, the formality of her surroundings, terrified her into muteness. She could never remember the proceedings clearly, except for what the magistrate had said. The severity of her crime, the solid evidence of the police, her lack of morals and sheer audacity to plead not guilty. There was no mention of the fact that this was her first offence. At the pronouncement 'Twelve months hard labour!' she uttered a scream and clung to the constable at her side. Then she was half carried back to her cell.

She didn't know or care what time it was and when she heard the door being unlocked her expression was puzzled rather than fearful or expectant.

'You've got a visitor,' the young constable announced.

Slowly Maggie got to her feet and stared at the man. He was middle-aged and very well dressed. 'Who are you?' her voice was a hoarse whisper.

'I'm Alfred Compton, Miss May.'

She looked from him to the constable who stood with his back to the door, his arms folded over his chest. 'You . . . why didn't you help me?'

'There was nothing I could do, Miss May.' Despite her appearance he could see what had captivated Callan O'Shea. 'Miss May, I tried, believe me I did, most earnestly. They had irrefutable evidence. I offered to be a character witness but it was of no use. I didn't . . . don't know you. I'm so sorry.'

She couldn't reply. Why had he come here if he couldn't help her?

'This will all be sorted out when Mr O'Shea returns.'

'They won't believe him. They won't.'

'I think they will have to, my dear. He is a man of some standing.'

'But that won't be for . . . for weeks. What . . . what will happen to me now?'

'I'm afraid they will take you to Walton Jail. You'll be a third division prisoner, hard labour, but don't despair!'

Her eyes were swimming with tears and Alfred Compton was certain she had committed no crime and wondered sadly how she would cope with the harshness of Walton Jail.

'Time's up, sir, I'm sorry.'

He nodded curtly and took Maggie's hand. 'Keep your spirits up, my dear. We'll sort it all out.'

When they'd gone she sank down on the stool and buried her face in her hands. Walton Jail! Oh, the times she'd heard her da tell of the brutality of that place. He'd deserved it, she hadn't, but even the name struck fear into her heart.

Callan took the stairs two at a time. God how he'd missed her. He'd never known a trip to take so long! 'Maggie! Maggie!' he yelled, hammering on the door with his fist. There was no reply. 'Maggie! Maggie it's me, Callan!' He was greeted with silence and he began to feel uneasy, pressing his ear close to the door, listening for any sound from within. He turned as a fat, blowsy woman came puffing and panting down the stairs, her face puce with her exertions.

'She ain't there!'

'What do you mean? Where's Maggie gone?'

'That bloody little bitch! The scuffers took her. A nice carry on I must say and this a respectable 'ouse. Incitement to Riot they had her for.'

Callan grabbed her by her shoulder and she yelled in pain. 'Where did they take her? Where? I'll knock it out of you!'

'Down to Cheapside but it won't do you no good going there, she's been tried and found guilty!'

He released her and headed for the stairs. By the Holy Saints! He'd sort this out before the hour was over! He turned back. 'If you or anyone else touches a single thing of Maggie's, I'll break your bloody neck, do you hear me, you fat, dirty, old whore!' His rage was so consuming that his dark eyes sparked and his handsome features contorted. Ma Nevitt nodded hastily, knowing he meant every word. She'd have to be quick and round up all the stuff they'd taken or there'd be hell to pay, she knew his type, he'd see them all on the street – or worse!

When he got outside, he tried to think rationally. It wouldn't be any use going to the Bridewell at Cheapside, the old bitch was right, but where should he go? To Compton. He'd know what the procedure was for a miscarriage of justice. Wherever she was, he'd have her out and damned quickly too and by God someone would pay for it!

The minute Alfred Comptom set eyes on his client he knew what he'd come for. 'I did what I could for her, but they had hard evidence. They had witnesses! Their case was watertight.'

'What evidence? What witnesses?'

'Three men and a woman, who looked very

respectable, swore they saw her in the centre of a crowd. Screaming and shouting abuse at everyone. Then they say she smashed the shop window.'

'Ah, don't give me that! Do you take me for an eejit? I know Maggie, she could never carry on like that. She's been set up. They must have watched her and planned it all. She was afraid of someone called Mick Devanney who was hanged for murder. Those witnesses will be friends of his. She's innocent.'

'Of course she is, I never doubted it. You'd only just sailed, there was no one who could verify her version of the events. They came here on the Monday morning but there was little I could do. At that time I'd never set eyes on the girl and I couldn't vouch for your movements! I couldn't perjure myself.'

Callan ran a hand impatiently through his hair. 'Where is she now?'

'In Walton Jail, she got a year's hard labour.'

'A year! You mean they've locked her up in that . . . that place for a year!' Callan was beside himself.

'I tried! I offered myself as a character witness but even then I couldn't do anything. I didn't know her and they knew it!'

'But you saw her?' Callan stood up and began to pace the room. Maggie! Maggie locked up in Walton Jail. It didn't bear thinking about.

'I did, she's a very lovely girl, even though she was nearly demented, I could see that. I promised her I'd do everything I could, that I'd see you the minute you got back. I was packing up to come down to see you.' He indicated his case.

'For God's sake, Compton, what can we do?'

'Appeal and try and find those "witnesses", but that will take time and money, I'm afraid.'

'I don't care how much it costs, find someone of their own kind to track them down. Offer them all a reward. Money makes most people talk. Start the procedure right away! I've got to get her out of that place!'

Compton nodded sagely. Distraught and dishevelled though Maggie had been, he could see why O'Shea was so concerned about her. The women in Walton were the lowest of the low and the wardresses were not much better. He'd felt so sorry for the girl, desperately sorry. 'I have to warn you that this could all take months, these things move very slowly.'

'Then do whatever you must do. Can I see her?'

Compton looked perturbed. 'Visiting is restricted to once a month and then only after the first month has been served.'

'Jesus Christ! It's inhuman! I have to leave in two days! Can I send things in to her?'

'Nothing much I'm afraid and whether she gets what you send is quite another matter.'

Callan felt like putting his fist through the window. He'd never felt so helpless or quite so furious! 'As an Irishman I've never had much faith in British justice! It's a bloody sham and this proves it!'

'No, this is a miscarriage. It happens sometimes in the best of legal systems. Don't judge the whole on one error, please.'

Callan sat down. 'There's something else I want you to do. Something I should have done before this. If I had she wouldn't be in this mess. Dear God, I'm a bloody eejit! When she comes out she's not going back to that house! I want you to find a house, big enough for her to take in a few lodgers, selected lodgers, no riff-raff. She'll have to have an income and I want her to be secure. You know well enough my commitments in Ireland. I have a family to support.' He paused, thinking of how pale and listless Breda had been the last time he'd seen her. How she refused to see the doctor, how both his sons had told him she really wasn't well at all. He pushed the stab of guilt from his mind. 'But I have enough to buy Maggie a house. Buy not rent, I want her name on the deeds, Compton.'

'I'll see to it.'

'And I want all her things moved from Brick Street. I threatened that old bitch that I'd break her neck if anything was missing and, by Jaysus, I've never been more serious in my life!'

Compton was making notes.

Callan wondered how she'd cope. Whether she'd change, but dear God, how could anyone not change after spending time in Walton Jail, and she'd been in there a month now!

* * *

Maggie's back felt as though it was breaking but if she slowed her pace she knew the respite would result in a kick or the crushing of her fingers by Bella Banks' heavy boots. She'd lost track of time, how long she'd been in Walton she couldn't remember clearly.

When she'd arrived, in a state of shock, she'd been taken into a small room and told to strip. She'd been given a bath in an old, chipped and filthy bath, but the water had been hot. It had been the first time she'd met Bella Banks. The woman had stood, tall, stiff and unbending in her dark blue dress, her brown hair scraped back under the small black bonnet, her dark eyes malicious and mocking and Maggie had felt nothing but humiliation at her nakedness.

As a third division prisoner she'd been handed the regulation clothes: a low-necked flannel undershirt, yellowish-grey with age and use and badly patched; a chemise of unbleached calico striped with red; a pair of very stiff canvas stays; flannel drawers; a petticoat of coarse cotton; and the brown prison dress, marked with broad white arrows. A small white calico cap that tied under the chin, a pair of thick woollen stockings and a pair of hard, heavy shoes completed the outfit. Second and first division prisoners wore dark green and dark blue respectively.

The days became a routine of drudgery. Her cell was similar to that at the Bridewell except that there was a table attached to the wall and a mattress and pillow stuffed with chaff. This had to be rolled up each morning, then the cell had to be scrubbed, the tin plate and mug polished. Breakfast consisted of porridge, lunch of fish or meat and potatoes and supper of more porridge or rice pudding. Each afternoon a group of them walked in single file in the prison yard, the rest of the time was spent sewing women's and men's underclothes. At five o'clock the cell door was locked and the never-ending night began.

Days merged together. It seemed like eternity and it would be another eternity before she was released. It wasn't the food or the loss of freedom or the terrible conditions that she hated most, it was the lack of privacy, the utter humiliation and degradation. Most of the wardresses, or 'officers' as she must call them, were stern but not vindictive. Except Bella Banks, who picked on her at every opportunity.

Every day she'd waited for someone to come and tell her it had all been a terrible mistake, that she was free to walk away, but gradually that hope had faded. She'd quickly reverted back to the girl she'd been when she lived in Bowers Court. She'd learned how to fight then, to defend herself, and they were lessons that stood her in good stead now. When she'd shown she could stand up for herself, she'd been left alone by most of the other prisoners but not by Bella Banks.

She kept her head down, concentrating on the circular movements of the scrubbing brush, as a pair of highly polished black buttoned boots came into view.

'You! May! Get up, her ladyship wants to see you, now!' Bella bawled.

Maggie slowly got to her feet, pressing her hands into the small of her back, feeling dizzy.

'Tidy yerself up!'

Maggie refused to look at the woman.

'Know of any reason why she should take such an interest in you, May?'

Maggie shrugged, tucking loose strands of hair under her cap. She was at a loss to know why the matron had sent for her. Mrs Fairchild was her name but Bella always referred to her as 'her ladyship'.

'Answer properly!' Bella yelled at her.

'No. I know of no reason, Mrs Banks,' Maggie said dully.

She followed the wardress down the long narrow corridor, her eyes downcast. She dare not hope . . . she dare not even think that there could be the possibility that the matron would say the words she had dreamed of and prayed for in her every waking moment.

The room was at the end of the corridor and she noticed that other corridors ran off from it in a star shape. She had only seen the matron twice and on both those occasions Mrs Fairchild had come to her cell to inspect it.

Mrs Fairchild was a severe woman in her fifties, her iron-grey hair confined under the regulation black bonnet, but her dress was of a much finer quality than Bella's. She wore a small gold fob-watch pinned to the right side of the bodice which she looked at impatiently, then cast a disapproving glance at Bella. It was very obvious by her manner that this interview was not to her liking at all.

Maggie dipped a bob and then let out a cry, startled to see Mr Compton sitting in a chair on the other side of the room.

'Thank you, Mrs Banks, you may return to your duties.' Mrs Fairchild dismissed Bella brusquely and addressed Maggie.

'Well, girl, Mr Compton has something to tell you.' She turned her head away, as though disgusted by the very presence of Mr Compton.

'Thank you, ma'am,' Maggie said quietly.

Mr Compton walked towards her, smiling and her heart leapt into her throat. 'Miss May, I'm here to tell you that Mr O'Shea intends to find the real criminals and bring them to book, to prove to everyone that you have been convicted unfairly. He has also lodged an appeal to the Crown Court on your behalf.'

Maggie twisted her hands together, not quite able to grasp what he was telling her. 'Does that mean that they know I'm not guilty?'

'What it means, Miss May, is that they will have to look at the case again and, in the light of fresh evidence, I'm certain you'll be completely vindicated and freed!'

The room began to spin sickeningly and she tried to grasp Mr Compton's hands but there was a great rushing sound in her ears and everything was receding into darkness.

When she came to, she was lying on the floor, her head in Mr Compton's lap and he was smiling down at her.

Mrs Fairchild remained standing, looking down at her with ill-concealed fury that she had dared to faint in her office.

'Don't worry, Miss May, I'll push as hard as I can, we'll have you out of here soon,' Mr Compton said softly, as he helped her up.

She bowed her head towards the matron. 'I'm sorry, ma'am . . . it was the shock,' she muttered, but Mrs Fairchild turned away from her.

Mr Compton was still holding her hand and she looked at him with eyes brimming with tears. Why had she given up hope? She should have known that Callan would move heaven and earth to get her out. Soon, oh, soon, all this would be behind her!

'If you have to blame someone, then blame your father. He left you a legacy of hate and revenge, for I know that you were "set up" as you put it. I know you are completely innocent.' He raised his voice so that the matron could not fail to hear his words nor misunderstand his meaning. It would all be reported to the governor, word for word, but his letters were already on the governor's desk.

It was all too much for Maggie to take in, she shook her head, dazedly.

'I think you'd better be leaving now, Mr Compton, the girl has her duties and, until I receive any instructions to the contrary, she will continue with the routine of this establishment! We can show no favouritism.'

Maggie got to her feet as he picked up his hat and case and Mrs Fairchild pressed a bell set in the wall.

A superintendent wardress appeared to escort Mr Compton out and Maggie turned to go too.

'Not you, *Miss* May. Not yet.'

Maggie turned to face the matron who waited until the door had closed firmly behind Mr Compton before she spoke.

'How far gone are you, *Miss* May?' Again the word 'Miss' was stressed.

Maggie looked at her blankly. 'I'm sorry, ma'am, I . . . I don't understand?'

'Don't insult my intelligence, girl! You may fool the likes of him with your virginal airs and graces and your swooning fits, but not me! I have dealt with women like you for too long. When is your child due?'

Maggie's hands went to her mouth. Dear God, she was pregnant! She had been through so much that she hadn't even missed the 'curse' and lately she'd felt ill in the morning but she'd thought it was just the prison routine and the strain. It must have been that first time. That very first time.

Mrs Fairchild turned away from her in disgust and signalled for her to depart with a dismissive wave of her hand. 'Let's hope that the appeal will be over and done with before the birth! We are already overstretched,' she said with chilling finality.

When she reached her cell, Maggie still felt dazed. Was it true or had the matron been mistaken? No, it must be true, things all began to add up. But how would she cope? How on earth could she bring a child into this terrible place? She twisted her hands together. She *had* to get out now and soon! If only she could get word to Mr Compton, to beg him to speed things up. A child! She was carrying Callan's child! She should be filled with joy, but all she felt was despair, fear and foreboding.

Chapter Eighteen

'MAGGIE! MAGGIE, ARE YOU all right? Is it time?'

Maggie looked up into the plain face, filled with concern. 'I don't know, I think it might be.' She heaved herself to the edge of the mattress and managed a grim smile that turned into a grimace at the onset of another knife-like pain.

Philippa Barton twisted her hands together nervously, yet anger filled her. Maggie didn't belong in here, she should have been released long ago. The way things were going Maggie would have served out her sentence before that damned appeal was even heard! Men! Pompous, inefficient, heartless pigs they were, with very few exceptions!

The pain receded and Maggie watched her new friend pacing the small cell, her tall thin body hunched, annoyance evident in every movement and gesture. She'd almost lost all hope of being released. She had served nine months of her sentence.

After Mr Compton's visit her moods had alternated between hope and despair, joy and depression. Hope and joy that her release would come soon, despair and depression at the knowledge that she was carrying Callan's child. A child that would be born a bastard, an outcast. No matter how much he loved her he could never marry her. Would he still even love her? That was the fear that haunted her.

Before she'd known about her pregnancy she'd been glad that Callan was so much older than herself. From conversations with the other prisoners she'd realized that many of them had men to blame for their present plight. Young men who had deserted or betrayed them in one form or another. And she'd seen many examples of how thoughtless and irresponsible young men could be throughout her childhood. No, she'd been glad he was older, until now. His sons were grown up, he was settled in his ways, he wouldn't want to be saddled with a baby.

He had not visited her. It was unfortunate that his leave did not coincide with visiting days, Mr Compton had told her. 'Unfortunate.' What a poor way to describe his absence, she'd thought.

Mr Compton had been very kind to her. He'd tried to explain in great detail the progress, or lack of it, of her appeal. It wasn't his fault that she didn't understand all the long words and legal ramifications.

When her condition had become unavoidably clear to him, she had made him promise he would not tell Callan.

'But, my dear, why not?' he'd asked, looking very perturbed.

'What can he do? He's married already and there is no divorce in Ireland.'

'But he can provide for you and the child. He will insist on it, I'm certain.'

'And what difference will that make, Mr Compton? It won't change the wording on the birth certificate. It won't stop the taunts. I know what it's like to be mocked and tormented. Names *do* hurt. They hurt terribly. Please, I want to sort . . . this out myself. Promise you'll say nothing, please?'

'Very well, if that's what you wish, but if you ever need help, my dear, you know who to come to.'

She'd thanked him gratefully.

Her routine had not changed but she'd been treated very warily by the wardresses. There was no more abuse, either physical or verbal, from Bella Banks, for now no one was sure that she was even guilty of the crime she'd been accused of and there could be serious repercussions.

Then just before Christmas, Philippa Barton had arrived. Maggie had been startled when the cell door had been opened and the very tall, thin woman had been pushed roughly in by Bella Banks.

'We'll take you down a peg or two, Miss high and bloody mighty!' Bella had barked before slamming the cell door shut. She had stared at her new cell-mate, taking in her smooth white hands and the complete absence of fear in the woman's eyes. She wore the drab brown dress of a third division prisoner but instinctively Maggie had known she was not a common felon.

'Hello, I'm Philippa Barton,' she'd announced in a quiet, cultured voice.

'I'm Maggie, Maggie May, miss.'

Philippa had smiled. 'There's no need to call me "miss", we are all equal in here,' had been Philippa's reply.

She had known little then about women's suffrage. Oh, she'd heard of suffragettes. Wealthy ladies who, for reasons that she couldn't understand, chained themselves to railings and held protest meetings and marches. In the long night that followed she learned a great deal and not only about women's suffrage.

Philippa Barton was a well-educated woman in her early thirties and she was wealthy. Her father had been a banker and her mother the youngest daughter of an impoverished earl. Philippa had been their only surviving child and she'd been sickly, and, Maggie suspected, very spoiled, from the way Philippa spoke about her childhood. Even now, she'd told Maggie, she had a weak heart and suffered with pains in her joints, the legacy of scarlet fever. She had never been married because the only suitors she'd had had only been interested in spending the money her father and paternal grandmother had left her. 'Why else would a man take on a plain sickly woman?' she'd said in a tone that was totally devoid of self-pity.

She lived in a large house in Birkdale near Southport and she had Hetty who had been with her since childhood, and her friends in the women's movement, her dear friend Elizabeth MacKenzie in particular. They'd been at school together although Elizabeth lived in Scotland. It had been through Elizabeth that she had become involved in the campaign for women's rights, one of the many causes she'd espoused. Indeed Elizabeth had been arrested with her and she was here in Walton Jail, too.

'What did you do?' Maggie had asked.

'I threw a stone and it broke a window in the governor's house, it's next to the jail. We were having a protest meeting. Elizabeth was arrested for Causing an Affray. She won't be in here for as long as I will be.'

'How long did you get?'

'A month.'

'A month, just for throwing a stone and breaking a window!' Maggie had been incredulous, no wonder she'd been given a year.

'Don't worry about me, I deserve my sentence. I welcomed it, but there are women in prisons all over the country whose crimes are none of their own making. They are the victims of poverty, desertion and betrayal in one form or another, by men.'

'I know,' Maggie had answered and, bit by bit, she'd related her own life-story to Philippa Barton.

When she had finished, Philippa had looked at her with undisguised triumph. 'You see the part men have played in your life, Maggie, and you have never had the right to challenge them.'

'But we've never had any rights, as you call them.'

'Exactly, Maggie! We're treated like chattels, little better than slaves in some cases! We have no control over our lives. Look at your poor mother, killing herself with work and worry so your father could indulge his vices and take no responsibility for his family. But things must change, Maggie! This is the twentieth century not the Middle Ages, though you'd never think so by some people's attitudes, this government's in particular. Only by drawing people's attention to our cause, by civil disobedience and protest and by every woman in the land demanding that the laws be changed, will things improve!'

'But there must be thousands of girls who've never even heard of suffrage.' It was incomprehensible to her that someone should give up a secure, comfortable, even luxurious life in exchange for the privation, humiliation and degradation of prison and all for a cause.

'There are! But they will learn, in time, and if enough of them join us we'll be a force to be reckoned with! There are many working-class women in our movement, it's for all women, not just gentlewomen. Although, because of our . . . well, education and position those in power will have to take us more seriously. It won't always be like that though.'

Maggie was totally unaware of how patronizing

Philippa's attitude was, she was astonished by the glow that had transformed Philippa's face, by the zeal and energy and hope that burned in her eyes.

Philippa had refused all food and drink. 'I'm on hunger strike,' she'd announced quietly to Bella Banks.

'We'll soon see about that!' had been Bella's reply as she'd stormed off.

'I know it's awful, especially after what you've been used to, but you've got to eat. You'll make yourself ill,' Maggie had advised.

'It has nothing to do with the food, Maggie. It's another form of protest.'

'You're going to deliberately starve for a month?'

'Yes.' A frown had creased Philippa's forehead. 'At least I hope I will have the courage to. They will try to force-feed me and I've heard that it is so vile and painful.'

'What do they do?'

'They hold you down and force your mouth open with a steel gag. Then . . . then they push a rubber tube down your throat into your stomach and . . . and pour food down it, milk and glucose, Bovril, things like that.' Philippa had tried not to shudder at her own words.

Maggie was horrified. 'God Almighty! You . . . you mean you'd go through all that so . . . so girls like me can vote?'

'I hope I can, Maggie, but I must admit that . . . that it terrifies me.'

Maggie had thought, with something akin to wonder, that she had never met anyone so unselfish . . . so noble, yes that was the word, she told herself. Philippa Barton was noble. Maggie had never seen the burning fervour of a zealot, the intensity of determination for an ideal. She had no way of knowing the true nature of her new cellmate.

They came for Philippa the following night. The matron, Bella Banks and four other wardresses and the prison doctor.

'You still refuse to eat, Miss Barton?' Mrs Fairchild had asked in a cold voice.

'I do,' Philippa had replied firmly, gazing steadily at the matron.

'Then we have no alternative but to feed you forcibly. You will come with me, Miss Barton.'

With an apprehensive glance at Maggie, Philippa had followed the matron and the doctor, flanked on all sides by the wardresses.

Maggie had sat on the edge of her mattress and had prayed that it wouldn't be too bad for her.

An hour later they had brought Philippa back. They had half dragged, half carried her into the cell.

Maggie's eyes had widened with shock and horror. Philippa's dress, hair and cap were covered in vomit, her mouth was bleeding and her face was a ghastly shade of grey. Bella Banks carried a bucket of water and Maggie noticed that both hers and the other wardress's dress were also badly stained.

'Clean yourself up, you dirty bitch!' Bella had snapped as Philippa had been laid on her mattress.

Maggie flew at her. 'Don't you dare speak to her like that, she's a lady! It's you who is the bitch! God Almighty, what have you done to her! You've killed her!'

Bella had stormed out and it had been the other woman who had answered, glaring at Maggie. 'She looks worse than she is.'

'You've half killed her! She's got a weak heart. Haven't you got any pity, any sense? If she dies it's your fault!' Maggie had screamed.

The woman hadn't answered.

Maggie had tried to clean Philippa up and make her comfortable but she had burned with rage at the inhuman treatment meted out to Philippa.

Philippa had cried for two hours and Maggie hadn't been able to comfort her.

'They won't dare to do it again!' she had soothed.

'They will. Oh, Maggie, Maggie, I'm so weak! I don't know if I can stand it. I kept being sick.'

'For God's sake give it up. They'll kill you and nothing . . . nothing is worth that!'

'I . . . I have to try, Maggie, I can't give in so soon.' Philippa had wept.

Nothing Maggie had said could alter her decision and when next day they came and took Philippa away again, Maggie had knelt on the stone floor and had prayed as she'd never prayed before, that Philippa Barton would see sense.

This time when they brought her back she was in an even worse state and Maggie had screamed such abuse at the wardresses that Mrs Fairchild had come and threatened Maggie with the punishment cell.

'It's Miss Barton's own fault. It is her decision entirely,' the matron had said icily,

'She's doing it for the likes of me and you, too, ma'am, if you'd realize it!'

'This is not your affair, Miss May. You have been warned, kindly remember that.'

When they'd gone Maggie had pleaded with Philippa. 'Please, please give it up! You've got to, it's killing you. Can't you see it's no use and that Bella Banks takes a delight in hurting people? Please, Philippa, give it up!'

Philippa was broken. It had been far worse than she had imagined. There had been moments when she had thought she would die. Maggie was right. Force-feeding would kill her and what would have been gained? Now she knew she was not the stuff that martyrs are made of. Oh, she'd really believed in what the suffragettes were fighting for, but they were such strong-minded women with great determination. She was a coward, a weak coward and she despised her weakness. Oh, it was all so unfair that women should have to suffer like this, all because men were so narrow-minded and biased against them! But she couldn't go on, she just couldn't!

That evening she'd asked to see the matron and had

told her that she capitulated. Her heart wouldn't stand it and her death would achieve nothing.

'I'm glad you have seen sense, Miss Barton. However, the doctor has already decided that the risk to your health is too great to continue with feeding you forcibly. Your release is being considered on those grounds.'

Philippa had straightened her shoulders, giving no sign of the utter humiliation she felt. 'I have no wish to be released. I will serve out my sentence. I am perfectly fit to do so now.'

'As you wish,' had been the dismissive reply.

Maggie was incredulous. 'You turned down the chance to get out?'

'Oh, Maggie, you don't understand. I was so humiliated when she told me that . . . that my suffering had been in vain. That they had already decided to stop it. I wasn't going to give her the satisfaction of thinking that they had beaten me entirely. I could see that the woman is a vindictive snob!'

Maggie had smiled ruefully. 'You're mad, you do know that?'

Philippa had also smiled sadly. 'I think you are right.'

They had discussed Maggie's predicament but the week before Philippa was due to be released she had asked Maggie to discuss it again with her more seriously. Time was running out.

Philippa's experience of prison had weakened her

considerably and now she felt that Hetty had been right all along in telling her she was mad to go along with women's suffrage. Hetty had been most vociferous on the subject, blaming Elizabeth MacKenzie for her involvement, but she knew Elizabeth wasn't fully to blame. She had thrown herself into the cause zealously.

There had been other projects in her life in which she'd become equally involved and just as disillusioned by. Looking back they'd all been dubious ideas that had seemed so sensible, so important and all-consuming at the time. A steadying influence in her life, that's what Hetty had said she needed and ruefully she'd admitted that Hetty was right, for Hetty had watched her grow up. Now that this horrendous experience was nearly over she *had* to think seriously about her future, and a plan was beginning to form in her mind.

'Have you decided what you are going to do yet, Maggie? Your time is getting nearer.'

'I know, but . . . but he can't marry me, I've told you that.'

'But he must support you and the child, it's his duty, Mr Compton has told you that!'

'Oh, I know he would, but . . . well, at the end of the day my baby will be a bastard and you don't know what that means for someone like me.'

Philippa did know what Maggie meant. An illegitimate child was treated shamefully by society, scorned and rejected, an object of derision or pity. 'I do know, Maggie. Society is very cruel, people are cruel.'

'What chance will he or she have? I don't want my baby to grow up living the way I did, except that it will be even worse. I had a da, though much good he did me! I know Callan would see that we were well cared for but when I do get out I know there will be a fuss in the newspapers and then everyone will know about . . . about the baby. And anyway he hasn't been to see me – he hasn't even written. Perhaps he doesn't love me after all.'

While she had been speaking Philippa had been nodding in agreement. What more steadying influence in her life could there be than a child? She was resigned to spinsterhood, she would never have children of her own, but if she were to take Maggie's baby and bring it up, then she would have something in her life. Something tangible, something that wouldn't fail her. Someone to plan for, to share the future with. For the future looked very empty.

'Maggie, let me take the baby. I have the legacy left me by my father and that from my grandmother. I can bring the child up in a good home. It will want for nothing; the best education, trips to Europe, a chance in life, all the things you never had, Maggie!' Her thin face had been earnest, her tone pleading.

'But . . . but you're not married either.'

'I will say it is my cousin's child. That my cousin died in childbirth. No one would refute it, Maggie. Think about it, please?'

'But what if you go to prison again?'

'I won't.' Philippa had sounded weary. She had lain awake pondering her future, wondering why it was that the aims and ambitions she'd sought had always eluded her, why fate had been unkind. Now at least something seemed about to happen for the good. Maybe all her energies would be better spent in rescuing one poor unfortunate child from a life of misery.

Maggie had thought about it long and hard. It did make sound sense. She'd grown up fighting the stigma of her name and she didn't want her child to have to fight an even harder battle. Her child would never be cold and hungry. Nor would he or she have to walk the streets in all weathers selling matches and firewood, or be denied the chance of a good education and a good job. It would never be at the mercy of a system that had no time or compassion for the weak and helpless. At last she'd agreed to Philippa's request and it had been arranged that when the baby was born, either Philippa herself or Elizabeth MacKenzie would take it straight to the house in Southport Philippa owned. If Philippa had not been released then her maid, Hetty, would care for the child until Philippa was free.

A stronger pain gripped Maggie and she screamed.

'Oh, my God!' Philippa cried, and, taking off her shoe, she hammered as hard as she could on the cell door.

The door was eventually opened by Mrs Connell, a stern but fair-minded woman.

'Her time's arrived! You've got to get her to the hospital! She's in labour!' Philippa informed the wardress.

Mrs Connell turned away and shouted down the corridor. Maggie gripped Philippa's hand tightly, beads of sweat on her forehead. 'Philippa, I'm frightened! I'm terrified! Stay with me, please!'

'Maggie, you know they won't let me, but you'll be just fine and I'll get word to Hetty and Elizabeth and I'll be out myself at the end of the week. Don't worry, Maggie, everything will be all right!'

She'd begged them to let Philippa go with her to the small hospital wing but her pleas had fallen on deaf ears as had all her screams of pain. She'd never experienced such pain. Wave after wave of it racked her, leaving her exhausted and shaking in the minutes between the spasms. Only when she had the terrible urge to bear down, and knew instinctively that her baby was to be born very soon, did a nurse appear, as grim-faced and unsympathetic as all the other wardresses.

'Stop that noise, girl! There's nothing wrong with you, childbirth is natural!'

Maggie wanted to kill her but the pain gripped her again. Sweat blinded her and she sank her teeth into the back of her hand to stop the screams. There was a great wave of pain, then a sensation of everything being washed away from her insides and then she heard the thin wail, and she sank back on the bed and closed her eyes. It was over. It was over and her baby had been born. But with the relief came the bitter knowledge that she must give it away.

'It's a girl. Quite healthy and perfectly formed.'

The nurse held out a tiny bundle, hastily wrapped in a towel.

Maggie took her daughter in her arms and looked down into the tiny, screwed-up face above which was a thick mop of black hair. A sob caught in her throat. 'Callan! Oh, Callan, why couldn't you be free?' she sobbed silently.

'You'll have to give her a name.'

Through her tears Maggie looked up at the woman and saw a slight softening of her expression. There was no hesitation. She knew what she would call her. 'Laura,' she said firmly. 'I'll call her Laura.'

'Very pretty. Rather fanciful for a child born in here, but pretty.'

Her words dispelled some of Maggie's euphoria. Yes, she'd been born in a prison, the child of a father unable to give her his name and legal birthright, but it wouldn't matter. Her Laura, the name her mam had wanted to give her, would never know the circumstances of her birth, she would never know poverty or injustice. Everything that had been denied to Maggie, synonymous with the terrible name Nago May had bestowed on her, would not be denied her child. It was as if she had been born again, but with the name Dora had chosen, a talisman against all the harshness and evil that had been Maggie's lot.

She hoped that somewhere Mam was watching her and smiling down with approval. Setting the seal on such a great sacrifice, the sacrifice that meant that Laura May Barton, as she would be called, would grow up to be a lady. Maggie held the baby to her and closed her eyes and two large, bitter tears rolled slowly down her thin cheeks.

Philippa had been released and so it was she, accompanied by Hetty, who came to take the baby. Philippa had hoped that Elizabeth would accompany her but Elizabeth had surprised her with her sharp words.

'Is this another of your "schemes", Philippa?' she'd asked tersely.

'What do you mean? You're angry with me because I couldn't stand the force-feeding, that's it, isn't it?'

'No, it's not. You were wonderful to have stuck it at all, but have you thought about this? I mean really thought about it?'

'Of course I have,' Philippa had replied hotly, becoming impatient with her close friend.

'Philippa, I've known you for years and you are my dearest friend, but I have to say this. Give this matter a great deal more thought, please.'

'I have thought about it.'

Elizabeth had sighed. 'Oh, Philippa, all your life

you've been chasing ideas . . . dreams . . . but you never seem to fulfil them, you seem to just . . . well, lose heart.'

'You *are* angry with me! I know you are!' Philippa had interrupted.

'I'm *not*! Will you just listen to me, please? All I'm saying is consider everything before you take this child. If things don't turn out as you expect . . . well, you can't just discard a child.'

Philippa's mouth had set in an obstinate line. 'I have thought about it. All of it. I expected you to support me.'

Elizabeth had given up. 'I will, but please don't do anything really rash.'

'Like what?' Philippa had demanded. She couldn't understand why Elizabeth was so against her giving Maggie's child a chance in life and what did she mean about 'chasing ideas and dreams and losing heart'?

Elizabeth had looked at her levelly. 'Like adopting the baby.'

'Why not?'

Elizabeth had wondered how anyone who had been incarcerated in prison could be so unworldly, but that was part of Philippa's problem and had been for as long as she'd known her. 'Philippa, you hardly know this girl, Maggie. What kind of a family did she come from? What is the baby's father like?'

'What does all that matter?' Philippa had cried.

'What if there is insanity . . . or hereditary illness in

the family? There is no way of knowing.'

Philippa had been stunned. 'Of course Laura's not . . . like that! She's perfect! You can see in a baby's face the signs of . . . well . . . signs!'

'You are sure about that?'

'Very sure! I've made up my mind, Elizabeth, so nothing you can say will deter me!'

'Very well, I suppose you know what you're doing, but just don't legally adopt her, please Philippa.'

'Oh, all right, if you are going to make such a fuss! Really, Elizabeth, I don't understand why you are taking this attitude!'

Elizabeth had smiled at her friend. 'Because I'm your friend and I have your interests at heart, that's why. I don't want to see you hurt or disappointed.' She had refrained from adding the word 'again'.

Philippa had smiled back, but after she'd left Elizabeth MacKenzie was troubled. What she'd said had been the truth. All her life Philippa had had the money and the freedom to pursue whatever ideal or dream that presented itself. There had been times when Hetty had been able to prevail with common sense and times when she hadn't. She had thought that Philippa's zeal for women's suffrage, which she believed in with firm conviction, would last. That this would be one ideal that Philippa would sustain, but she seemed to have lost all interest. She couldn't blame her for not being able to withstand force-feeding, it was inhuman and Philippa had been brave enough to endure it twice, but she seemed to have lost all interest in the cause now that another had presented itself. But perhaps she was misjudging Philippa. Perhaps taking on this poor unfortunate little soul would be the making of her, but if it wasn't or if the child was retarded, then at least if the process of law were not involved Philippa wouldn't have to shoulder an intolerable burden for the rest of her life.

Philippa had looked down anxiously into the tiny face and had then smiled. The baby was perfect. She felt a strange excitement surge through her. Oh, she was sure she was doing the right thing. She would nurse her, play with her, dress her in lace and silk, teach her to sew, make sure she had music and dancing lessons and she would take her everywhere and bask in the admiration that was certain to be showered on the little girl. Life looked so sunny now. Now that she had Laura, a child of her own.

Maggie hadn't been able to speak. Pain twisted the knife in her heart and constricted her throat as Laura had been placed in Philippa's arms. She nodded when both Philippa and Hetty promised she would be well cared for and in Hetty's eyes she had seen something of her pain mirrored. Mrs Connell had led her away, for her eyes were so full of tears that she was blinded.

In the middle of February Maggie was released. After Philippa had gone she'd felt desolate and bereft. She'd tried to bolster her spirits by telling herself firmly that she'd done the right thing, the sensible thing. It hadn't helped to ease the heartache.

Mr Compton was waiting for her as she stepped outside the small door set into the massive wooden gates. He had been standing by a black taxi but he smiled and walked towards her. She smiled back as she took great gulps of clean, fresh, crisp air. She was free! She was out, away from the likes of Bella Banks and Mrs Fairchild. Away from the dismal cells, the misery and the all-pervading odours of prison.

'Welcome to freedom, my dear. I'm only sorry that it took so long.' Mr Compton took her hand and shook it gently.

'It wasn't your fault. Oh, it's . . . it's just wonderful to be out! to breathe clean air!'

Mr Compton grimaced. 'It's not so clean. Come along, the sooner we leave here the better.'

'Where are we going?'

'To Walton. Walton Village to be precise.'

'But I've no clothes . . . nothing. Shouldn't we go to Brick Street?'

'No. Everything has been moved to the new place.'

'The new place?'

'Yes, Mr O'Shea has purchased a house for you and I have a couple of suitable ladies who are interested in boarding.'

'He bought me a house!' she gasped.

'He wanted a secure future for you, Miss May.'

Maggie was fighting back the incipient tears. It

must have cost a fortune, as must the appeal, and he'd said he wasn't a man of great wealth. Doubt was mingled with her happiness. Would she have been better to have told him about Laura? She pushed the question from her mind. No, he could buy her a dozen houses but nothing would alter the fact that Laura was illegitimate.

'How are you really, Miss May? There's still time to change your mind about . . . the other matter.' Mr Compton looked pointedly at the back of the driver.

'No. I won't change my mind about that. I'll get over this feeling of loss. I will. I really will.'

She remained silent for the rest of the journey, drinking in the sights and sounds until the car stopped in Elm Road and Mr Compton helped her out. While he paid off the taxi she looked at the row of neat, red brick houses. They were two-storeyed, modest terraced houses but to Maggie they looked like mansions.

Mr Compton opened the front door and made her an exaggerated bow, something that was totally out of character. Some of her excitement had transmitted itself to him and he liked her a great deal, for she was a lovely girl and he greatly admired her spirit.

She wandered from room to room, her hands clasped over her mouth. All this was hers! She couldn't take it in, it was all too much. It was unbelievable and after the privations of Brick Street it was a veritable palace.

'I'll leave you to get settled in then. There is food in the larder and the press, and coal in the yard. Oh, and Mr O'Shea asked me to give you this.' He handed her an envelope. 'Shall I write to the ladies who wish to board, so you can interview them?'

'Yes, please. But not too soon.'

Mr Compton smiled. 'I understand.' She was like a child let loose in a sweet shop, he thought.

After he'd gone she sat down at the kitchen table and opened the envelope. Inside was a short letter and a white five-pound note.

> My dearest Maggie,
>
> When you receive this you will at last be free. I have cursed myself over and over for being such a fool for allowing everything to happen and for not being able to visit you. I've missed you so much and have suffered agonies of despair at the thought of you being in that terrible place. But now it is all over and we can start afresh, put it all behind us. I will be home on the first of March and can't wait to hold you in my arms, until then, my dearest, Maggie, I love you, Callan

She hugged the letter to her and closed her eyes. He loved her and in a matter of days he would be home and they could start afresh. Yes, it would be a new beginning.

The two ladies came to see her on the Sunday and she had liked them both. Miss Tifnell was a secretary to the manager of a manufacturing company and was rather strait-laced but she seemed pleasant enough. Mrs Ashley was a widow who worked as a floor supervisor at Frost's on County Road and who wanted somewhere nearer her place of work than her present accommodation. Her two sons had left Liverpool years ago. One to America, the other to Australia and she had no other family at all. Maggie liked her instantly.

'You must call me Carrie,' she'd smiled after Maggie had asked when she would like to move in.

'Then you must call me Maggie, no more of this "Mrs O'Shea" nonsense.' Maggie wondered what she would think if she knew she wasn't married at all.

'It will be nice to live somewhere where there's a bit of lively company, more like a little family.'

'I hope we can all be like a little family, although Miss Tifnell may not be too talkative.'

'Oh, she'll thaw a bit when she gets to know us. So, I'll move my things in tomorrow night, if that's convenient?'

'You could have brought them with you,' Maggie had replied, warming to Carrie Ashley, for in a way the woman reminded her of Mam.

Both ladies had settled in when Callan arrived home and Maggie had found that she got on so well with Carrie that she could talk to her for hours. She felt as though she could confide in Carrie, but it was too soon, much too soon.

Early spring sunlight slanted down between the houses in Elm Road. It made windows sparkle and the grey slate roof tiles gleamed as though they had been polished. Maggie had been up since the crack of dawn, cleaning and polishing so that the house looked spotless. She had great plans to redecorate but they could wait for a while. She'd dressed with care in the dark-green-and-black chequered wool dress that he'd bought her on one of their shopping expeditions before things had gone so wrong. She was still pale and thin she thought anxiously as she stood before the mirror in the bedroom.

Her heart started racing and the palms of her hands had started to sweat as she stood by the parlour window, concealed from the outside by the white cotton-lace curtain. When she saw him walking up the road she caught hold of the windowsill to steady herself. Oh, he hadn't changed one bit and he was so handsome.

He didn't have time to knock, the door was flung open and she was in his arms and neither of them could speak for a few minutes.

She clung to him, sobbing with happiness.

'Oh, Maggie, Maggie! I've missed you so much.' Callan's voice was harsh with emotion.

'I thought I'd never see you again.'

'It's all over now, my darling.'

'Oh, Callan, I love you so much.'

He held her tightly. 'And I love you, Maggie, and you'll never be frightened or cold or hungry ever again. I tried to tell you all that in my letters, about the way I feel, the house . . .'

She lifted her head from his shoulder. 'Your letters? What letters?'

'Maggie, I wrote every single week.'

'I never got them.'

Callan felt the bile rise in his throat. He'd thought that she would be comforted and reassured by his letters but they'd kept them from her. What good would it do now to create an almighty fuss? She wanted to put the past behind her.

'They don't matter, Maggie, not now. I have you.'

Chapter Nineteen

THE SUMMER SUN WAS bright and the sky was a bowl of azure with not a cloud in sight. The day would be hot. The soft breeze lifted the white lace curtain and sent it billowing like a cloud in the small parlour where Maggie sat, the letter on the table in front of her.

The parlour was small, but furnished with good pieces, all lovingly cared for. A deep crimson carpet with fringed ends covered the floor, and crimson curtains and mantel cover gave the room added richness. The buttoned chair and low sofa were covered in a bright chintz, and an aspidistra stood on a tall wooden stand in the corner by the fireplace. A clock and two china figurines adorned the small overmantel, above which was a mirror. The house was modest but in Maggie's eyes it was a palace. Her kitchen was spotless, the range black-leaded every morning, the bright rag rugs beaten in the yard, the copper pans and utensils burnished until they gleamed, the deal table scrubbed white. The dishes on the small dresser all matched and were of good quality. All the bedrooms had been redecorated with floral wallpaper. There were pretty curtains and bedspreads. Colourful rugs were scattered on floors covered with polished linoleum. It was everything she could have wished for and had never even dreamed she could own.

It was four years since she'd been released from Walton and it was a very different Maggie to the one who had stepped out into the fresh, clean air that winter morning. She was twenty-four years old and a woman, no longer a girl, a beautiful woman whose features bore the stamp of suffering. In this quiet, respectable street she'd begun a new life as Mrs O'Shea. Her neighbours were not aware that there had been no legal ceremony or that the gold band on her finger was there only to give credence to the title of Mrs and substantiate the deception. She didn't care about the subterfuge. In her heart and her mind she was Callan's wife and it was to her that he returned as often as he could.

Carrie knew the truth and, later on, Miss Tifnell had been told. In those early days Maggie had grown very close to Carrie Ashley; it was as though she had a mother again and Carrie, who had been so lonely, was so thankful to have found what she thought of as a proper home again, that she looked on Maggie as the daughter she'd never had.

It had been after her miscarriage, brought about by the frenzy of work she'd thrown herself into, decorating and cleaning the house to try to banish from her mind the memories of prison and Laura. There had been no need for her to involve herself physically, Callan had told her to employ people, but she'd stubbornly refused. Her pregnancy had been in the very early stages but she'd been racked with guilt and had been feeling very low one evening. The fits of depression had become less frequent as time passed by but they hadn't disappeared altogether. She missed Callan and she felt so guilty about concealing Laura's existence and she missed the child terribly. Carrie had come quietly into the kitchen that night and found Maggie sitting staring into the fire, her cheeks wet with tears.

'Maggie, luv, what is it?' Carrie had asked softly.

Maggie had turned towards her and there was such pain and suffering in her eyes that Carrie had been moved and had taken Maggie in her arms. 'What's wrong? Tell me, you know you can trust me and I know there's something been troubling you for months now.'

Maggie had told her and it was such a relief to unburden herself that when she'd finished she felt light-headed.

Carrie hadn't passed any judgement nor recoiled in horror. She'd just patted Maggie and let her cry. It would help, she knew that from experience, but her troubles had faded into insignificance beside Maggie's. She'd had good times when Kenneth had been alive and the boys had been young; Maggie had never had anything remotely like the blessings she'd had in life and whose disappearance she grieved over. The loss of a husband, the emigration of two sons. What was that compared to the loss of both parents, the estrangement from a brother she'd loved dearly, the grinding poverty and misery, the love of a man not at liberty to marry her, the injustice and suffering in Walton and the terrible sacrifice of giving away a child and the pain and loss of the miscarriage? Oh, her troubles were nothing at all compared to Maggie's.

There were times when Maggie was happy and she knew she would have been happy every day but for one thing. Laura. Laura was the secret she had kept from Callan all these years, but Laura was always in her heart and her thoughts.

There had been times over the years when she'd been desolate. When nothing could console her, when she told herself she must have been out of her mind. There were the nights when sleep wouldn't come, when she cried for hours, the longing an almost physical pain. Twice she had actually gone to Southport. The first time she had caught the train back immediately. The second time she had gone as far as Birkdale. There had been a third time, when she had actually got as far as the street in which Philippa lived. Each time she'd told herself it was just to perhaps catch a glimpse of Laura, to see how she'd grown, to see that Philippa was caring for her. In the end common sense had prevailed. Laura was better off with Philippa. She told herself that the pain would lessen with time and when she had another child. There had been that one miscarriage and then . . . nothing. Often she wondered was she now incapable of bearing children. Had the miscarriage in some way affected her or was this her punishment for living in sin with Callan.

She had heard from Philippa regularly at first, letters that gave her pain, yet letters she looked forward to. They had become less frequent over the past year, but now her child was ill and Philippa had written to tell her how worried she was.

Maggie picked up the letter again and re-read it. All Philippa's money hadn't saved Laura from the epidemic of diphtheria that was raging. The very word sent icy fingers of terror clutching at Maggie's heart. Very few recovered, choking to death as the membrane of the throat closed. She got to her feet, her mind made up. She was going to Southport. She'd promised Philippa that she would never attempt to see the child but now . . . even now she might be too late.

She cleared the breakfast dishes and then packed a few things in a Gladstone bag, then she wrote a note to Carrie asking could she possibly serve the meals she had left prepared. 'Tell Miss Tifnell that my aunt is ill, near to death,' she wrote. 'I have to go, Carrie,' she'd scrawled, while she prayed for forgiveness for the lie.

She spent the whole journey silently praying that she wouldn't be too late and blaming herself, illogically, that this was her fault for living out the lie that she was Callan's wife.

She took a cab from the station to Crescent Road in Birkdale and she was too worried to notice much about the house, except that it was very big and had steps leading up to the double doors of the vestibule and a sort of small drive. When Hetty opened the door she burst into tears.

Hetty remembered her. She remembered how Maggie had looked the morning she had accompanied Philippa to the jail; she remembered the tearful, heart-wrenching scene when Maggie had handed her baby over to Philippa.

'Hush now, miss! They say she's not going to die! Miss Philippa's at the hospital, she's been there all night!'

'The hospital!' All the terrors from her past, bound up in that word, seized Maggie.

'The doctor said there was no other course, he couldn't do any more for her. But they've done some sort of operation and it's working, it is!'

Maggie steadied herself. Telling herself not to be stupid. Philippa could afford the best treatment, for she was a wealthy woman.

'You come in and I'll make you a nice cup of tea, then you can go up to the hospital.'

Maggie shook her head. 'No, no, thank you, Hetty. I'll go straight there.' She was gripped by a terrible longing to see her child, to hold her in her arms. Something she hadn't done since the day, four years ago, when she'd placed Laura in Philippa's arms.

Hetty understood. She took Maggie into the house, into the kitchen, while she packed some food in a basket.

'Shall I get you a taxi or will you go on the train? The station isn't far, it's just around the corner, halfway up Dover Road.'

'Where is the hospital?' Maggie asked, wishing she would hurry up.

'It's on the Promenade. You can't miss it, it's a huge red-brick building.'

'I'll get a taxi.' Speed was of the essence and money was of no consequence now, not while her child's life was at risk.

Hetty sent the little kitchen maid out to find a cab.

The journey wasn't long but to Maggie it seemed an eternity. She stared unseeingly at the banks of flowers in their well-tended beds along the Promenade. Nor did she notice the big hotels, the pier, or the crowds, taking full advantage of the warm weather. Many of the people were on holiday and looked fit and carefree. As she paid the driver she realized that her hands were shaking.

It was a very big, imposing building that faced the sea and it looked new, not like the begrimed and shabby

Infirmary in Liverpool whose past as a workhouse gave it an appearance and an air of doom and decay. She enquired at the reception desk and then followed the sister along the white tiled corridors that smelled of ether and carbolic, smells that caused her stomach to heave. She was not taken to a ward, but a small room. The blind was pulled down over the window, making it dark. Her hand went to her mouth to stifle the cry that sprang to her lips as she caught sight of the narrow iron bed and the small figure that lay in it.

'Maggie! Maggie!' Philippa, her face pale and strained, her eyes dark circled with exhaustion and worry, looked at Maggie with undisguised fear.

Maggie moved towards her slowly. 'I'm sorry, I'm sorry, but I had to come. I just had to come.'

'I've been demented with worry. I've felt so helpless, so very, very helpless.' Never in her life had Philippa had to contend with such anxiety. She'd always been able to exact some form of control over circumstances, except when she'd been in prison – a time she tried not to think about. Then events had been out of her control but not since. This realization frightened her and for the first time in four years she let doubt enter her mind. To see a child at the mercy of such a terrible disease frightened her and focused her thoughts on the size of the commitment she had so lightly taken on. She passed a hand over her eyes. 'She's nearly out of danger, Maggie. They said if I'd have left it any longer . . .'

Maggie wasn't listening, her eyes were fixed on the child. On the long, dark curly hair spread across the white pillow, the dark lashes that formed two crescents as they rested on the alabaster cheeks. Her heart missed a beat. Dear God, but she was the very image of Callan but so pale, so very pale and fragile. She wanted to reach out and scoop her up in her arms and hold her tightly, never to let her go. All the feelings she had suppressed over the years wouldn't be held back. They rose with such force that she began to tremble all over. This was her child, her child, and yet she must restrain herself. She reached out and gently touched the pale cheek. 'Laura. Oh, Laura,' she whispered.

'They had to operate . . . it was the only way,' Philippa said quietly.

Maggie noticed the small red gash and the tiny piece of tube protruding from the child's throat, above the frilled collar of the white lawn nightgown sprigged with rosebuds. 'What have they done to her?' she whispered.

'Inserted a tube, so she could breathe. She . . . she was choking, Maggie! I never want to hear such a terrible sound again in my whole life! It brought back all the terrible memories of that force-feeding. Choking as though you were being strangled. I was so afraid and there was nothing I could do.'

Maggie had taken the small hand in her own, her whole being aching with longing to hold her child. 'Will . . . will it have to stay there?'

'No, once the fever has abated and she can breathe normally, they will take it out.'

Maggie felt a surge of gratitude. 'Why don't you go home and get some rest? I'll stay with her.'

'I don't think they'll allow it, I'm here under sufferance. Only Mr Fellow's authority has allowed me to stay.' Suddenly Philippa was angry. Two bright spots of colour appeared on her cheeks, making her look like a Dutch doll. 'All these damned rules and regulations! Institutions! They're all the same!'

Maggie shuddered. 'Let me stay for a while longer, please?' she pleaded.

Philippa agreed reluctantly, but how could she refuse after Maggie had come all this way and indeed she had written to her?

She stayed, sitting just holding Laura's hand, drinking in the sight of her child, noticing every minute detail of her face and expression. Trying to imprint them indelibly on her memory. The child slept peacefully, waking occasionally and staring at Maggie uncertainly with her huge dark eyes before Philippa spoke and soothed her and she drifted back to sleep, reassured.

Maggie stayed that night with Philippa but sleep wouldn't come and she sat at the dressing table, staring at her reflection in the mirror. The bedroom was large and very elegant with its expensive furniture, its dusky blue and plum-coloured curtains and bedspread, and blue and old rose thick carpet. The beauty of the room had overawed her, as had the other rooms she'd seen. The drawing room with its long windows covered by green velvet curtains, green and gold carpet, the carved fireplace and mahogany bookcases, bureau and side tables, the deep comfortable sofas and chairs covered in green and gold brocade. The fine pictures, the dainty porcelain figures, the solid silver tea service and fine bone china that Hetty had brought in on a tray when they had returned from the hospital. Everything seemed to impress upon her the fact that Philippa was wealthy and she was not.

She looked tired, miserable and gaunt, she thought, trying to sort out the confusion that filled her mind. Every instinct screamed out that she should take Laura back with her, no matter what the consequences would be. Then her common sense told her that had she kept Laura, her child would have been more likely to have died. And what of the little girl herself? How could she selfishly shatter the child's safe, secure little world – this world epitomized by the room she now sat in – and take her to a strange city, a strange house, to live with people she didn't know? And what could she offer her? Oh, her situation had changed since the dark days in Brick Street but she could offer nothing like this and nothing could alter the fact that Laura had been born out of wedlock, a fact that would soon become known. How would she explain away the sudden appearance of a four-year-old child who looked so like Callan that even a fool would know he was her father? And Callan, what would she tell him?

Hour after hour she tormented herself, until at last, totally exhausted, she lay down on the bed and cried herself to sleep. Common sense had prevailed. She could never take Laura back to Liverpool.

She left for the station next morning, before Philippa went to the hospital.

'Oh, Maggie, don't think I don't know what you must be feeling, but it's for the best that you don't see her again. Better for her and better for you,' Philippa had said before she had left.

Maggie's gaze had wandered over the large hall with its plaster-moulded ceiling, its fine staircase and richly carpeted stairs and she nodded silently. Laura would want for nothing here but would Laura be happy? Really happy? Don't be such a fool! she told herself. Of course she would be happy!

'I'll write and keep you informed about everything, but I'm sure that now she will recover quickly, thank God.'

Thank God and your money for the best treatment, Maggie thought bitterly. 'Promise me you'll write every week, Philippa?'

'I promise. Now you'd better go or you'll miss your train,' Philippa advised a little sharply. She was tired, very tired, for the whole experience had shaken her. Until now she had never fully realized the extent of the responsibilities she had so lightly taken on.

Exchange Station was busy but Maggie hardly noticed as she made her way to the tram stop. She felt as though she had been drained of all emotions, that she had left a part of herself in Southport. The tram rattled and swayed along the tracks and she gazed aimlessly out of the window, feeling as though she were imprisoned in a metal cocoon. She didn't care that the sun shone brightly or that fluffy white clouds moved slowly across a sky of forget-me-not blue. Or that the leaves on the trees that lined the suburban streets rustled like silk in the breeze. She felt dead, as though winter had returned and encased her heart in ice.

Absently, she greeted the few neighbours she met and they, thinking she had suffered a family bereavement, nodded and thought they understood.

The house was still and warm as she let herself in. She went into the kitchen and let out a startled cry. Callan was sitting in the ladder-backed chair by the empty kitchen range.

He looked at her with relief. He'd been worried. In fact worries seemed to be crowding in on him. He had had news that Breda's illness had become worse. Much worse. The specialist in Dublin that Richard had insisted on calling in, had confirmed his son's fears. Breda had cancer and his eldest son had written to inform him of the fact.

'Maggie, where've you been? What's all this nonsense about a dying aunt in Southport?'

She caught her breath, not knowing what to say, yet thankful that Carrie hadn't betrayed her. 'I didn't expect you until tomorrow.'

'Obviously. What on earth's the matter? Have you been to Southport at all? I've been worried sick.'

Her shoulders slumped. What possible excuse could she give? If she had just gone shopping it might have been all right, although the shops on Lord Street were too expensive for her. Philippa's station in life was too far above her own to have just gone visiting. But she had stayed overnight. Oh, she was so weary of all the deception. Weary and drained from the trauma of the last twenty-four hours. The time for lying was over now and it would be a relief. She took off her hat and placed it on the table. 'Yes, I've been to Southport. To see Philippa Barton.'

'Philippa Barton? The suffragette who was in prison?'

'Yes. We kept in touch, there was a reason.' As she looked at him, his dark hair greying at the temples, she saw in her mind's eye the child who was so like him.

'You're not involved in this women's suffrage thing, are you, Maggie?'

'No, although I agree with what they're trying to do. No, I went because . . . because Laura had diphtheria.' She held his gaze steadily. Outwardly she was calm but her insides were knotted with fear.

'Laura?' He was totally confused. He'd never heard her mention anyone of that name before.

She looked down and started to pluck at the hem of the white linen jacket she wore.

'My daughter. Your daughter, she's four years old.'

The silence was so heavy between them that she felt she could have cut it with a knife. Only the ticking of the clock on the overmantel could be heard, loud and seemingly strident.

Callan's face registered a gamut of emotions, shock, disbelief, confusion. He gripped her by her shoulders. 'My daughter! My daughter! Maggie! Maggie, what are you saying, girl?'

'I didn't know I was pregnant when I went to Walton Jail. Mr Compton knew but I made him swear he wouldn't tell you, and then Philippa came and we talked . . . and . . . Oh, Callan, it was for the best! I couldn't let her grow up with the stigma of being branded a bastard! I couldn't! I know what it feels like to be jeered at. Mam tried to protect me but I had to learn how to cope with it, I had to learn how to fight the kids who mocked me. I didn't want that for her. And besides, you hadn't visited me – I never got your letters. I wasn't sure whether you still loved me or not. Philippa is supposed to be her aunt, her legal guardian. Laura will be known to everyone as her niece. Philippa is rich, she can give her everything that both you and I can't afford. It was for her, for Laura!'

He released her abruptly, his eyes dark with barely controlled hurt and anger. 'What about me, Maggie? Did you never even think about me and what my feelings would be? Do I count for nothing?' Compton knew, Philippa Barton and the prison staff knew, yet she had denied him that knowledge.

'You have children, remember! Your sons!'

He groaned. 'Jesus, Mary and Joseph, what does that matter? Yes, yes I have sons but I also have a daughter!'

'How was I to know how you would react? How was I to know if you'd even want her, acknowledge her, or if you'd still want me?' she cried.

'Maggie you should have trusted me enough to know that I love you, that I would love her too and I would have provided for you both.'

'Mr Compton said that. He said that you'd provide for us, that I shouldn't doubt you and really I didn't.'

'Then for God's sake, why didn't you tell me?' he shouted. He couldn't take it in, not yet, but he was hurt and angry.

'Because you can't marry me and make her legitimate, can you?' she cried.

'No! But would that have mattered, Maggie? No one need ever have known! No one in this neighbourhood thinks you are Miss May, do they? They don't know you've been to prison. No, to them you are the respectable Mrs O'Shea!' The anger was building, taking over from the hurt.

'Callan, it would have come out. You know it would! Birth certificates are needed for all kinds of things these days! I *had* to think of her!'

'And yourself.' He was too furious to even think of her feelings, to try to understand. What she had done was too monstrous for calm consideration.

'That's not fair! Don't you think it nearly broke my heart to give her to Philippa? Don't you think that every day and every night I long for her? Three times I've gone to Southport. I just wanted to see her, nothing else. Each time I turned back because I knew I was only torturing myself. I'm her mother, for God's sake! I nearly lost her! She nearly died!'

He drew away from her, his shoulders squared, his back stiff, his dark eyes filled with bitter anger. 'And I'm her father and you kept her very existence from me. That was cruel, Maggie. Cruel and wicked! You denied me the chance to see her grow, to smile, to talk, to walk. I always wanted a daughter.'

A sob caught in Maggie's throat and she tried to tell him that Laura was so like him, but the words wouldn't come. 'I did it for her sake, for her sake!' she choked. 'She'll grow up a lady.'

'I don't care if she will be the bloody queen, you had no right to do it, Maggie! No bloody right at all!'

She shrank back from the force of his anger, suddenly afraid of him and with horror she watched him pick up his hat. 'Callan! Where are you going?'

He was shaking with fury. 'Away, Maggie. Back to Ireland, where I belong. Back to my family, I have a wife and two sons, as you so readily reminded me! I'll never forgive you for this, Maggie. Never.'

She couldn't speak. It was as though her throat had been gripped in a strangulating grasp and when she heard the front door slam, she slumped forward. Even in the darkest days in Walton she had never felt so alone or so defeated.

Chapter Twenty

THROUGHOUT SUPPER Miss Tifnell noticed nothing amiss. She complained about the heat and the traffic and ate sparingly of her meal. Then she announced that she would change her clothes and take a walk in the park as she had a slight headache.

'The fresh air will clear it, Harriet. It will be pleasant now, the fiery heat has gone and I don't wonder you get so many headaches stuck in that poky office all day, hammering away on that typewriting machine,' Carrie encouraged her. She herself had a headache, an airless sales floor was almost as bad as an airless office, but her sharp eyes had noticed Maggie's pallor and her wooden movements and lack of conversation. There was something wrong and there was no sign of Mr O'Shea.

When Miss Tifnell had at last gone for her evening stroll, Carrie went into the kitchen.

Maggie was sitting at the table, her head in her hands.

'What's the matter, Maggie?'

Maggie lifted her head. 'He's gone, Carrie.'

'I suspected that much.' She crossed to Maggie's side. 'He'll be back, luv.'

'No, Carrie. I . . . I told him about Laura.'

'Oh, God!'

'I had no excuse for being away overnight and I was so weary of the lies. Oh, Carrie, he was so mad. I've never seen him so angry.'

In a way Carrie wasn't surprised at his anger. 'Maggie, give him time, a day or two to think about it rationally. He'll come back. He'll understand.'

'He won't. He said he was going home, to Ireland. Oh, Carrie, what will I do? What will I do without him?'

Carrie held her in her arms until her sobs quieted. 'Maggie, how was Laura?'

'Over the worst. Philippa has paid for the best treatment. But she's so like him, Carrie, and it broke my heart to look at her and not be able to hold her in my arms.'

Carrie tutted and shook her head. 'Money isn't everything. If I were you, Maggie, I'd go and see him and then together go and fetch your child and bring her home. Here, where she belongs, with you and her father.'

The thought was so tempting, the idea balm to her aching heart. 'I wish it was so simple.'

'It is, Maggie, girl. You're tearing yourself apart

over them both. You've always been a fighter, go and get them both.'

'I can never bring her here, Carrie. Philippa can give her so much.'

'She can't give her a mother's love and in my book that's something that has no price.'

'Carrie, don't you understand? I won't have anyone calling her names. How could I explain about her, people will soon realize.'

'It will be a nine day wonder.'

'No, she'll have to go to school and then people will know.'

'Why are you meeting all these obstacles before you reach them? There are ways and means.'

'I can't, Carrie. I can't deprive her of a chance in life or let her suffer the way I did.'

Carrie sighed deeply. Maggie was so determined. A determination fired by bitter experience. 'Then at least go after Mr O'Shea.'

'What good would that do? I have no claim on him. I can't turn up on his wife's doorstep, can I? I can't wreck a family, destroy a wife.'

Carrie had to agree, but she felt so helpless, so desperately sorry for Maggie. Twenty-four years old and her future so bleak. 'He'll be back. I know he will. Just you believe that,' she said firmly, with far more conviction than she felt.

Maggie had waited day after day for him to come back, to receive a letter, a note, a message, but there had been nothing. The summer days dragged on, hot and dusty, the brazen sun sapping what little resolve Maggie had left. She wouldn't look any further ahead than the next week, she was afraid to. Afraid to face so bleak a future.

Carrie watched with growing fear as Maggie became thinner, paler and more listless. As the talk of war increased daily she wondered if she should try and contact Mr O'Shea herself. Germany had now amassed a huge fleet and was boosting its army. Greece, Serbia and the Balkan States were already at war with Bulgaria, and Russia and Turkey were on the brink of joining in. The world was going mad, Carrie thought. Although she didn't understand the complicated treaties, she'd heard, read and understood enough to know that there was cause for grave concern.

There was trouble at every turn it seemed. Trouble in Ireland; the Unionists in the north were up in arms over the Home Rule Bill, while in the south there was anger at its rejection by the House of Lords. And, as for the suffragettes, Carrie was of a generation that thought they'd gone too far. Mrs Pankhurst inciting women to all kinds of terrible deeds. Arson at Kew Gardens, destroying telephone lines, bombing Mr Lloyd George's new house and that woman, Emily Davidson, throwing herself in front of the king's horse at Epsom and killing herself. What in the name of God was the world coming to? She asked Harriet Tifnell. Harriet had agreed with her. Mankind seemed bent on going to perdition at breakneck speed.

In the end, Carrie went to see Alfred Compton. She told him how worried she was about Maggie and begged his help. Sadly, he informed her that there was little he could do. He could not interfere in personal matters, he told her regretfully, much as he would like to. If the request to contact Mr O'Shea had come from Miss May, who was also his client, it would have been different.

'I've got to do something! I can't just watch her fading before my eyes, she'll go into a decline.'

'I understand your predicament, your concern. But would either of them appreciate your interference?'

Carrie bit her lip. He was right. Another idea had been hovering in her mind, born of desperation. 'Maggie has a brother, Tommy. They haven't spoken for years but maybe . . . maybe now with all this talk of war . . . ?'

Mr Compton pressed the tips of his fingers together and looked hopeful. 'A reconciliation?'

'He lives in Glasgow. At least that's where Maggie said he was.'

'You have an address, a place of work?'

'No. Don't you have anything?'

'Why should I?'

Carrie looked defeated.

'Glasgow is a big city. If we had a place of work even. Why not ask Miss May?'

'How can I do that? She might say she doesn't want to find him, she might not even know.'

'Can you do it surreptitiously?'

'What does that mean?' Carrie was becoming impatient with the old man.

'By means of stealth, bring the conversation around to Glasgow, sound Miss May out.'

Carrie wondered how on earth she would bring any conversation around to Glasgow without Maggie knowing what was on her mind. 'I'll try,' she said, flatly. Her visit had been totally useless and she felt frustrated, impatient and even more dispirited.

She had tried, but all Maggie had said was that Tommy had gone to Glasgow. He'd been living with Florrie and Andy Mcsomething and was working at a place with a strange name.

'Strange? How strange?' Carrie had pressed.

'Something Blazes, I can't remember. Carrie, I don't want to talk about our Tommy, please.'

Carrie had had no option but to change the subject.

The Indian summer lingered on but in the second week of October the weather broke. The skies clouded, the leaves began to turn from dusty green to gold and orange until they fell and formed thick carpets on the ground in the parks and leafy suburban streets. By the end of the month there was a sharpness in the air and very soon the first frost glinted with silver tracery across the windows and the November gales stripped the remaining leaves from the trees, leaving them to wave skeletal branches at the scudding clouds above.

Maggie got through each day like an automated doll, the loss and longing never left her. Philippa had been true to her word throughout August and September but then the letters had become less frequent. As Christmas approached, Maggie felt desperate. If only she could see Laura again it would help. The image of the child lying ill haunted her day and night. She bought sweets and toys and took the tram to Exchange Station.

She stood outside the house in Crescent Road for five minutes, just staring at it, trying to overcome her fears. Trying not to let the sheer size of it demoralize her. The first time she'd come here she'd been too worried to notice much about it, but now, in the weak December sunlight, her gaze wandered over the imposing façade. The ivy-covered walls, the tall windows, the steps, flanked by large stone urns, that led up to the double doors. She clutched the paper carrier bag tightly and took a deep breath.

'Maggie!' Hetty stared at her as though she'd seen a ghost.

'I'm sorry I didn't write and let you know, Hetty. Is Philippa in?'

Hetty nodded slowly, wondering how her mistress would greet Maggie. Ever since the little girl's illness she'd noticed a change in Philippa's attitude to the child. It worried Hetty, it worried her deeply for she'd seen such signs in the past and they only led to trouble. From experience she knew that her mistress was losing interest, but this time it was different. This time it wasn't a cause or a committee or something equally inconsequential. It was a child and a child Hetty had become very fond of. She prayed that Philippa would think carefully before speaking to Maggie.

'Who is it, Hetty?' Philippa entered the hallway, dressed in a dusky pink, merino wool dress edged with black braid, a gold and amber brooch fastened to its high neck. Her hair was dressed high in elaborate puffs and rolls, which suited her long, thin face. 'Maggie!' She quickly overcame her shock. 'Why didn't you let us know you were coming? Come here and let me look at you, you look pale.'

'I'm sorry, Philippa, but I just had to come.' Maggie had noted the coolness beneath Philippa's cordial welcome. 'I brought some things for . . . Laura.' It hurt to even speak the child's name.

'Come in to the fire, you look perished. I'm afraid Laura's not here.'

'Not here!' Maggie almost screamed the words.

'Now don't get upset, she's at a birthday party, she'll be back at four o'clock. Sit down and Hetty will bring us some tea.' Philippa was disturbed. Maggie looked ill and there was a restlessness in her manner. 'Have you been reading about Mrs Pankhurst?' she asked, conversationally. 'They arrested her as soon as she set foot in Plymouth. She had been to America, you know. It was absolutely dreadful the way she was treated after that bomb affair, and Sylvia in jail for three months!

Mind you, I don't agree with the lengths she has gone to. Demonstrations, protests and petitions, yes, but not this "guerrilla warfare" as she calls it. There is quite enough open warfare going on in Europe. I dread to think what the future holds.'

Maggie couldn't have cared less if Mrs Pankhurst or her daughters had flown to the moon. 'I don't read much, the newspapers depress me.'

Philippa could see that Maggie was becoming more agitated. 'Oh, they depress me, too!'

'I hadn't heard from you for quite a while,' Maggie interrupted impatiently. 'I didn't know what to think, if everything was all right . . .'

'Oh, Maggie, everything is just perfect,' Philippa said flippantly. 'I'm sorry I've been so lax, I kept meaning to write, I just don't know where the time goes to. I hardly seem to have a minute.'

Maggie thought of how the hours in her day dragged, but said nothing. Hetty appeared with the tea-tray and Maggie watched Philippa pour from the silver teapot, feeling more and more uneasy and uncomfortable. Philippa had changed. There was a more self-confident air about her. She seemed aloof, her attitude a little disdainful, Maggie thought bitterly, glancing around the room at the fine mahogany furniture, the velvet curtains, the deep-piled oriental carpet and the numerous expensive porcelain and ivory ornaments. Oh, yes, Philippa could be confident and patronizing. She had Laura, while she . . . she had very little and no one in the world who really cared for her now.

The atmosphere was strained. Philippa made light conversation while Maggie grew more and more tense until at last the sound of the doorbell echoed through the hall, causing Maggie to jump nervously.

Philippa got to her feet. 'Ah, here she is!' She moved quickly from the room, unsure of how Maggie would react. There was obviously something very wrong with Maggie's state of mind.

'How was the party? Did you enjoy it? I do hope you behaved nicely. We have a visitor, she's come all the way from Liverpool.' Philippa let Hetty divest Laura of her coat, hat and muff before ushering the child into the room.

The little girl said nothing, her eyes moving from Philippa's face to Maggie's.

'Don't you want to know who she is, Laura?' Philippa's tone was a little brusque. She felt irritated by the child's reticence. Reticence that seemed to have increased since her illness. 'She's . . . a friend. I knew her when I lived in Liverpool. I did live there for a little time, just before you were born.' Philippa smiled brightly and gently pushed Laura towards Maggie.

'Say hello to Miss May, Laura, or she'll think you are very rude.' Philippa's tone was sharp.

Maggie got to her feet slowly with a quick intake of breath. The older she had become, the more like her father Laura was.

'Hello, I'm Laura.' The voice was cultured but quiet.

Maggie swallowed hard, there was a lump in her throat.

Philippa smiled. 'That's better. This is Miss May. She's brought you something, presents, I think.'

'Yes, I . . . I thought you might like these.' Maggie thrust the parcels she had brought towards the child, feeling as though the smile, nailed to her face, would splinter and crack in the same way that her heart was doing. This was her child, she'd carried her inside her body for nine months, she'd spent hours of agonizing pain bringing her into the world, and yet she was afraid to speak, afraid to reach out and touch her.

'Can I open it, Aunt Pippa, please?' Laura didn't look at Philippa.

Maggie managed to suppress the cry that rose to her lips. At least Laura hadn't addressed Philippa as mama or mother, something she'd expected and tried to steel herself against.

'Well, I really think Maggie meant them for Christmas, but, seeing as she can't stay very long, I think you can open them.'

Her words drove the knife deeper into Maggie's heart, but she said nothing. Her hands were clasped tightly together in her lap. She just watched the child as she opened the gifts. A small doll, a picture book and the brightly coloured top and whip, something the child had obviously never seen before, which surprised her. When she'd been Laura's age, all she had wanted – longed for – was a top and whip but she'd never had one. The nearest she'd ever got was begging the loan of one for a few minutes.

'How quaint,' Philippa murmured as she explained how it worked to Laura, and Maggie suddenly knew that once she had left, the toy would be quietly disposed of. It was a toy of the working classes, a toy to be used in the street and she knew that Laura would never be allowed to do something as common as play in the street. Never more had Maggie been made to realize how humble were her origins, how wide the divide between herself and Philippa Barton.

Nor did Philippa approve of the postcards she had brought of Liverpool, she could tell that. 'I thought you might like to see where . . . where I live. You see, we have a lot of big ships coming in and out of the river.' She held out a postcard of the *Mauretania* and *Lusitania* in the Canada Dock basin.

At last the child showed enthusiasm. 'Look, Aunt Pippa, two big ships!'

'They are the biggest and fastest in the whole world,' Maggie said softly.

'Maybe we'll go on them, one day, when you're older,' Philippa said coldly, without looking at Maggie.

As the minutes passed Maggie began to notice how quiet and withdrawn the child was and how Philippa was a little sharp with her. It seemed as though Philippa wasn't really listening to the child, that her mind was elsewhere, that Laura actually irritated or annoyed her, but she could find no reason for this in Laura's behaviour. She told herself she was being over emotional, that she was imagining it. The ways of the rich were different, their manners more formal.

After half an hour Philippa rose and took Laura's hand. 'I think you should say thank you now to Miss May for all these lovely things. It's time for your bath and she has a long way to go home.'

Reluctantly, Maggie stood up and the child came forward. Unable to help herself, Maggie bent and kissed the soft cheek, catching the sweet freshness of the shining, dark hair. Instantly the tears welled in her eyes and she fought hard to smile.

'Maggie will come and see you again . . . soon. Now off you go with Hetty.'

Maggie hadn't seen Philippa's hand reach for the bell and was surprised to see the maid standing in the doorway. As though relieved, Laura ran to her, but before she left the room, she turned. 'Goodbye, Miss May.'

Maggie somehow managed to smile and raise her hand.

Philippa closed the door firmly. She had noted Maggie's battle to keep her composure and was determined to quell any hysterics. She wanted no scenes. 'Maggie, I don't think it would be very . . . wise of you to see Laura again. It would only . . . unsettle her.' Her tone was clipped and authoritative.

'How would it unsettle her?' Maggie's voice was equally cold.

'Maggie, be reasonable. It was your decision for Laura to be brought up by me. She adores Hetty. She is bright and intelligent and I don't want anything to spoil all I have accomplished.' Philippa thought of all the expense, all the disruptions, all the worry she had undertaken for Laura's benefit and that of Maggie, too. It was far from easy to bring up a child on your own, she'd come to realize that only too well lately.

'And you think that if she sees me, she will be . . . tainted!'

'Maggie! That's not what I meant at all.' Two spots of red burned on Philippa's cheeks.

'If you want me to beg, Philippa, then I will. Can I come and see her, perhaps once a month, for a few hours, like today? That's all I'm asking. A few hours, that can't do any harm, can it? I . . . I have nothing, now. No one.'

This was exactly what Philippa had feared when Maggie had written to say that Mr O'Shea had left her. 'I hate to be so harsh, Maggie, but I think it would be harmful. Not for Laura but for you.'

'For me?' Maggie cried.

Philippa was trying to be patient. 'Yes. Look how upset you are now. What good will it do for you to torture yourself every time you have to leave her here with me?'

'Oh, I'm used to being "tortured". All my life I've been tortured and tormented.'

Colour suffused Philippa's cheeks. She should have sent Maggie away without seeing the child. Now she seemed determined to cause a scene. Determined to jeopardize everything she had done over the last four years. Maggie had wanted Laura to have the best in life and no expense had been spared, to say nothing of the time and attention that had been lavished on the child. Time she could have spent pleasing herself without even considering Laura. 'No, Maggie. I must insist. No more visits!'

Maggie's reserve broke. 'She's mine! She's my child not yours! You have everything! Look around you, Philippa! You have money and time and people like Hetty and Elizabeth MacKenzie. You can fill your life with your charities or you can shut yourself away from the harshness of it. I have nothing, nothing to look forward to. I'm twenty-four and I have no future without Laura!'

Philippa's colour heightened and her eyes narrowed. 'For God's sake keep your voice down, Maggie! Do you want to throw away everything? Do you want to take Laura back to that . . . that hovel in Liverpool? To play in the dirty streets sharing that . . . that toy you brought her with urchins?'

'It's not a hovel! I have a respectable house in a nice area!'

'And what about her future? Where will she go to

school? Will you be able to afford the music lessons, the dancing and painting classes, all the extras? Don't be a fool, Maggie!'

Maggie was shaking and she didn't care if the whole road heard her. 'Callan was right. I should have told him. I should never have let her go!'

'Oh, I see! You've lost Mr O'Shea, so now you want Laura as some sort of consolation prize! Well, you won't get her! I have spent a great deal of time and money on her!'

'But she's not happy!' Maggie interrupted furiously. 'Any fool can see she's not happy with you. She's frightened to open her mouth! She never smiled, not once, let alone laughed!'

'Don't be ridiculous! Of course she's happy, what child would be unhappy with all she has? With everything she's been given?'

'You don't love her, Philippa, and that's all that matters! Not money or pretty clothes or dancing lessons! It's love that really counts!'

Philippa was becoming tired of Maggie. Tired and exasperated. She'd given the child a home. She'd had the best of everything. What more did Maggie want? Did she honestly think she could come here and visit regularly? Undo, by her speech and manners and ideas, everything that she and Hetty had achieved? Did she want to turn Laura from the quiet, nicely spoken, genteel child that she was into a hoyden? 'That's enough, Maggie! I have influence and, as you so rightly pointed out, money, and I'll make sure that you never see her again. Now I think you'd better leave for, if you cause a fuss, I won't hesitate to call the police and then what will Laura think of you?'

Maggie knew she was beaten. She hadn't come here with the intention of seeing Laura regularly, but how could she help not wanting to see her own child, her own flesh and blood? Philippa was inhuman. Oh, she pretended to feel deeply for women and all their trials and tribulations, but what did she really know of the conditions that governed the lives of thousands of women who did not have the benefits of money and education and status? She picked up her bag and walked from the room with as much dignity as she could muster, but her mind was made up. She didn't care how much money Philippa Barton had, Laura was 'her' child.

She'd had doubts, her resolve had wavered on the journey home, but when she walked from Exchange Station, she knew where she was going. To the office of Compton, Skyes and Radnage, Solicitors.

She'd told the officious-looking clerk that she had no appointment but begged him to ask Mr Compton to see her.

Mr Compton himself came out to greet her and useher her into his office.

'Miss May, this is a surprise.' He smiled at her, but his sharp eyes took in her thinness and the dark circles beneath her eyes. Eyes that were suspiciously bright. It was months since he'd seen her friend and he wondered had the woman prevailed upon her to reconcile herself with Mr O'Shea or her brother. 'What can I do for you? How can I be of service, my dear?'

'Mr Compton, I've just come from Southport. From Miss Barton's house.' She fiddled nervously with her handkerchief.

Ah, that was it, Alfred Compton realized. 'You want your daughter back, Miss May?'

'How did you know?'

'It's very easy. It was a hasty decision you made four, nearly five, years ago. You and Mr O'Shea are estranged and you must be very unhappy and lonely.'

'Oh, Mr Compton, I'm so miserable. Since Callan left there's been nothing, no purpose to my life. As soon as I saw her today, I knew. I want her back desperately. I know she's not happy there, despite all Philippa's money. Will it be hard?'

'Miss Barton never legally adopted her or applied to be her guardian? You never signed anything, no papers, no documents, no matter how innocuous they might have looked?'

'No. I signed nothing.'

'Then in the eyes of the law, Laura is your child. How does Miss Barton feel, is she aware of your intention?'

'Yes. I told her.'

'Do you think she will protest?'

'Yes. I know she will.'

Alfred Compton looked thoughtful. 'She has wealth and status on her side, that cannot be underestimated. She may also have some very influential friends.'

'The only friends she seems to have are in the women's suffrage movement.'

He frowned and twisted his pen between his fingers. He totally disapproved of suffragettes and all they stood for. 'Of course, and I'm certain that no judge will look kindly on all that nonsense that resulted in her being in prison.'

'But won't they hold it against me that I was in prison, too?'

'You were imprisoned quite wrongly, Miss May. She was very definitely guilty of an act of deliberate vandalism, and she flouted the authorities by going on hunger strike. All that will go against her. Now you are a very respectable woman, owning your own house and earning an income.'

'A very small one, Mr Compton. I don't know how I can afford to pay you.'

'We'll worry about that later on, shall we?' He smiled.

She felt all the tension leave her. 'What must I do? Shall I go and fetch Laura?'

'Oh, no, my dear! It must all be done properly, by the book. That would look very bad, very irresponsible. I will write a formal letter to Miss Barton, informing her of your decision and setting out a time and a place for the child to be officially handed over.'

'How soon will that be?'

'I don't expect Miss Barton to comply, my dear. Not immediately. A letter from her solicitor will be received, most likely, but there is little they can do except prevaricate, put off the day when Miss Barton must return your child. Don't worry, you go on home and leave everything to me.'

She'd informed Carrie of her decision and Carrie had agreed and applauded it. 'I told you you've nothing to worry about, Maggie. No amount of money can buy a mother's love or the right to her own child. You won't regret it.'

'But what about Laura? What will I tell her?'

'Maggie, it may take a little while for her to get used to things here, but stop worrying. Why don't you start and get things ready for her? That will take your mind off the other things. She can have that little attic room.'

'Yes, yes she can. I'll start tomorrow. Oh, Carrie, I'm so happy.'

Chapter Twenty-one

SHE HAD THE TINY ATTIC room freshly decorated with white wallpaper, embellished with tiny bunches of rosebuds and forget-me-nots. She bought material from Frost's, Carrie got it at a discount, and she made curtains and a bedspread. She draped yards of bleached muslin to form a skirt over an old, second-hand dressing table and attached pink satin bows to it. From the same second-hand shop she bought a large wooden chest and painted it white, it would do for Laura's toys. Even Harriet Tifnell had bought two pictures of kittens for the wall. Maggie had expected that Harriet would be shocked and disapproving, but to her surprise she took it very well. The preparations completely absorbed Maggie and she lost the air of dejection that had clung to her since Callan had left. She smiled and she began to put on weight again.

Ten days later she received a letter from Mr Compton, informing her that Philippa's solicitor had written to inform him that Miss Barton intended to contest the matter and if necessary would appeal to the highest court in the land.

Maggie was so disappointed, but Mr Compton had warned her, she told herself, trying to bolster her spirits. But still she couldn't see why she must wait. Philippa had no legal claim, so why was she fighting it? Surely Philippa knew that in the end she couldn't win.

'Why don't you go and see her again?' Carrie suggested, after Maggie had unburdened herself to her.

'Mr Compton said not to, Carrie.'

'Oh, what does a dried-up old stick like him know about people's feelings? He's been stuck in that dusty old office with all those books for years! She must see that now you really mean to have Laura back. Go and talk to her, Maggie. I always found it better to talk, face to face, like. She must know that you've got the law on your side and by dragging it all out it will only make it worse in the end, for herself and for the little one.'

Maggie could see her point. Maybe she was right. What did Mr Compton know about 'feelings' as Carrie called them? Maybe if she did point out that it would be better for everyone, for Laura especially, if the matter be resolved quickly.

'Well, will you go?'

Maggie smiled. 'Yes. You're an old meddler, Carrie, did you know that?'

'Oh, I love meddling in people's lives, it's what

keeps me going!' Carrie laughed. 'Go on, get your hat and coat, I'll see to everything here.'

'You mean go now?'

'Yes.'

Impulsively Maggie bent and kissed her. 'What would I do without you?'

'Oh, get off with you, girl!' Carrie said, 'I hate being fussed,' but she was touched by Maggie's show of affection.

All the way to Southport, Maggie rehearsed her speech. She would be calm but firm, there would be no hysterics, no shouting or crying. That would only upset everyone, but she couldn't suppress the joy that made her heart beat like a frightened bird in her chest. In a few hours, she would hold her child in her arms. There would be no need for restraint. She would explain that she had been too poor to look after her, so Philippa had been very kind and taken her to live with her and Hetty. But now she loved her and missed her and she could well be bringing Laura home.

Her steps were quick and light and she smiled to herself as she walked up the quiet road. Just a few more minutes now, a few more steps. Her smile and euphoria vanished when she arrived at number forty-seven, replaced by stark horror. The house was closed up. Shutters were fastened over the windows. She ran up the steps and hammered on the door, shouting Philippa's name, until her strength deserted her. They'd gone! Philippa had gone and she'd taken Laura with her! She looked with disbelief down the quiet road, not knowing what to do. She must be calm, she must think, she told herself. Surely someone would know where they'd gone. The neighbours. She ran to the house next door and rang the bell impatiently.

A young maid answered.

'Oh, please, please, can you tell me where Miss Barton from next door has gone?'

The girl looked at her with surprise. 'I don't know.'

'Surely your mistress must know. Ask her, please, it's so important!' she begged, nearly in tears.

She waited for what seemed like an interminable age before the girl returned.

'Sorry, but madam doesn't know. She never really had much to do with Miss Barton. Didn't approve of all that suffrage thing, years ago. She was in prison, you know. A nice carry-on for a lady!' The girl looked over her shoulder furtively and lowered her voice. 'Stuck-up lot they are round here! Won't pass the time of day unless they can't avoid one another! She,' she jerked her head in the direction of a closed door, 'didn't think it right Miss Barton having that child, her being a single lady. Oh, the little girl was supposed to be some sort of relative, orphaned, but she said there was more to it than met the eye.'

'There was. Laura is my child. I want her back and now she's run off with her.'

The girl's eyes widened and she tutted sympathetically. 'I'm sorry, I honestly don't know where they've gone. Even that Hetty kept to herself. The first thing we knew was when a cab arrived and they were piling all the luggage in it and off they went.'

Maggie nodded, mute misery in her eyes.

'I'd ask you in for a cup of tea, you look as though you need one, but she'd have a blue fit! Wait until she knows she was right about the little girl.'

Maggie turned away, not even thanking the girl for her sympathy.

Mr Compton looked very grave after she'd related to him the details of her visit to Southport. 'Now that really puts the cat among the pigeons! Absconding with the child, the law will take a very dim view of that!'

'That's if she's found! What can I do?' she pleaded.

'I'll write immediately to her solicitors. It's their duty to find her.'

'But what if they can't?' What if they don't know where she's gone and how long will it all take?'

'Now, Miss May, don't upset yourself. It will all be resolved, I promise you.'

She wanted to scream at him. Everything was so slow. By the time they caught up with Philippa, she could well have moved again. She could even have taken Laura abroad to somewhere where the long arm of British justice didn't reach.

'Go home, my dear,' Alfred Compton advised, kindly.

Home, she thought emptily. What was there at home for her? But she had no alternative.

It was to Carrie that she cried and raged against Philippa and the abominable slowness of the law. 'I should have just gone and taken her, the way I wanted to do. It's his fault, he said it had to be done "correctly"! God knows where she is now. She has the money to take her anywhere in the world!' She buried her head in her arms and sobbed.

Carrie looked grim. Philippa Barton was a selfish woman and that Compton was an old fool! 'Then there's nothing for it, Maggie, you'll have to go and see Mr O'Shea. He's her father and he has the right to know that this woman has run off with Laura. He might be able to do something about it.'

Maggie raised her head, her face blotched and tear-stained. 'Carrie, I couldn't! What can he do? He has a wife and two sons!'

'So, he also has a daughter and didn't you say he'd always wanted one? Maggie, she's gone outside the law. She thinks she's above it because she's got money! You need his help! You've got to try! You can't do it on your own, there are some things men are better at; he may know something, anything. After all, he travels the world!'

'What if he won't see me?'

'You won't know unless you try, girl, will you? Where's all that spirit gone? You were such a fighter, Maggie!'

Maggie knew she was right. All her life it seemed she had fought against adversity, yet lately she had just . . . given up. 'You're right, Carrie. I'll go and if he won't see me then . . .'

'He will, Maggie. I'm certain of it,' Carrie replied firmly.

The next day Maggie again sat facing Alfred Compton, the strain showing on her face but determination sat on her like a cloak. She wasn't going to be fobbed off again.

'I've always trusted you, Mr Compton, but now I'm not too sure. I hope you'll forgive me, but if I hadn't listened to you, I would have my child.'

'Miss May, I'm sorry and I'm sorry you feel that way, but no one could have foreseen that Miss Barton would take the child away.'

'No, I'll give you that.'

'What can I do, Miss May?'

'I . . . I've decided to go and see Mr O'Shea, to see if he can help me. Laura's his daughter.'

'Do you wish me to inform Mr O'Shea?'

'No. No more letters, Mr Compton. They don't do any good, they're too stiff . . . too formal. I'm going to see him.'

'Is that wise, his family . . . ?'

'I won't go and hammer on his door. I'll send a note. I'll stay in an hotel or guest house but I don't know exactly where he lives. He didn't tell me and I never wanted to know, I never wanted to know anything about . . . them.'

'He may not be home, Miss May, have you thought of that?'

'I have, but please, Mr Compton, this is something I *have* to do! I . . . I need him now!'

Alfred Compton hesitated. It was a difficult situation and one that he really wanted no part in exacerbating, for she was so desperate that the consequences for the whole O'Shea family could be disastrous. He nodded and drew a sheet of paper across the desk towards him. 'Miss May, I beg of you to be cautious, tread lightly. I know I sound like a fussy old man but I know what is at stake and what is at risk.'

She managed a smile as she put the address in her bag. 'I promise I will try my best to be discreet.'

Carrie went with her for the midnight ferry to Dublin. It was a miserable night. The wind driving in from the river was raw and the rain spiteful and cold, stinging their cheeks.

'I wish you'd leave it until tomorrow, Maggie, it's going to be bad out beyond the Bar and on nights like this I can never get the *Ellan Vannin* out of my mind.'

'Carrie, that was five years ago and the weather was ten times worse than this. I've got to go now, there's no time to wait for the weather,' but she shuddered, remembering the Isle of Man mail steamer that had sunk with the loss of all hands.

'Go on then, girl, and take care.' Carrie hugged her,

praying her journey wouldn't be a waste of time.

As Maggie walked down the floating roadway towards the ferry she suddenly remembered the night she'd stood here in the fog and the gentleman who had given her a sixpence for a box of matches. It seemed a lifetime ago, years and years in the past. She'd had a family then. Mam and Da, Tommy. Well they'd all gone now, one way or another, even her child had been taken from her, and across the Irish Sea was a man whose love and support she had lost. Or had she?

'It's a disgrace, that's what it is! A disgrace!' Andy MacKinnon rattled the newspaper in annoyance.

'What is it now?' Florrie asked. The older Andy became, the more tetchy he seemed to be. 'Is there more fighting?'

'There will be in Ulster soon, but look at this. These infernal women!'

Florrie glanced over the article he'd been reading and sighed. The suffragettes again. This time two fine mansions had been burned to the ground. She didn't approve of course, but if no one would take them and their demands seriously, then what else was left for them to do? Secretly she did admire them and she believed that the young women should have rights. Not women of her age, they were settled, their lives half over. She had no complaints but young lassies were different. The world was changing and the future for the next generation looked far from rosy.

She thought of young Kirstie, Tommy's wife. What lay ahead for her and for Tommy for that matter. 'Aye, it's a disgrace, I'll give you that, she agreed, returning to her knitting. 'Andy, do you think there will be a war?'

He looked up. 'Aren't there wars going on everywhere now.'

'I mean a big one. Everyone is saying there will be, that the kaiser is getting too big for his boots with all those ships and soldiers.'

'Haven't we just launched the *Tiger*, the biggest battle cruiser in the world and hasn't Mr Asquith scorned the need for compulsory military service? Don't you go listening to the scaremongers, hen.'

'Don't treat me like a wain, Andy MacKinnon. I know what's going on, didn't Kirstie tell me it's all the talk in Craig's? She's worried about Tommy.'

'Tommy's nae fool, he won't be listening to the blatherin' of women.'

'Did they say they'd be over the night?' Florrie changed the subject.

'Aye.'

They relapsed into silence, Andy thinking of his conversation with Tommy. It was a conversation that centred on war and he was more worried than he would ever admit to Florrie. He was remembering another war and Mafeking. He knew the evils of war, he'd argued with Tommy. Tommy was of a different mind. In his quiet, serious way he had talked about duty and patriotism and the rights of small nations. Tommy had taken the place of the boy he'd lost in South Africa. He'd worked hard to get his position and he was well liked. He'd married Kirstie MacDonald, the first and only lassie he'd walked out with, the eldest daughter of the MacDonalds who lived at the end of the street. They had a small house a few streets away, but visited three or four times a week. If war came Tommy would volunteer and if anything happened to him Andy knew that neither he nor Florrie could stand the shock.

Florrie was thinking on the same lines as her husband. Kirstie had told her how they argued over the prospect of war. It was the only thing she and Tommy had ever disagreed on. They hadn't even had words over Kirstie keeping her job at Craig's tearooms. It would only be until there was a bairn on the way and they were saving up for that day. Florrie could see Kirstie's point and she sympathized with her. There was another matter they'd discussed, something she intended to speak to Tommy about tonight. With or without Andy's approval.

Only the crackling of the fire broke the silence in the warm, cosy kitchen until there came the awaited knock on the door.

'Come on in with you, 'tis a bitter night.' Florrie ushered them in, taking coats, hats and mufflers, while Andy pushed the kettle on the hob.

'Sit down and warm yourself, lassie.' Andy indicated the chair by the range.

Tommy smiled at his wife, thinking how pretty she was with her cheeks glowing from the cold night air. Her light brown hair was swept up in a roll like a halo around her head and her blue eyes softened as she looked at him. Her dress was plain, but the severity suited her and she'd never been one for frills.

Kirstie returned his smile. She was so lucky to have him for a husband. He was tall and well built, his hair a reddish brown, his eyes blue like her own. And if she had searched Glasgow she couldn't have found a more honest, hard-working and loving man. She couldn't envisage a life without him, which was why she prayed every night that there'd be no war.

'Florrie and me were just saying what a disgrace these women are.' Andy jabbed at the newspaper while Florrie and Kirstie exchanged glances.

'It's not right, all this violence, but can't you see it's got to come. We'll have the vote one day soon,' Kirstie said mildly.

'Aye, well, there'll be no arguing over that in this house, not tonight,' Florrie stated firmly.

Kirstie looked at her with surprise. Florrie wasn't usually so terse.

'And no talk of war either,' Kirstie added, not looking at Tommy. 'This is a social visit.'

Florrie poured the tea and when everyone had a cup she sat down. 'Well, it's something I want to talk about the night.'

Kirstie looked at her with hurt surprise. Tommy and Andy with mild amazement.

'There's all this talk, and let's hope that's all it amounts to – talk, but if not then . . . Well, Tommy, there's something you should do.' She held up her hand to silence Tommy.

'Andy and me know about separation, grief and loss. Part of me died at Mafeking and the worst part was that we'd had words, me and Billy. Och, only a wee bit of a row and over a lassie. It wasn't much but I never got the chance to tell him I was sorry.'

'I never knew that,' Tommy said quietly.

'No, I never told anyone.'

'What's all this leading up to, hen? I know you too well. I can read you like a book after forty years.'

Florrie smiled at her husband. 'It would be a poor thing if you could nae, Andy MacKinnon.' She turned to Tommy. 'Your sister, Maggie, Tommy. That's what I'm talking about.'

Tommy's face became set, his eyes hard. 'I don't want to talk about her.'

'You must, Tommy May! If war comes and you have to go, then you must go with no hatred in your heart. No anger or bitterness. You must go with a pure and forgiving heart.'

'No!'

'What harm would it do, Tommy, just to find her, to make your peace?' Florrie persisted.

'You know what she is!' Tommy was resentful.

Maggie had become just a faint and infrequent memory.

'I know what she is, she's your sister! She loved you, she cared for you. No matter what she's done you can't deny that. Tommy, she can't be that bad.'

Tommy looked down at his boots for he could sense that Kirstie was watching him and agreeing with Florrie.

'Tommy, lad, think on it. It may be too late soon.' Andy added his voice to the argument. 'It's too late when . . .'

Kirstie uttered a cry. 'No! Don't say it. Don't say that word!'

Florrie patted her shoulder. 'Hush now, hen. Please God it will never come to that. But it's wrong to let a wound fester, it should be washed so it will heal. Tommy, please, laddie, do this for me?'

Tommy shook his head. 'I . . . I don't know if I can. I'll have to think on it. It's too . . . painful, Florrie. She betrayed me.'

'And is she to be punished for ever, Tommy? "Forgive us our trespasses, as we forgive those who trespass against us." Remember the Lord's own words, Tommy, and we all have need of the Lord these days.'

'All right, I'll think on it,' Tommy answered, shaken by the vehemence of Florrie's pleading. It would need a great deal of thought. A great deal of soul-searching and forgiveness, but as she'd said, how could any of them hope for forgiveness if they gave none themselves.

Chapter Twenty-two

THE BITTER WIND WAS still blowing strongly off the sea and Maggie drew her coat tightly around her. The grey horizon merged with grey sea and the clouds scudded overhead, but the rain had stopped.

White-crested waves laved the shore and threw spray high into the air as they hit the rocks, the shingle they dislodged clattering as they ebbed. As Carrie had predicted, the crossing to Dublin had been rough and nearly everyone had been sick. Maggie had also been terrified, never having been on a ship in her life – not even the Mersey ferries. Somehow she'd got through it, sustained by relentless determination and desperation. She had been weak, tired and very thankful when she had arrived at the small boarding house in Killiney and had been able to wash and change her clothes.

The breakfast the landlady had provided had made her feel much better and she had written a short, pleading note, which had been taken by hand to the large house set back from the main road, perched above the sea overlooking Killiney Bay. But she hadn't been able to sit and wait under the scrutiny of the talkative and avidly curious Mrs Doyle, who'd informed her that her visit had come at a very bad time for Mr O'Shea.

'Would you be related then, to himself? Very distantly, is it?'

She'd looked at the woman blankly but she'd inclined her head. Let her think that, it might be for the best.

'Ah, shocking it is. Expected, but a shock just the same. Wasn't it a good thing he was home? Thanks be to God and the holy saints.' Mrs Doyle had crossed herself and Maggie had begun to wonder if the woman had lost her wits.

'Ah, now, there was a time when no one saw hide nor hair of him for months on end. Away he was. Oh, it was a fine thing to have such an important job but never to come home, now that was odd. Sure, he wasn't travelling around the world non-stop. But these last months he'd been home more regularly, she'd been failing and, well, the last month it had been downhill all the way, poor soul. And not a word of complaint out of her and how she must have suffered. Well, she's in heaven now. All that suffering would ensure it.'

Maggie thought she was rambling until she'd finally deduced that Breda O'Shea had been ill for a long time and had finally died. And Callan had never even told her of Breda's illness. With a feeling of utter dismay she learned that by the worst possible stroke of luck she'd arrived on the day of the funeral.

'But there was no wake, mind. Oh, he wouldn't hear of it.' Mrs Doyle had finished with a disapproving shake of her head.

The sand was firm beneath her feet and the wind tore at her clothes. She wondered if he could see her from the house. She wouldn't see him today, that much was obvious, if he would see her at all, and yet . . . now . . . a faint spark of hope flickered in her heart. He was a free man. She quelled it, he was a man who had just lost his wife in tragic circumstances. Would he be interested in finding his daughter, a child he had never even seen?

She couldn't stay on the beach all day, for the tide had turned and was coming in and the sky had become more ominously leaden. Slowly she retraced her steps, wondering how she was to face the avid curiosity and incessant chatter of Mrs Doyle for the rest of the day. She'd plead a headache, a legacy of her long and nauseous journey, and stay in her room.

She had drifted into a restless sleep when the rapping on the door wakened her. She sat up and peered sleepily into the gloom at the unfamiliar surroundings for the room was in darkness.

'Miss May! Miss May! Are you asleep in there?

There's a carriage come for you, and Paddy Power says he has to wait for you!'

Quickly she got up and grabbed her coat and hat.

There was no time to feel nervous or to plan what she was going to say, suddenly she was sitting in the darkness of the carriage and he was sitting opposite her.

'Drive on, Power!' he instructed sharply.

'And where shall I be driving to, sir?' the question was shouted back with unmistakable disapproval.

'The headland.' Callan sank back and studied her closely, noting the pale thinness of her face and the dark shadows of fatigue beneath her eyes. He wondered how she'd known about Breda's death. Or had she? he wondered tiredly. It had been a long day and a harrowing one. He and Breda had grown closer over the past months. She had never reproached him, never alluded to his long absences. The passion of the early days of their marriage had long gone and she'd built a life for herself, until her health had failed.

Maggie felt she could stand the silence no longer.

'I'm sorry about . . . your wife. You never told me she was ill.' She couldn't see his face with a great degree of clarity, yet he didn't seem to have changed. He was a little greyer around the temples, a little heavier in build, but that was only to be expected.

'How did you find out? Who told you?'

'No one and I didn't know until I arrived and Mrs Doyle told me. She thinks I'm a distant relative. It was the worst time I could have picked. I'm sorry. I really mean that.'

He leaned forward. 'How are you, Maggie? You look tired.'

'I am. It was a rough crossing and I was sick.' She was acutely aware of the driver and was loath to say anything about her reasons for coming.

He leaned back and the silence prevailed, broken only by the steady clip-clop of the horse's hooves on the road until she could hear the sound of the waves crashing against the rocks and the carriage gradually slowed down and stopped.

Callan stood up and helped her out. 'I'll walk back, Paddy. It's been a long day and I need some air.'

There was a grunt of disapproval and muttering about 'wild goose chases' from the driver before he clucked to the horse and it moved off slowly.

She stood facing into the wind, staring out into the darkness, suddenly afraid.

'So, why did you come, Maggie?' His question was spoken softly. He was cautious, she'd hurt him once, very badly, and he wasn't about to let it happen again.

'It's about Laura. I . . . I need your help, Callan.' Still she didn't look at him, she couldn't bring herself to turn her head and look into his eyes.

'You didn't need it before, Maggie, when you took the decision to give her away!'

He couldn't keep the bitterness from his voice. It pained him still, a deep physical pain, to even think about the child. His sons were grown men. Self-assured and independent, they didn't need him. If the truth be told they were like strangers, polite and pleasant strangers. Breda had brought them up. It had been to her that they'd turned for affection, guidance and companionship. All the things he should have given them. He couldn't blame them for the way they were, but Laura – his daughter – oh, he would have given her all the love he had and all the time in the world. Maggie's voice broke into his reverie.

'I want her back, Callan.'

'Ah, so now you've decided you want to be a mother. What about the stigma of her birth, Maggie, that so-important thing that had to be concealed, from everyone?' There was bitter mockery in his voice.

At last she turned to him, her eyes brimming with tears, the heartbreak tearing down the barrier of composure she'd tried to maintain. 'She's all I have in the world! You came back here, remember. You had . . . your wife, and your sons. I had no one. No one! I don't blame you, Callan, for leaving me. I was wrong, I was so very, very wrong, but at the time . . .'

'It seemed you picked your time fortuitously, Maggie. Now I'm a free man, I can give Laura my name, is that what you were thinking?'

'No! No! I didn't even know she was ill! Don't make me out to be heartless and calculating, because you know I'm not! I'm not!' All her resolve broke and she dissolved into tears. Hanging her head she sobbed quietly into her hands.

She looked so like the young girl he'd picked up from the street outside the Yankee Clipper that his heart softened and he reached out and gently drew her to him. He'd lost one woman who had once played an important part in his life, and what was the point in carrying on old quarrels? Life was too precious and death so sudden.

Instantly her arms went around his neck and she buried her face against his broad shoulder.

'Oh, Maggie! Maggie! I've missed you. I thought I'd never be able to think of you again without anger and bitterness.'

She raised her head. 'I need you, Callan, I need you so much! My life has had no meaning, no purpose!'

'What's wrong with Laura, what's brought you all this way?'

She clung to him and for the first time in weeks she felt sheer relief. 'I went to see Laura, before Christmas, and Philippa and I argued. She wouldn't let me visit Laura and Laura didn't seem happy there. Oh, Philippa's changed, Callan! All she seemed to think of was the money she'd spent on Laura. She doesn't love her! I know she doesn't, but she's taken her away, I don't know where to and I think she's doing it just to spite me!'

'Did she know you wanted her back?'

'Yes. Mr Compton wrote to her. She has no legal

right to Laura! I never gave her that right, I signed nothing!'

'So she's abducted . . . kidnapped her?'

'Yes. I went to fetch her. I couldn't wait for the law to sort it out and she'd gone. I should never have listened to Mr Compton. I wanted to go and get her that day, but he said it had to be done by the book.'

'And what has Compton done about it?'

'He's written to her solicitors, telling them what she's done, telling them to find out where she is. I couldn't wait, I didn't know what to do! She could have taken her anywhere, she has the money. I may never see her again.' Her face was wet with tears.

He held her tightly. Hadn't she suffered enough without this? And Laura, his precious child, where was she? Anger and grim determination welled up in him. 'No amount of money can make what she's done right, Maggie. We'll find her, if it takes years and I have to search every country on this earth, I'll find her! I swear I will!'

She sagged in his arms. Carrie had been right and now she knew that ever since she'd left Liverpool, those were the words she longed to hear.

'Have you eaten?'

'Hours ago. I've felt sick at the thought of meeting you, wondering if you'd even see me.'

He held her away from him. 'Look at you, Maggie. You're exhausted. I'll take you back to Mrs Doyle's. Damn! I wish I hadn't sent Power away.' He placed his arm firmly around her. 'Tomorrow I'll send Power down for you. You'll feel better, we both will. Then we can make plans.'

'Callan, I can't come to the house, not after . . .'

'Didn't you say Mrs Doyle thinks you're a distant relative? Then let them all think that and that you arrived too late.'

'But your sons will know.'

'They will both be in Dublin. They have work to go to. We can't talk at Mrs Doyle's nor anywhere public, there are too many gossips in this place. No, it must be the house.'

She'd slept deeply, for the first time in months an untroubled, peaceful sleep. Mrs Doyle had commented that it was very inhospitable of him not to have had her sleep there, after all wasn't it a great barn of a place with hundreds of bedrooms. This was an exaggeration as there were only five, but she seemed content with the explanation Maggie had given. That it was too late, she hadn't been expected and the room wasn't prepared and she was going there in the morning, before she returned to Dublin for the ferry back to Liverpool.

The morning was fine, cold but crisp. The wind had dropped and the rain clouds were far out on the horizon. Even the greenish-grey sea looked calmer, Maggie thought. Was it a good omen?

At close quarters the house reminded her of Philippa's home in Southport. The walls were covered in evergreen creepers, the windows were long, reaching almost to the floor but there were no steps, no grand entrance, just a white-painted door with a brass knocker.

Callan himself opened it before she had alighted from the carriage.

'You're welcome, cousin,' he said gravely, as he handed her down. The greeting was solely for the benefit of Paddy Power.

Maggie nodded as he ushered her inside, showing her into a small room that was obviously his study.

'Sit down, Maggie. Would you like some tea?'

'No. I don't want to trouble anyone.'

'It's no trouble.'

'No, please, nothing.'

He looked at the Waterford decanter, half-full of Jameson's. It was too early in the day for him, but he poured her a glass of Madeira wine. 'Drink this, you look so pale.' In the morning light he saw clearly the ravages of suffering in her face. He sat down on the leather chesterfield beside her and took her hand.

'I've been thinking . . . planning all night, Maggie, and there are a few matters here I have to attend to, but then I'll come back to Liverpool. I don't have to travel abroad again until the end of the month. I'll go and see Compton myself.'

'But, Callan, where do we start to look?' she asked bleakly.

'Philippa must have some relatives, no matter how distant. We'll start with them. And friends, Maggie, did she ever mention any friends? Think hard. What about all those suffragettes she mixed with?'

'Miss MacKenzie . . . Elizabeth MacKenzie is her close friend. She lives in Scotland, Glasgow I think, but I don't know exactly where.'

'Good, that's something else Compton can look into, there are lists at town halls and, despite his prejudices, he can contact the women's suffrage movement.' He smiled grimly. 'It won't be long, Maggie. I'll put a bomb under Compton if I have to.'

She felt so much better, stronger, more in control of herself. She'd been right to come. Right to trust him. Oh, why had she been such a fool, such a stubborn, dogmatic fool when Laura had been born?

'Have you never heard anything from your brother?' he asked suddenly.

She was surprised. 'No. Not a word in all this time. I don't know if he's still in Glasgow. I think about him sometimes, I try to picture how he looks. Is he like me or Mam or even Da? And I wonder is he married, has he children?'

'Ah, the older you become, Maggie, the more important family becomes,' he answered heavily.

'That's a fine statement coming from you.'

Startled, they both turned and Callan's expression became sober as he saw his youngest son standing in the doorway. He got to his feet. 'I always thought it polite to knock before entering a room, Sean. Besides, I thought you were back in Dublin.'

Sean moved forward into the room and Maggie's eyes were fixed on him for he was the very image of his father.

'Obviously, but we both decided it was too soon. Work would wait for another day. Paddy said we had a guest, a cousin.' His voice was cold, his stare hostile.

'Maggie is an old friend.'

'Is that the way of it? A friend. From Liverpool, perhaps?' He did not disguise the mockery in his voice. They'd all known he had a woman in Liverpool, even his mother had known but she had stubbornly refused to even admit she knew.

Callan was in no mood to pursue placatory measures, besides, with Sean they wouldn't work. He was not the type who could be appealed to, he was hot-headed and idealistic. Reason, explanation, worked with Richard but not Sean. 'Yes she's from Liverpool and yes I lived with her, not that it's any concern of yours.'

Sean gripped the neck of the decanter tightly, his eyes narrowing. 'Is that right? You've got a bloody neck! Bringing her here and my poor mother, God rest her, not cold in her grave!'

Maggie rose. She had no wish to be the cause of a scene, not now. Sean was right. She shouldn't have come to the house. 'I agree with you, but please don't blame your father. It's my fault. I didn't know when I arrived . . . about your . . . mother.'

'Don't you dare to even mention her, you slut!' Sean yelled.

The colour drained from Maggie's face, but Callan put his arm around her. 'One more word, Sean, and you'll leave this house – for ever! It's my house, remember that!'

'In the name of God, what's going on? The whole house can hear your yelling and bawling!' Richard O'Shea quickly took in the scene that met his eyes. His brother red-faced and furiously angry, his father cold yet just as furious and the tall, slim, beautiful woman with striking auburn hair and large amber-coloured eyes. He let out his breath slowly, feeling his own temper rise. So this was she, the woman who'd claimed his father's affections for so long. She had no right in this house, especially not now, this day. 'Was it necessary to bring her here?' he asked Callan, his voice clipped, his tone icy.

'Oh, he's told everyone she's family – a cousin! A bloody cousin!' Sean interrupted.

Callan ignored him. 'Yes, Richard, it was.' They both deserved an explanation and he would not have Maggie thought of as a slut, a common tart and she was so sensitive about her name.

Maggie made to speak but he silenced her with a quick gesture of his hand. 'No, Maggie, I'll say it, they both have to know.'

'Know! Know! We all "know" what's been going on for bloody years!' Sean cried.

Richard shot him a warning glance. Yelling would solve nothing.

'I left Maggie six months ago. I thought it was all over between us, there was a reason.'

'Isn't there always?' Sean jeered.

Callan rounded on him. 'One more word from you and I'll take my belt to you, big as you are!'

'Try it! Go on, Father, try it!' Sean was beside himself with rage and humiliation, but his father had turned to Richard.

'I'm not proud of my behaviour, towards either your mother or Maggie. Your mother was a good woman and I was fond of her, I respected her. But I won't have you condemning Maggie out of hand. She is good and kind, gentle and faithful. But I never felt for Breda what I feel for Maggie, that is the simple truth. Right or wrong I can't change it. Your mother knew, I think, but she was a proud woman.' He paused and Richard folded his arms over his chest and waited to hear the rest of his father's words. Sean could hardly contain himself.

'Maggie came here because she was desperate, she knew nothing of . . . of your mother's illness and . . . death. You see, she has lost someone very dear to her and had nowhere else to turn. And that someone is also very dear to me. You have a sister. A half-sister. She's five years old, and her name is Laura.'

Maggie closed her eyes and waited for the storm to erupt about her but there was only silence.

'Well, Sean, have you nothing to say to that? No insults, no cruel jibes about "my bastard"?'

Sean's face had turned an ugly shade of puce. 'You bitch! You bloody bitch!' he spat at Maggie, then, turning on his heel, he stalked from the room, slamming the door so hard that the glasses on the tray shook and rattled.

'Well, Richard, will you follow him?'

Richard O'Shea was controlling his anger with great difficulty. 'There is more, isn't there?'

Callan sighed heavily. 'Yes, there's more. To protect the child, Maggie gave her to a wealthy young woman she knew, Philippa Barton. I didn't even know I had a child until six months ago.'

'Which was when you began to come home to us more often?' Richard interrupted contemptuously.

'Yes. But now . . . now Maggie wants Laura back and so do I, but this woman has run off with her – God knows where to. I have to help to find her, Richard, she's my flesh and blood every bit as much as you and Sean. I don't expect you to understand. I'm just explaining why I have to go back to Liverpool.'

Richard unfolded his arms and walked to the door. 'No, I don't understand and maybe I never will, but you've always been your own man, Father! We were never consulted or considered. So why should you change the habits of a lifetime? I don't expect we'll see you again, will we?'

'I hope so, there's no need for us to be estranged, so to speak.'

Richard shook his head. 'Oh, there is, we buried the

reason yesterday. I wish you luck, Father. I hope you find the child and I hope you give her more time and affection than you ever gave to Sean and me.'

As the door closed Callan's hands fell to his side and his shoulders slumped. Maggie caught his hands. 'Oh, Callan, I'm sorry. I'm so sorry.'

'He's right, Maggie. I didn't play fair with them, either of them, and it hurts to hear it from his lips, but it's true, every word of it. I've lost them, but I'll not lose you or Laura.'

A week later, Callan faced Alfred Compton across the width of the desk. 'I want no shilly-shallying, no prevaricating, no dragging of feet over this, Compton. You let her slip through your fingers once.'

'Mr O'Shea, at that time I couldn't sanction Miss May to go and snatch the child.'

'But Philippa Barton could up stakes and run!'

'There was no way of knowing she would do that.'

'Well, she did, Compton, so let's not waste time arguing the legal niceties. I want my daughter found and quickly!'

'Miss Barton's solicitors are being very secretive.'

'To hell with them. Employ a solicitor in Glasgow to look up the rolls and find this Elizabeth MacKenzie, she's our strongest bet.'

'Advocates.'

'Pardon?'

'They are called advocates.'

Callan could have shaken the man, heedless of his age. What did it matter what they were called? No wonder the legal profession was so dilatory if it argued over every single word. 'Then find an advocate.'

'Certainly, but I must warn you that there are differences in Scottish law.'

'What does that mean?'

'It means just that. Mr O'Shea, believe me, I am as anxious as you are in this matter. Miss May has suffered more than any woman should ever have to, and what Miss Barton has done is cruel and very, very wrong. Please believe me I did everything possible.'

Callan relented a little. 'I'm sorry, Compton.'

'I realize it must have been a shock to find out about the child, and then there was the death of your wife.'

'Quite!'

'When do you leave?'

'Not for another week. Do you think there will be some progress by then?'

'It's hard to say but I do hope so.' Alfred Compton paused. 'You will still be away and Miss May will be alone, so I will keep her informed, try to keep her spirits up.'

'Thank you.'

'Things are looking bad in Europe. If war comes, what will you do?'

'They won't want me, Compton, I'm too old to be called up to fight.'

'Be thankful for that. I know how dreadful war is. I was seventeen when I went to the Crimea. There is nothing glorious about war, as I know only too well. I'm an old man now, I should be retired.'

'It's not a prospect I relish, but I'm hoping there may be some way I can help. If they blockade us, we'll starve.'

'The way the Southern States of America starved in their Civil War?'

'Exactly, but let's hope it won't come to that. The king, the kaiser and the tsar are first cousins, for God's sake, surely they can sit down as a family and sort it out?'

'Can you and your sons sit down and sort it out, Mr O'Shea?' Compton asked quietly.

'No. I see your point.' Callan rose and shook the old man's hand, feeling more out of sorts than he'd ever done before. War was for young men, not men like himself and Alfred Compton.

Chapter Twenty-three

KIRSTIE MAY GLANCED SURREPTITIOUSLY at her husband from beneath her lashes. She knew he was troubled and she knew what caused his restlessness, his moods. It was Maggie. There were times when she caught him smiling to himself, a rueful smile, and times when his eyes were bright with tears. She knew of the battle that was raging within him, the conflicting emotions, the pricking of conscience.

A coal fell from the fire on to the hearth and she bent to pick it up with the tongs and replace it. Then she sat back on her heels at Tommy's feet, her hand on his knee.

'A penny for them, Tom?'

He shook himself mentally. 'They're not worth it.'

'Oh, Tom, will you stop tearing yourself apart? Don't you think I canna see what's wrong? It's Maggie, and what Florrie said you must do.'

He took her hand. 'Kirstie, I don't know what to think or what to do.'

'I know that, Tom. But I think Florrie's right. Go and find her, make your peace with her.'

'What if . . . what if she's on the streets, Kirstie? That's what's been eating away at me. What if I find her with her face raddled with paint, in some alehouse on the Dock Road, touting for business?'

'Then you'll come home, Tom, and you'll have some peace. But what if she's not a hairy?'

Tommy's brows rushed together. 'I hate to hear that word from you, Kirstie.'

'Och, what does it matter what they're called? Go, for heaven's sake, Tom, for you'll not rest easy until you've seen her.'

Tommy got to his feet. 'I wish to God that Florrie had never mentioned her.'

Kirstie got up and placed her hands on his shoulder. 'You're a bonny lad and I love you dearly, but go! Go to Liverpool or we'll both end up in the asylum.' She reached up and kissed him.

He smiled slowly. 'All right, I can't hold out against you, Florrie and Andy. Maybe I'll be able to sleep at night now.'

'When will you go?'

'As soon as I can arrange it, but, Kirstie, where will I start?'

'Where you left her.'

'In Brick Street?' He shuddered at the memory.

'Even if she's not there, someone might know where she is.'

Tommy bent and kissed his wife's forehead. Please God, if she's on the streets then don't let me find her, he prayed, but he knew that if she were, finding her would present no problem. A walk down Canning Place or Lime Street would be enough and then there was her name. The name that had caused all the trouble.

Across the city in the almost rural district of Newton Mearns, Philippa Barton sat facing her dear friend Elizabeth MacKenzie. The curtains in the large villa were closed, shutting out the wind and the sleet that rattled against the windows. Across the room, near the blazing fire, Laura sat quietly looking at a picture book. She was confused and frightened. She couldn't understand why they'd had to leave their nice house. Hetty had told her it was for a little holiday. That Aunt Pippa wasn't very well. That must be why Aunt Pippa always seemed so cross with her.

Since she'd been in the hospital, Aunt Pippa had become more and more cross, that was when she saw her at all. It was Hetty who looked after her now. After Maggie had visited them, both Aunt Pippa and Hetty had seemed different and she'd heard them quarrelling too. She looked cautiously across the room. She didn't like Miss Elizabeth, Aunt Pippa's friend, for she knew Miss Elizabeth didn't like her. She seemed cross that

Aunt Pippa had brought her with her. She wished she could go home and that Miss May would come and visit her again. She'd liked Maggie. She'd brought her presents but Aunt Pippa had taken them away, telling her that Santa Claus would bring her things that were much nicer. But he hadn't. He'd brought her books and a slate and chalks and a needlework basket and silks. She couldn't play with them. Hetty had told her that only common little girls played with things like tops.

'It will only be a matter of time before *she* knows,' Elizabeth said, her voice lowered. 'Does she have a solicitor?' Elizabeth MacKenzie was small, plump and fair and she remembered the beautiful, distraught girl in Walton Jail, Laura's natural mother, but Philippa was her friend.

'Yes. Don't you remember I had a letter, he'll write to my solicitor and I think they will be bound to divulge . . .' Philippa looked quickly at the child who seemed absorbed in the book. 'She has the most infernal cheek! After everything I've done for . . . for "you know who".'

'Philippa, I did warn you to think deeply about this. I hate to say "I told you so" but well . . . it's a responsibility for life, isn't it?'

'If you're implying that I have just given up you're mistaken, Elizabeth! I won't give up, I won't give in to her! How dare she?'

'Keep your voice down!' Elizabeth hissed, glancing

towards Laura. This really had nothing to do with the child as such. Now it was just a battle of wills, at least for Philippa. She would have counselled giving the child back to Maggie, but she could see that would be useless. Philippa was as obstinate as a mule when she wanted to be. 'Well, let's give this some rational thought. Your solicitor won't divulge anything. It's client privilege, it's like the Catholic confessional.'

'I don't know, Elizabeth. Legally she's Laura's . . .' Her voice dropped to a mere whisper '. . . mother. She's not mine, legally. It was you who talked me out of adopting her, if you remember.'

Elizabeth did remember but she didn't regret it. If the worst came to the worst and Maggie got Laura back it wouldn't break Philippa's heart. She would get over it, in time she would be thankful she was rid of the responsibility. She knew her friend very well.

'I shouldn't have come here but I didn't know what to do. I won't give her up! I won't!'

'You won't have to, Philippa.'

'But she'll find out where we are, she's not a fool. She'll remember you, Elizabeth.'

'Does she have the address, the area even?'

'No.'

'Then it will be hard. Not impossible, but hard.'

'Just a matter of time, as you said. What am I to do?'

Elizabeth's round face furrowed as she put her mind to the problem. 'Have you absolutely no relations?'

'A distant cousin on my father's side. No one has heard from him for years and he must be quite old, he may even be dead.'

'Someone must know, surely? Your solicitor?'

'Yes, I suppose they would have some records. They've been the family solicitors for years and years.'

'Well, then, there you are. Have them trace him or his family.'

'Elizabeth, they live in New Jersey. In America.'

Elizabeth leaned back in her chair. 'Oh, I see. There's no one else?'

'No.'

'Then it's the only solution. I know it's so far away, a drastic step, but it may only be for a little while. If Maggie thinks you've left the country, she'll give up. She can't possibly afford to go following you, or paying people to follow you. She'll give up and then you can come back. Take a house here.'

Philippa was silent. It did seem to be the only solution but it was a strange country with a cold and hostile ocean between her and home.

'And it might be best, with all this talk of war. Not that I think anything will come of it. Men are always posturing and strutting. Vain, pompous little men, both the kaiser and the tsar. It won't amount to much but you may well be better off in New Jersey.'

It was another reason to leave, Philippa thought. 'But we'll need documents, passports, there may be a problem.'

'What problem? She's your cousin's child. Your cousin is dead, you have her birth certificate. You won't need a death certificate. It states she's illegitimate, Philippa. What are you worrying about? Write to your solicitor and trace this cousin or his family. In the meantime you can apply for documents.'

Philippa looked at the little girl and felt a pang of annoyance and regret, but she wasn't going to let Maggie best her. Maggie should be eternally grateful to her for taking the child and making her into a lady, for what was Maggie, anyway? An ignorant slum girl, a suspected felon; and the child's father, what kind of a man was he? An adulterer. Maggie was a fool to try to protect such a man. No, no one was going to throw her generosity back in her face. Maggie would never take Laura from her. Elizabeth was right, she had no choice but to take her away – far away. Then she would consider carefully the child's future. There were boarding schools even in America.

The spring sunlight slanted down through the glass-domed roof of Lime Street Station. It dappled the platform and picked out the dull brasswork on the great steam engine, now hissing slowly as though sighing with relief that the journey had ended, its work was done. Tommy made his way down the platform towards the barrier with the crowd. It didn't seem to have changed much, he thought as he stepped out into the bright sunshine and stood staring at St George's

Hall, its magnificent façade already begrimed, the huge lions looking down on the crowds in Lime Street.

He had thought he would feel a sense of belonging and nostalgia for his native city, but all he felt was apprehension. A fear of what lay ahead. Would he be glad or sorry he'd come before this day was over? He caught a tram to the Pierhead and, as it clanked along, he stared at the familiar streets and buildings, not with interest but impassively, his mind elsewhere. Would he even find her? It was a big city. What would she look like? The innocent memory he had of her was that of a young girl standing in the sunlight at the door of the cottage in Kirkby so many years ago. He'd closed his mind to all other memories, especially the one of the day he'd left.

She'd been happy in Kirkby but he'd hated it. If they had stayed he wondered how things would have turned out. She would never have taken up with that man, there would have been no rift between them, but he would never have realized his ambition. Never known Andy and Florrie and he'd never have married Kirstie.

''Ere, lad, are yer thinkin' of doin' a round trip?'

The conductor's bellicose question jolted him into reality. They had reached the terminus. He walked towards the landing stage and stood for a long time just gazing at the sun-dappled waters of the Mersey, watching the ferries and dredgers and tugs. Further out three liners were anchored in the Sloyne. A sailing barge, the *Lucy*, was being towed towards the Albert Dock for there was no wind to speak of.

Now the memories came flooding back. The cold winter evenings when he'd stood here, barefoot and in rags, trying to earn a few coppers by carrying luggage and parcels, and later, selling matches, kindling and papers. The long hot summer days when he and the other street arabs had sneaked aboard a ferry for a free ride, hiding from the deck hands. Clinging precariously to the back of a tram, seeing how far they could ride before they were discovered. The games played on the dirty cobbles and amidst the debris of the gutters. Ollies, cherrywobs and grid fishing. Grid fishing was sometimes profitable for people often accidentally dropped coins down the grids and fishing them out with a bit of bent wire and an equally bent spoon, had often provided them with money for food.

His favourite game had been flattie throwing. Hurling your cap beneath the moving vehicles to the other side of the street. It often resulted in the loss of the cap, and a belt around the ear from Da was the consequence. He smiled wryly, knowing he was only remembering the rosy side of things, the happy memories. The time for games had been very scarce. It had been too much of an effort to keep body and soul together to find time and energy for leisure activities.

He turned away and began to walk down towards

Canning Place. The docks were busy and he savoured the sights, sounds and smells, the hustle and bustle of a working port that dealt with hundreds of ships every day.

The buildings became more closely packed, more dilapidated, the streets and alleys more noisome and filthy, and he shuddered. It was even worse than he remembered it. There were no pleasant, rose-coloured memories of Bowers Court. Somehow he'd imagined that the festering courts would have been cleared but they survived, slowly degenerating into even worse slums.

Like the rest, Brick Street looked dirty and depressing and he stood looking at the house for some minutes, very tempted to turn and retrace his steps to the station, but what would be the point in that? He pushed open the door and climbed the narrow, stinking stairs to the room where they had once lived.

A thickset man, clad in his trousers and a dirty singlet, his face covered in dark stubble, opened the door.

'Does Maggie May still live here?' Tommy asked flatly.

The man's eyes narrowed. 'Are yer some kind of bloody comedian?'

'No. It's her name, she's my sister.'

'Well, she ain't 'ere. I've never 'eard of anyone called that, except 'er in the song, now bugger off!'

'Does Ma Nevitt still live upstairs?' Tommy

shouted as the door closed. He thought he heard an answering grunt and he began to climb the final flight.

Ma Nevitt answered his knock.

She hadn't changed much, Tommy thought. Grown a bit stouter that was all.

'What do yer want?' she asked suspiciously.

'I'm looking for someone, my sister.'

'Oh, aye. What's 'er name then?'

'Maggie. Maggie May, she used to live downstairs.'

Ma Nevitt vaguely remembered Tommy. He wasn't doing too badly she thought, eyeing up his clothes and noting the slight trace of an accent she hadn't heard before, at least not in Brick Street. 'She hasn't lived 'ere for years. I never saw 'er after the scuffers took her away. I heard she went to jail, some posh legal feller came 'ere an' got her stuff moved out.'

Tommy's heart dropped like a stone and his stomach felt awash with ice water. Jail! Jail! It was worse than he had imagined. 'What . . . what did she do?' he managed to get out.

'Oh, causing trouble. Breaking windows, something about rioting. I can't remember.'

Tommy couldn't believe it. Maggie breaking windows? 'Can you remember what the legal bloke's name was?'

Ma Nevitt wasn't a woman to pass up the chance of easy money. 'Me memory gets better when there's a few coppers in me hand,' she whined.

Tommy was tempted to tell her to go to hell, but

he'd come this far and now he found himself wondering about Maggie. He placed a silver threepenny bit in her fat, grubby hand.

'Compton, his name was. Compton, from Compton, Sykes and Radnage in some posh office, I can't remember where. He threatened me, he did, and me an' owld woman. Said if I touched anything of hers he'd have the scuffers on me.'

Tommy looked confused. Why should a solicitor come here on Maggie's behalf and take away her things? He turned away. He'd have to take a tram up to Dale Street and ask someone for the office.

It was nearly three o'clock when he finally found the place. At first the clerk was very officious. No appointment? Well, Mr Compton couldn't see him then. People just couldn't walk in off the street as though it were a public house.

'Will you just go and give him my name and tell him I've come about my sister. I've come all the way from Glasgow so I'm not going back until I've seen him.'

The clerk glared at him but disappeared along a corridor. Tommy looked around. The place was dark, dusty, cluttered and it smelled musty.

It wasn't the arrogant little clerk who came out to see him but an old man, white haired and a little stooped, his clothes those of another age. He was smiling.

'So, you are Tommy May!' He held out his hand

and Tommy shook it, surprised by the firmness of the grip.

Tommy decided to be direct. 'I've come to see if you know where I can find my sister, Maggie?'

'Come through, your visit couldn't have come at a better time for your sister.'

Again Tommy wondered why a solicitor was so interested in Maggie. He knew her well, that was obvious.

He sat in the chair Alfred Compton indicated.

'I am Miss May's solicitor and I have been since that terrible unjust charge was brought against her. I have her address but I have to ask the nature of your business? I must protect my client first and foremost, Mr May. You do understand that?'

Tommy nodded, now totally mystified. 'What's this "unjust charge" business? That old hag, Ma Nevitt, said Maggie had been to jail. Look, I've come to . . . well . . . to make it up with her. We fell out years ago.'

Alfred Compton smiled thankfully. Now more than ever Maggie needed the support of family. 'I'll let Miss May tell you herself of all she's been through. It's not my place to enlighten you, but I would impress upon you, Mr May, that she has suffered greatly and is still suffering. She lives in Walton Village. Number ten, Elm Road.'

Tommy stood up. Walton Village, that was a very respectable area. All his fears melted away. She couldn't have been on the streets to have ended up there and what was all this suffering that Mr Compton was talking about? Suddenly he felt very guilty as he thanked the old man.

Alfred Compton watched him leave with a smile and heartfelt relief. He looked a fine young man and he'd obviously done well for himself. His clothes were good, not expensive or flashy, but good. He spoke well, the Liverpool accent slight, diminished by the Gaelic inflections in his speech.

The more Tommy thought about Maggie the more confused he became. Each footstep seemed to echo down the quiet street. He was certain he saw curtains twitching but he looked straight ahead, his heart pounding in rhythm with his feet. What would he say to her? What would she say? How would she look? Would she turn him away?

By the time he reached number ten, beads of sweat stood out on his forehead and his hand shook as he lifted the knocker. And then she was there, standing before him. No painted face, no gaudy finery, just the Maggie he had always loved.

Maggie just stood and stared, unable to believe her eyes. It couldn't be! It just couldn't be, not after all this time! Then with a cry she flung her arms around him. 'Tommy! Oh, Tommy, is it really you?' Tears were streaming down her cheeks and soaking into his jacket.

Tommy buried his head in her hair, his face working, the lump in his throat so big he couldn't speak. How could he ever have thought he'd find her walking the streets of Liverpool like her namesake?

She pulled him inside and stood back, drinking in the sight of him, her hand against his cheek.

'Tommy, you're grown up! Oh, you look great, you really do.'

Tommy found his voice. 'Maggie! Maggie, you're . . . beautiful, do you know that?'

She laughed. 'You daft ha'peth, Tommy May! I was never beautiful. Oh, Tommy, I've missed you so much, come on in and tell me everything! Everything!'

The hours passed and the light faded as they talked, catching up on the lost years. Tommy listened with horror to the story of her trial and imprisonment; her love and devotion for Callan O'Shea and the child she had borne and given away; the quarrel with Callan; Philippa's flight and the anguish she now lived with, despite the fact that Callan had returned to her.

Maggie learned from Tommy of his deep affection for the MacKinnons, that he had a good job and a nice home and that she had a sister-in-law. He told her that it had been Florrie and Kirstie who had persuaded him to come to find her and to patch up the old quarrel.

At last as darkness fell they were both silent and she sat with her head on his shoulder, feeling more tranquil than she had been for many weeks.

'When do you think Mr Compton will find out about this Miss MacKenzie?'

'I don't know.'

Tommy was still struggling to come to terms with

the fact that he had a niece. 'Maybe I can help. If he could just find out the district, I could go and ask people.'

She looked up at him eagerly. 'Would you? Would you really do that, Tommy?'

'Of course, Maggie, from now on you can rely on me to help you.'

'Tommy, you'll never know how glad I am you came now. This feeling of helplessness and loneliness is terrible when Callan is away and he won't be back for another ten days. He didn't want to go. I have been so low and he said he wanted to be here, but he couldn't stay. I know you'll like him, Tommy. He's a good man. He's just as miserable about Laura as I am.'

'Do you think he'll marry you, Maggie?'

'It's something we've never spoken of. His wife hasn't been dead long.'

Tommy said nothing. He had more than enough to cope with at this moment in time. He needed time to think, sort things out in his mind, to get used to everything before he met the man that Maggie loved, but who it seemed to him had played a big part in the tragedies in her life. 'I always remembered you standing in the doorway of the cottage, Maggie, with the sun on your hair, do you remember?'

She smiled. 'You hated it there, Tommy, didn't you? You weren't cut out for that kind of life. The only bit of excitement was that fair.'

'And look where that got us, Maggie. Many's the

time I've thought of that lad, Dinny, and wished I'd never set eyes on him.'

A memory came suddenly into her mind. The memory of Dinny's mother. 'His mother came to warn me,' she said, 'the night he stole the money. "Beware of a man connected with distant lands, he'll bring you grief", that's what she said.'

'In a way she was right, Maggie. If you had never met him things would have been so very different.'

'I'd have starved Tommy, or maybe even worse, I'd have been forced to live up to my name.'

'No, you wouldn't. I'd have been home and we would have gone to Glasgow.'

'It wasn't to be, Tommy. It wasn't our destiny.' A silence fell between them again, but a silence not of regret or remorse but of compassion, understanding and love.

Tommy could only stay for two days and on the day before he was due to leave, a message arrived by telegram from Mr Compton, giving the address of Miss Elizabeth MacKenzie.

'He's found her! He's found her, Tommy!'

Maggie's hands were shaking as Tommy took the telegram from her and read it.

'I know where this is, Maggie. Come back with me and we'll go and see her together.'

'Tommy, I'm afraid. Afraid of what will happen when we get there.'

He caught her by the shoulders and looked down

into her eyes. 'Maggie, you've always been a fighter, you wouldn't have survived otherwise. We'll go and get Laura. We'll just go and take her and to hell with all the legal stuff.'

'Oh, I wish Callan were here.'

'Well, you'll just have to make do with me, Maggie.'

She hugged him. 'I love you just as much, but in a different way, of course.'

'Then get your things together, in a day or so it will all be over and we'll be together again. A family.'

'Yes, a family, Tommy. A real family. You, Kirstie, Callan and me and Laura.'

Chapter Twenty-four

KIRSTIE MAY SMILED WITH relief when Tommy arrived home. She was pleasantly surprised when Tommy gently drew Maggie into the room. Kirstie had not expected her sister-in-law to be quite so strikingly lovely. She was tall, nearly as tall as Tommy, and, beneath her wide-brimmed cream hat, her thick auburn hair framed her pale, oval face. But Maggie's large amber-coloured eyes were what held Kirstie's gaze. Eyes that were misty with tears.

'This is Maggie, Kirstie. I brought her home with me and tomorrow we're going to Newton Mearns to bring back Maggie's little girl, Laura. Our niece.'

Maggie hung back shyly. The only thing she knew about this girl was that Tommy loved her. This was Kirstie's house and she felt defensive. Her sister-in-law was pretty in a plump, dimpled way. Her light brown hair was taken up neatly in a roll, but a few tendrils had escaped and curled on her forehead. Her blue eyes were wide and shining and to Maggie she radiated openness and simplicity. Her lips were parted in a smile and there was warmth in her eyes.

She reached out and took Maggie's hand. 'Maggie, I'm glad you've come. You don't know how happy I am to see you. I've prayed and prayed that he'd find you and that you'd both forget all about the past.'

The tenseness dropped from Maggie and she smiled. 'It's you I have to thank for making it all possible.'

'Och, no. It was all Florrie's idea. I just helped a wee bit. Florrie lost her son at Mafeking and with all this warmongering, well, let bygones be bygones, we told him.' Kirstie turned to her husband. 'Tom, when you've had a bite to eat, go over to see Andy and Florrie and tell them the good news. Give Maggie and me time to get better acquainted and she must be tired, too.'

'I am, it's a very long journey,' Maggie answered, remembering how Tommy had taken weeks to get here the first time, walking and begging rides.

After supper Tommy left to visit the MacKinnons and Kirstie ushered Maggie upstairs to the small bedroom with the narrow bed covered with a plain white counterpane. The other furnishings were a simple washstand, a small wardrobe and a narrow chest.

'It's lovely, Kirstie,' Maggie said truthfully. The whole house was spotlessly clean and Kirstie was a good cook, too. A far better one than she was herself.

'Can I ask you why Laura is here in Glasgow?' Kirstie asked, rearranging the jug and bowl on the washstand.

Maggie sat down on the bed and told her the whole story.

When she'd finished, Kirstie looked anxious. 'Will she be all right in here with you? I've no more rooms or furniture and if she's been used to a grand house, well . . .'

'Of course she will,' Maggie interrupted.

'Ah, the poor wain will be confused and upset.'

Maggie agreed. 'It upsets me the thought of taking her away from Philippa, but I'll try and explain it all to her. Oh, I just hope there won't be any really ugly scenes.'

'Well, they will only be of her making. She's the one who is in the wrong, not you. Running off like that, dragging the poor wain all over the country. What kind of a woman is she?'

'A rich, spoiled and determined one,' Maggie answered sadly.

Kirstie went with them to Newton Mearns. She felt she had to, that Maggie needed some feminine support. She knew Maggie had been awake all night. She'd heard her pacing the small bedroom for hours and this morning she looked pale and drawn.

'It'll be all right, Maggie, dinna fret. Tom and me

are with you.' Kirstie gripped Maggie's hand tightly as Tommy rang the doorbell.

It was answered by a young girl in a cap and apron who stared at them with annoyance. 'What is it ye want? I canna get on with me work for all this runnin' tae the door!'

It was Maggie who spoke, her voice sharp for her throat had suddenly constricted. 'We want to see Miss MacKenzie, please.'

'Who shall I say ye are?'

'Maggie O'Shea.'

'An' are they kin?' she nodded in the direction of Tommy and Kirstie.

'Aye, we are.' Tommy answered.

'Step in then an' stay there. Dinna go trampin' all over me clean floor.'

'Well, that's no' polite, now is it!' Kirstie commented acidly.

They waited in the hall until the girl came back looking pained. 'She says I've tae take ye through.'

They followed her into a large drawing room and Tommy and Kirstie stood a few paces behind Maggie, Kirstie's sharp eyes noting the signs of wealth.

Tommy was trying to form an opinion of the woman who sat, stiff and upright, at a small writing desk.

Elizabeth MacKenzie was in her mid-thirties, middle-aged by the standards of her day. Her fair hair was drawn up into an elaborate coiffure and she had fine clear grey eyes. The white lawn blouse with its tucks and ruffles didn't suit her, it was too fussy for a woman of her age and build, Tommy thought. She was plump and even though she was seated, it was obvious that she was of short stature. One small white hand rested in her lap, the other held a pen. They were hands that had never seen a day's work, he thought.

Elizabeth indicated that they should sit down but Maggie shook her head, summoning all her courage. 'This isn't a social call, Miss MacKenzie. I want to know if Philippa is here with Laura? I think you already know that Philippa has run off with my child.'

Elizabeth stared at Maggie, thinking that if she had been possessed of such beauty there would have been a legion of suitors beating their way to her door. Maggie had changed from a thin, bowed and demoralized girl. She was a woman now and filled with determination. It radiated from her and shone in those large lustrous eyes.

'I seem to remember that you were most anxious, not to say insistent, that Philippa take her. And it is Philippa who has cared for her all these years, nor can you deny that the child has wanted for anything.'

'I'm not here to argue the rights and wrongs of the past. Circumstances have changed. Her father and I want her back. I have the law on my side, Philippa doesn't and you both know that.'

Elizabeth stood up, closing the lid of the desk very

carefully. 'She's not here. Neither of them are here.'

'You're lying!' Maggie's voice rose and cracked with emotion.

'I never lie!' came the icy reply. She had been in the middle of writing to Philippa.

'Then where is she, you of all people must know?' Tommy asked bluntly. He didn't like Elizabeth MacKenzie. She was too sure of herself, too arrogant and condescending.

Kirstie slipped her arm around Maggie's waist. She, too, didn't like the older woman and she was certain that she was hiding something in that desk.

'They have gone to stay with relatives,' Elizabeth said coldly. How dare they insult her in her own home! Interrogate her as though she were a common criminal!

'Where?' Tommy demanded.

'In America. They sailed from Greenock last week.'

Kirstie's grip tightened as she felt Maggie sway and heard the strangled sob in her throat.

Maggie was unable to speak. It was as though Elizabeth MacKenzie had just announced the end of the world.

'Where in America? Laura is my niece and I have a right to know. We all have a right to know,' Tommy demanded, becoming angry.

'Somewhere in New England. I don't know exactly where. Philippa said she would write when they were settled,' Elizabeth lied.

'You do know. You're hiding something in that desk!' Kirstie cried.

'Indeed I do not and what is in my desk is my affair!'

'You let them go, knowing she'd taken Laura against Maggie's wishes, against the law.' Tommy's voice was harsh.

'The child is better off with Philippa. You would destroy her life by dragging her back to Liverpool.' Elizabeth was furious that Philippa had placed her in this position. She should have told Philippa that she washed her hands of the whole affair. 'I would have thought you could have put the child's welfare before your own selfish feelings.'

Maggie was so devastated that she still couldn't speak, she just clung to Kirstie.

Tommy was furious at the slur cast on Maggie.

'You cold, dried-up old maid! What would you know about Maggie's feelings, a mother's feelings, something you'll never be! She didn't give Laura away without thinking hard about it! Well, this isn't the end. Oh, no! We'll see what the police have to say about your part in this, *Miss* MacKenzie!'

Elizabeth was white with anger and humiliation. 'Get out of my house, all of you, before I call the police myself! Get out and don't you dare to come here again or threaten me! A fine life that child would have with you . . . you low, common . . . individuals! Get out of my house!'

* * *

'Well, wasn't she a bitch! She canna talk to people like that, Tom! We'll go to the police!' Kirstie's cheeks were flushed and her eyes flashed with a rare show of temper.

'People like us don't go to the scuffers, the police,' Tommy amended. 'They won't even listen.'

'But they'll have to!' Kirstie argued. She'd never felt so angry in all her life.

'They won't, luv, they're more likely to listen to her! Money talks and besides, what can they do? She's done nothing wrong,' Tommy said bitterly.

'She's been aiding and abetting, that's what she's done, Tom May!'

'Kirstie, he's right. They won't listen to us. Let's go . . . let's just go home, please?' Maggie choked. She just wanted to be alone to cry out her hurt and terrible disappointment.

'When is Callan home, Maggie?' Tommy asked.

'Next week.'

'He sails to America, doesn't he?'

'Yes, but he never has much time there and we don't know where she is. We don't even know how big a place New England is, do we?'

'Callan will know, Maggie. It's not the end. You can't give up, you've got to go on believing you'll find her!' Tommy urged, for Maggie looked so stunned that he was afraid that this further setback would destroy her sanity.

She hardly slept that night. America! Oh, it was so

far away. Laura! Laura! She sobbed into the pillow, afraid to wake Tommy and Kirstie. She thanked God for them both. They'd tried their best to help her. She was thankful that the years of silence between them had not irreparably damaged the deep affection they had for each other. And Kirstie, she couldn't wish for a sweeter, kinder sister-in-law, but everything had been in vain. She'd fallen into a restless, shallow sleep as dawn crept into the room.

She'd clung to Tommy before he'd left for work, for Kirstie was going with her to the station.

'Come and see us soon, Maggie, promise?'

'I will, Tommy. And . . . and I'll write when Callan gets home.' She'd hugged him wishing he were going home with her. Then she'd realized that this was his home now.

At the barrier Kirstie took her hands. 'I'm sorry it's all been for nothing, Maggie. I really mean that.'

'No, it's not been wasted, you've been so kind and good to me, Kirstie, and the one thing that stands out in this terrible mess, is that you and Tommy are so happy and that means so much to me.'

'Think about what Tom said, Maggie. Dinna give up hope, you'll get her back.'

A great outrush of steam and a deafening whistle from the engine drowned out Maggie's reply and the two women hugged each other before Maggie walked down the platform, leaving Kirstie May's cheeks wet with tears.

When Carrie and Harriet both heard from a still-distraught Maggie what had happened, both were outraged.

'Self! Self! Self! That's all that woman thinks about. To take the little one all that way! Well, it's just wicked, downright wicked!' Carrie raged.

'Just wait until Mr O'Shea gets home, Maggie. He'll know what to do,' Harriet said grimly.

The days had dragged by and April was nearly over. Across the English Channel the rumblings of war grew louder, but Maggie cared little for politics. She stood at the window in the parlour watching the sparrows and starlings as they flitted from roof to roof and envied them their carefree existence. Her heart was so heavy. Was she doomed never to see her child again? What if Callan could think of nothing, where would all her dreams and hopes be then? And why was he so long in coming? She prayed he hadn't been delayed.

At last she saw him walking quickly down the road and she flew to the door and wrenched it open. His pace quickened and then she was in his arms.

'Maggie, I got your letter. Have you been to see Elizabeth MacKenzie?'

'Yes, I went with Tommy. Oh, Callan, I was so sure, so absolutely certain that it was all over . . . that I'd have her back, that we'd both be waiting here for you.' She swallowed hard but she couldn't go on. She drew him into the hall and closed the door.

As soon as he'd seen her face he'd known something was wrong. 'What happened, Maggie?'

'She . . . she's taken her to America. To New England. They . . . they sailed from Greenock.'

He drew her to him. Her grief was almost tangible and it seemed to pass from her body into his own. 'Maggie, come and tell me what happened?' he said gently, leading her into the parlour. He sat on the sofa and held her to him, stroking her hair, sharing her pain.

'We've lost her, Callan. America is such a big place, what can we do?'

'We can check every passenger manifest, every purser's list, that's what we can do! And when we find out which ship they took we'll find out where they've gone for they will have addresses. They have people over there, Maggie. Investigators for the Pinkerton Agency who will track them down.'

She looked up at him.

'Maggie, we'll get her back, I promise you! When they find her, we'll go there. We'll both go and bring her home and we'll take proof, legal proof that she's ours!'

Maggie's eyes lost their glaze of despair. What a fool she'd been to have almost given up. She should have known he would have a solution. He wasn't an ignorant product of the slums as she was.

'This has all been too much for you to bear alone, Maggie. I'm going to take you with me this time. You need a rest. I'm only going to France, but a few days away will do you good. We'll look on it as a honeymoon.'

She stared at him blankly.

'Are you turning me down, Maggie?' A smile hovered around his lips.

'Callan, do you mean . . .?'

'I do. That's what I meant about legal proof. Our marriage lines. We're her parents and we'll be married. Just let Philippa Barton try and find a way around that!'

There was no need for words, her heart was too full.

The memory of those glorious days in May 1914 were to stay with Maggie for the rest of her life. The beginning of summer, the last summer of peace. The end of the world as she and so many thousands of others had known it.

They'd been married by special licence at Brougham Terrace, with Carrie and Alfred Compton as witnesses. She had been saddened that Tommy and Kirstie had not been able to come to Liverpool, but Tommy had written and Kirstie sent her a small porcelain trinket box with a Highland scene painted on the lid. Not an expensive gfit, but one Maggie treasured.

She'd been treated with great deference by everyone. She was now Mrs O'Shea in reality, a fact that she still couldn't believe was true. She, the once scrawny and often barefoot waif from the slums of Liverpool, daughter of a drunken jailbird, with the name of a whore, was now waited on hand and foot and treated with respect. She slept between crisp cotton sheets, her clothes were of fashionable linen, crêpe and corded bombazine, her underclothes of soft embroidered lawn. She spent those halcyon days reading or just watching the sea. The evenings she spent with Callan and if she could have had her child at her side she would have been the happiest woman on earth.

The rest, the change of air, had done her good, Carrie and Harriet had agreed when she'd returned, her cheeks pink, her skin glowing. But the long, warm days brought no real sense of progress and as the summer dragged on, war fever gripped the nation. On a hot day in June, in a country Maggie had never heard of – Bosnia – the Archduke Franz Ferdinand was assassinated. Nor did she understand the political ramifications. She was unaware that the lines were being drawn, the armies were assembling from the Baltic Sea to the Adriatic and the English Channel.

Through Callan's influence they had found out that Philippa had sailed on the *Clan MacGregor* and the address she had given was not in New England as Elizabeth MacKenzie had told them, but in New Jersey.

Callan had contacted the Pinkerton Agency in New

York and the search had begun, but it was taking so long, Maggie thought.

On the 5th August she could no longer ignore the events of the world. The possibility had become fact. Great Britain and her Empire had declared war on Germany and the Austro-Hungarian Empire.

Crowds thronged the streets in all the major cities. Cheering, roistering crowds of men and boys, all eager to join up to fight the Hun. To experience the excitement and the glory for it would only last until Christmas, everyone knew that, and no one wanted to miss it.

There was no rejoicing in the house in Elm Road. The three women sat quietly in the parlour. Maggie was afraid for Tommy, not knowing whether he would be called up to fight. Carrie was thinking of her two sons. Harry in America would be safe enough, but what of young Georgie as she always thought of him? Australia was part of the Empire. Would Australian men be called to fight in this war on the other side of their world? Harriet was remembering a young man in uniform, standing proudly stiff and formal for the photograph that she kept in a small case in her bag. A photograph no one had ever seen of the young man she had loved and who had died beneath the blazing sun of the Transvaal, half a world away.

Two days later came the letter from Ireland. It was from Callan's solicitor, informing him that Richard and Sean O'Shea had joined the British army.

Chapter Twenty-five

THE SNOW WAS FINALLY melting, Philippa thought thankfully as she looked out of the window and across the back yard, where patches of dull green grass were now showing through the thin layer of snow. She'd been here almost a year and she had still not come to terms with the American way of life. Yard. That word in itself summed up the differences. At home, in England, it was called a garden. A yard was a paved area, usually at the back of business premises or small terraced houses. It was an incongruous word for a garden. Gardens here were public parks or large formal stretches of greenery. When they weren't covered with snow and ice.

She had never been so cold in her entire life these past four months, despite the heated pipes and radiators that were standard fitments in all the rooms. Wilma and Edgar had been amazed to learn that English houses were heated only by means of open coal or log fires. They looked at each other, eyebrows raised and Wilma had said, 'Is that a fact, Philly?' She hated Wilma's accent, more pronounced than Edgar's. New Jersey she pronounced 'Noo Joysey' and many other words of what was loosely called the 'English' language received the same enunciation. She hated being called 'Philly' it made her sound like a horse. No, she wasn't happy here.

At first she'd enthusiastically told Hetty that they would get used to things. It was a different way of life and they had different attitudes and values; she had meant it, at the time, but the enthusiasm had faded. The feeling of impatience and annoyance had not diminished, instead it had increased. Maybe the fault lay within herself. Was she set in her ways, a middle-aged spinster?

She had finally admitted to herself a few weeks ago that she was homesick and that she'd never get used to living here. She leaned against the radiator and watched as Alvin, the boy her second cousin Edgar employed to help around the place, began to brush the now greyish slushy snow from the path that led down to the end of the yard.

Winter hung on with grim determination here, she thought. At home, the daffodils and crocuses would be starting to bloom and the snowdrops would already be drooping their heads. She searched her memory for the line of a poem.

'Oh, to be in England now that April's here.'

There were two more weeks to April, but the mere thought of an English spring brought tears to her eyes. Eyes now jaded by this North American landscape.

It had been a lovely spring morning when they'd sailed up the Hudson River. They'd stood on deck and watched as the ship had passed beneath the Verrazano Narrows Bridge and the Statue of Liberty had become larger, an impressive sight. The mist swirling around its base had made it appear as though the statue was rising from the waters of the river.

Most of the passengers had been taken off at Ellis Island, to be processed like cattle by the immigration department. The steerage passengers far outnumbered those in first class. Then they'd sailed on and she, Hetty and Laura had been completely overawed as the skyscrapers of lower Manhattan had emerged from the mist.

Edgar and Wilma had been waiting at Pier 19. Middle-aged and rather overweight, both of them, but they'd welcomed them warmly enough. There had been a bit of a delay with the luggage and Edgar had remarked that she'd put the wrong address on the labels. They'd moved from their old place ten years ago. She'd pleaded a lapse of memory with the flurry of activity of packing up. In reality it had been done deliberately at Elizabeth's suggestion, a final precaution against Maggie's determination. Edgar Barton's 'new' place was twenty miles from his 'old' one.

They'd driven north through Manhattan and she'd

noted how the streets were set out in grid-like squares, quite unlike anything she'd ever seen before and that the buildings were so tall that the streets appeared dark and narrow to eyes that were used to wide, airy and open neighbourhoods. And the traffic! Hetty had exclaimed that she was absolutely terrified, and swore that she would never cross a road. It was taking your life in your hands, but Laura had appeared to enjoy it. But now she was not sure that Laura had really settled here. The children she played with were very precocious and boisterous.

Once across the George Washington Bridge they had left the tall buildings behind and the scenery became more rural as they drove through New Jersey.

Edgar and Wilma had kept up a continuous commentary throughout the journey and had extolled the virtues of Atlantic City, which apparently was a seaside resort, until they had finally arrived at the house.

Philippa's sombre reverie was broken by Hetty's entry into the room and she turned away from the window with some relief.

'Well, at last it's finally started to thaw,' Hetty said grumpily, her arms full of clean bed linen.

'Yes, I thought spring would never come,' Philippa answered, beginning to tidy the top of her bureau. 'Is there any news from home, Hetty?'

'No, miss. Except that the German blockade is starting to bite, according to the newspaper. It seems as though there is still a stalemate on the Western Front but there's some speculation that there will be a spring offensive.' Hetty began to strip the bed.

Philippa bit her lip worriedly. That had been the worst part of being here in America. The news was so late and not as detailed as she would have wished it to be. Her country was at war, a war which now looked as though it would drag on and on and neither Wilma nor Edgar seemed to understand how important it was to her. Paris and even London had been bombed, something utterly unimaginable. Towns like Scarborough and Whitby, pleasant little holiday resorts, had been shelled by German warships. At Ypres there had been 100,000 casualties, but when she had read aloud that appalling figure, Edgar had announced firmly that it was a European war and if Europe wanted to tear itself apart, it was no concern of America's. She'd had to bite her tongue to stop herself from screaming at him. When she'd heard that ex-President Roosevelt had criticized America for 'tame and spiritless neutrality' she had repeated his words with great satisfaction.

'But, Philly, we're providing billions of dollars to help!' Wilma had said accusingly. She had wanted to tell her that friends, allies, were supposed to support each other in time of trouble, not just hand out money and think that that fulfilled their obligations.

'Hetty, I think when the weather is better we will go home,' she announced.

'Will it be safe?'

'I had a letter from Elizabeth last week and she said she hadn't heard a thing from either Maggie or any of her relations.'

'Will it be safe to travel with all those submarine things?' Hetty's mind had been on the war, not Maggie.

'Of course it will. They don't attack merchant ships, flying the American flag. We'll go in May or early June, I think. It should be a good crossing, just as it was when we travelled here.'

'Oh, I know I shouldn't say this, but I'll be so glad to get home, miss. War, shortages and all. I just can't take to life here. It's all too . . . fast. All these new-fangled inventions, all these motor cars. I'm getting too old and set.'

Philippa smiled. 'I am myself, Hetty, and we can get Laura settled into a good boarding school.' She had been annoyed and disappointed that Wilma had said quite tartly that she didn't approve of the English custom of sending children away to school for others to bring up. They had been her exact words. Wilma just didn't understand that it was in the child's best interests. Wilma had just stated that she didn't know of any such schools and that had been that. Laura went to the local school, an institution Philippa disapproved of for she considered the discipline far too lax and the educational standard not up to scratch. She was forever correcting and reprimanding the child who lately seemed bent on annoying her.

Now that the decision had been made she felt much brighter. 'I think I'll take a walk. I'll wrap up well and walk over to the schoolhouse. Perhaps I'll bring Laura home for lunch, although she insists on staying. She enjoys taking that lunch pail like the others. A lunch pail!' She sniffed disapprovingly. A pail was a bucket, something large and often used for feeding animals – not children. 'I don't know why they can't call it a hamper or even a box,' she muttered.

'Take care you don't slip now, it's still treacherous underfoot. Especially where the sidewalks haven't been cleared properly,' Hetty advised.

As she took her heavy outdoor clothes from the wardrobe as she insisted on calling it, Philippa raised her eyes to the ceiling. Sidewalks! Yes, she'd be glad to get home.

To her annoyance she hadn't been able to persuade Laura to come home for lunch, she'd pleaded to stay with her friends and Philippa's good humour had begun to disappear. Of course she could have insisted on it, but that awful teacher had been listening to every word and she'd refused to make a spectacle of herself or give the woman the satisfaction of seeing her lose her temper. She would speak to Laura later. She would have to tell her that their 'holiday' or 'vacation' here was over and that she was going to book their passage home, and she would stand for no tantrums or tears.

As she began to ascend the hill towards the house,

she had to stop for breath. She was getting very short-winded lately, she'd noticed. Perhaps it had something to do with the cold air. Some days the temperature was well below freezing even during the day. By the time she had reached the gate to the front yard, she couldn't breathe. The pain in her chest was intense and seemed to run down her left arm as well. She clung to the gatepost, feeling herself beginning to slip slowly towards the ground. The pain was excruciating. It was as though all the breath was being crushed out of her.

When she came to she was in bed and Hetty, Wilma and Dr Bernsen were standing around her. She knew it was Dr Bernsen for he'd stitched a nasty gash in Laura's leg when she'd fallen from a tree in the yard, while playing with the rough, tiresome Greely children from next door.

'Now just you take it easy, Miss Barton. You should have told us you had a heart condition. Hetty here says you've had it for years,' Dr Bernsen scolded mildly. He'd been concerned to learn from Hetty that the tall, thin, very formal English woman had always had a weak heart. Her condition should have been made known to him, he'd informed Wilma Barton who had appeared as surprised and concerned as he was.

Philippa tried to speak but her tongue felt numb and so did one side of her face. She tried to raise herself up but to her horror she seemed to have no feeling down one side of her body.

'No, no, you must lie still now, Miss Barton! You've

had a stroke. The paralysis may not be permanent, but you must be still and take it easy.'

She began to feel light-headed and sleepy and realized that he must have given her something.

When she awoke again, only Hetty remained, sitting beside the bed, and darkness must have fallen for the electric light was on, its brightness dimmed by a cloth draped over the shade.

'Oh, Miss Philippa, how are you feeling? You gave me a terrible fright!' Hetty was nearly in tears.

She tried again to talk but couldn't. She felt a bit stronger, although still a little woozy.

'Don't you worry, I'll stay with you. I won't leave your side. Go back to sleep now, you'll feel much better in the morning,' Hetty soothed.

She tried to fight it, but the drug was too strong and her eyelids dropped and closed again.

Over the next week she got stronger, but she was utterly dejected and humiliated that Hetty had to do everything for her. She now had a pad and a pencil and she could scrawl words, answers to Hetty's questions. The first thing she had written was 'Want to go home'.

Dr Bernsen came every day and had said very sharply and firmly that she must not travel. She had written 'Will I die?' He'd replied, 'You will if you intend to sail back to England.' 'Will I ever get better?' had been her next question. 'It will take time and you must do as I tell you' had been the reply to that.

As the weeks passed she became more and more

determined. The paralysis was showing no sign of improving. She was going home. If she was to be a bedridden invalid or if she were going to die, then it wasn't going to be here, in a foreign country, amongst people who were barely more than strangers. Kind, hospitable strangers, but strangers just the same.

Through Hetty Philippa made her intention clear and Hetty supported her argument vehemently to Wilma. 'Mrs Barton, I don't want to sound rude, but if you were as ill as she is, wouldn't you want to be in England? Wouldn't you want to look out of your window and see that?' she pointed to the trees, now beginning to burst into bud, 'instead of seeing some strange countryside? I know Miss Philippa, she'll not get well again here.'

'And if you go dragging her back across three thousands miles of ocean, she'll die!' Edgar remonstrated.

'Edgar, don't go on so, if it's what Philly really wants, then we shouldn't object. She's her own mistress after all and more than old enough to know her own mind.' Wilma had not found her husband's strait-laced cousin the easiest of people to get along with and she had no wish to have an invalid on her hands for God knows how long. And then there was the child. She and Edgar were too old to be saddled with a six-year-old girl. She was a cute, pert child, but in time she would become a burden and, if deprived of Philippa's restraining influence, would become a hoyden like that Careen Hamilton from the house on the corner of the block.

'Then I'll tell her you agree?'

Wilma nodded firmly. 'Edgar will see Dr Bernsen and make all the arrangements, Hetty. You go and set her mind at rest.'

Hetty was so relieved and she could see that Philippa was too, for her expression became more relaxed, her gaze less intense. They'd all be better when they were home. There were excellent doctors at home, too, and she'd be cared for on the ship. She was wealthy enough to pay for the best. Now there was only the matter of Laura. It was out of the question that she keep the child now, she herself was far too ill to be responsible for the child's future and Hetty would need all her energy to look after her. In fact it was too much for Hetty alone, once she was home a nurse would be employed. It was very probably the added strain of having to put up with the child and of having to leave England that had made her so ill. She must think of herself now, she must get better and not allow herself to get upset. She had been a fool to have let this affair get so out of hand. She hated to admit it, but Elizabeth had once again been right. Laura would have to go back to Maggie.

She'd written on her pad. 'Notepaper, envelope, pen.'

It hadn't been an easy letter to write. It hadn't been easy to even write anything so lengthy and she'd had to stop many many times, but at last it had gone, and she'd seen the tears well in Hetty's eyes although she'd never uttered a word of protest.

They had agreed that it should be Hetty who told Laura.

'Your Aunt Pippa is very sick, Laura, and we have to take her home, back to England.' Hetty had refused to tell the child yet that she would be going to live with her mother. One shock at a time was enough for any six year old.

The little girl looked at her questioningly. She'd heard the half-whispered conversations of Wilma and Edgar and she'd noticed the uneasy, tense atmosphere. 'Is she going to go and live with Jesus, Hetty?'

Hetty had never believed in lying to children, they were more resilient than people gave them credit for and lies were nearly always found out. 'I don't know. No one knows when Jesus will take them to heaven, but sometimes, when people are very sick or have a lot of pain, then it's best if they go to heaven, there's no pain or sickness in heaven.'

'Will Aunt Pippa be able to walk and talk in heaven?'

'Yes, but we don't know if she will go there just yet. But we have to go home, Laura lass.'

'We won't be going to Miss Elizabeth's?'

'No. We won't be going there. We'll be going on a big ship first though.'

'Like the one we came on?' Laura looked more interested.

Hetty could see that there were going to be no tantrums and she breathed a sigh of relief. 'Oh, much bigger than that one. And it has four red and black funnels, not just one, and there will probably be lots of other little girls you can play with, too.'

'Will Aunt Pippa let me play with them?'

'Of course she will.' Hetty knew that Philippa would have no objection, she was too ill. She also knew that Philippa would be anxious to know if Laura was going to be difficult over their departure. 'Why don't we go and tell her that you're glad we're going home? I know she'd like that.'

Laura didn't reply. She'd be sorry to leave Uncle Edgar and Aunt Wilma, even though they were very old. They weren't always telling her to be quiet, to sit still, to talk properly, to act like a little lady, the way Aunt Pippa used to, but she couldn't say that. It would only upset Hetty and make her aunt even more ill.

Hetty took the pad and pencil from the chest beside the bed and handed them to Philippa. She nodded quickly to let Philippa know that Laura had taken it well. Then she left them alone.

Slowly Philippa wrote. 'Do you remember Miss May? She gave you a top and whip and showed you pictures of ships.'

Laura read the words slowly, then nodded.

Laboriously, Philippa wrote, 'When we get home, I will be very sick, so you must go and stay with Maggie.'

Again Laura read the words. 'I don't want to!' Laura cried with spirit, everything familiar seemed to be disappearing and she was frightened.

'You liked Maggie,' Philippa scrawled.

Laura shook her head vehemently as she read. 'No! No! I want to go home!'

Philippa was very tired. Hetty would have to try to explain, there was time yet. Ten more days. Ten days here and then five days on the ship. In fifteen days she would be home.

Laura had calmed down for Hetty had come back into the room on hearing her cries and Hetty had soothed her and brought up the interesting and diverting subject of the ship that was to take them home. She extolled its virtues; it had lovely big rooms, just like bedrooms, she might even have a room all for herself. That would be very grown up. It had a big playroom, she'd heard, with all kinds of toys, and she could wear all her pretty dresses, even her Sunday best ones, every day if she wanted to.

Philippa watched the interest rekindle in the little girl's face and eyes. There was plenty of time to get her used to the idea of going to live with her mother. Hetty had a way of making things sound far more interesting and exciting than they really were. Hetty was very good with obstinate, fractious children.

'What's the name of the ship, Hetty? Is there a picture of it? Can I see it?' Laura had already forgotten Philippa's words about Maggie, they'd been pushed from her mind by the delights that Hetty had talked of.

'We don't have a picture of it, but perhaps Uncle Edgar can get one for you.'

'But what's it called, Hetty?' Laura persisted. She had a little sailor doll with 'R.M.S. Clan MacGregor' on its hat and she wondered would she be able to have another one.

Hetty smiled. 'I think we'll let Aunt Pippa tell you.'

Slowly Philippa wrote the name *Lusitania*.

Chapter Twenty-six

MAGGIE STARED AT THE rain as it beat against the window pane and impatiently she threw down the sock she was knitting. April was drawing to its close. It was supposed to be spring. The days should be getting warmer but it was more like February. The flowers in the park were bowed and broken, the trees and shrubs, their new leaves still tightly furled, dripped moisture. Even the birds were bedraggled and the month was nearly over.

It was a year since Philippa had gone to America and she was no nearer to getting Laura back. She'd lived in a highly agitated state of nerves for months, her moods vacillating, her temper short. She just couldn't understand it. Why was it taking so long? That was the demand she'd shouted and sobbed to Callan so many times. It had become more difficult because of the war, he'd told her. He was as impatient and frustrated as she was. The address Philippa had given had turned out to be an old one. Edgar Barton and his wife had moved from that address years ago. Philippa had lied to the shipping company, very probably encouraged by Elizabeth MacKenzie, Maggie had raged. Oh, they could be anywhere by now, they could have even left America, they would never find her.

Callan had held her and tried to calm and reassure her that he was certain that Philippa would never take Laura to another country. It was a setback, yes, but it would only be a matter of time, for the Pinkerton Agency was utterly reliable and even famous, they wouldn't fail. Like the Canadian Mounties they always got their man, or woman in this case. But the time he spent at home was very short nowadays, and when he was away she was terrified for his safety. In January three merchant ships had been sunk by U-boats in the Irish Sea and she knew that if she lost him, her spirit would be utterly broken and she would lose her mind.

She received letters regularly from Kirstie, letters in which her sister-in-law tried to cheer her, to urge her not to lose hope. Kirstie tried to hide her own fears, to make light of them, for Tommy was in France. It seemed to Maggie as though everything, fate, circumstances and conditions, were ranged against her. There was no brightness now in her life, the war had taken it all. Now even food was short, for daily it was getting harder and more dangerous for the ships to evade the U-boat blockade, and to avoid the mines that had been laid with complete disregard for the safety of all shipping, for mines could not distinguish between warships and neutral merchant ships.

More and more men were being urged to enlist and there was fighting from Belgium to Alsace and Lorraine in France. It seemed years ago since Queen Mary had appealed to all women to knit socks for the troops, 300,000 pairs she had asked for, yet that had only been in September, six months ago. Now women, too, were being urged to join the war effort, to take the jobs the men left vacant, to work in the munitions factories.

Harriet had said she would never be strong enough, her constitution wasn't exactly delicate but it was such heavy and dangerous work. Carrie had agreed it was dangerous but not all that heavy. It was a damned sight easier than lugging sacks of coal, which was what some women were doing. Both Maggie and Carrie had agreed to volunteer for war work, this would probably be the last pair of socks she had time to knit.

She picked up the knitting again and resolutely she resumed the difficult task of turning the heel, until she heard the front door slam.

Carrie was soaking wet. 'Oh, what a day! "Great day for ducks!" as my Ken used to say, but even the flaming ducks looked miserable when I passed the park. Well, I've done it!' Despite her bedraggled appearance, Carrie looked triumphant.

Maggie had taken Carrie's coat and had draped it over a chair by the fire. 'Done what?'

'I've been and put my name down for munitions!'

'Carrie, you haven't! You said you wouldn't. You said you would do something less dangerous, like taking the fares on the trams.'

'Well, I decided I'd sooner fill shells. The more shells our lads have, the more dead Huns there'll be and the sooner everyone can come home! Oh, let Harriet go and work on the trams! Mind you, they didn't seem very keen at first. They had the cheek to say wasn't I a bit old, but I said I was a widow and alone and did they think General Kitchener was too old?'

'Carrie, you make me feel ashamed. Here I am sitting by the fire knitting, I'll get my coat on now.'

'No, you won't. You can make me a cup of tea while I get changed, I'm frozen. You can go down tomorrow, one more day won't matter and you can take Harriet with you. You'd better get the kettle on, that will be her now.' Carrie smiled as they heard the rap on the knocker. 'She's forgotten her key, again. For someone so particular and meticulous about her work in that office, she's terribly forgetful about things like keys.'

When Carrie came back into the kitchen all trace of the smile had gone. In her hand she held a telegram.

Maggie's hand went to her throat. The buff-coloured envelopes had become such harbingers of tragedy. 'Oh, my God! No! No, Carrie! Not Callan! Not Callan!'

Carrie shook her head.

Instantly Maggie thought of Tommy. 'Carrie, I . . . I can't . . . you . . . you read it.'

'It's addressed to Mr O'Shea, Maggie.'

Relief flooded through her, making her dizzy and she caught the back of the chair for support. Thank God! Oh, thank God, it's not Callan or Tommy!

'Maggie, you'd better open it, just the same.'

Her hands were still shaking as she opened it and scanned the bald lines, then she passed it to Carrie.

'Oh, how am I going to tell him, Carrie? How? Both of them! Both his sons . . . gone! Ypres it says.'

'May God have mercy on them both, and on him as well, it will be a bitter blow for him, Maggie, even though they weren't close. He'll start feeling guilty and go blaming himself that they weren't on speaking terms,' Carrie said sadly.

'Carrie, I'm the one who should feel guilty. That quarrel was over me.'

'Don't you think like that, girl. You've been through enough and he'll need you now. You beating your breast with remorse won't help anyone.'

She went to meet him. He must have heard news of the terrible carnage of the second battle of Ypres, she thought. Hundreds of thousands of casualties and all for a few feet of mud. Where was the sense in it? The newspapers were full of it and the streets were crowded with women dressed in the black of mourning. Old women and young women, some only young girls.

Mr Daniels, the chief engineer, escorted her to Callan's cabin and he could see by the look on her face that there was something terribly wrong. They'd heard the news.

She couldn't speak. She couldn't utter the words, words that would bring him such pain. It was so cowardly, she knew that, but she handed him the telegram. He seemed to shrink and to age before her eyes as he sank down on to the bunk, his head in his hands.

She put her arms around him and held his head against her. 'Oh, Callan, I'd give anything . . . anything to have spared you this! Dear God! Where will it all end? They said it would be over by Christmas! They were so sure! They lied, they lied to us!'

She realized that he was quietly sobbing and she stroked his greying hair. He and his sons had never been close, indeed they'd never spoken or met since that day in Killiney, but they were his sons, his flesh and blood. Young men with their lives before them and now they lay buried in a foreign land.

He made an effort to control his grief and with shock and pain came anger. 'Why did they have to go, Maggie? They were Irishmen! Dear God, I'd have sooner they had joined the republicans. It wasn't their war!'

She'd never heard him talk like that before. He'd always condemned the republicans, back-stabbers he'd called them. Murderers and thugs, and now he was saying he wished they'd joined them. 'Callan, stop it! Stop it! Don't talk like that, you know you don't mean it! They volunteered as soon as war was declared. You were proud of them, you said so!'

'And they're dead, Maggie. I'd have sooner they were conscientious objectors and be alive! It's such a waste, a desperate, desperate waste. Richard, a fine young doctor and Sean, dedicated and passionate. Oh, he'd have made a good barrister but he'll never have the chance and that's the waste. That's the terrible pity of it.'

'How many more fathers must feel like you, Callan, how many in this city alone? There will be thousands of grieving fathers and mothers and hundreds of thousands throughout the land.' She knew it wouldn't help, this reminder of collective grief, but she could think of nothing else to console him.

'I'm glad Breda's dead, Maggie. She could never have stood this. They were her pride and joy. They meant everything to her.' The anger had gone, only a dull ache persisted now, that and a feeling of utter exhaustion. Each trip became more and more hazardous. She drew him to his feet. 'Let's go home, Callan.'

He nodded. Home. It was his home now and she was his wife, there was nothing left of that other home, that other family. Everything had gone. Part of his life had been wiped out by a few lines on a piece of paper.

Harriet had gone to her room, unable to bear the sight of poor Mr O'Shea's grief, she'd told Carrie, but remembering the photograph in her bag of another young soldier, dead before his time. Carrie said she'd wait, for the post had arrived. There had been a letter for her from Georgie, he had joined the army and was on his way to Europe. There were Australians and New Zealanders together, ANZACs he said they were called, and it was rumoured they were going to fight the Turks. The other letter was for Maggie and it bore an American stamp.

Carrie got to her feet when she heard the key in the door, steeling herself for the sight of Mr O'Shea's grief, but he went straight upstairs. Maggie came into the room alone.

'How did he take it, Maggie girl?'

Maggie's cheeks bore the trace of tears. 'Badly, Carrie. He says part of his life has been wiped out and that he's glad that she . . . Breda . . . is dead.' Maggie sat down wearily. 'Oh, Carrie, it's aged him. I watched him become an old man in minutes.'

Carrie held out the letter. 'It's from America, Maggie.'

Maggie snatched it from her and tore it open, not stopping to think, to deliberate or speculate. There had been too much speculation already today. As she read the spidery handwriting, the tears began to fall. The sobs rose from her chest painfully and caught in her throat.

'Maggie! Maggie, what's wrong! What does she say, girl?' Carrie cried.

'She's coming home, Carrie! She's ill, very ill! Oh, Carrie, she's bringing Laura home to me . . . and to Callan!' She was smiling through her tears.

Carrie smiled back. 'As one door closes, another opens, Maggie. Thank God, oh, thank God!'

Laura smiled happily across the dining table at Grace, her new friend. She was enjoying herself. Of course it was sad that Aunt Pippa was ill and Hetty had to look after her all day and all night, but Aunt Pippa had seemed to be cross with her all the time, even before she'd become sick, and she'd tried to be so good. At least now she could play nearly all day, instead of having to do her lessons.

Hetty had been right, there were quite a lot of children on the ship and she'd quickly made friends with Grace Meecock who was American but who was going to visit her grandmama who was terribly old and might even die before she'd seen Grace. Grace was also six but she wasn't allowed to play all day in the playroom or roam the decks, although Grace's mama was lovely and said that it was so nice for Grace to have a friend and that Laura must have her breakfast and lunch with them. And she had supper with Grace and all the other children in the huge, grown-ups' dining room. Before the ladies and gentlemen came for their supper, of course.

She'd tried not to think about what Aunt Pippa had said about her going to stay with Miss May when they got back. She had liked Maggie, but well, she couldn't understand why Hetty couldn't look after her. It was best not to think about it but now she couldn't help but do so for Grace's mama had just asked Grace's papa how long it would be before they reached Liverpool.

'Well, I guess this time tomorrow we should be coming up the River Mersey,' he answered, smiling at both Grace and Laura. 'Of course Laura knows what Liverpool looks like. We don't, but I hear it's a real fine city.'

Laura smiled at him. She liked him, too. She'd been very shy with him to start with, but he was much younger than Uncle Edgar and he laughed a lot and she'd soon got used to him. She wished she had a papa and mama and a sister like Grace, instead of just Hetty and Aunt Pippa.

'Tell us about Liverpool, Laura,' he asked.

Laura tried to think about the city, but she'd only been there twice. Her thoughts were distracted by a loud noise.

'Good grief, wouldn't you think they could close those doors more quietly!' Grace's mama interrupted.

Strangely, Grace's papa didn't answer. Instead he was getting to his feet. 'That wasn't a door slamming. Get yourself and these two up on deck, now!'

Grace's mama gave a little cry. 'George! George, what's wrong? Where are you going?'

'For the lifejackets! Get a move on, honey, I'll follow you!'

Laura noticed that people were beginning to get up and were rushing towards the doors. Then there was another, much louder bang and Grace and her mama both cried out.

'Papa! Papa, don't go! Papa!' Grace screamed.

At the sound of her voice he turned. 'Louisa! For God's sake, get those kids up on deck!' he yelled back.

Laura was frightened but she took Grace's mama's hand and clung to it tightly as they ran towards the door.

It seemed to Laura that there were crowds of people everywhere and they were all shouting, some were crying and screaming. The deck was slipping away under her feet and she lost her hold on Grace's mama's hand and began to slide. Her fear increased and she began to scream. 'Grace! Grace, where are you? Grace!' She managed to catch hold of a rail and pull herself up. High above her head she could see some of the lifeboats hanging crazily from their davits and men were trying to get them down. The ship seemed to be alive and was groaning aloud, there was a loud hissing noise and clouds of steam and smoke erupted from the four red-and-black funnels.

Panic swept over her. 'Hetty! Hetty! Where are you? Please come and find me, Hetty!' she screamed, the tears streaming down her face. Then she was swept up into someone's arms. It was Grace's papa and she clung to him, sobbing.

'Laura! Laura, where's Grace? Where's Grace and her ma?'

She was so terrified she couldn't speak, but her terror increased as he hastily passed her to another man. A man wearing a uniform this time.

'My wife! My wife and little girl! I've got to find them! This child was with them, she's on her own! Her aunt is below!' she heard Grace's papa yell at the man who was holding her.

'You can't go back, sir! She's listing badly! The port lifeboats are useless! You've no lifejackets, take the child and get into a boat!'

'I've *got* to find them! I can't just leave them!'

Laura was shaking with terror, her teeth chattering.

'For God's sake, get into a boat, man! We're going down!'

Turning her head, Laura saw two lifeboats hit the churning, seething water and turn upside down. People were thrashing about in the sea and she could hear their screams. She clung tightly to Grace's papa, still sobbing with terror.

Yet another man was yelling at them. 'All the boats have gone! They've all bloody well gone!'

'They can't have! For Christ's sake, pull yourself together, Johnson! They can't all have gone yet!'

'They 'ave, sir! Those were the last two, the port boats are useless! There's women an' kids still 'ere, God 'elp them!' The voice broke, cut off by a choking sob of fear and desperation.

'Then we'll all just have to take our chances! Get as

many people as you can into lifejackets! Get going, Johnson! Women and children first!'

Great gouts of water surged upwards as the stricken ship heeled further over to starboard.

'I want Hetty! I want Hetty!' Laura screamed.

'For the love of God, jump! Jump, sir! There's nothing else you can do now! She's so far over it's not far! She'll take us all down with her she's going that fast! Try and get to one of the boats! Jump, man! It's your only chance, we're going down!'

'No! Not without my Louisa and Gracie!' George Meecock was beside himself with fear and anxiety.

'They've probably gone! They'll be in one of the boats! Jump! Don't be a bloody fool! Jump!'

Laura felt the rush of cold air against her body, then she cried out as they hit the icy water and then she was being dragged along on her back, coughing and choking as the salt water filled her mouth and nostrils and blinded her. Numb with cold, terror and shock and only half-conscious she was pushed upwards and cold hands reached out for her. Her salt-caked lips moved but no sound came from them, but her voice shrieked inside her head, 'I want to go home! I want to go home!'

Chapter Twenty-seven

On the 8th and 9th of May, 1915, mobs roamed the streets of Liverpool, their targets anything Germanic. They had taken to the streets after a stunned and shocked city had learned of the sinking of the *Lusitania* by the German U-boat, U-20. She'd been Liverpool-bound and was off the Old Head of Kinsale, and she'd been carrying men, women and children. She'd gone down in eighteen minutes and one thousand, one hundred and ninety souls had been lost.

Irish fishing boats and drifters had set out to search for survivors and took in tow the pitifully few lifeboats that had got away from the stricken liner. The drifter *Elizabeth* took two boats in tow and then the naval tug *Stormcock* took the survivors to Queenstown.

In Elm Road the doctor had been called in by Carrie. Maggie had been sedated. Callan O'Shea had tried to find courage and solace in a bottle. Neither the whiskey nor the laudanum had worked.

Three days later, when the police had quelled the riots, they both stood at the landing stage watching the Dublin ferry *Connaught* making her way upriver. The last dregs of hope had been dredged up in both their hearts. Neither would even contemplate the future. The war still raged. There was no end in sight.

The time slipped by and the crowd was silent. Only the sound of the gulls overhead and the mournful hoot of the tugs could be heard across the calm, grey water. The hawsers were taken up and the *Connaught* had docked.

Maggie gripped Callan's hand tightly as the gangway was lowered and the first passengers began to descend. A few people pushed through the crowd, arms outstretched, as dear familiar faces were recognized.

High in the pale blue sky, the white cirrus clouds drifted away and the sun was clear and bright. It shone on the *Connaught*'s green-and-black funnel and silhouetted the figure of a stewardess and a child with long dark curls, who stood at the top of the gangway. Laura May O'Shea had come home.

Epilogue

TOMMY AND KIRSTIE MAY stood on the dockside gazing up at the towering white hull of the *Empress of China*. There was a carnival atmosphere that glorious summer day in 1920. Thousands of coloured streamers floated down from the decks above and the Liverpool City Police Band was playing its repertoire with gusto. Tommy's arm tightened around the now thickening waist of his pregnant wife and Kirstie smiled at him.

'Do you think they'll be happy, Tom?'

'Why shouldn't they be? It's a new start for them all. All the bad memories can be put behind them now and Maggie deserves to be happy.'

High up on the boat deck, Callan O'Shea looked with affection on his wife and daughter. His days of roaming the world were over.

Maggie turned and smiled at him. A smile of pure joy, yet it was tinged with just a little sadness that

Tommy and Kirstie were waiting until the baby had been born before following them. It would have been nice to have gone as one big family. Her smile vanished and her forehead creased in a frown for Callan was humming a song. A very familiar song.

'Will you stop humming *that* song, Callan O'Shea!'

He grinned. 'Why? It's not been your name for six years, Maggie, and everything is behind us now. *Her* as well.'

'What song, Ma?' Laura turned from the rail, her attention diverted.

'Oh, it's an old sea-shanty, it goes something like this,' Callan cleared his throat.

'Oh, gather round, you sailor boys, and listen to my plea.
And when you've heard my tale you'll pity me.
For I was a ruddy fool, in the port of Liverpool,
The first time that I came home from sea.

I was paid off in the Pool, from the Port of Sierra Leone,
Four pounds ten a month was all me pay.
With a pocket full of tin,
I was very soon taken in
By a girl with the name of Maggie May.

Oh, Maggie, Maggie May
They've taken her away

And she'll never walk down Canning Place no
   more,
For the Judge he guilty found her,
Of robbin' a homeward-bounder,
And paid her passage out to Botany Bay'.

Laura laughed. 'That was your name, Ma.'

'A long, long time ago. Almost as long ago as that Maggie May went "Cruising up and down old Canning Place",' Callan exaggerated, a trait of all Irishmen as he frequently said. He winked at Laura who turned back to the rail and began to wave to the tiny figures on the dockside below.

'You robbed this homeward-bounder of his heart, Maggie, and now you're off to Botany Bay – well, Australia anyway.' He drew her closer to him. 'A new country, a new life and a new name. All that's in the past now.' He pointed to the fine new buildings of the Liverpool waterfront.

'And so is that blasted song!' Maggie laughed.

There was a deafening blast from the steam whistle on one of the mustard-coloured funnels. The hawsers were cast off and slowly the *Empress of China* left Liverpool, bound for Sydney, Australia.